THE SECRET SCIENCE ALLIANCE
AND THE COPYCAT CROOK

THE SECRET SCIENCE ALLIANCE

→ AND THE **COPYCAT CROOK**

WILDERNESS BRANCH LIBRARY
6421 FLAT RUN ROAD
LOCUST GROVE, VA 22508

ELEANOR DAVIS

BLOOMSBURY

NEW YORK · BERLIN · LONDON

DEDICATED TO KINO SCHOOL AND EVERYONE
WHO HAS EVER LEARNED AND TAUGHT THERE

The Secret Science Alliance and the Copycat Crook

Created, written & drawn by Eleanor Davis
Inked by Drew Weing
Colored by Joey Weiser & Michele Chidester
Lettered by Bryant Paul Johnson
Art direction & book design by John Lind

Text and illustrations © 2009 by Eleanor Davis
All rights reserved. No part of this book may be used or reproduced in any manner whatsoever without written permission from the publisher, except in the case of brief quotations embodied in critical articles or reviews.

Published by Bloomsbury U.S.A. Children's Books
175 Fifth Avenue, New York, New York 10010

Produced for Bloomsbury U.S.A. Children's Books by Kitchen, Lind & Associates LLC
www.kitchenandlind.com

Library of Congress Cataloging-in-Publication Data
Davis, Eleanor.
Secret science alliance and the copycat crook / by Eleanor Davis. — 1st U.S. ed.
p.   cm.
Summary: Eleven-year-old Julian Calendar thought changing schools would mean leaving his "nerdy" persona behind, but instead he forms an alliance with fellow inventors Greta and Ben and works with them to prevent an adult from using one of their gadgets for nefarious purposes.
ISBN-13: 978-1-59990-142-8 · ISBN-10: 1-59990-142-0 (hardcover)
ISBN-13: 978-1-59990-396-5 · ISBN-10: 1-59990-396-2 (paperback)
1. Graphic novels. [1. Graphic novels. 2. Inventors—Fiction. 3. Schools—Fiction. 4. Clubs—Fiction. 5. Individuality—Fiction. 6. Youths' writings.] I. Title.
PZ7.7.D38Sec 2010   [Fic]—dc22   2008045399

First U.S. Edition 2009
Printed in China by SNP Leefung Printers Limited
(hardcover) 10 9 8 7 6 5 4 3 2 1
(paperback) 10 9 8 7 6 5 4 3 2 1

All papers used by Bloomsbury U.S.A. are natural, recyclable products made from wood grown in well-managed forests. The manufacturing processes conform to the environmental regulations of the country of origin.

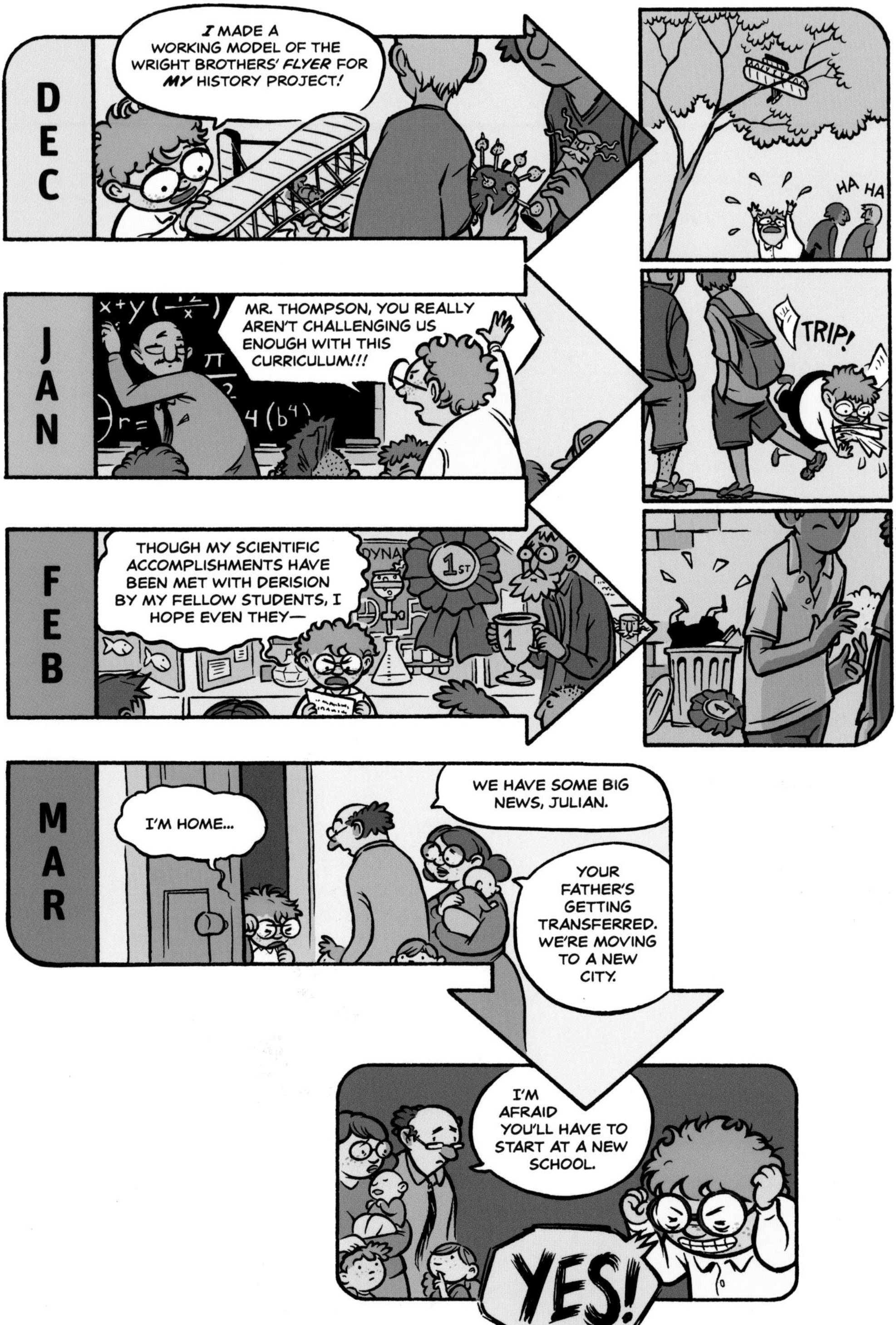
DEC
I MADE A WORKING MODEL OF THE WRIGHT BROTHERS' FLYER FOR MY HISTORY PROJECT!
HA HA
JAN
MR. THOMPSON, YOU REALLY AREN'T CHALLENGING US ENOUGH WITH THIS CURRICULUM!!!
TRIP!
FEB
THOUGH MY SCIENTIFIC ACCOMPLISHMENTS HAVE BEEN MET WITH DERISION BY MY FELLOW STUDENTS, I HOPE EVEN THEY—
1ST
MAR
I'M HOME...
WE HAVE SOME BIG NEWS, JULIAN.
YOUR FATHER'S GETTING TRANSFERRED. WE'RE MOVING TO A NEW CITY.
I'M AFRAID YOU'LL HAVE TO START AT A NEW SCHOOL.
YES!

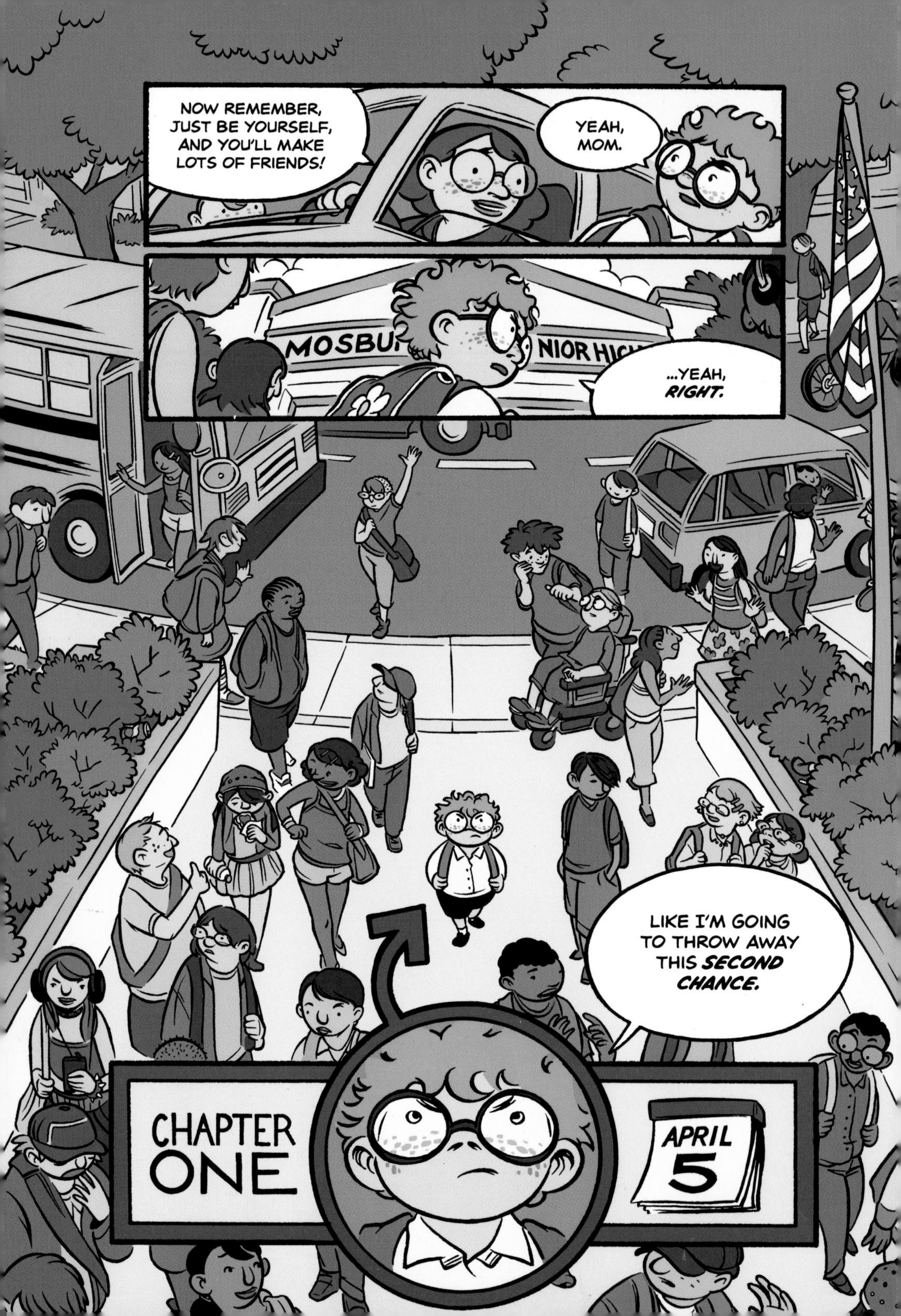
NOW REMEMBER, JUST BE YOURSELF, AND YOU'LL MAKE LOTS OF FRIENDS!
YEAH, MOM.
...YEAH, RIGHT.
LIKE I'M GOING TO THROW AWAY THIS SECOND CHANCE.
CHAPTER ONE
APRIL 5

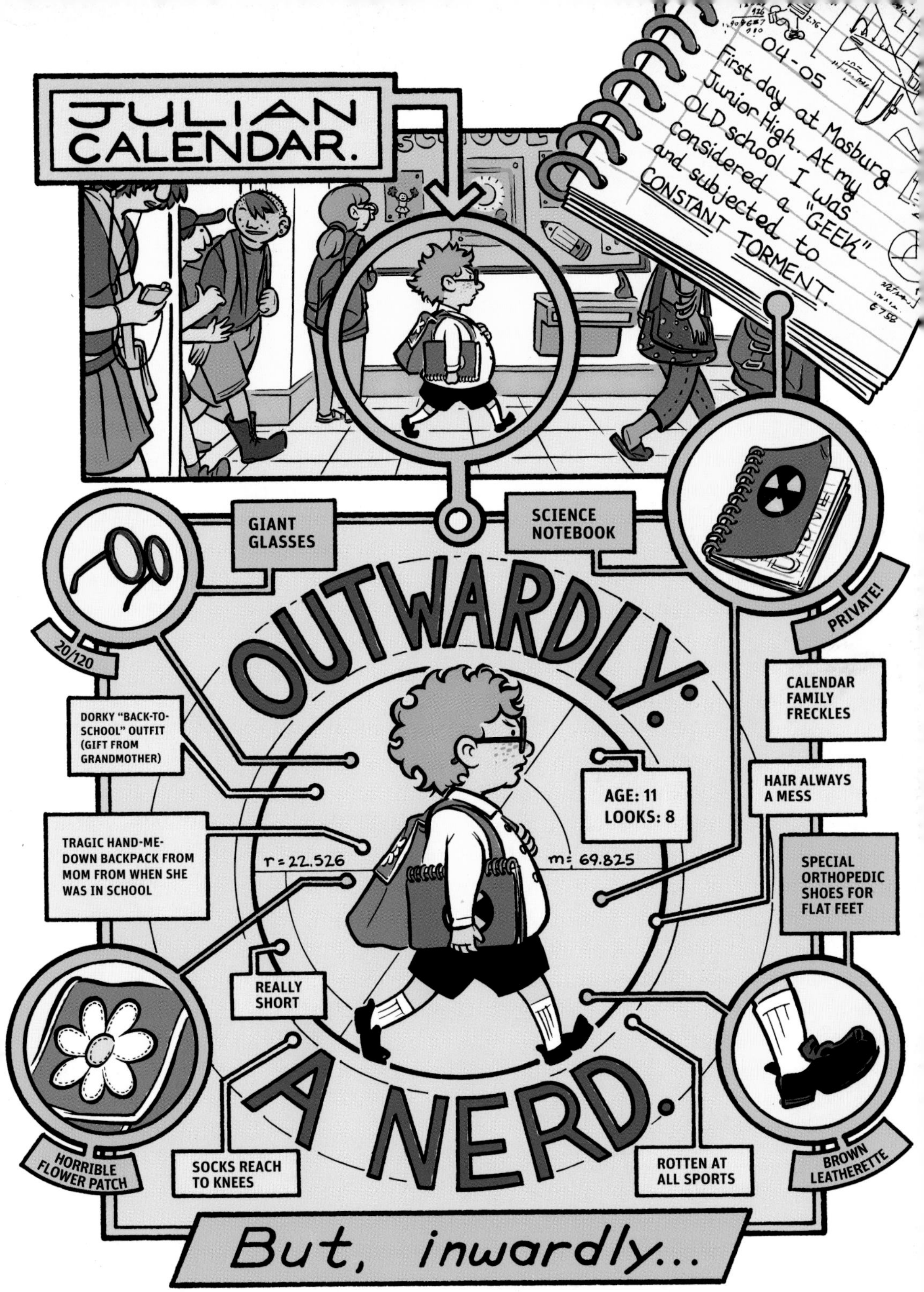

JULIAN CALENDAR.
04-05
First day at Mosburg Junior High. At my OLD school I was considered a "GEEK" and subjected to CONSTANT TORMENT.
GIANT GLASSES
20/120
SCIENCE NOTEBOOK
PRIVATE!
OUTWARDLY:
DORKY "BACK-TO-SCHOOL" OUTFIT (GIFT FROM GRANDMOTHER)
CALENDAR FAMILY FRECKLES
AGE: 11
LOOKS: 8
HAIR ALWAYS A MESS
TRAGIC HAND-ME-DOWN BACKPACK FROM MOM FROM WHEN SHE WAS IN SCHOOL
r = 22.526
m: 69.825
SPECIAL ORTHOPEDIC SHOES FOR FLAT FEET
REALLY SHORT
A NERD.
HORRIBLE FLOWER PATCH
SOCKS REACH TO KNEES
ROTTEN AT ALL SPORTS
BROWN LEATHERETTE
But, inwardly...

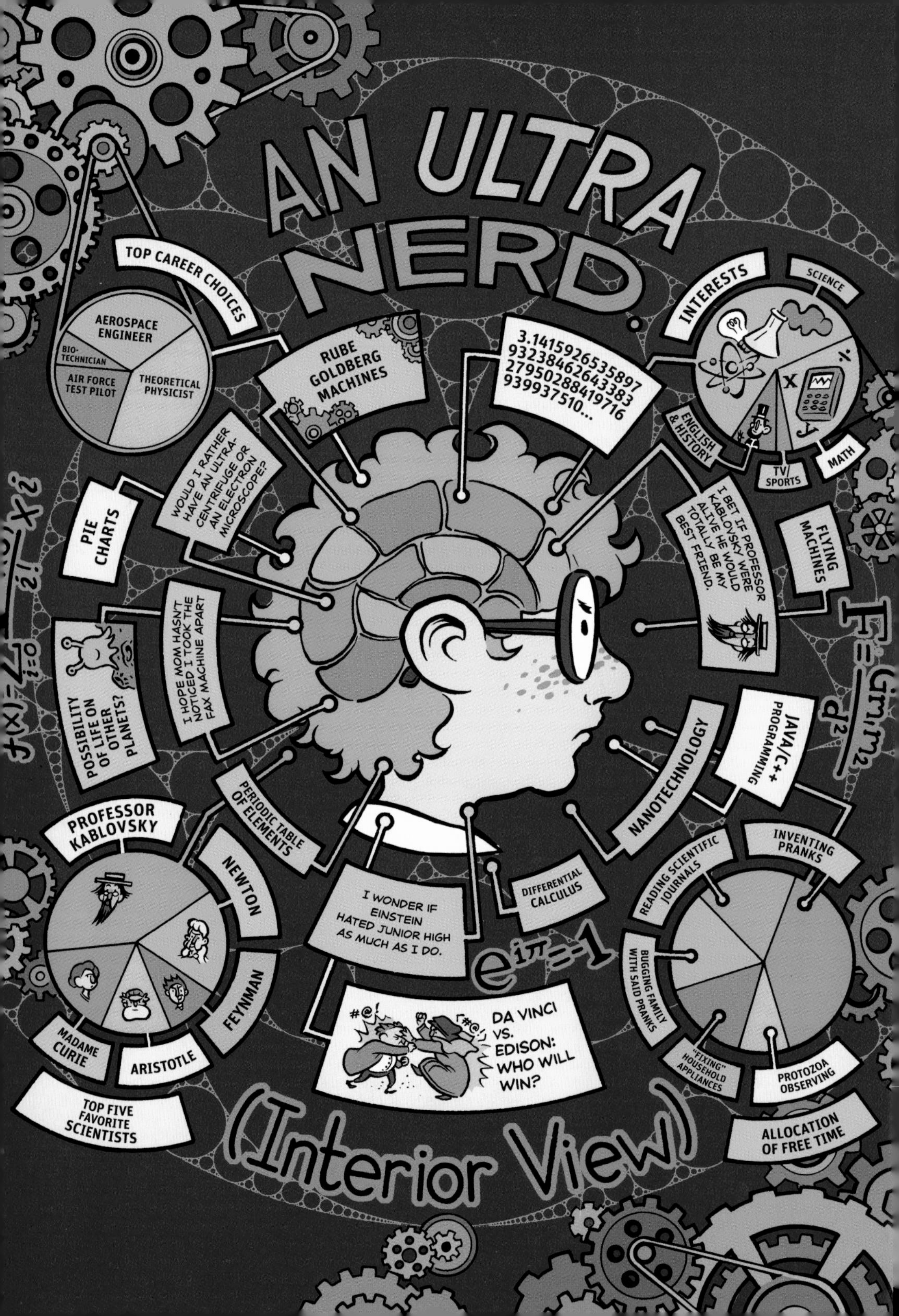
AN ULTRA NERD
(Interior View)
TOP CAREER CHOICES
AEROSPACE ENGINEER
BIO-TECHNICIAN
AIR FORCE TEST PILOT
THEORETICAL PHYSICIST
RUBE GOLDBERG MACHINES
3.14159265358979323846264338327950288419716939937510...
INTERESTS
SCIENCE
ENGLISH & HISTORY
TV/SPORTS
MATH
WOULD I RATHER HAVE AN ULTRA-CENTRIFUGE OR AN ELECTRON MICROSCOPE?
PIE CHARTS
I BET IF PROFESSOR KABLOVSKY WERE ALIVE HE WOULD TOTALLY BE MY BEST FRIEND.
FLYING MACHINES
I HOPE MOM HASN'T NOTICED I TOOK THE FAX MACHINE APART
POSSIBILITY OF LIFE ON OTHER PLANETS?
NANOTECHNOLOGY
JAVA/C++ PROGRAMMING
PERIODIC TABLE OF ELEMENTS
PROFESSOR KABLOVSKY
NEWTON
FEYNMAN
ARISTOTLE
MADAME CURIE
TOP FIVE FAVORITE SCIENTISTS
I WONDER IF EINSTEIN HATED JUNIOR HIGH AS MUCH AS I DO.
DIFFERENTIAL CALCULUS
#@!
#@!
DA VINCI VS. EDISON: WHO WILL WIN?
INVENTING PRANKS
READING SCIENTIFIC JOURNALS
BUGGING FAMILY WITH SAID PRANKS
"FIXING" HOUSEHOLD APPLIANCES
PROTOZOA OBSERVING
ALLOCATION OF FREE TIME
$f(x)=\sum_{i=0}^{\infty}\frac{x^i}{i!}$
$F=\frac{Gm_1m_2}{d^2}$
$e^{i\pi}=-1$

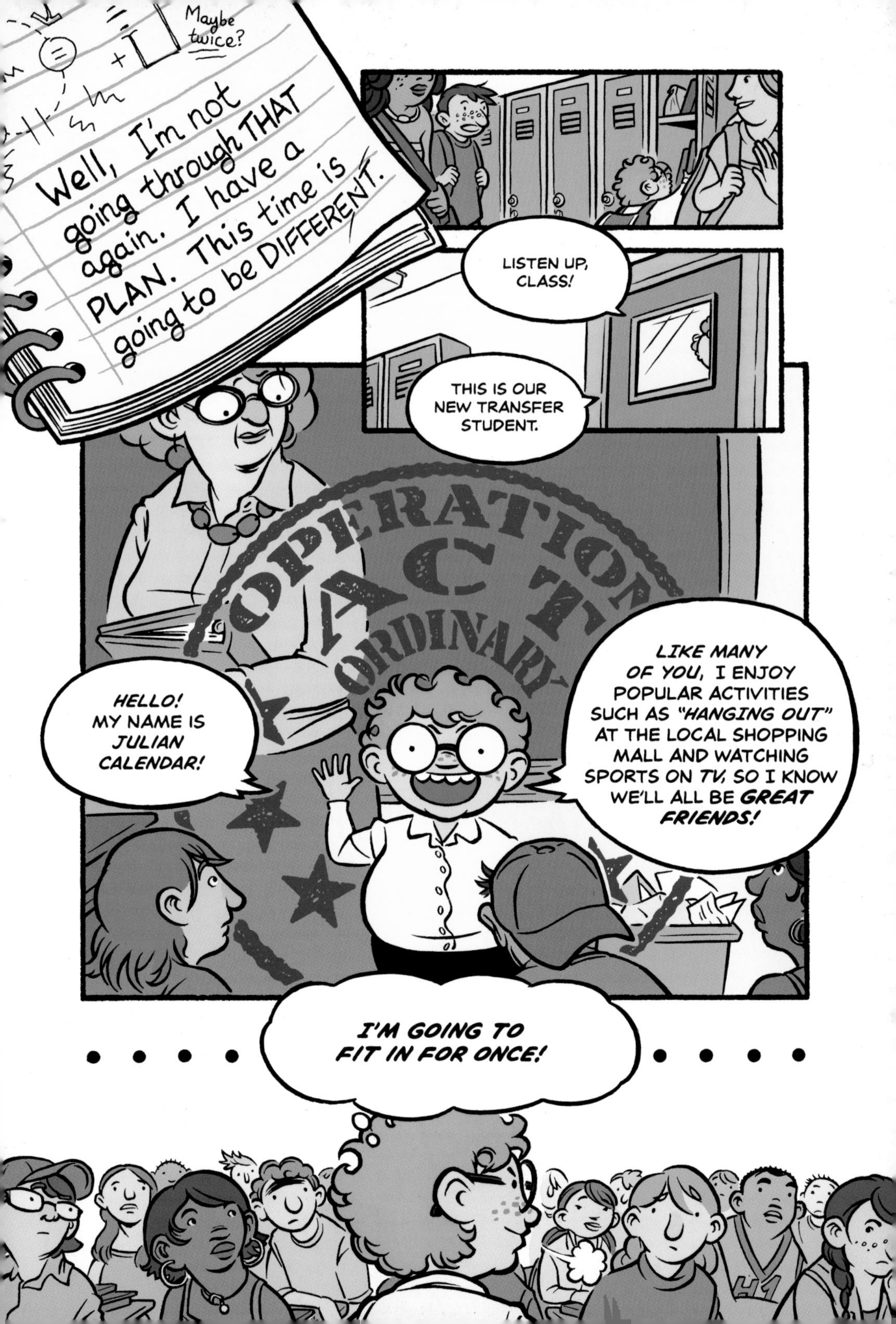
Maybe twice?
Well, I'm not going through THAT again. I have a PLAN. This time is going to be DIFFERENT.
LISTEN UP, CLASS!
THIS IS OUR NEW TRANSFER STUDENT.
OPERATION ACT ORDINARY
HELLO! MY NAME IS JULIAN CALENDAR!
LIKE MANY OF YOU, I ENJOY POPULAR ACTIVITIES SUCH AS "HANGING OUT" AT THE LOCAL SHOPPING MALL AND WATCHING SPORTS ON TV, SO I KNOW WE'LL ALL BE GREAT FRIENDS!
I'M GOING TO FIT IN FOR ONCE!

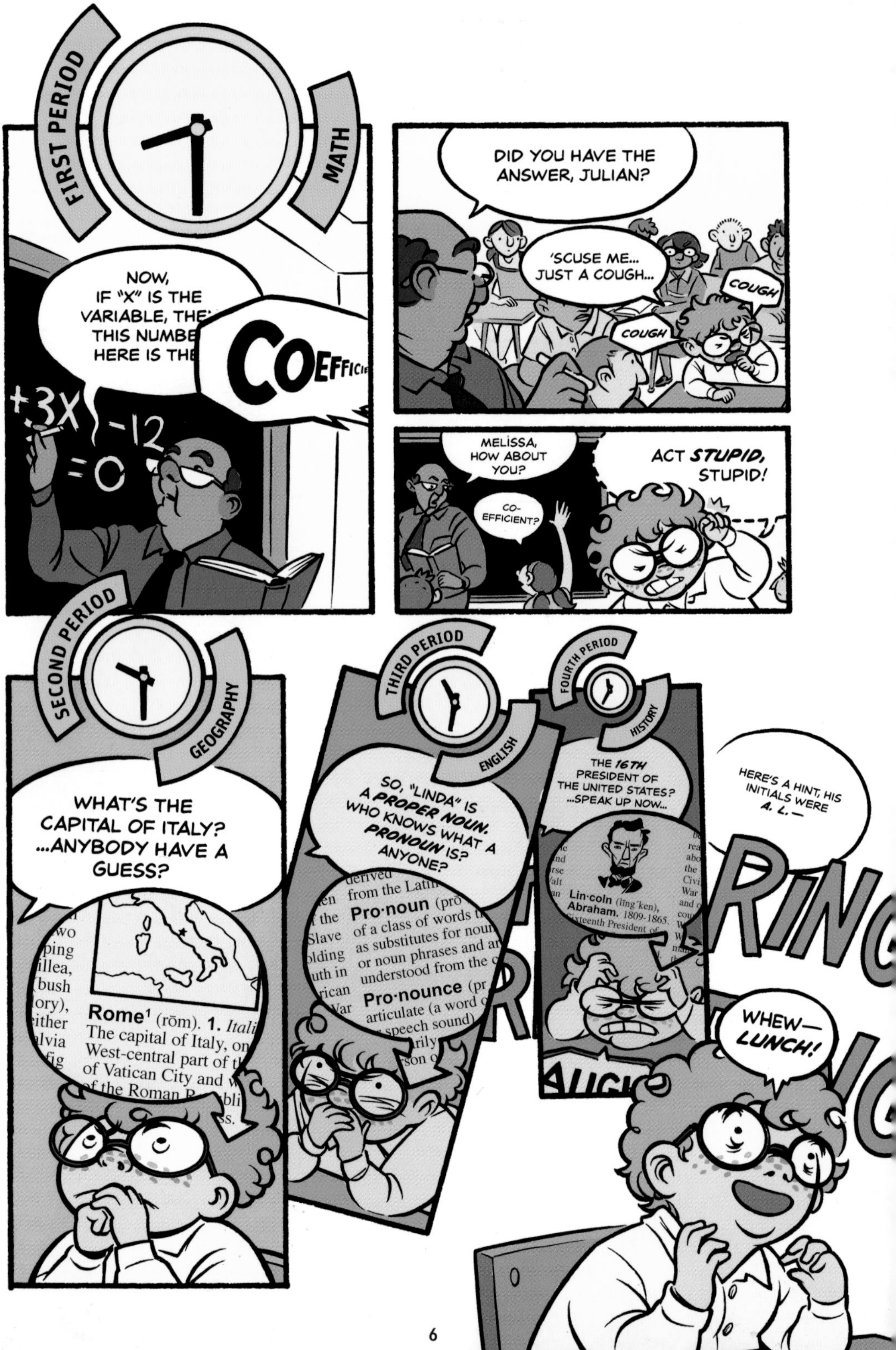
FIRST PERIOD
MATH
NOW, IF "X" IS THE VARIABLE, THE
THIS NUMBE
HERE IS THE
COEFFICI
+3X -12 =0
DID YOU HAVE THE ANSWER, JULIAN?
'SCUSE ME... JUST A COUGH...
COUGH
COUGH
MELISSA, HOW ABOUT YOU?
CO-EFFICIENT?
ACT STUPID, STUPID!
SECOND PERIOD
GEOGRAPHY
WHAT'S THE CAPITAL OF ITALY? ...ANYBODY HAVE A GUESS?
Rome¹ (rōm). 1. Itali
The capital of Italy, on
West-central part of th
of Vatican City and w
of the Roman Re
THIRD PERIOD
ENGLISH
SO, "LINDA" IS A PROPER NOUN. WHO KNOWS WHAT A PRONOUN IS? ANYONE?
derived
from the Latin
Pro·noun (prō
of a class of words t
as substitutes for noun
or noun phrases and a
understood from the c
Pro·nounce (pr
articulate (a word o
speech sound)
FOURTH PERIOD
HISTORY
THE 16TH PRESIDENT OF THE UNITED STATES? ...SPEAK UP NOW...
Lin·coln (lĭng'kən), Abraham. 1809-1865.
Sixteenth President of
HERE'S A HINT, HIS INITIALS WERE A. L.—
RING
WHEW— LUNCH!

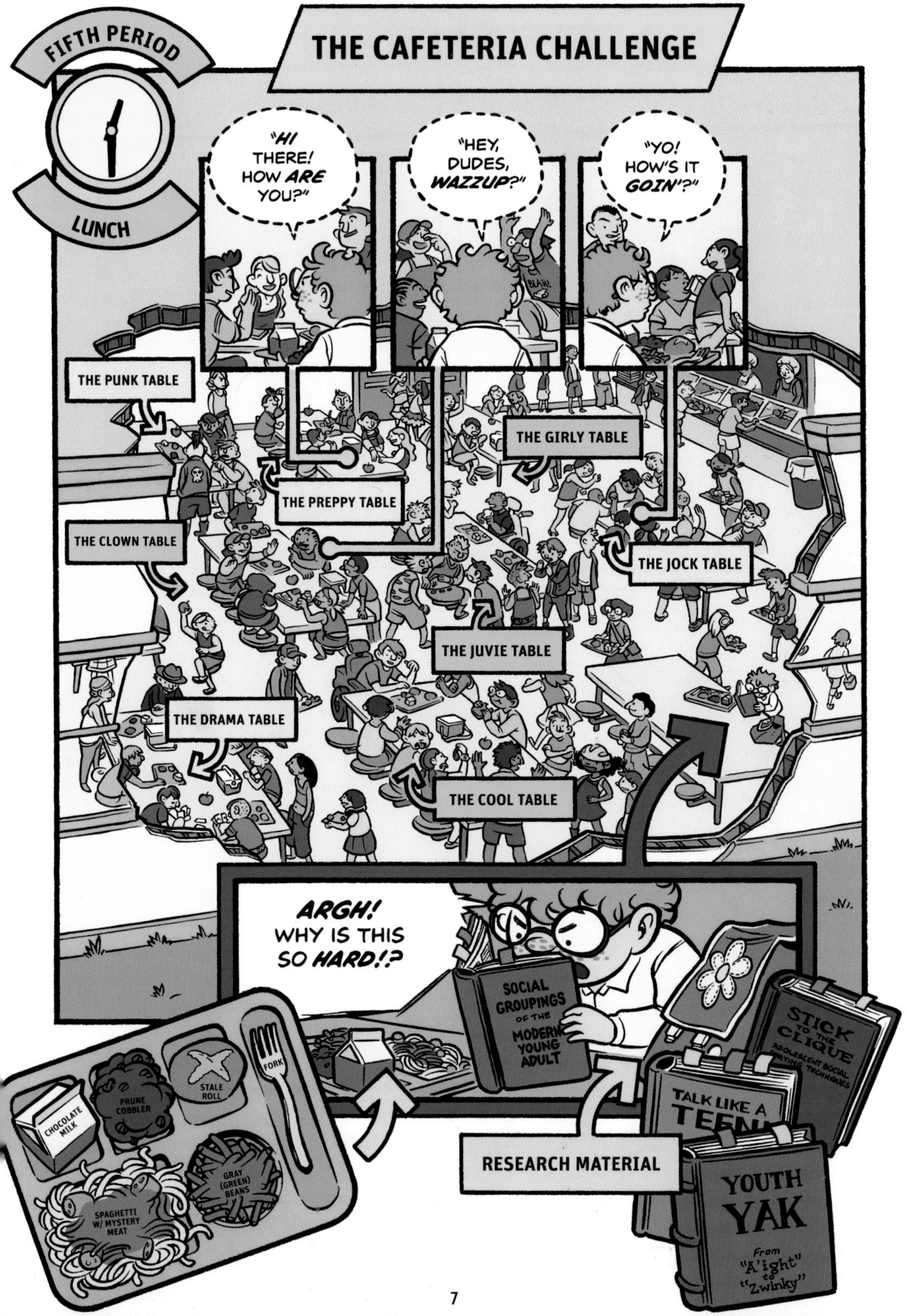

FIFTH PERIOD
LUNCH
THE CAFETERIA CHALLENGE
"HI THERE! HOW ARE YOU?"
"HEY, DUDES, WAZZUP?"
"YO! HOW'S IT GOIN'?"
BLAH!
THE PUNK TABLE
THE PREPPY TABLE
THE GIRLY TABLE
THE CLOWN TABLE
THE JOCK TABLE
THE JUVIE TABLE
THE DRAMA TABLE
THE COOL TABLE
ARGH! WHY IS THIS SO HARD!?
SOCIAL GROUPINGS OF THE MODERN YOUNG ADULT
STICK TO THE CLIQUE ADOLESCENT SOCIAL SORTING TECHNIQUES
TALK LIKE A TEEN
YOUTH YAK From "A'ight" to "Zwinky"
RESEARCH MATERIAL
CHOCOLATE MILK
PRUNE COBBLER
STALE ROLL
FORK
GRAY (GREEN) BEANS
SPAGHETTI W/ MYSTERY MEAT

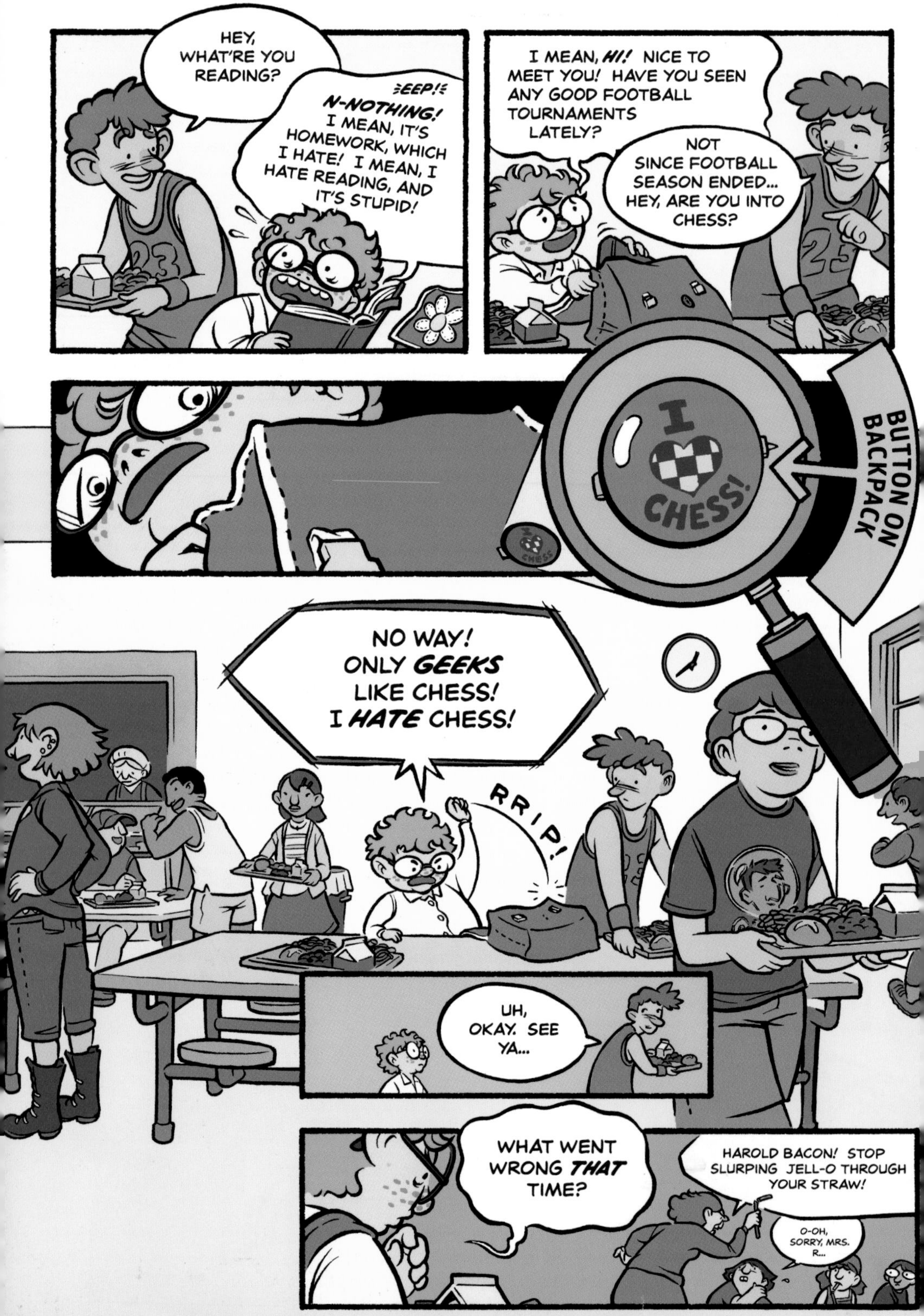

HEY, WHAT'RE YOU READING?
EEP!
N-NOTHING! I MEAN, IT'S HOMEWORK, WHICH I HATE! I MEAN, I HATE READING, AND IT'S STUPID!
I MEAN, HI! NICE TO MEET YOU! HAVE YOU SEEN ANY GOOD FOOTBALL TOURNAMENTS LATELY?
NOT SINCE FOOTBALL SEASON ENDED... HEY, ARE YOU INTO CHESS?
I ♥ CHESS!
BUTTON ON BACKPACK
NO WAY! ONLY GEEKS LIKE CHESS! I HATE CHESS!
RRIP!
UH, OKAY. SEE YA...
WHAT WENT WRONG THAT TIME?
HAROLD BACON! STOP SLURPING JELL-O THROUGH YOUR STRAW!
O-OH, SORRY, MRS. R...

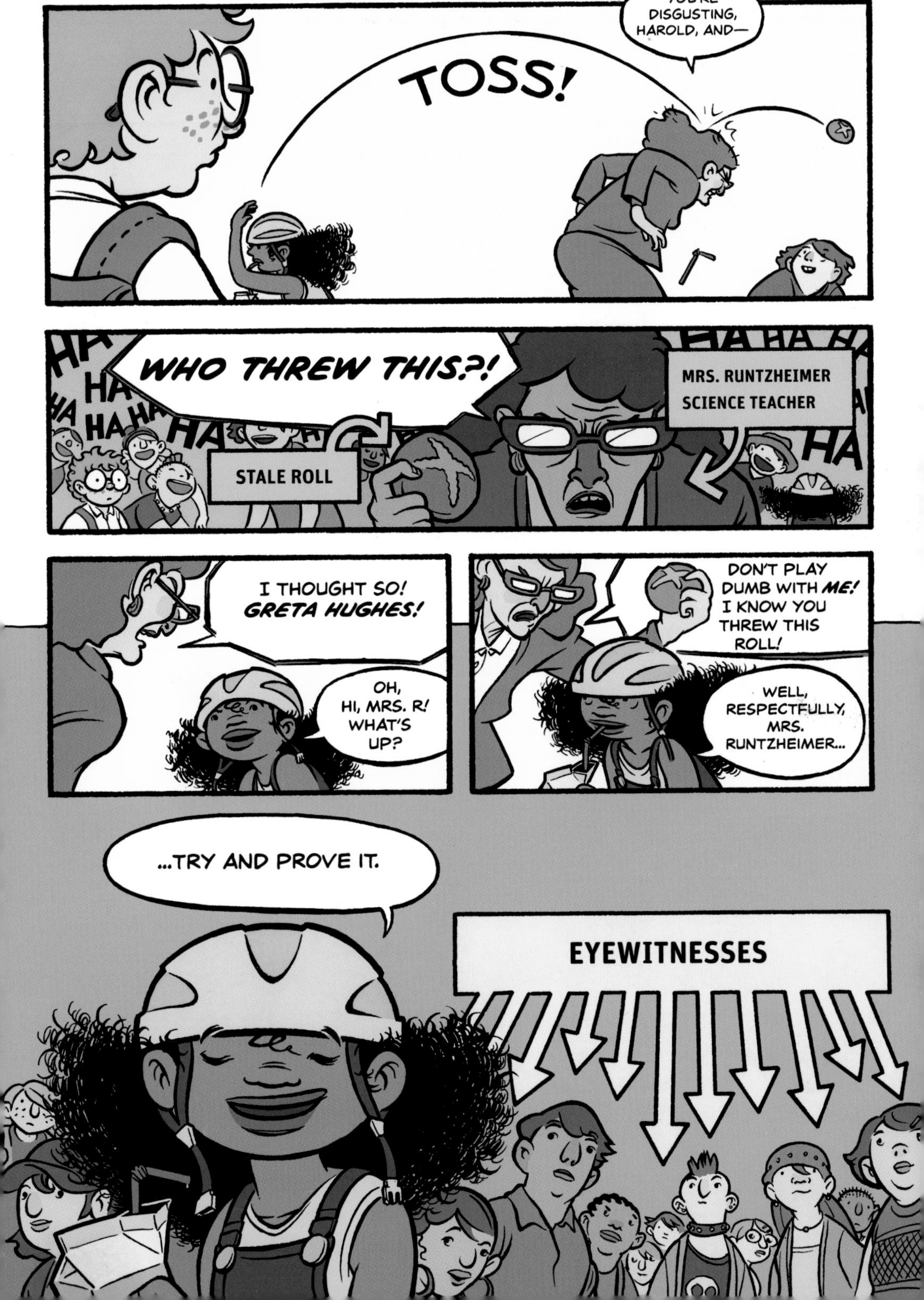

YOU'RE DISGUSTING, HAROLD, AND—
TOSS!
WHO THREW THIS?!
MRS. RUNTZHEIMER SCIENCE TEACHER
STALE ROLL
HA HA HA HA HA HA HA HA HA HA
I THOUGHT SO! GRETA HUGHES!
OH, HI, MRS. R! WHAT'S UP?
DON'T PLAY DUMB WITH ME! I KNOW YOU THREW THIS ROLL!
WELL, RESPECTFULLY, MRS. RUNTZHEIMER...
...TRY AND PROVE IT.
EYEWITNESSES

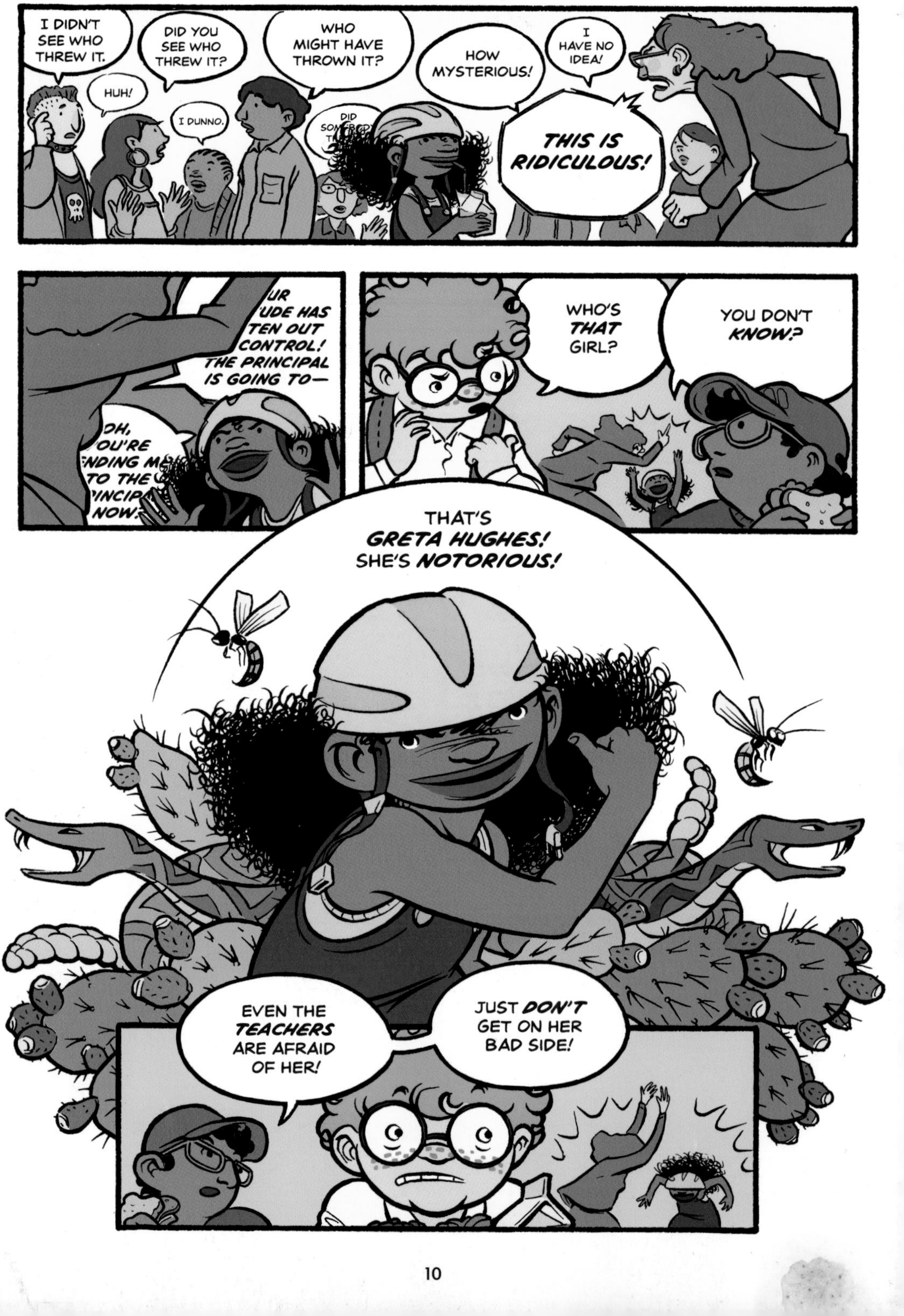

I DIDN'T SEE WHO THREW IT.
HUH!
DID YOU SEE WHO THREW IT?
I DUNNO.
WHO MIGHT HAVE THROWN IT?
HOW MYSTERIOUS!
I HAVE NO IDEA!
THIS IS RIDICULOUS!
UR 'UDE HAS TEN OUT CONTROL! THE PRINCIPAL IS GOING TO—
OH, OU'RE ENDING M TO THE RINCIP NOW?
WHO'S THAT GIRL?
YOU DON'T KNOW?
THAT'S GRETA HUGHES! SHE'S NOTORIOUS!
EVEN THE TEACHERS ARE AFRAID OF HER!
JUST DON'T GET ON HER BAD SIDE!

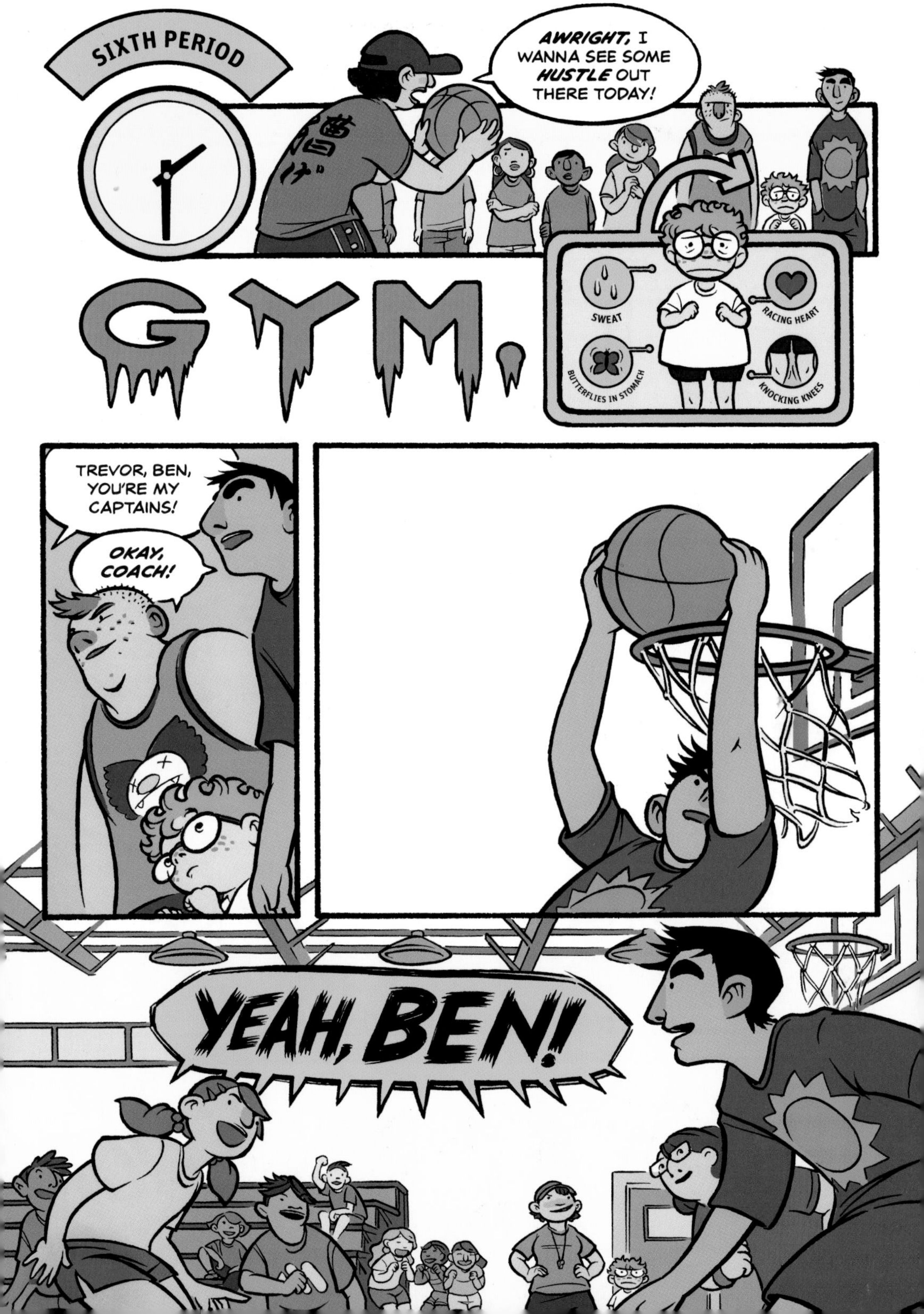
SIXTH PERIOD
AWRIGHT, I WANNA SEE SOME HUSTLE OUT THERE TODAY!
GYM.
SWEAT
RACING HEART
BUTTERFLIES IN STOMACH
KNOCKING KNEES
TREVOR, BEN, YOU'RE MY CAPTAINS!
OKAY, COACH!
YEAH, BEN!

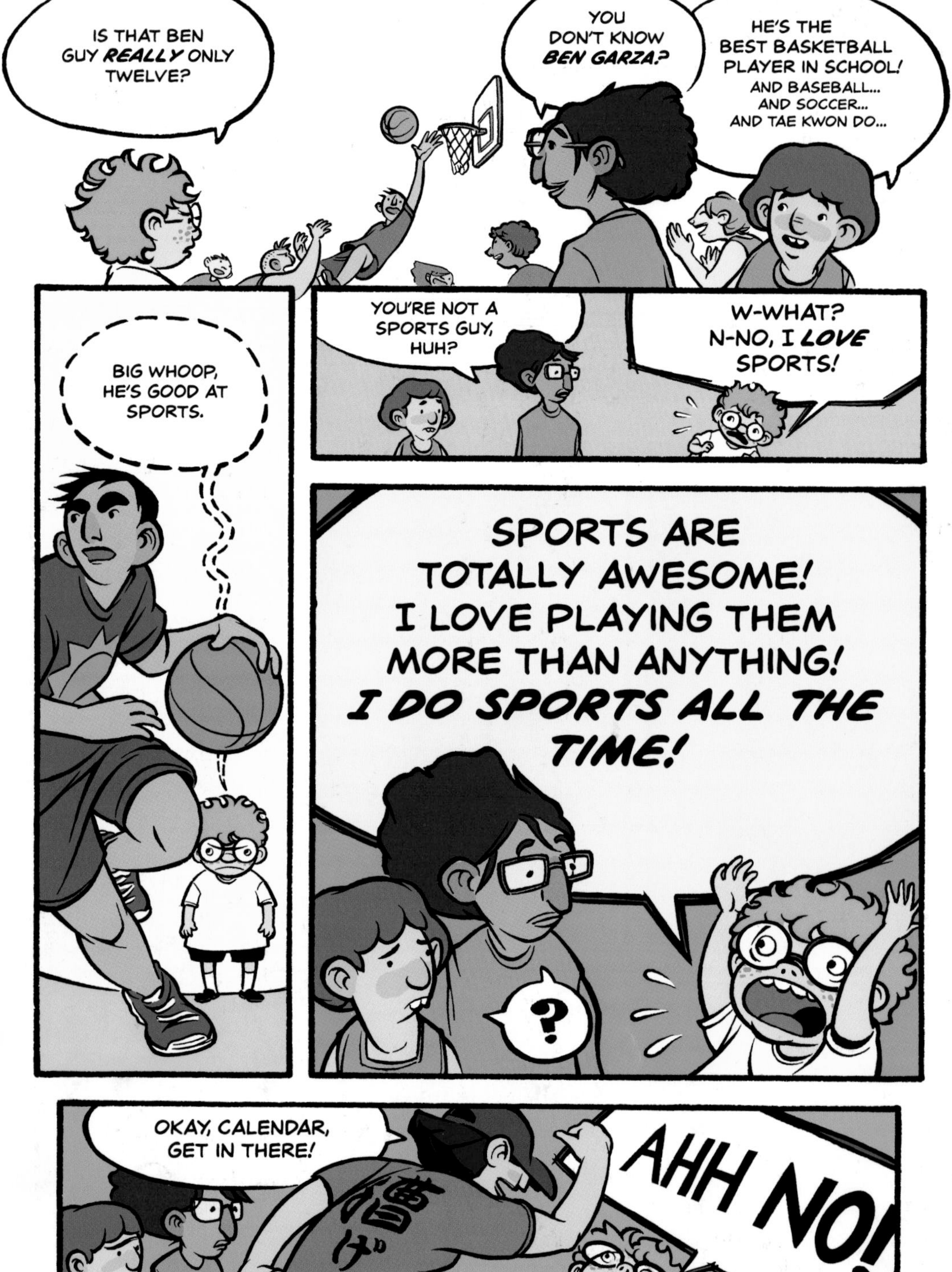

IS THAT BEN GUY *REALLY* ONLY TWELVE?
YOU DON'T KNOW *BEN GARZA?*
HE'S THE BEST BASKETBALL PLAYER IN SCHOOL! AND BASEBALL... AND SOCCER... AND TAE KWON DO...
BIG WHOOP, HE'S GOOD AT SPORTS.
YOU'RE NOT A SPORTS GUY, HUH?
W-WHAT? N-NO, I *LOVE* SPORTS!
SPORTS ARE TOTALLY AWESOME! I LOVE PLAYING THEM MORE THAN ANYTHING! *I DO SPORTS ALL THE TIME!*
?
OKAY, CALENDAR, GET IN THERE!
AHH NO!

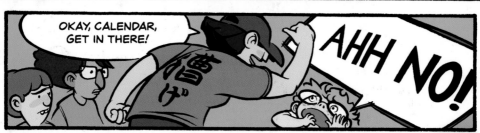

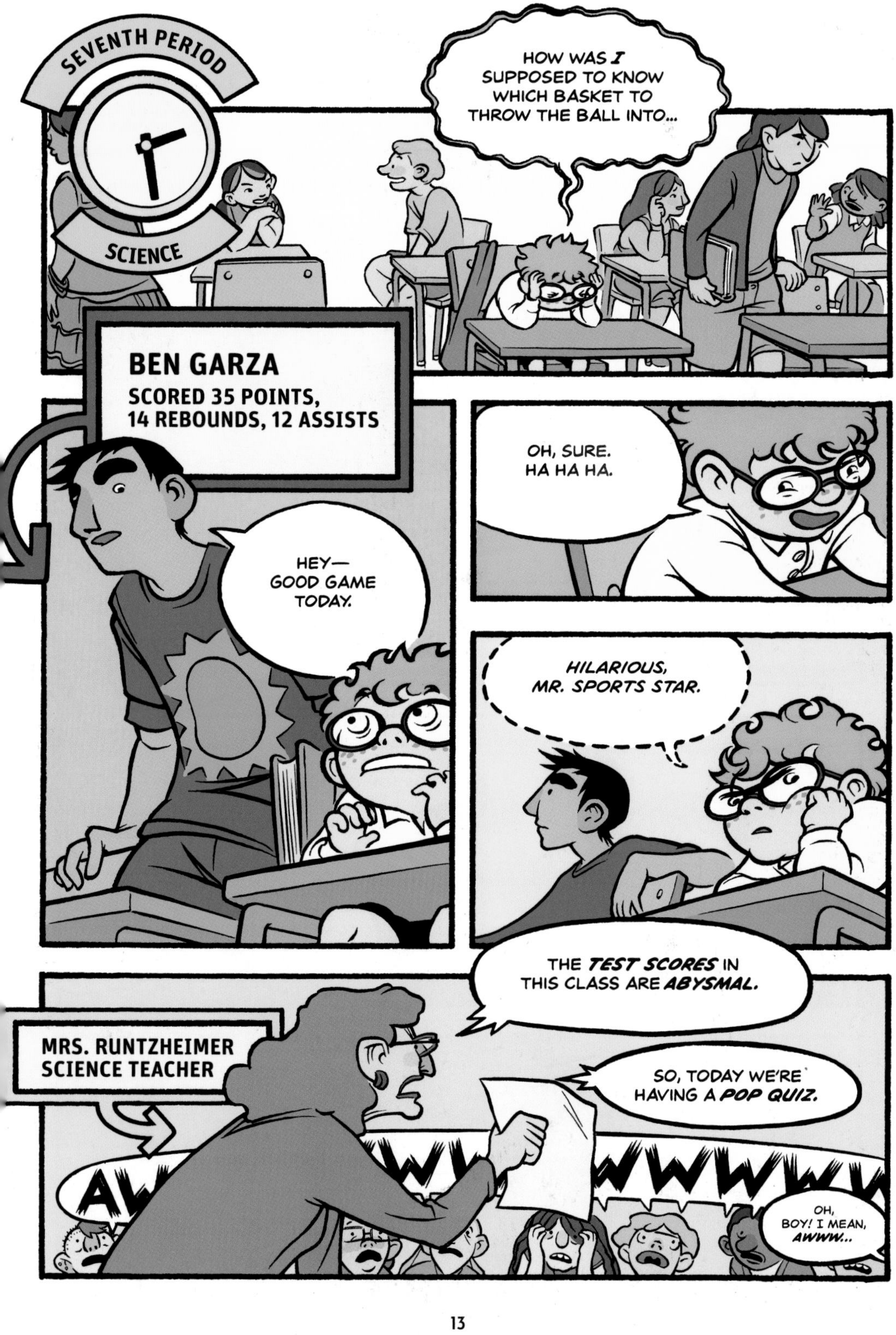
SEVENTH PERIOD
SCIENCE
HOW WAS *I* SUPPOSED TO KNOW WHICH BASKET TO THROW THE BALL INTO...
BEN GARZA
SCORED 35 POINTS, 14 REBOUNDS, 12 ASSISTS
HEY— GOOD GAME TODAY.
OH, SURE. HA HA HA.
HILARIOUS, MR. SPORTS STAR.
THE ***TEST SCORES*** IN THIS CLASS ARE ***ABYSMAL.***
MRS. RUNTZHEIMER
SCIENCE TEACHER
SO, TODAY WE'RE HAVING A ***POP QUIZ.***
AW WWWWWWWWW
OH, BOY! I MEAN, ***AWWW...***

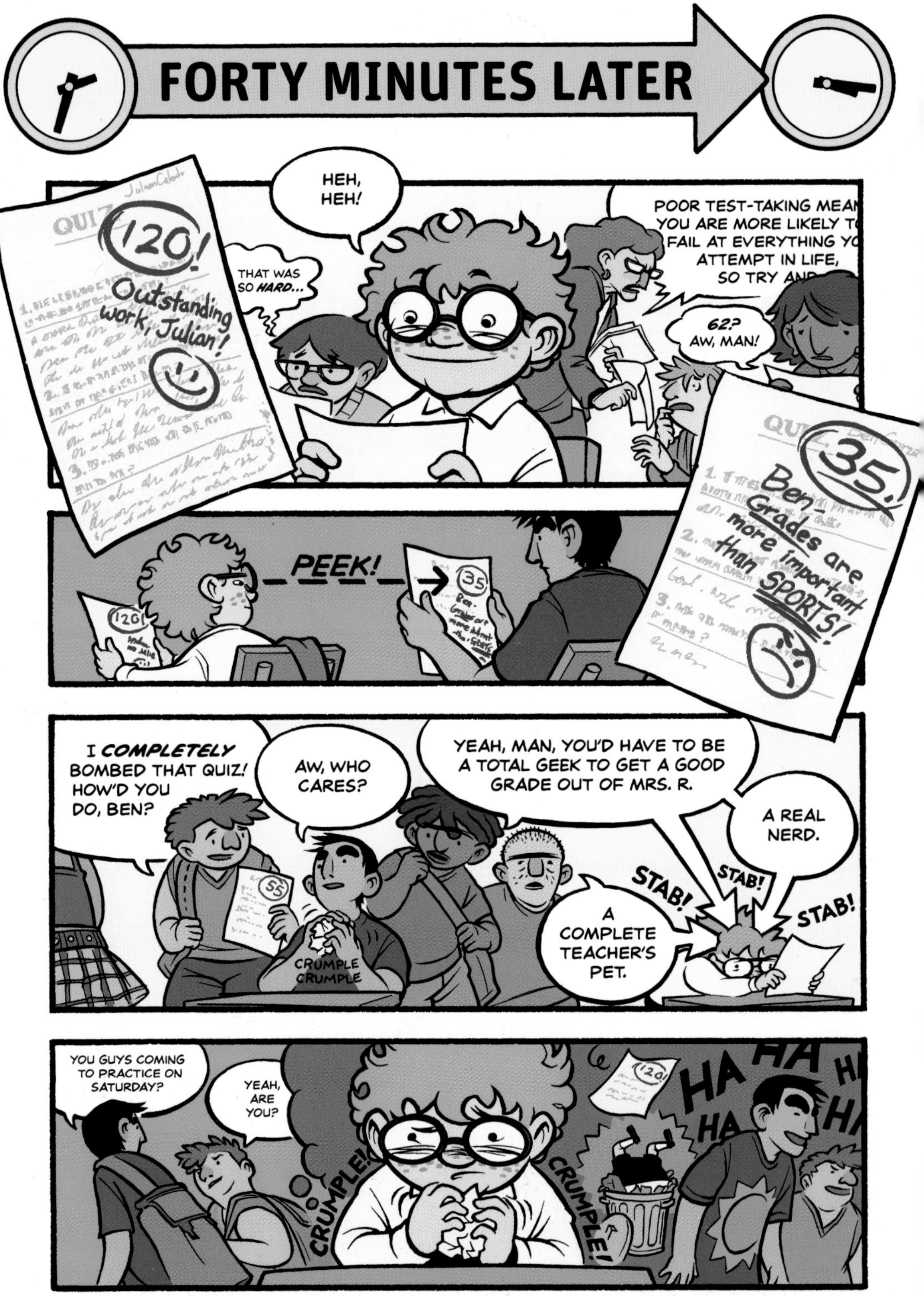
FORTY MINUTES LATER
QUIZ
120!
Outstanding work, Julian!
THAT WAS SO HARD...
HEH, HEH!
POOR TEST-TAKING MEAN
YOU ARE MORE LIKELY T
FAIL AT EVERYTHING YO
ATTEMPT IN LIFE,
SO TRY AN
62?
AW, MAN!
QUIZ
35!
Ben- Grades are more important than SPORTS!
PEEK!
I COMPLETELY BOMBED THAT QUIZ! HOW'D YOU DO, BEN?
AW, WHO CARES?
YEAH, MAN, YOU'D HAVE TO BE A TOTAL GEEK TO GET A GOOD GRADE OUT OF MRS. R.
A REAL NERD.
A COMPLETE TEACHER'S PET.
STAB!
STAB!
STAB!
CRUMPLE CRUMPLE
YOU GUYS COMING TO PRACTICE ON SATURDAY?
YEAH, ARE YOU?
CRUMPLE!
CRUMPLE!
HA HA HA HA HA

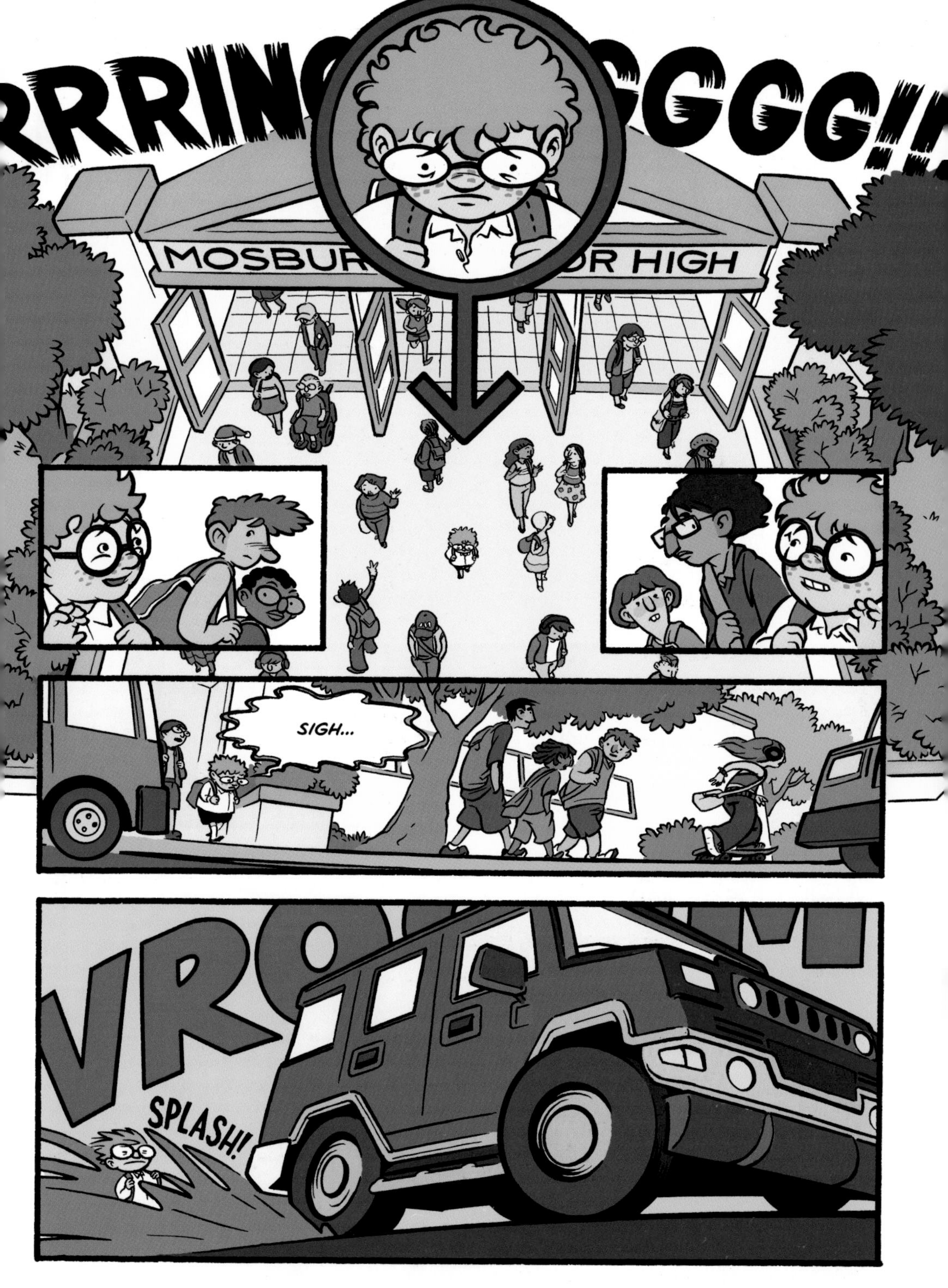
RRRINGGGGG!!
MOSBUR… …R HIGH
SIGH...
VROOM
SPLASH!

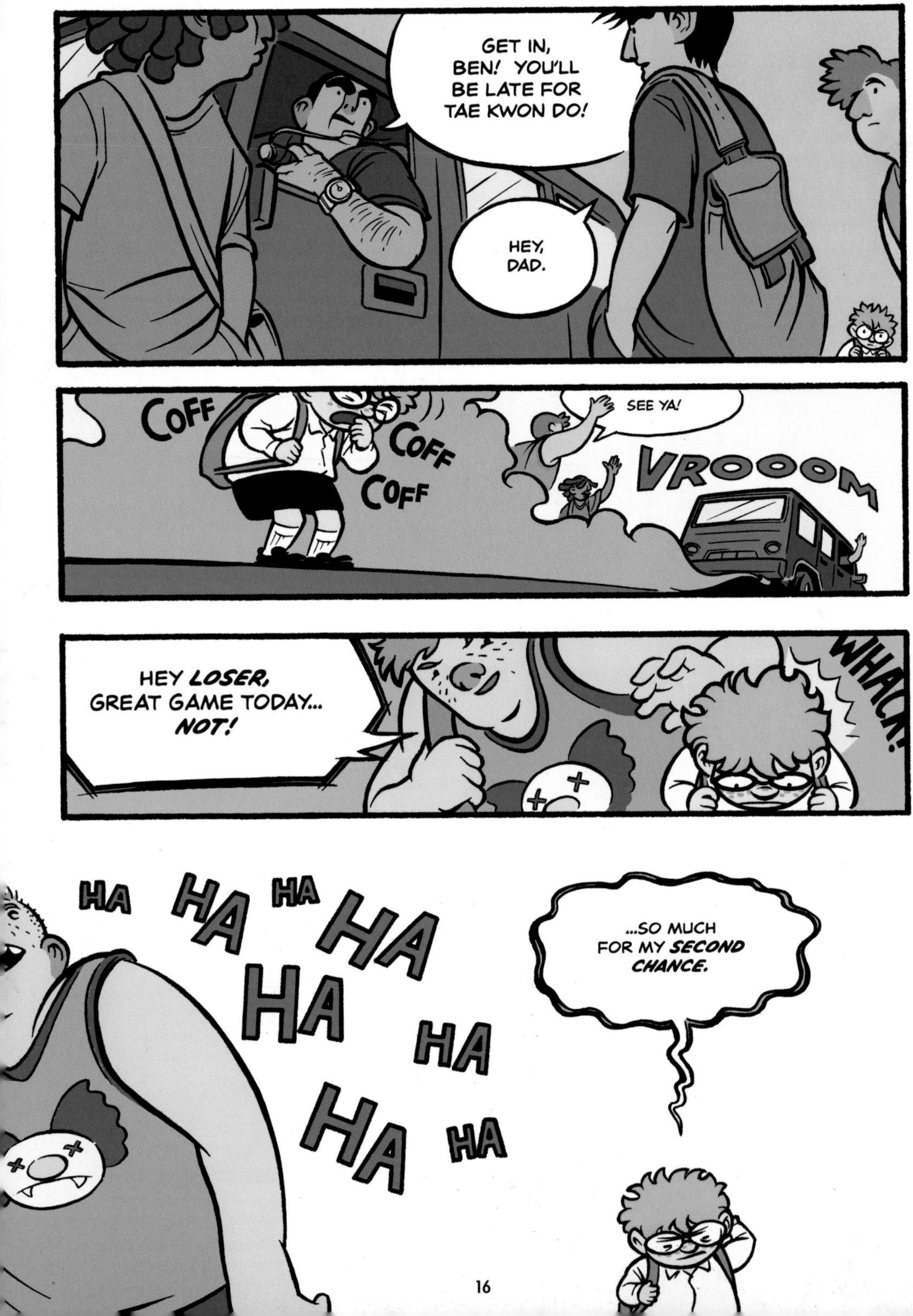
GET IN, BEN! YOU'LL BE LATE FOR TAE KWON DO!
HEY, DAD.
COFF
COFF
COFF
SEE YA!
VROOOM
HEY LOSER, GREAT GAME TODAY... NOT!
WHACK!
HA HA HA HA HA HA HA HA
...SO MUCH FOR MY SECOND CHANCE.

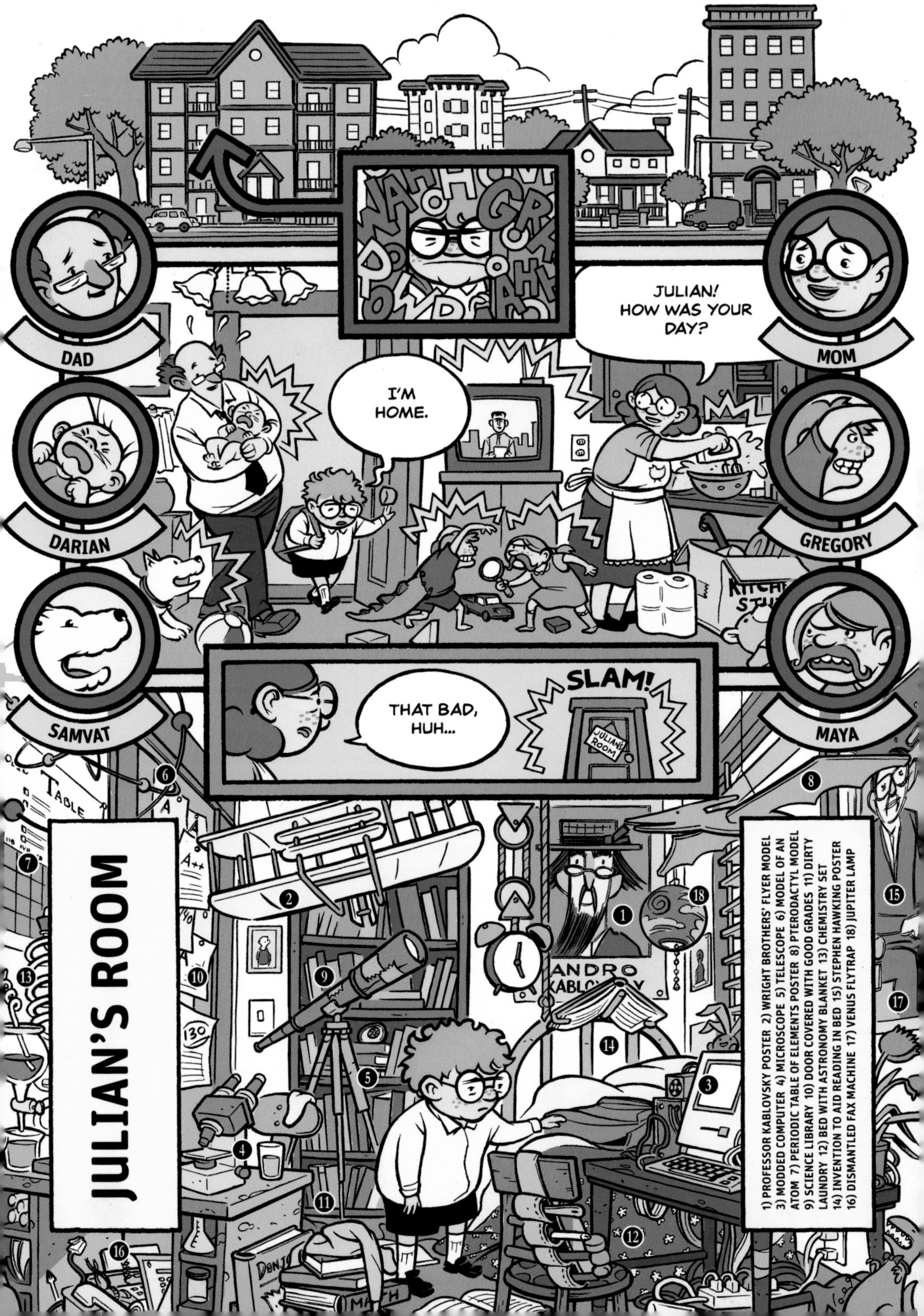
DAD
MOM
JULIAN! HOW WAS YOUR DAY?
DARIAN
I'M HOME.
GREGORY
SAMVAT
MAYA
THAT BAD, HUH...
SLAM!
JULIAN'S ROOM
JULIAN'S ROOM
1) PROFESSOR KABLOVSKY POSTER 2) WRIGHT BROTHERS' FLYER MODEL 3) MODDED COMPUTER 4) MICROSCOPE 5) TELESCOPE 6) MODEL OF AN ATOM 7) PERIODIC TABLE OF ELEMENTS POSTER 8) PTERODACTYL MODEL 9) SCIENCE LIBRARY 10) DOOR COVERED WITH GOOD GRADES 11) DIRTY LAUNDRY 12) BED WITH ASTRONOMY BLANKET 13) CHEMISTRY SET 14) INVENTION TO AID READING IN BED 15) STEPHEN HAWKING POSTER 16) DISMANTLED FAX MACHINE 17) VENUS FLYTRAP 18) JUPITER LAMP

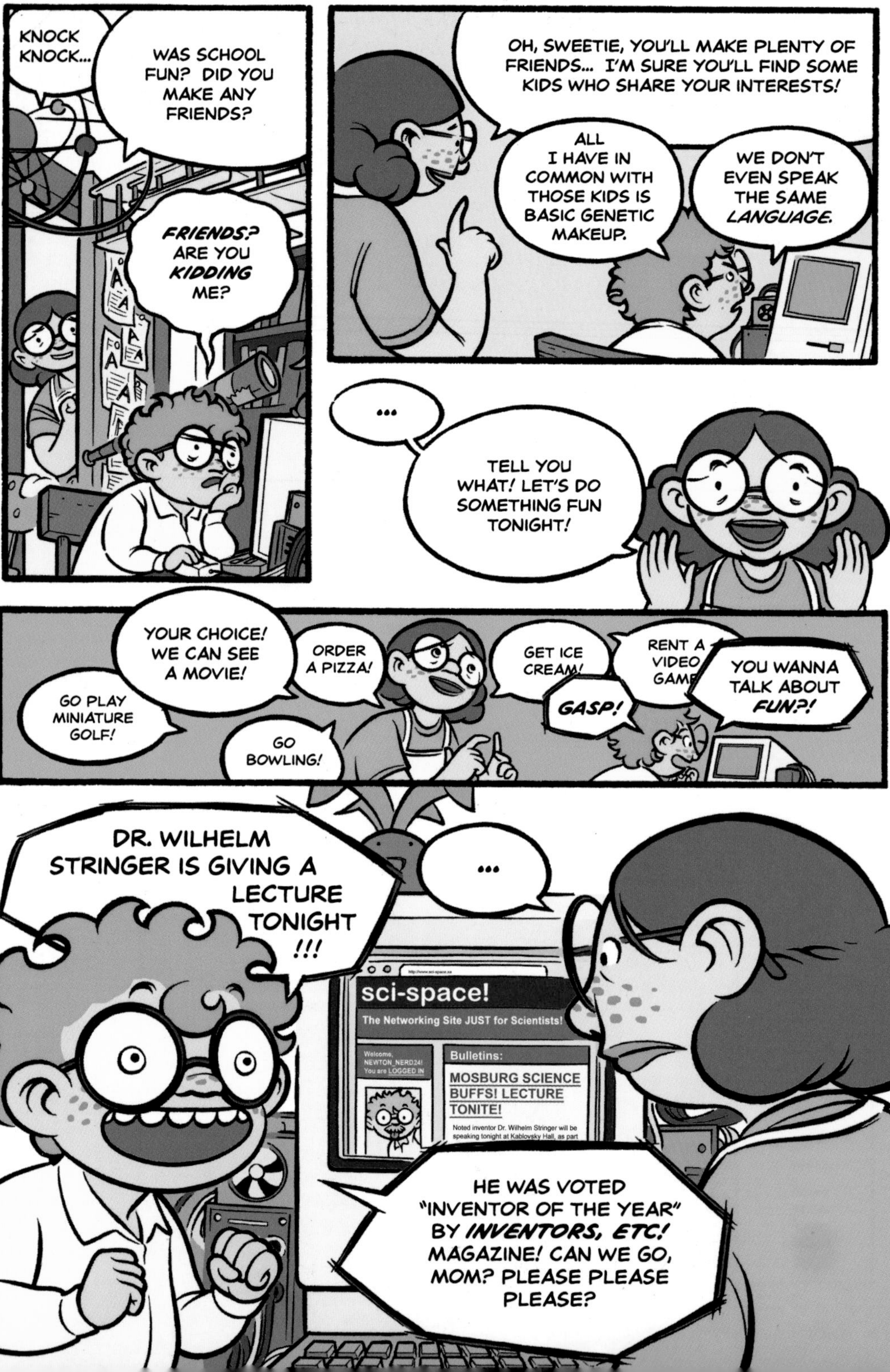
KNOCK KNOCK...
WAS SCHOOL FUN? DID YOU MAKE ANY FRIENDS?
FRIENDS? ARE YOU *KIDDING* ME?
OH, SWEETIE, YOU'LL MAKE PLENTY OF FRIENDS... I'M SURE YOU'LL FIND SOME KIDS WHO SHARE YOUR INTERESTS!
ALL I HAVE IN COMMON WITH THOSE KIDS IS BASIC GENETIC MAKEUP.
WE DON'T EVEN SPEAK THE SAME *LANGUAGE.*
...
TELL YOU WHAT! LET'S DO SOMETHING FUN TONIGHT!
GO PLAY MINIATURE GOLF!
YOUR CHOICE! WE CAN SEE A MOVIE!
GO BOWLING!
ORDER A PIZZA!
GET ICE CREAM!
RENT A VIDEO GAM
GASP!
YOU WANNA TALK ABOUT *FUN?!*
DR. WILHELM STRINGER IS GIVING A LECTURE TONIGHT !!!
...
sci-space!
The Networking Site JUST for Scientists!
Welcome, NEWTON_NERD24! You are LOGGED IN
Bulletins:
MOSBURG SCIENCE BUFFS! LECTURE TONITE!
Noted inventor Dr. Wilhelm Stringer will be speaking tonight at Kablovsky Hall, as part
HE WAS VOTED "INVENTOR OF THE YEAR" BY *INVENTORS, ETC!* MAGAZINE! CAN WE GO, MOM? PLEASE PLEASE PLEASE?

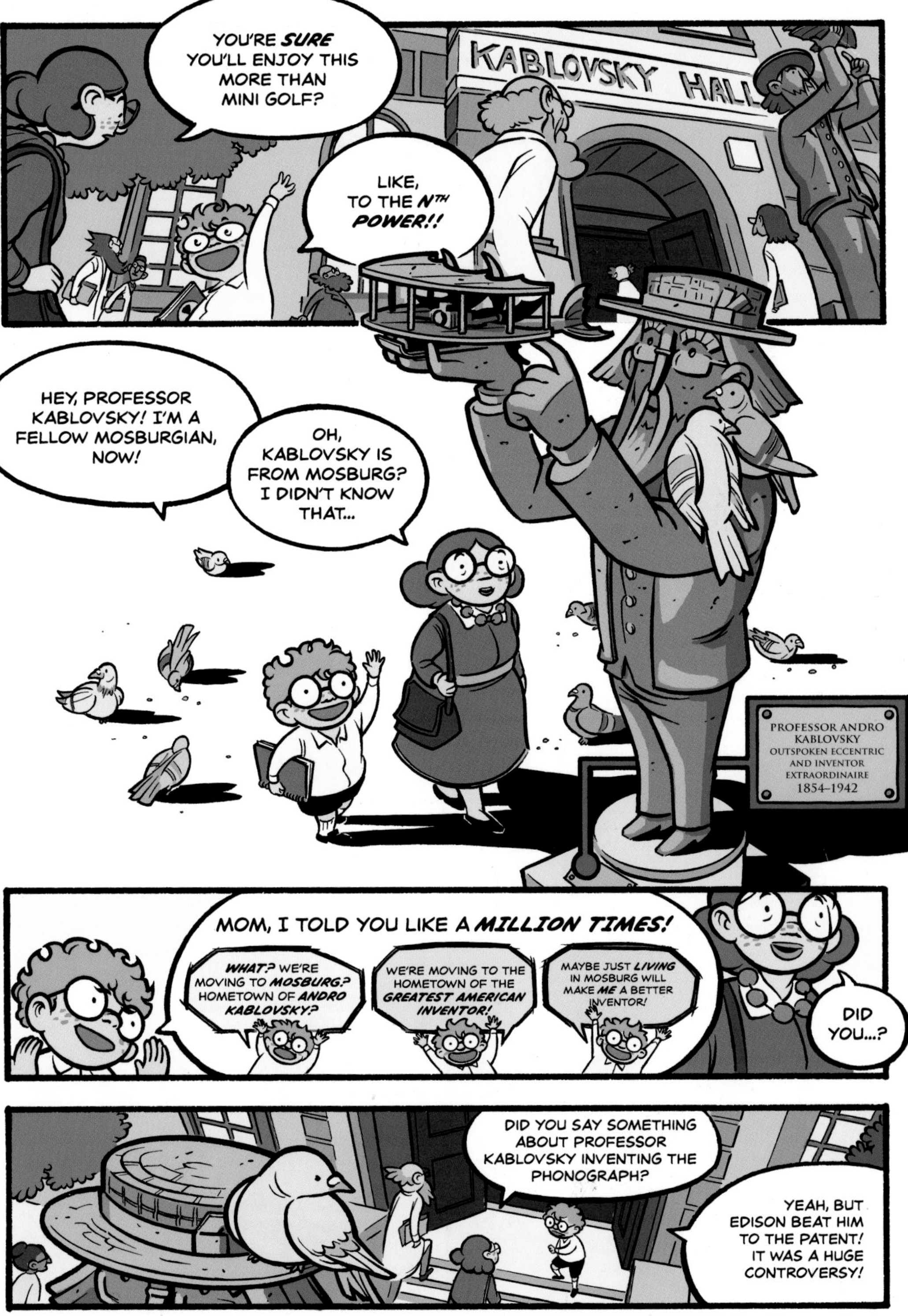

KABLOVSKY HALL
YOU'RE *SURE* YOU'LL ENJOY THIS MORE THAN MINI GOLF?
LIKE, TO THE N^{TH} *POWER!!*
HEY, PROFESSOR KABLOVSKY! I'M A FELLOW MOSBURGIAN, NOW!
OH, KABLOVSKY IS FROM MOSBURG? I DIDN'T KNOW THAT...
PROFESSOR ANDRO KABLOVSKY
OUTSPOKEN ECCENTRIC AND INVENTOR EXTRAORDINAIRE
1854–1942
MOM, I TOLD YOU LIKE A *MILLION TIMES!*
WHAT? WE'RE MOVING TO *MOSBURG?* HOMETOWN OF *ANDRO KABLOVSKY?*
WE'RE MOVING TO THE HOMETOWN OF THE *GREATEST AMERICAN INVENTOR!*
MAYBE JUST *LIVING* IN MOSBURG WILL MAKE *ME* A BETTER INVENTOR!
DID YOU...?
DID YOU SAY SOMETHING ABOUT PROFESSOR KABLOVSKY INVENTING THE PHONOGRAPH?
YEAH, BUT EDISON BEAT HIM TO THE PATENT! IT WAS A HUGE CONTROVERSY!

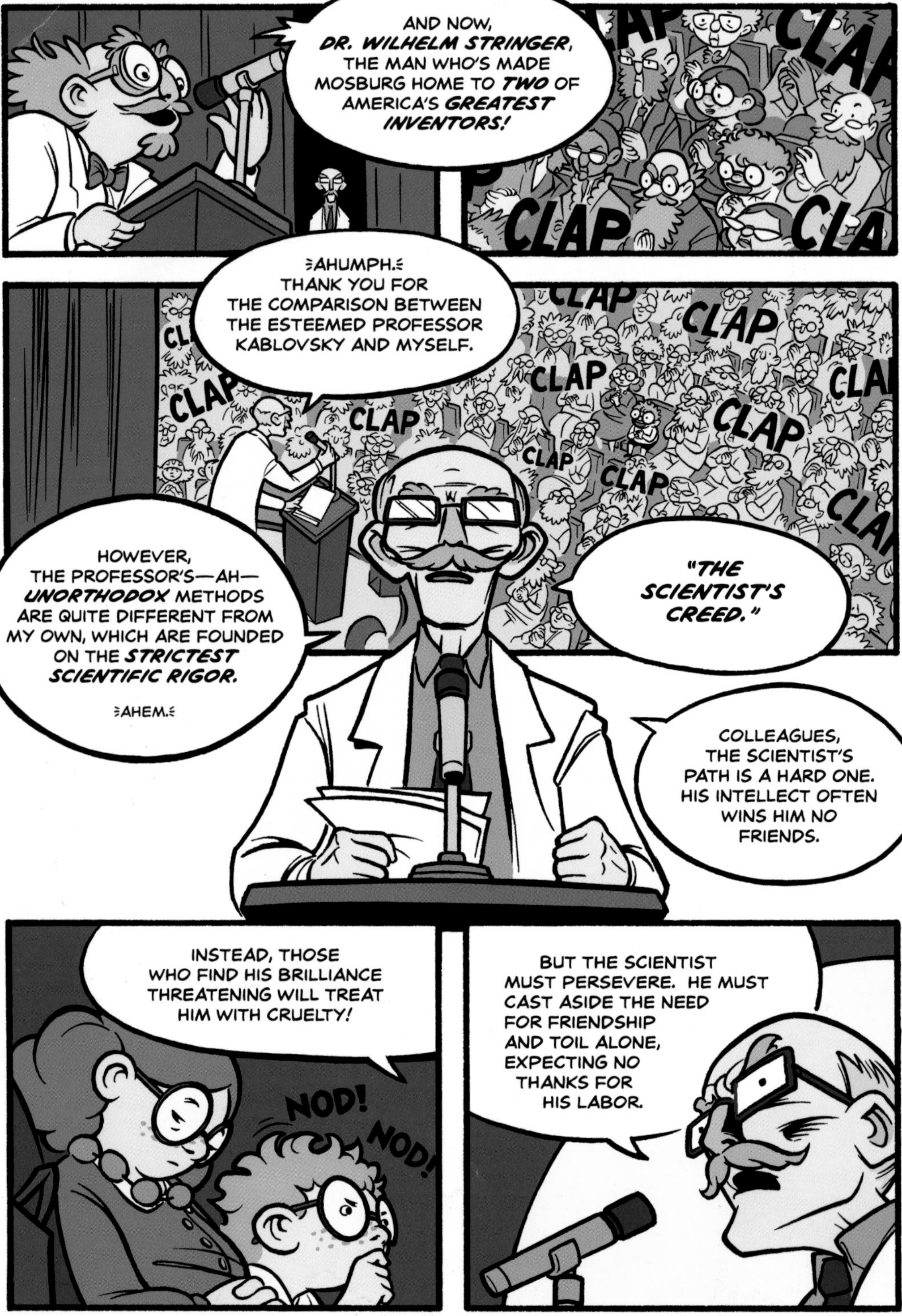
AND NOW, DR. WILHELM STRINGER, THE MAN WHO'S MADE MOSBURG HOME TO TWO OF AMERICA'S GREATEST INVENTORS!
CLAP CLAP CLAP CLAP CLAP
AHUMPH. THANK YOU FOR THE COMPARISON BETWEEN THE ESTEEMED PROFESSOR KABLOVSKY AND MYSELF.
CLAP CLAP CLAP CLAP CLAP CLAP CLAP CLAP
HOWEVER, THE PROFESSOR'S—AH—UNORTHODOX METHODS ARE QUITE DIFFERENT FROM MY OWN, WHICH ARE FOUNDED ON THE STRICTEST SCIENTIFIC RIGOR.
AHEM.
"THE SCIENTIST'S CREED."
COLLEAGUES, THE SCIENTIST'S PATH IS A HARD ONE. HIS INTELLECT OFTEN WINS HIM NO FRIENDS.
INSTEAD, THOSE WHO FIND HIS BRILLIANCE THREATENING WILL TREAT HIM WITH CRUELTY!
NOD! NOD!
BUT THE SCIENTIST MUST PERSEVERE. HE MUST CAST ASIDE THE NEED FOR FRIENDSHIP AND TOIL ALONE, EXPECTING NO THANKS FOR HIS LABOR.

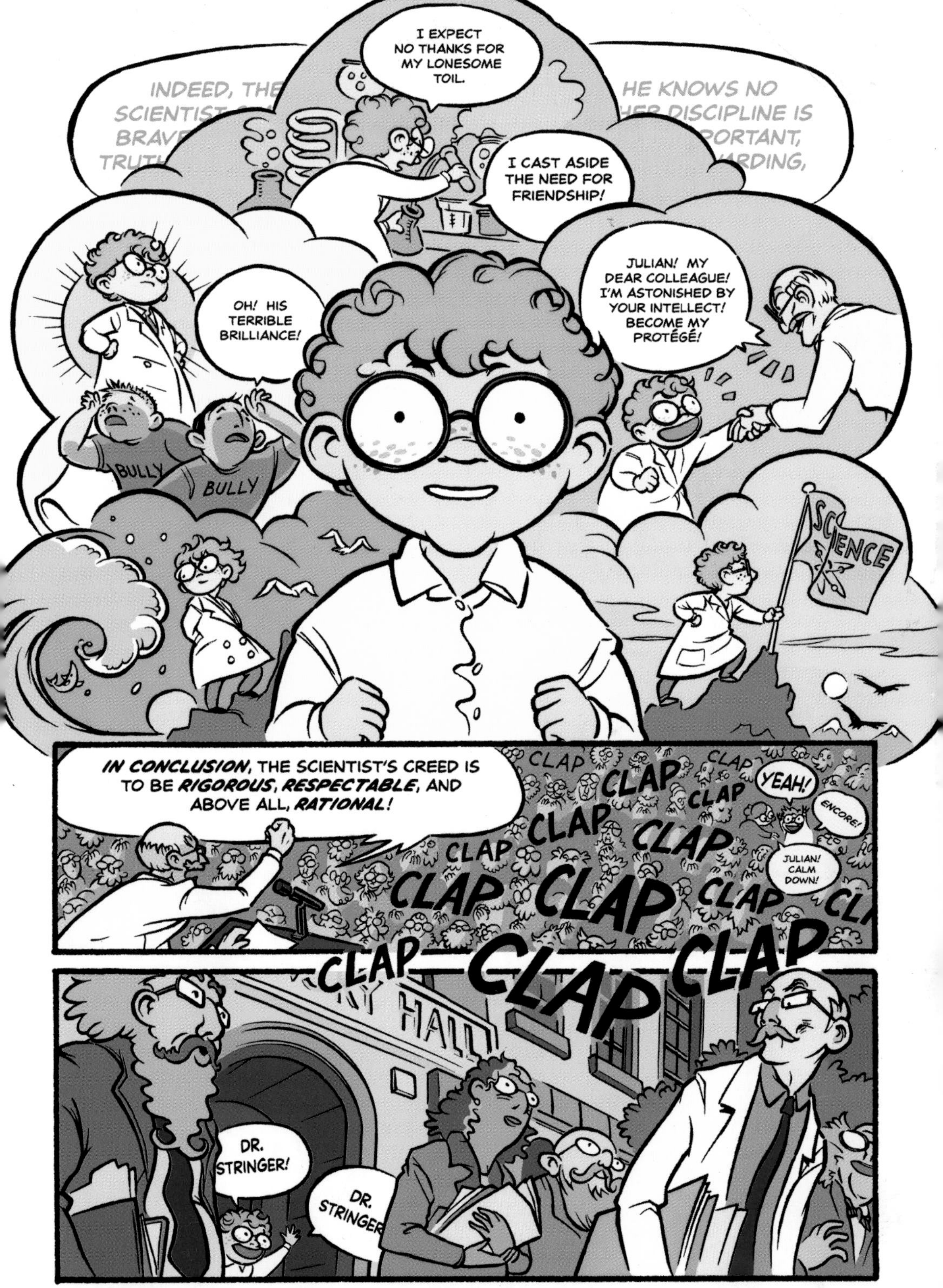
INDEED, THE SCIENTIST ... BRAVE ... TRUTH
I EXPECT NO THANKS FOR MY LONESOME TOIL.
HE KNOWS NO ... DISCIPLINE IS ... PORTANT, ... ARDING,
I CAST ASIDE THE NEED FOR FRIENDSHIP!
OH! HIS TERRIBLE BRILLIANCE!
BULLY
BULLY
JULIAN! MY DEAR COLLEAGUE! I'M ASTONISHED BY YOUR INTELLECT! BECOME MY PROTÉGÉ!
SCIENCE
IN CONCLUSION, THE SCIENTIST'S CREED IS TO BE RIGOROUS, RESPECTABLE, AND ABOVE ALL, RATIONAL!
CLAP CLAP CLAP CLAP CLAP CLAP CLAP CLAP CLAP CLAP CLAP
YEAH!
ENCORE!
JULIAN! CALM DOWN!
CLAP CLAP CLAP
HALL
DR. STRINGER!
DR. STRINGER

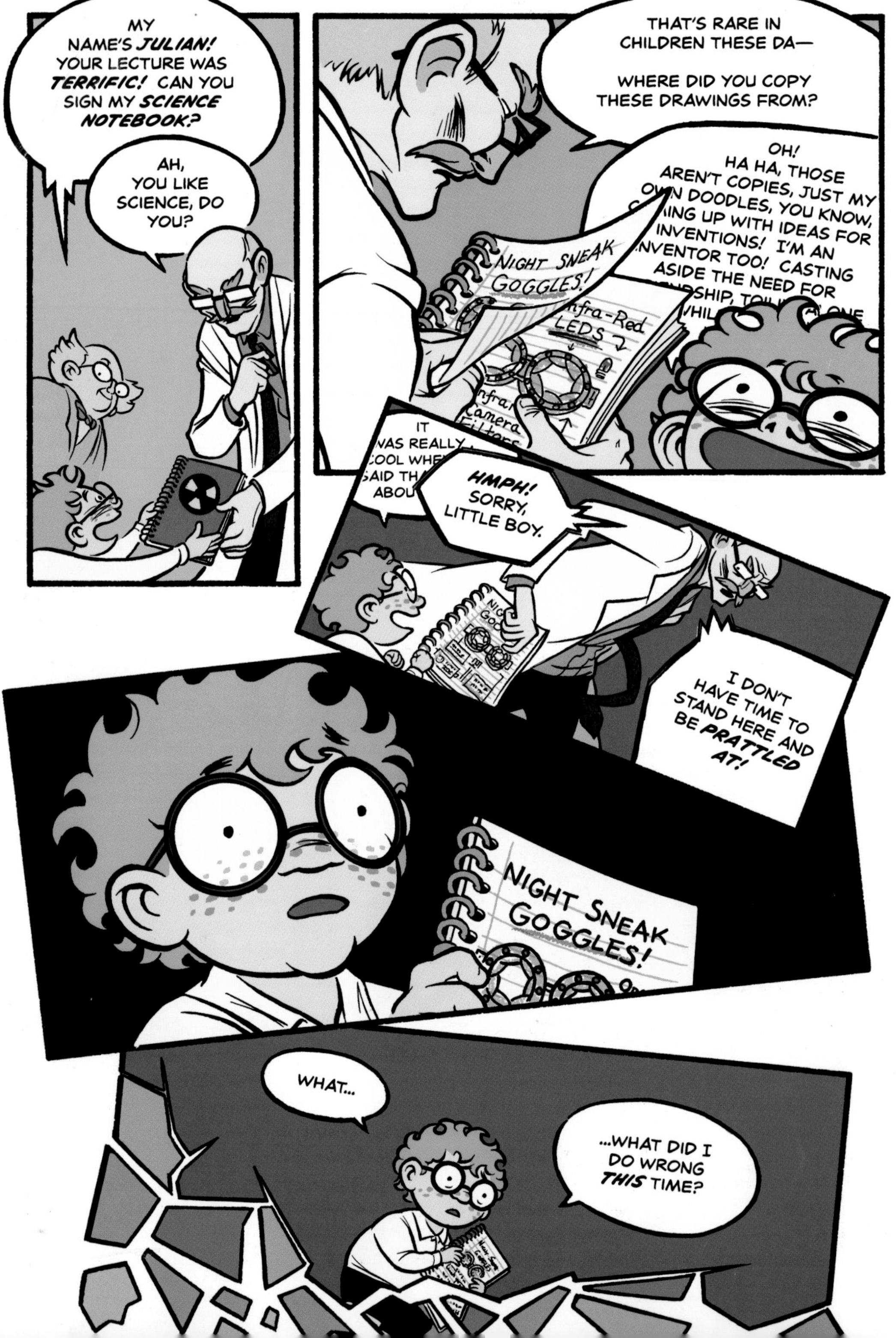
MY NAME'S JULIAN! YOUR LECTURE WAS TERRIFIC! CAN YOU SIGN MY SCIENCE NOTEBOOK?
AH, YOU LIKE SCIENCE, DO YOU?
THAT'S RARE IN CHILDREN THESE DA—
WHERE DID YOU COPY THESE DRAWINGS FROM?
OH! HA HA, THOSE AREN'T COPIES, JUST MY OWN DOODLES, YOU KNOW, ...ING UP WITH IDEAS FOR INVENTIONS! I'M AN ...NVENTOR TOO! CASTING ASIDE THE NEED FOR ...NDSHIP, TOIL... WHIL...
NIGHT SNEAK GOGGLES!
IT WAS REALLY COOL WHE... SAID TH... ABOU...
HMPH! SORRY, LITTLE BOY.
I DON'T HAVE TIME TO STAND HERE AND BE PRATTLED AT!
NIGHT SNEAK GOGGLES!
WHAT...
...WHAT DID I DO WRONG THIS TIME?

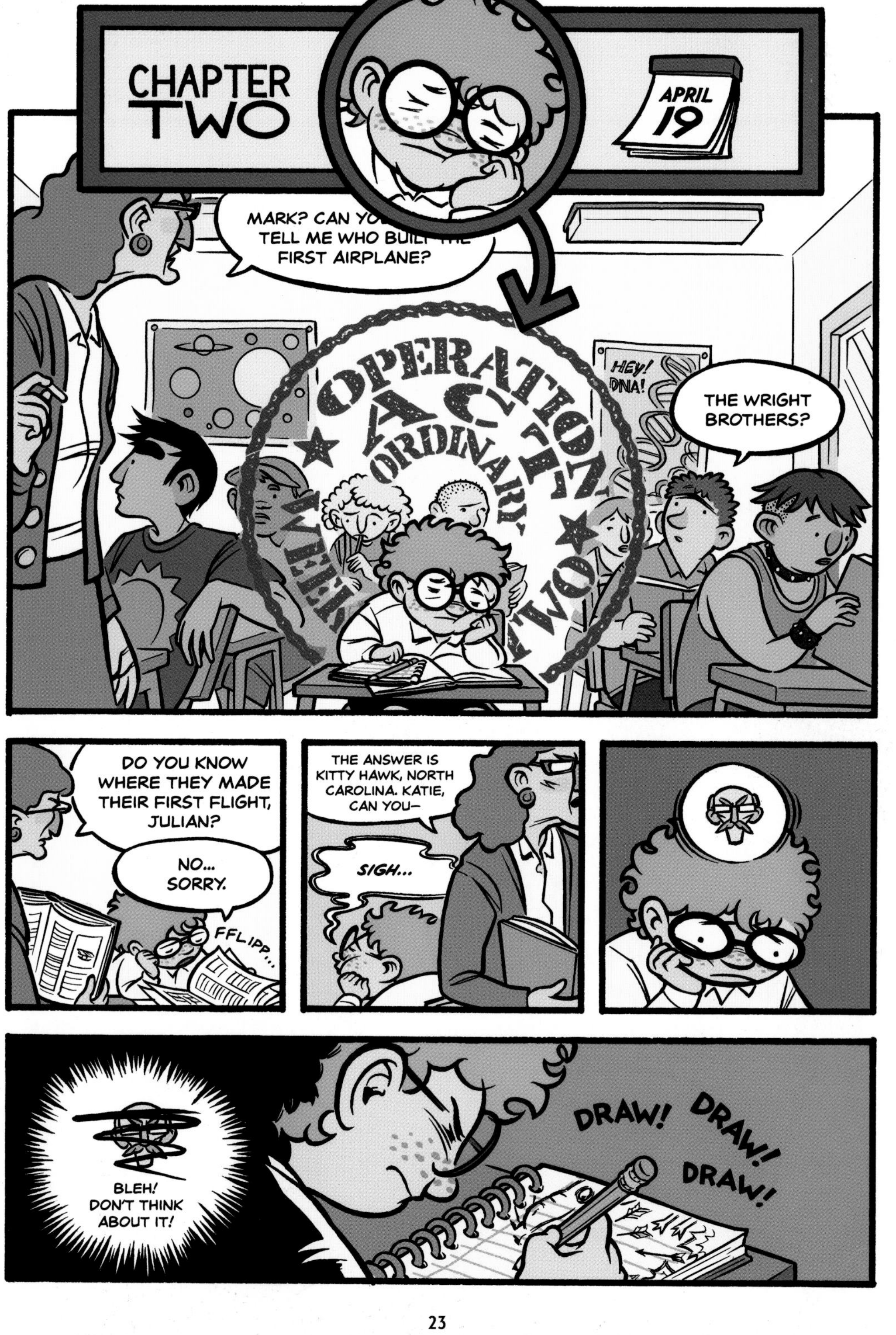
CHAPTER TWO
APRIL 19
MARK? CAN YOU TELL ME WHO BUILT THE FIRST AIRPLANE?
OPERATION A CUT WEEK ORDINARY TWO
HEY! DNA!
THE WRIGHT BROTHERS?
DO YOU KNOW WHERE THEY MADE THEIR FIRST FLIGHT, JULIAN?
NO... SORRY.
FFLIPP...
THE ANSWER IS KITTY HAWK, NORTH CAROLINA. KATIE, CAN YOU—
SIGH...
BLEH! DON'T THINK ABOUT IT!
DRAW! DRAW! DRAW!

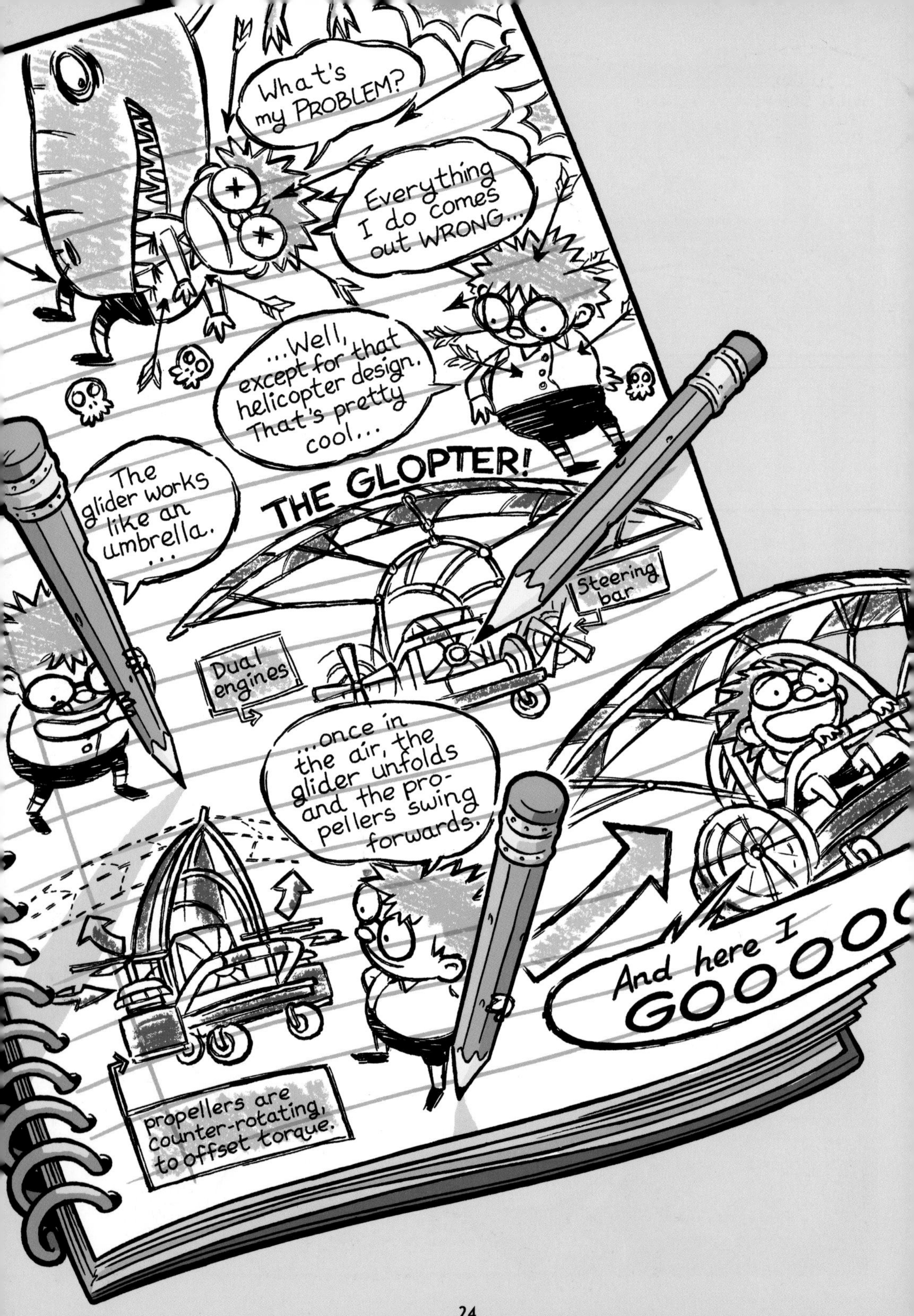
What's my PROBLEM?
Everything I do comes out WRONG...
...Well, except for that helicopter design. That's pretty cool...
THE GLOPTER!
The glider works like an umbrella. ...
Steering bar
Dual engines
...once in the air, the glider unfolds and the propellers swing forwards.
propellers are counter-rotating, to offset torque.
And here I GOOOOO

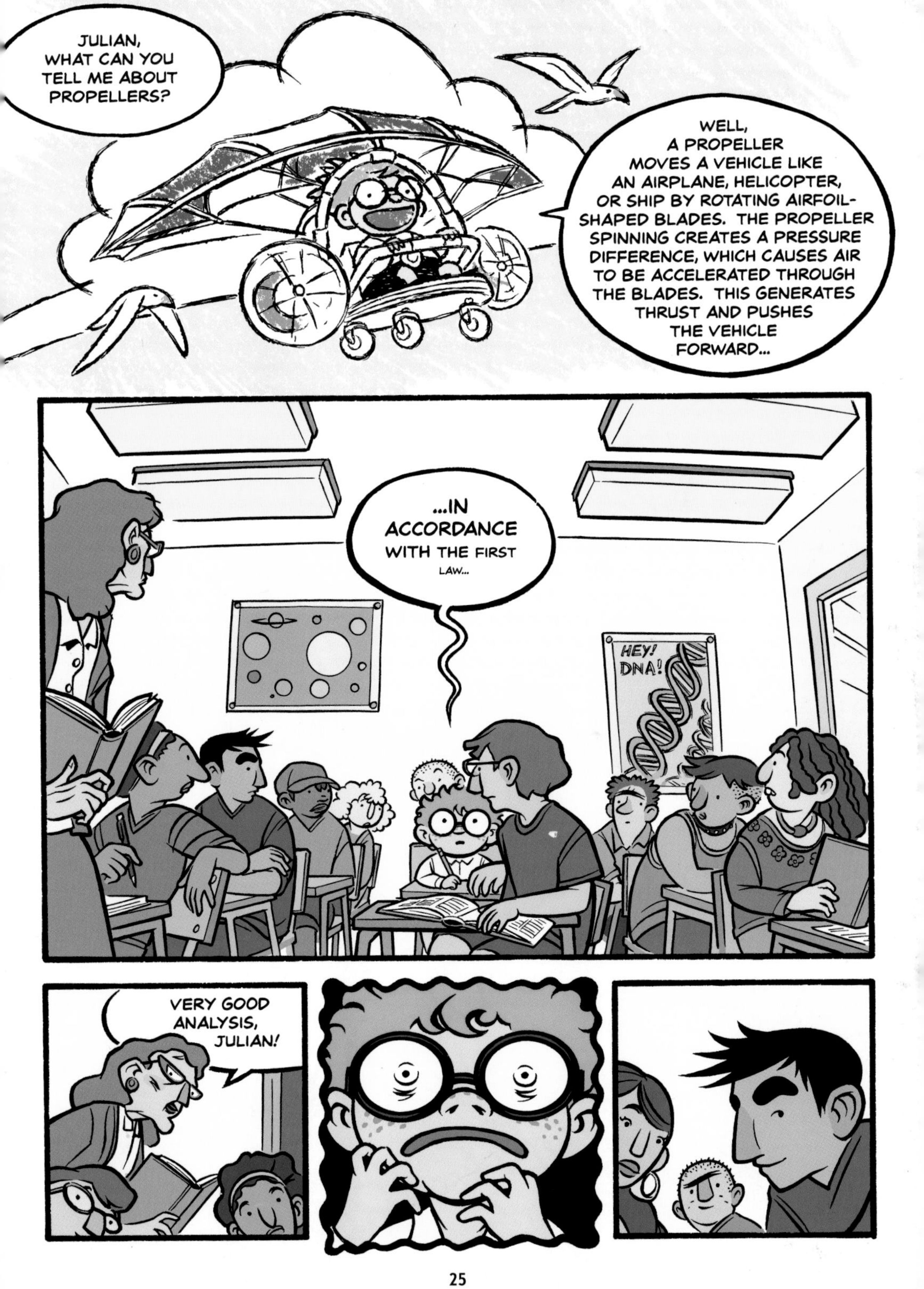
JULIAN, WHAT CAN YOU TELL ME ABOUT PROPELLERS?
WELL, A PROPELLER MOVES A VEHICLE LIKE AN AIRPLANE, HELICOPTER, OR SHIP BY ROTATING AIRFOIL-SHAPED BLADES. THE PROPELLER SPINNING CREATES A PRESSURE DIFFERENCE, WHICH CAUSES AIR TO BE ACCELERATED THROUGH THE BLADES. THIS GENERATES THRUST AND PUSHES THE VEHICLE FORWARD...
...IN ACCORDANCE WITH THE FIRST LAW...
HEY! DNA!
VERY GOOD ANALYSIS, JULIAN!

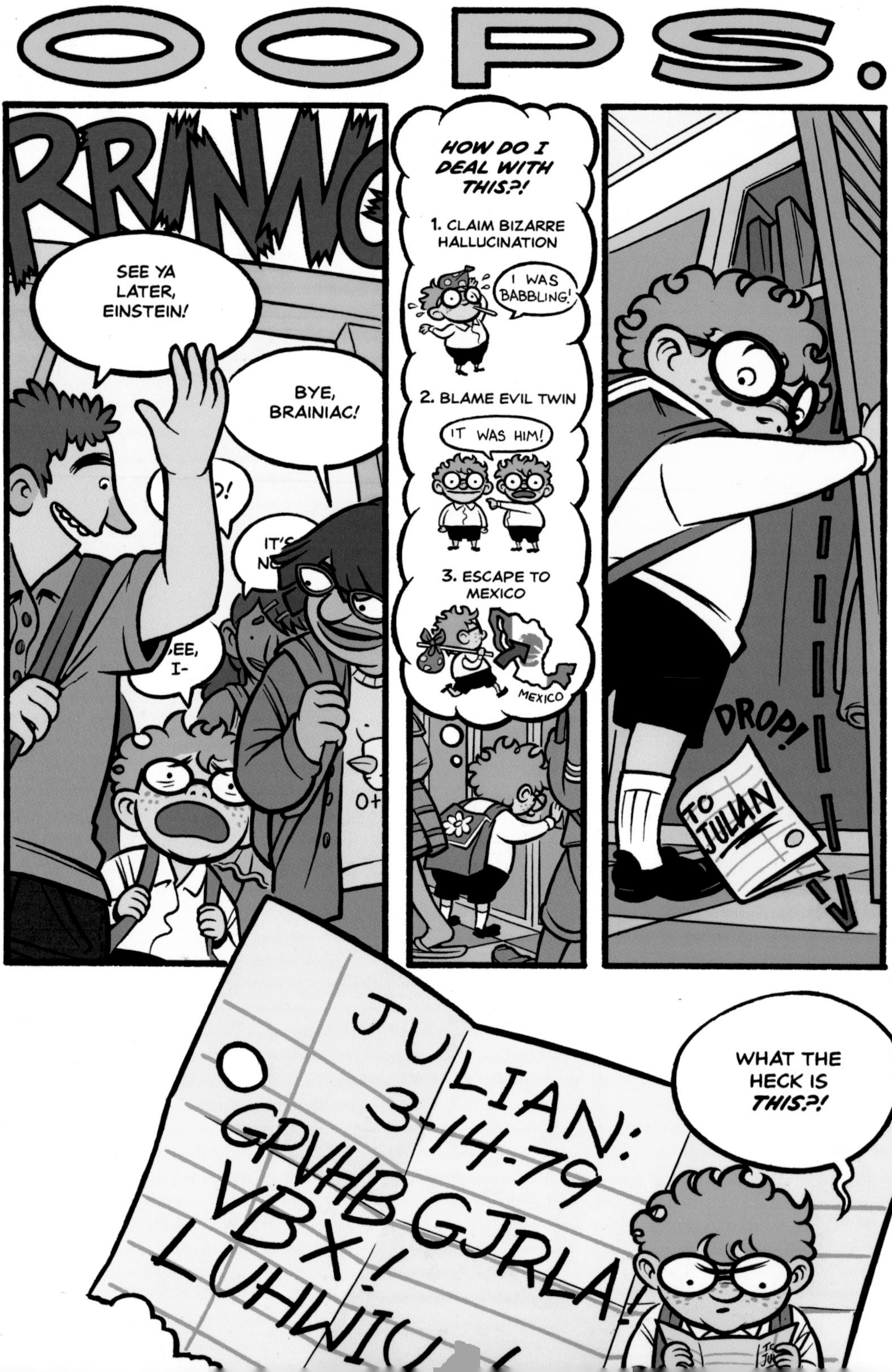
OOPS.
RRINNG
SEE YA LATER, EINSTEIN!
BYE, BRAINIAC!
HOW DO I DEAL WITH THIS?!
1. CLAIM BIZARRE HALLUCINATION
I WAS BABBLING!
2. BLAME EVIL TWIN
IT WAS HIM!
3. ESCAPE TO MEXICO
MEXICO
DROP!
TO JULIAN
JULIAN: 3-14-79
GPVHB GJRLA!
VBX!
WHAT THE HECK IS THIS?!

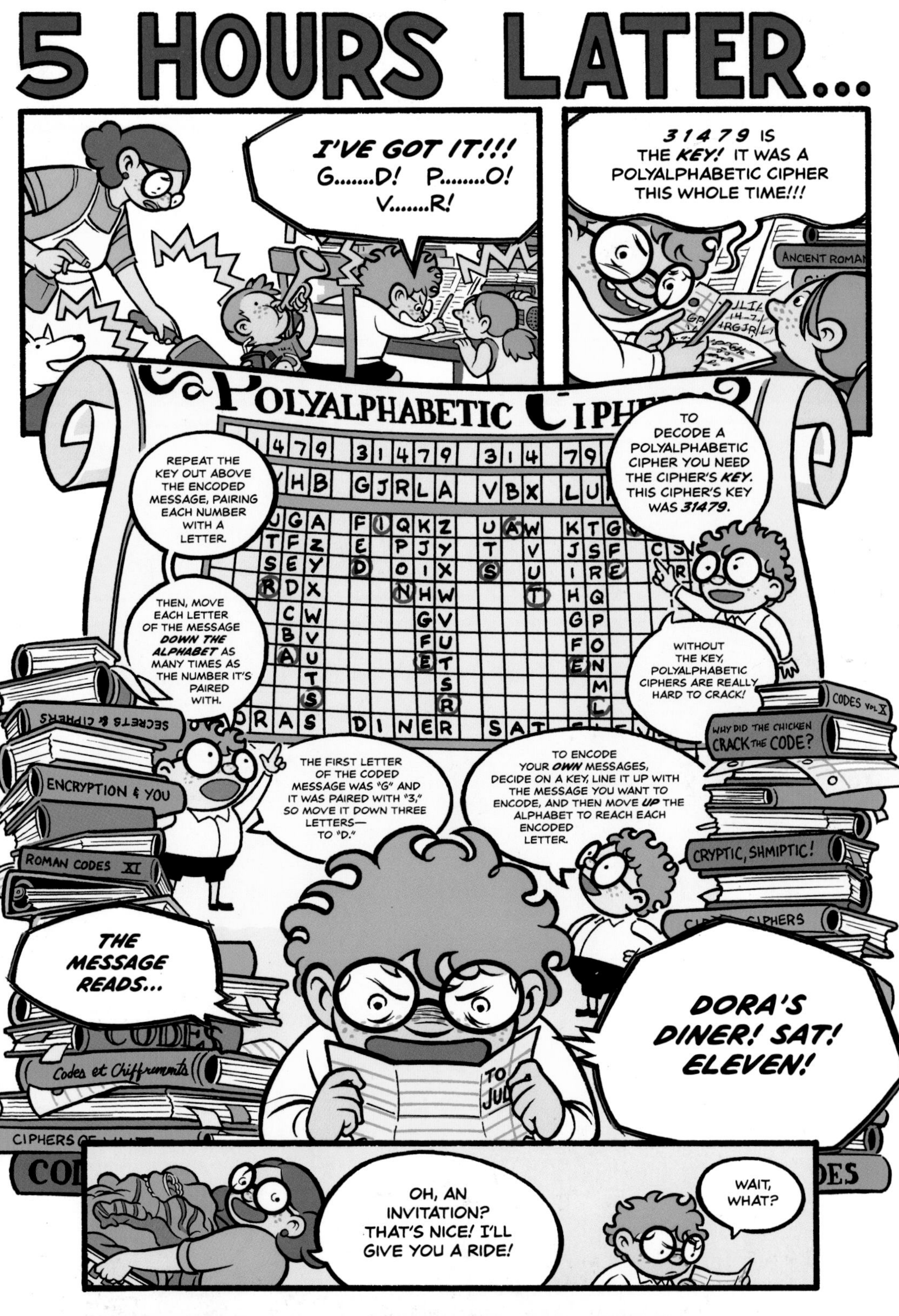
5 HOURS LATER...
I'VE GOT IT!!! G.......D! P.......O! V.......R!
31479 IS THE KEY! IT WAS A POLYALPHABETIC CIPHER THIS WHOLE TIME!!!
ANCIENT ROMAN
POLYALPHABETIC CIPHERS
REPEAT THE KEY OUT ABOVE THE ENCODED MESSAGE, PAIRING EACH NUMBER WITH A LETTER.
THEN, MOVE EACH LETTER OF THE MESSAGE DOWN THE ALPHABET AS MANY TIMES AS THE NUMBER IT'S PAIRED WITH.
TO DECODE A POLYALPHABETIC CIPHER YOU NEED THE CIPHER'S KEY. THIS CIPHER'S KEY WAS 31479.
WITHOUT THE KEY, POLYALPHABETIC CIPHERS ARE REALLY HARD TO CRACK!
THE FIRST LETTER OF THE CODED MESSAGE WAS "G" AND IT WAS PAIRED WITH "3," SO MOVE IT DOWN THREE LETTERS— TO "D."
TO ENCODE YOUR OWN MESSAGES, DECIDE ON A KEY, LINE IT UP WITH THE MESSAGE YOU WANT TO ENCODE, AND THEN MOVE UP THE ALPHABET TO REACH EACH ENCODED LETTER.
SECRETS & CIPHERS
ENCRYPTION & YOU
ROMAN CODES XI
CODES VOL X
WHY DID THE CHICKEN CRACK THE CODE?
CRYPTIC, SHMIPTIC!
THE MESSAGE READS...
DORA'S DINER! SAT! ELEVEN!
Codes et Chiffrements
CIPHERS OF
OH, AN INVITATION? THAT'S NICE! I'LL GIVE YOU A RIDE!
WAIT, WHAT?

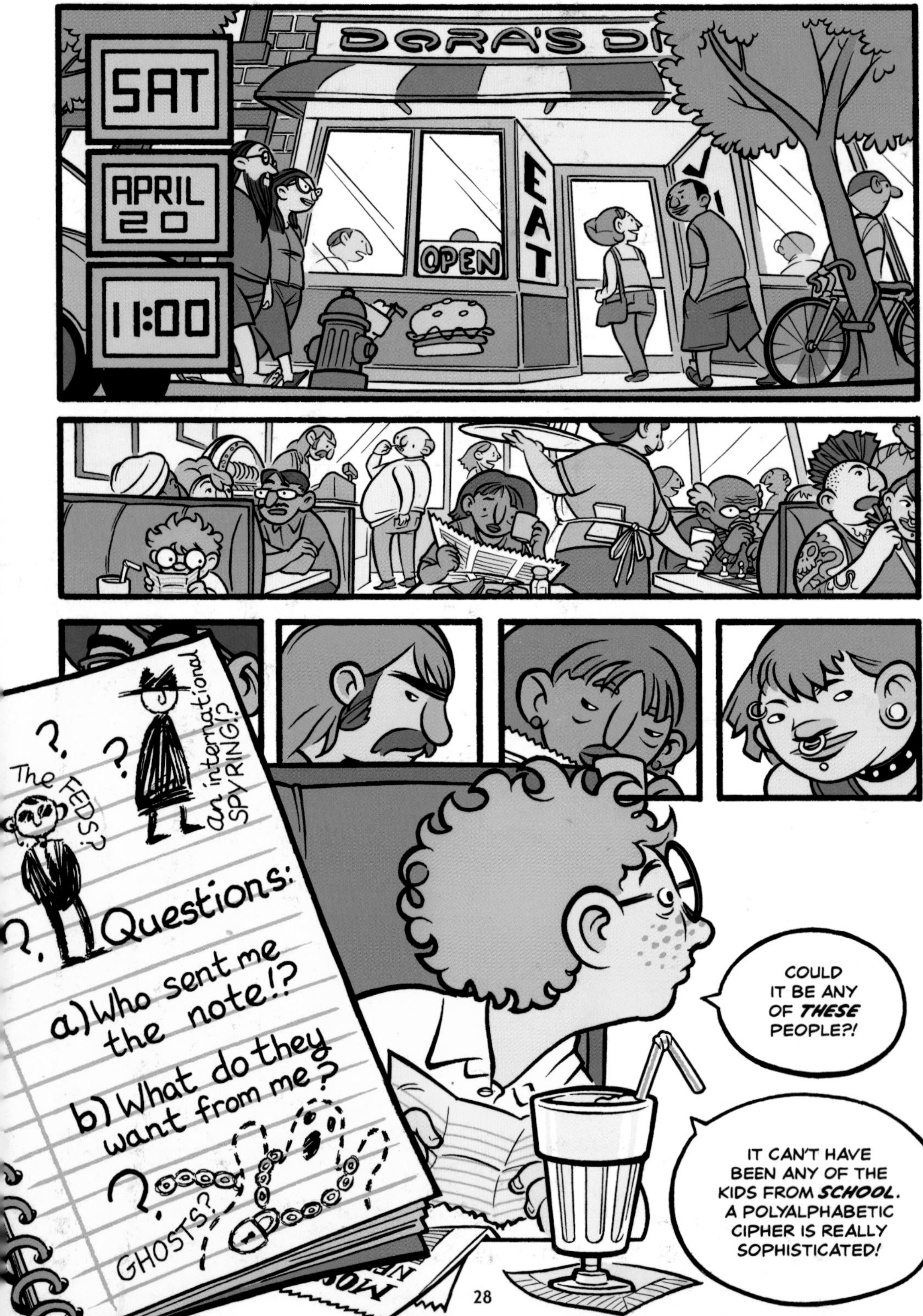
DORA'S DI
SAT
APRIL 20
11:00
EAT
OPEN
The FEDS?
an international SPYRING!?
Questions:
a) Who sent me the note!?
b) What do they want from me?
GHOSTS?
COULD IT BE ANY OF *THESE* PEOPLE?!
IT CAN'T HAVE BEEN ANY OF THE KIDS FROM *SCHOOL*. A POLYALPHABETIC CIPHER IS REALLY SOPHISTICATED!

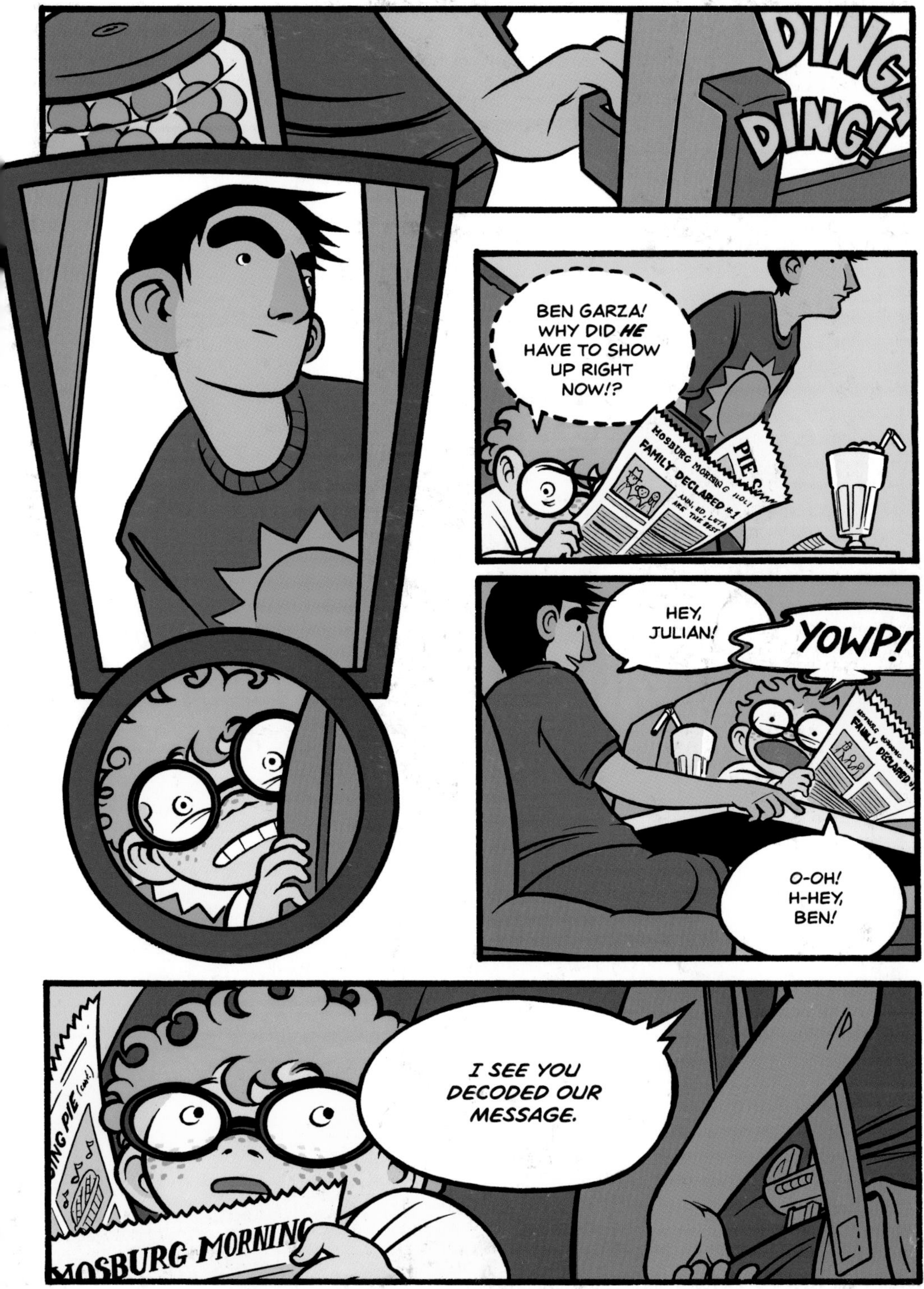
DING! DING!
BEN GARZA! WHY DID HE HAVE TO SHOW UP RIGHT NOW!?
MOSBURG MORNING
FAMILY DECLARED #1
ANN, ED, LETA ARE THE BEST
PIE S
HEY, JULIAN!
YOWP!
FAMILY DECLARED
O-OH! H-HEY, BEN!
I SEE YOU DECODED OUR MESSAGE.
PIE (cont.)
MOSBURG MORNING

I'M **GRETA HUGHES.** I HEAR YOU'RE A **BIG EXPERT** IN **AERODYNAMICS.**

WH-WHAT?!

NO! I DON'T KNOW ANYTHING ABOUT SCIENCE! SEE, IT WAS MY IDENTICAL TWIN FROM MEXICO WHO GETS THESE BIZARRE HALLUCINATIONS!

WHAT?

HEH

HEH

...OH, **CAGEY,** HUH?

WELL NICE TO SEE YOU GUYS! I GOTTA GO!

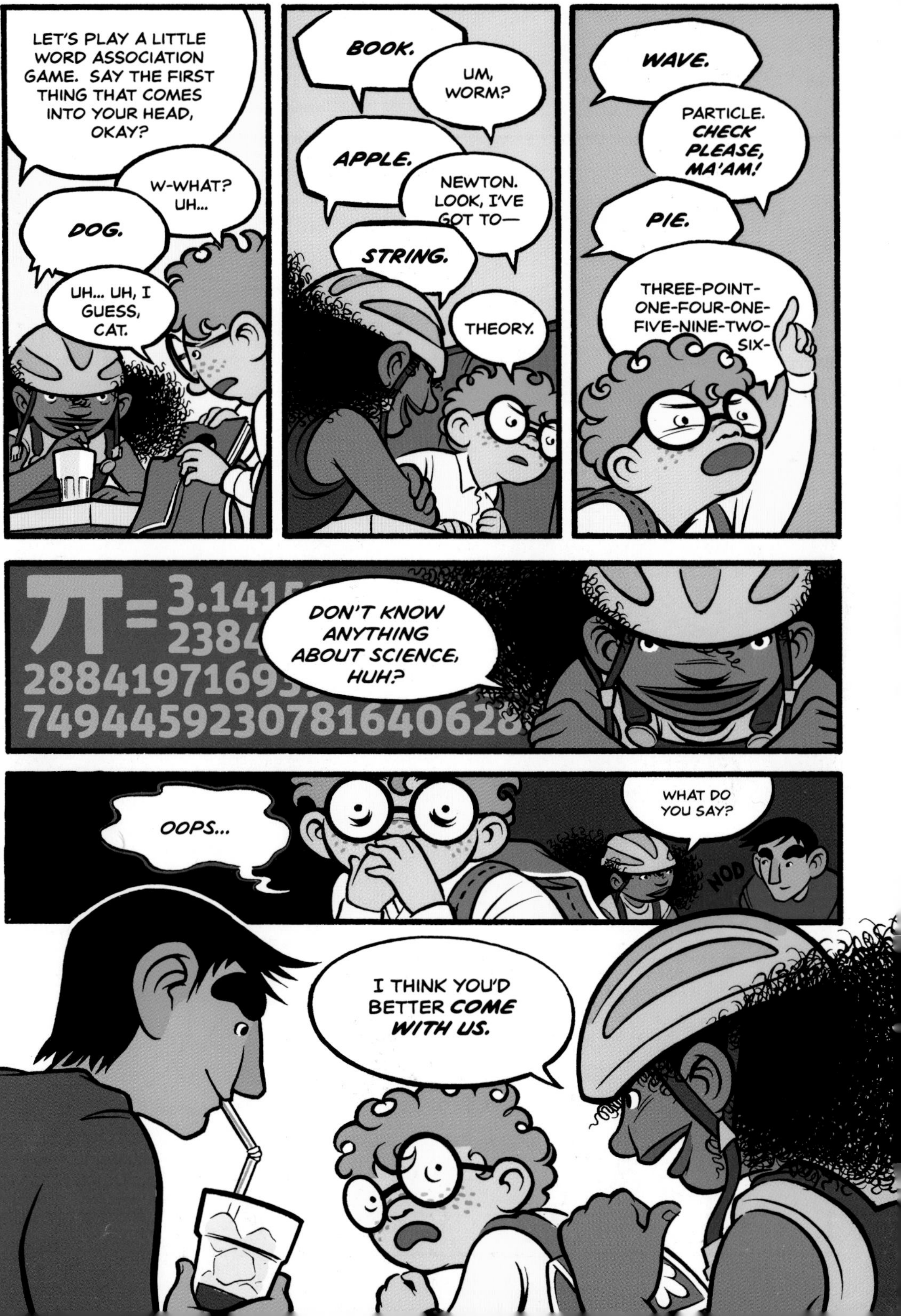
LET'S PLAY A LITTLE WORD ASSOCIATION GAME. SAY THE FIRST THING THAT COMES INTO YOUR HEAD, OKAY?
W-WHAT? UH...
DOG.
UH... UH, I GUESS, CAT.
BOOK.
UM, WORM?
APPLE.
NEWTON. LOOK, I'VE GOT TO—
STRING.
THEORY.
WAVE.
PARTICLE. CHECK PLEASE, MA'AM!
PIE.
THREE-POINT-ONE-FOUR-ONE-FIVE-NINE-TWO-SIX-
π=3.1415
2384
2884197169
7494459230781640628
DON'T KNOW ANYTHING ABOUT SCIENCE, HUH?
OOPS...
WHAT DO YOU SAY?
NOD
I THINK YOU'D BETTER COME WITH US.

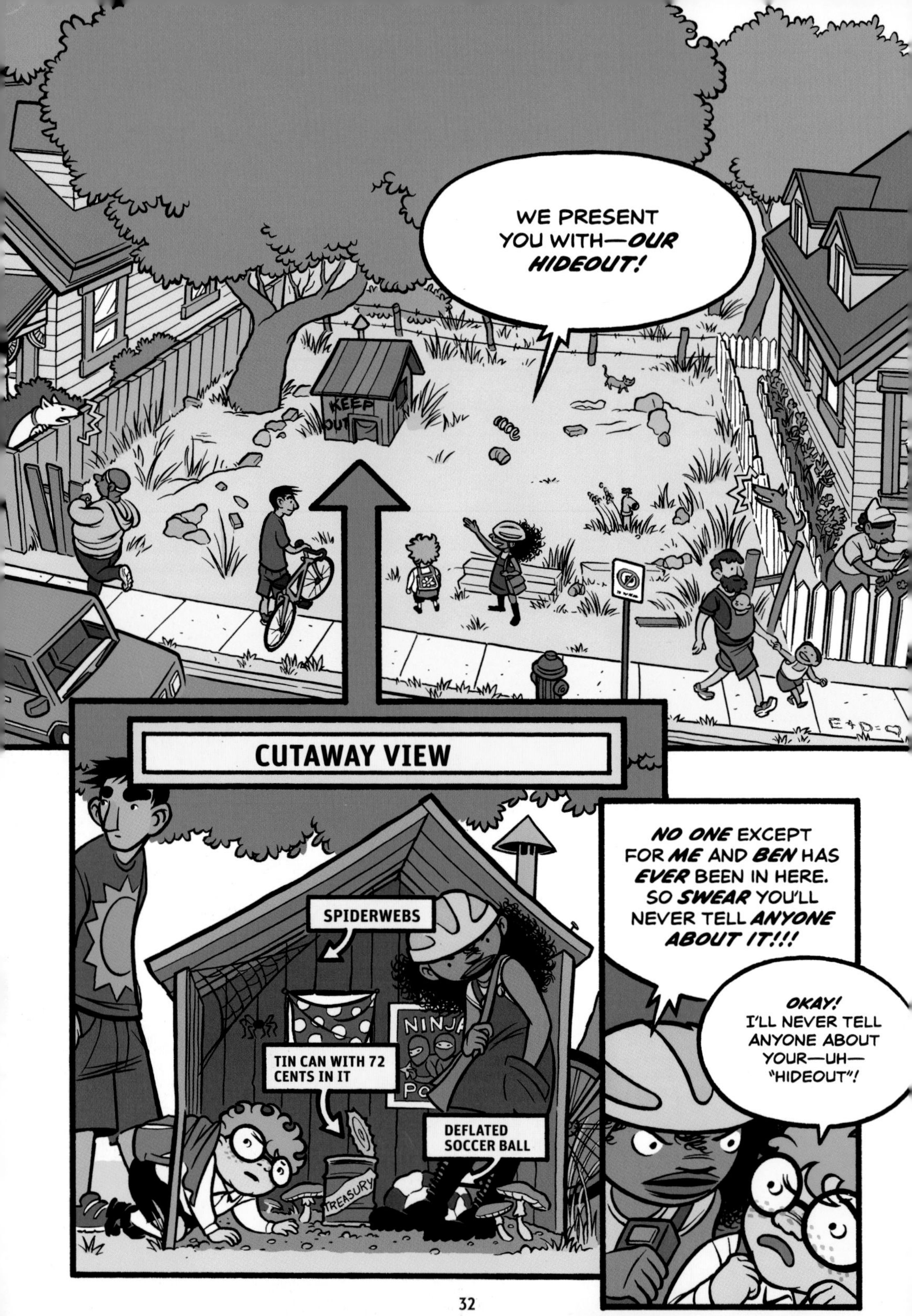
WE PRESENT YOU WITH—*OUR HIDEOUT!*
KEEP OUT
CUTAWAY VIEW
SPIDERWEBS
TIN CAN WITH 72 CENTS IN IT
TREASURY
DEFLATED SOCCER BALL
NO ONE EXCEPT FOR *ME* AND *BEN* HAS *EVER* BEEN IN HERE. SO *SWEAR* YOU'LL NEVER TELL *ANYONE ABOUT IT!!!*
OKAY! I'LL NEVER TELL ANYONE ABOUT YOUR—UH— "HIDEOUT"!

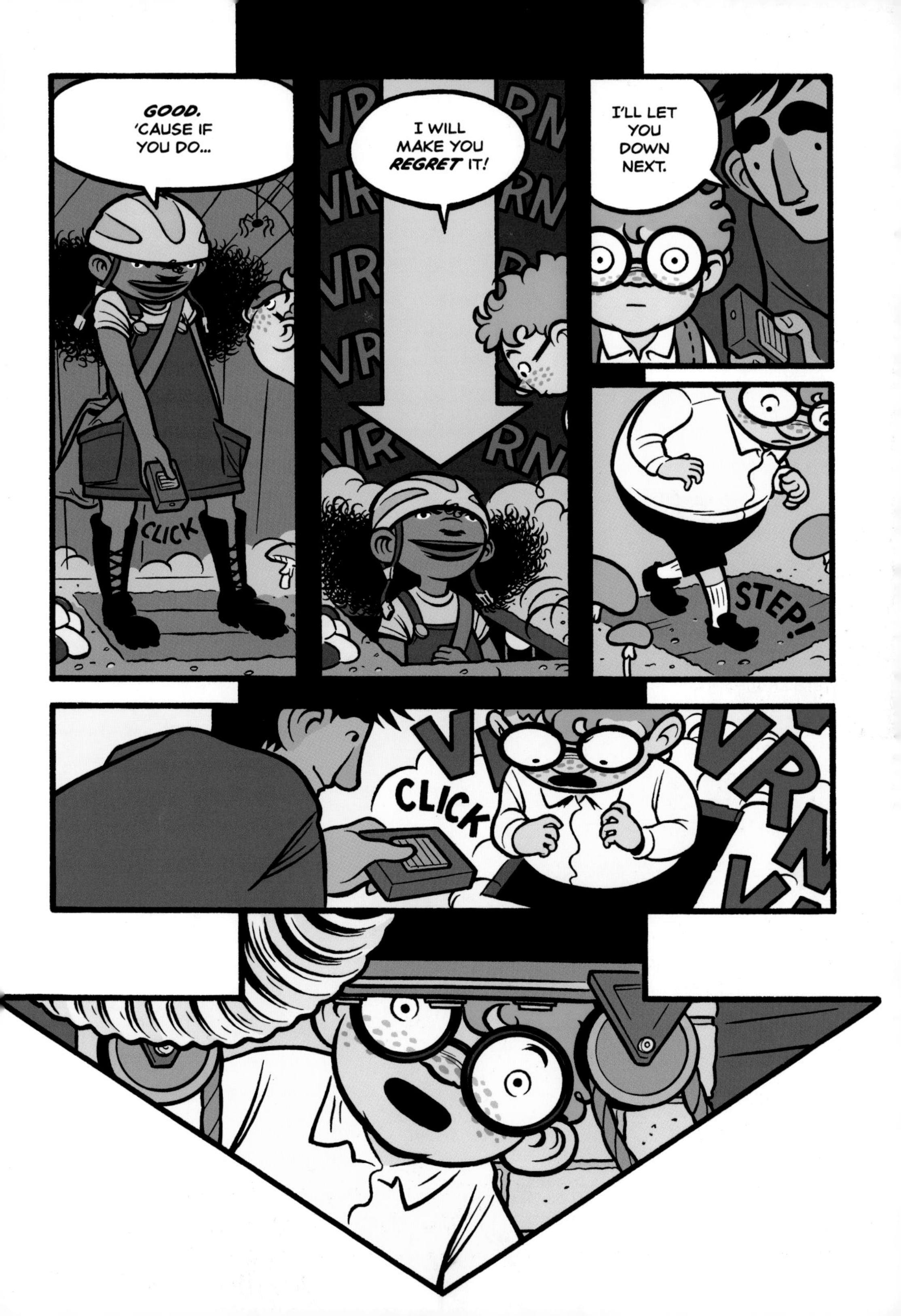
GOOD. 'CAUSE IF YOU DO...
CLICK
I WILL MAKE YOU REGRET IT!
VRN
I'LL LET YOU DOWN NEXT.
STEP!
CLICK
VRN

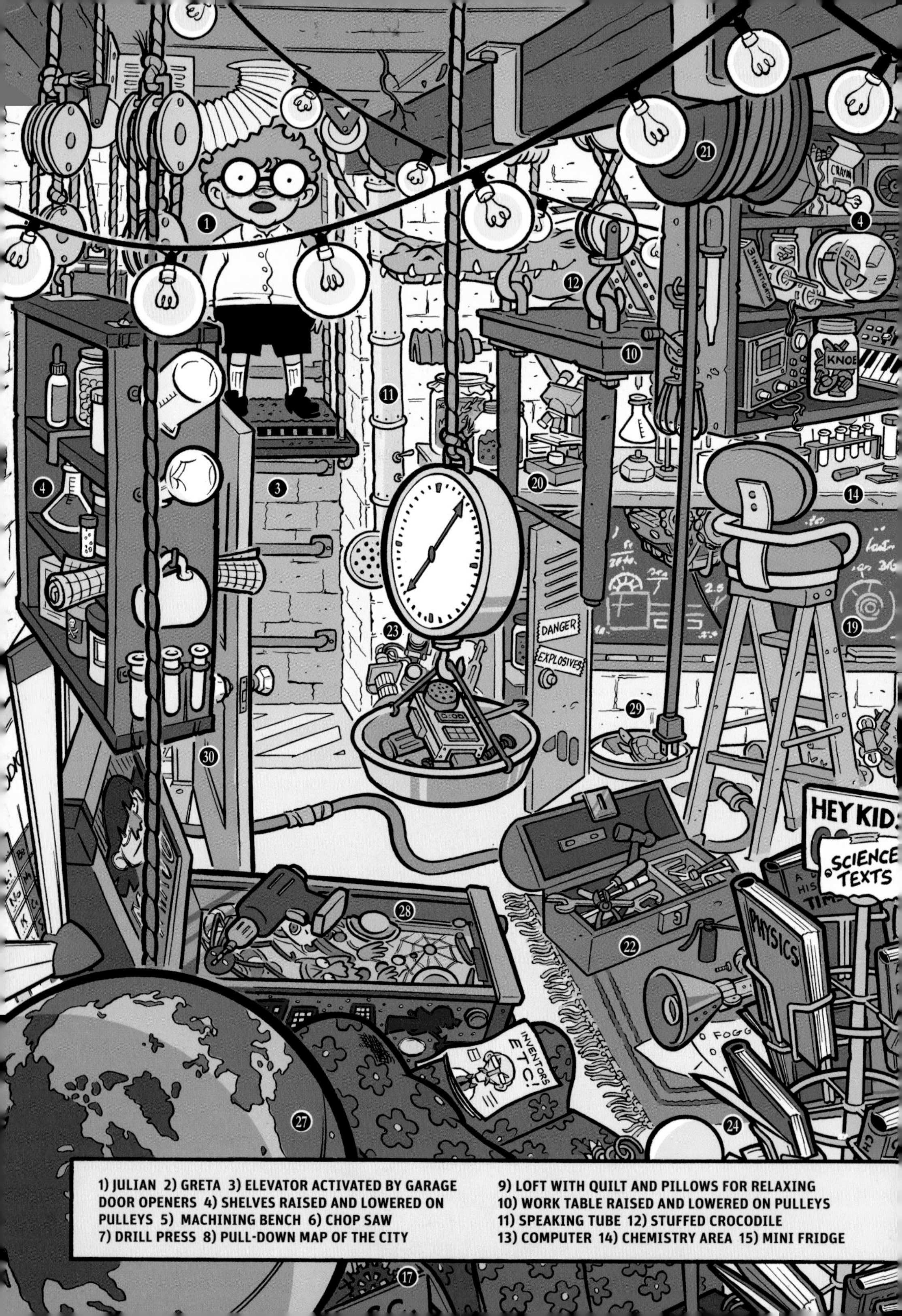
DANGER
EXPLOSIVES
HEY KIDS!
SCIENCE TEXTS
PHYSICS
INVENTORS ETC!

1) JULIAN 2) GRETA 3) ELEVATOR ACTIVATED BY GARAGE DOOR OPENERS 4) SHELVES RAISED AND LOWERED ON PULLEYS 5) MACHINING BENCH 6) CHOP SAW 7) DRILL PRESS 8) PULL-DOWN MAP OF THE CITY

9) LOFT WITH QUILT AND PILLOWS FOR RELAXING 10) WORK TABLE RAISED AND LOWERED ON PULLEYS 11) SPEAKING TUBE 12) STUFFED CROCODILE 13) COMPUTER 14) CHEMISTRY AREA 15) MINI FRIDGE

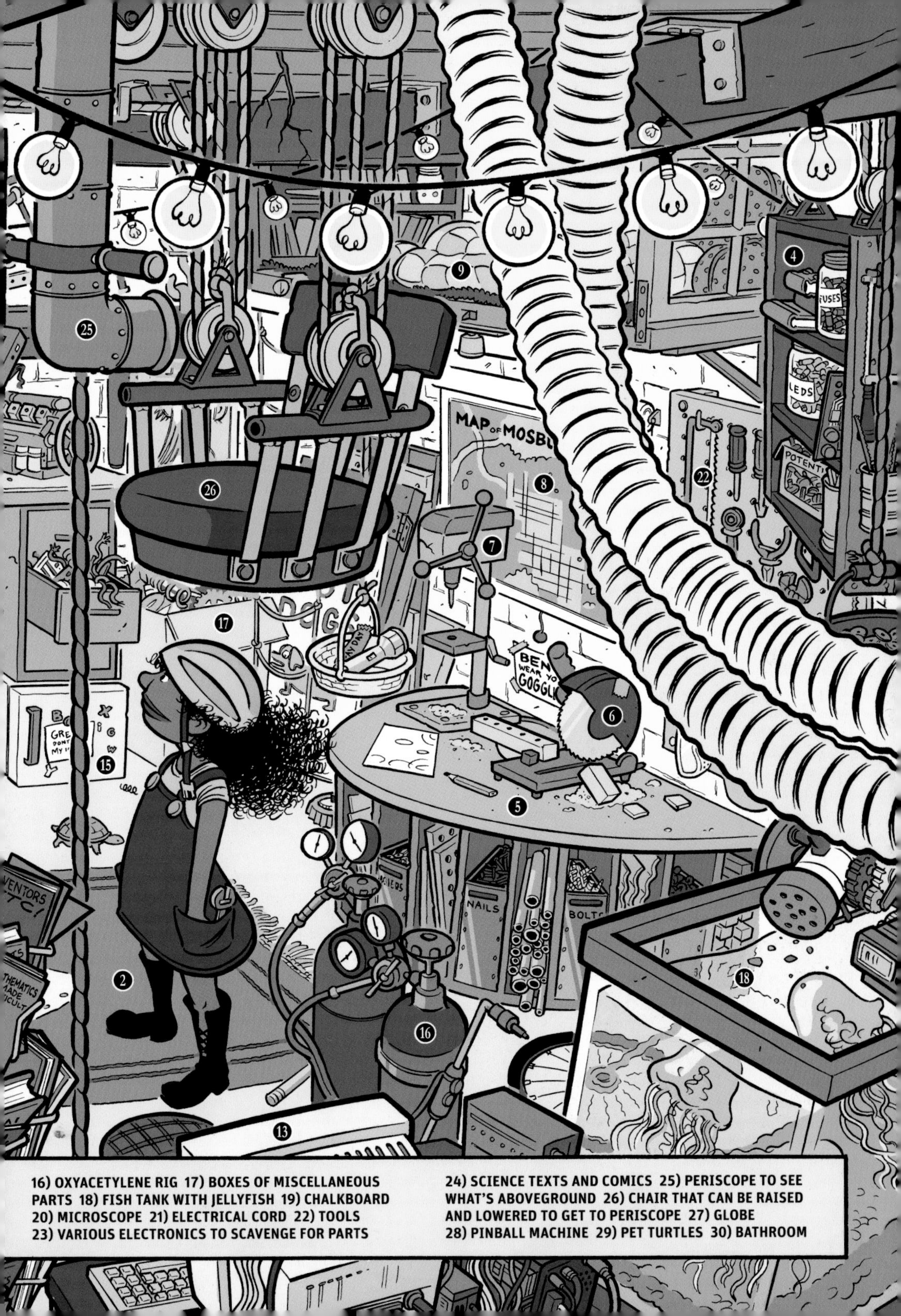
FUSES
LEDS
NAILS
25
9
4
26
8
22
7
17
6
15
5
2
16
18
13

16) OXYACETYLENE RIG 17) BOXES OF MISCELLANEOUS PARTS 18) FISH TANK WITH JELLYFISH 19) CHALKBOARD 20) MICROSCOPE 21) ELECTRICAL CORD 22) TOOLS 23) VARIOUS ELECTRONICS TO SCAVENGE FOR PARTS

24) SCIENCE TEXTS AND COMICS 25) PERISCOPE TO SEE WHAT'S ABOVEGROUND 26) CHAIR THAT CAN BE RAISED AND LOWERED TO GET TO PERISCOPE 27) GLOBE 28) PINBALL MACHINE 29) PET TURTLES 30) BATHROOM

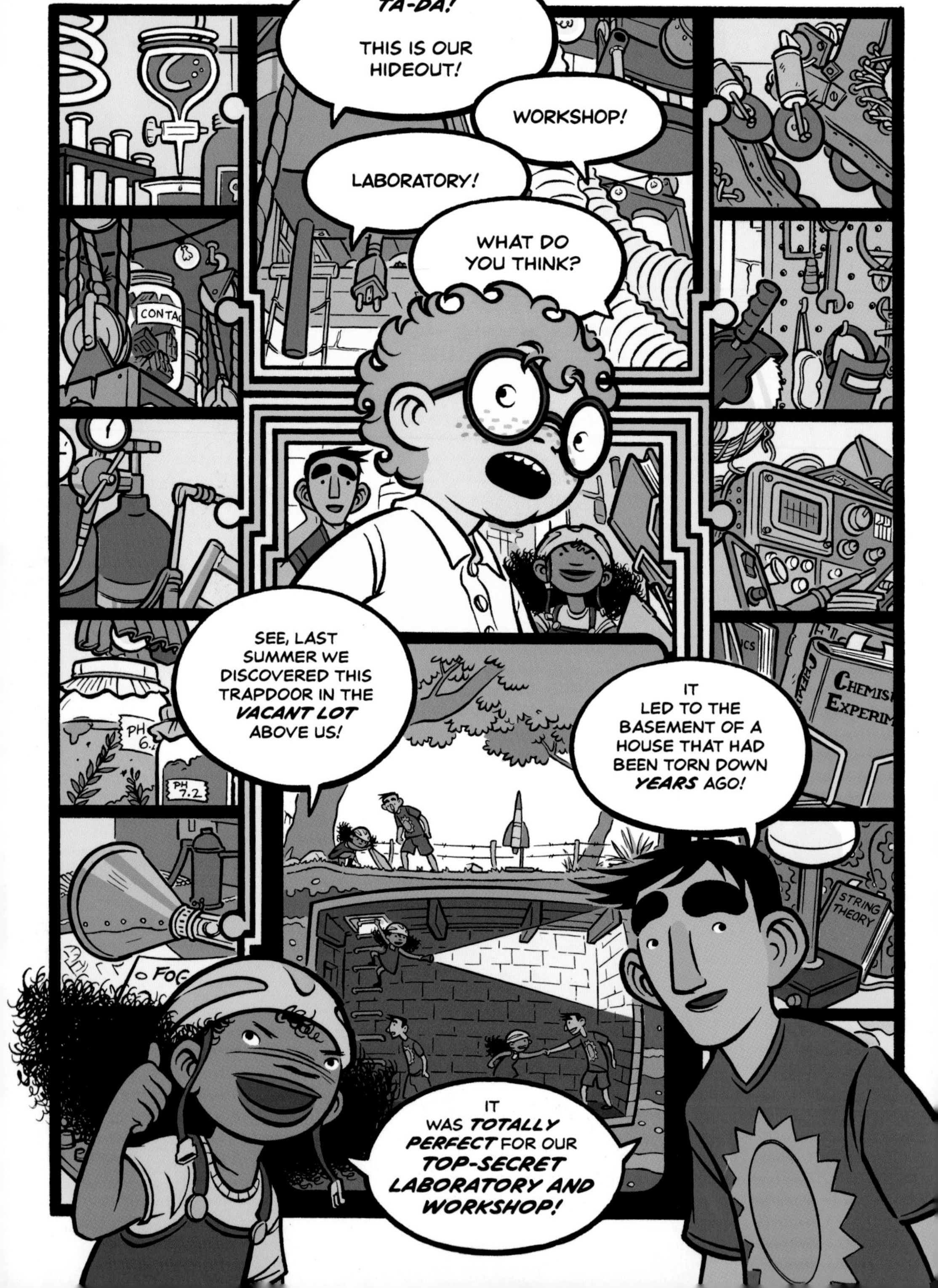
TA-DA!
THIS IS OUR HIDEOUT!
WORKSHOP!
LABORATORY!
WHAT DO YOU THINK?
SEE, LAST SUMMER WE DISCOVERED THIS TRAPDOOR IN THE VACANT LOT ABOVE US!
IT LED TO THE BASEMENT OF A HOUSE THAT HAD BEEN TORN DOWN YEARS AGO!
IT WAS TOTALLY PERFECT FOR OUR TOP-SECRET LABORATORY AND WORKSHOP!
STRING THEORY
PH 7.2

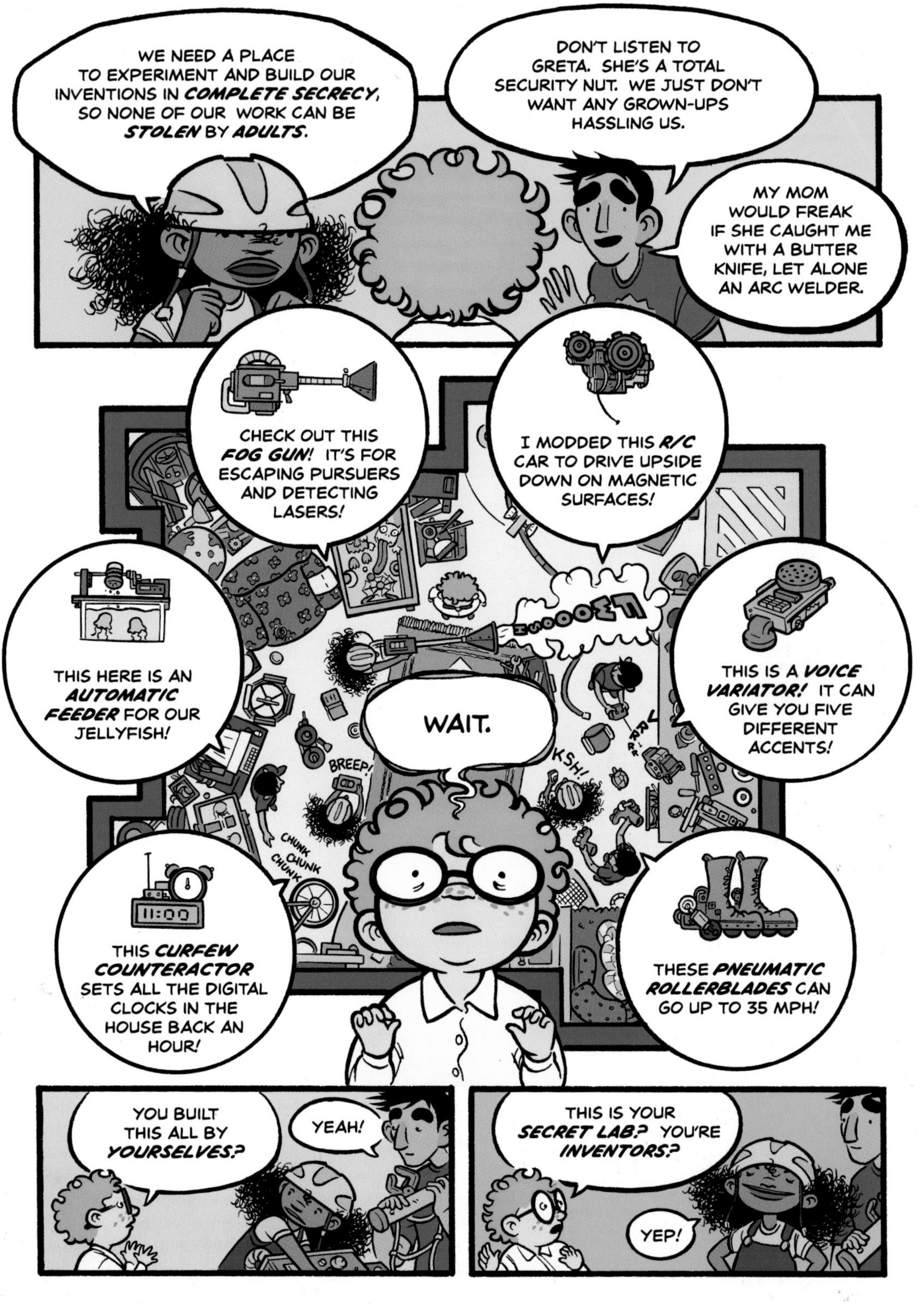

WE NEED A PLACE TO EXPERIMENT AND BUILD OUR INVENTIONS IN *COMPLETE SECRECY*, SO NONE OF OUR WORK CAN BE *STOLEN* BY *ADULTS*.
DON'T LISTEN TO GRETA. SHE'S A TOTAL SECURITY NUT. WE JUST DON'T WANT ANY GROWN-UPS HASSLING US.
MY MOM WOULD FREAK IF SHE CAUGHT ME WITH A BUTTER KNIFE, LET ALONE AN ARC WELDER.
CHECK OUT THIS *FOG GUN*! IT'S FOR ESCAPING PURSUERS AND DETECTING LASERS!
I MODDED THIS *R/C* CAR TO DRIVE UPSIDE DOWN ON MAGNETIC SURFACES!
FWOOOSH
THIS HERE IS AN *AUTOMATIC FEEDER* FOR OUR JELLYFISH!
THIS IS A *VOICE VARIATOR!* IT CAN GIVE YOU FIVE DIFFERENT ACCENTS!
WAIT.
BREEP!
KSH!
CHUNK CHUNK CHUNK
11:00
THIS *CURFEW COUNTERACTOR* SETS ALL THE DIGITAL CLOCKS IN THE HOUSE BACK AN HOUR!
THESE *PNEUMATIC ROLLERBLADES* CAN GO UP TO 35 MPH!
YOU BUILT THIS ALL BY *YOURSELVES?*
YEAH!
THIS IS YOUR *SECRET LAB?* YOU'RE *INVENTORS?*
YEP!

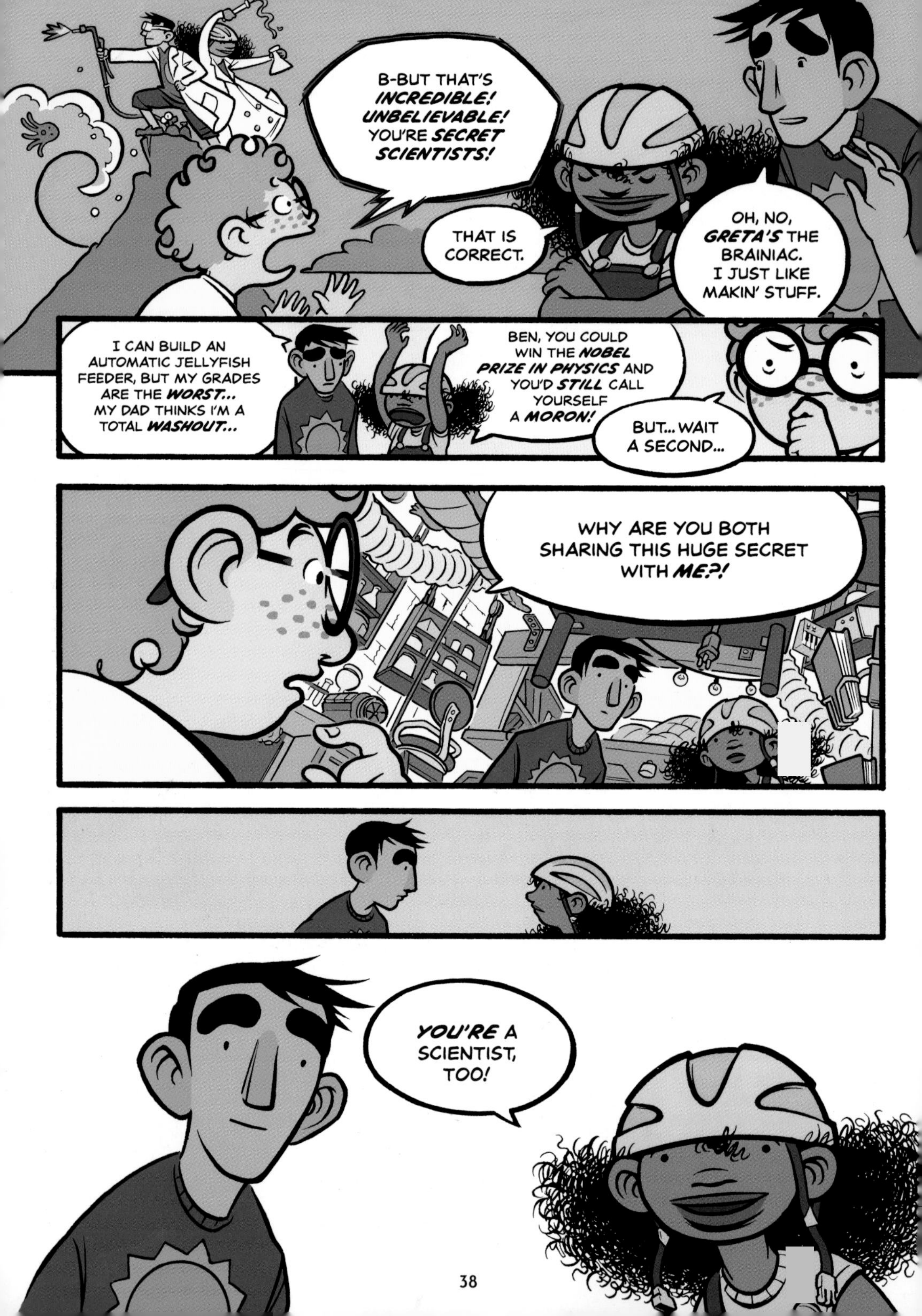

B-BUT THAT'S *INCREDIBLE! UNBELIEVABLE!* YOU'RE *SECRET SCIENTISTS!*
THAT IS CORRECT.
OH, NO, *GRETA'S* THE BRAINIAC. I JUST LIKE MAKIN' STUFF.
I CAN BUILD AN AUTOMATIC JELLYFISH FEEDER, BUT MY GRADES ARE THE *WORST...* MY DAD THINKS I'M A TOTAL *WASHOUT...*
BEN, YOU COULD WIN THE *NOBEL PRIZE IN PHYSICS* AND YOU'D *STILL* CALL YOURSELF A *MORON!*
BUT... WAIT A SECOND...
WHY ARE YOU BOTH SHARING THIS HUGE SECRET WITH *ME?!*
YOU'RE A SCIENTIST, TOO!

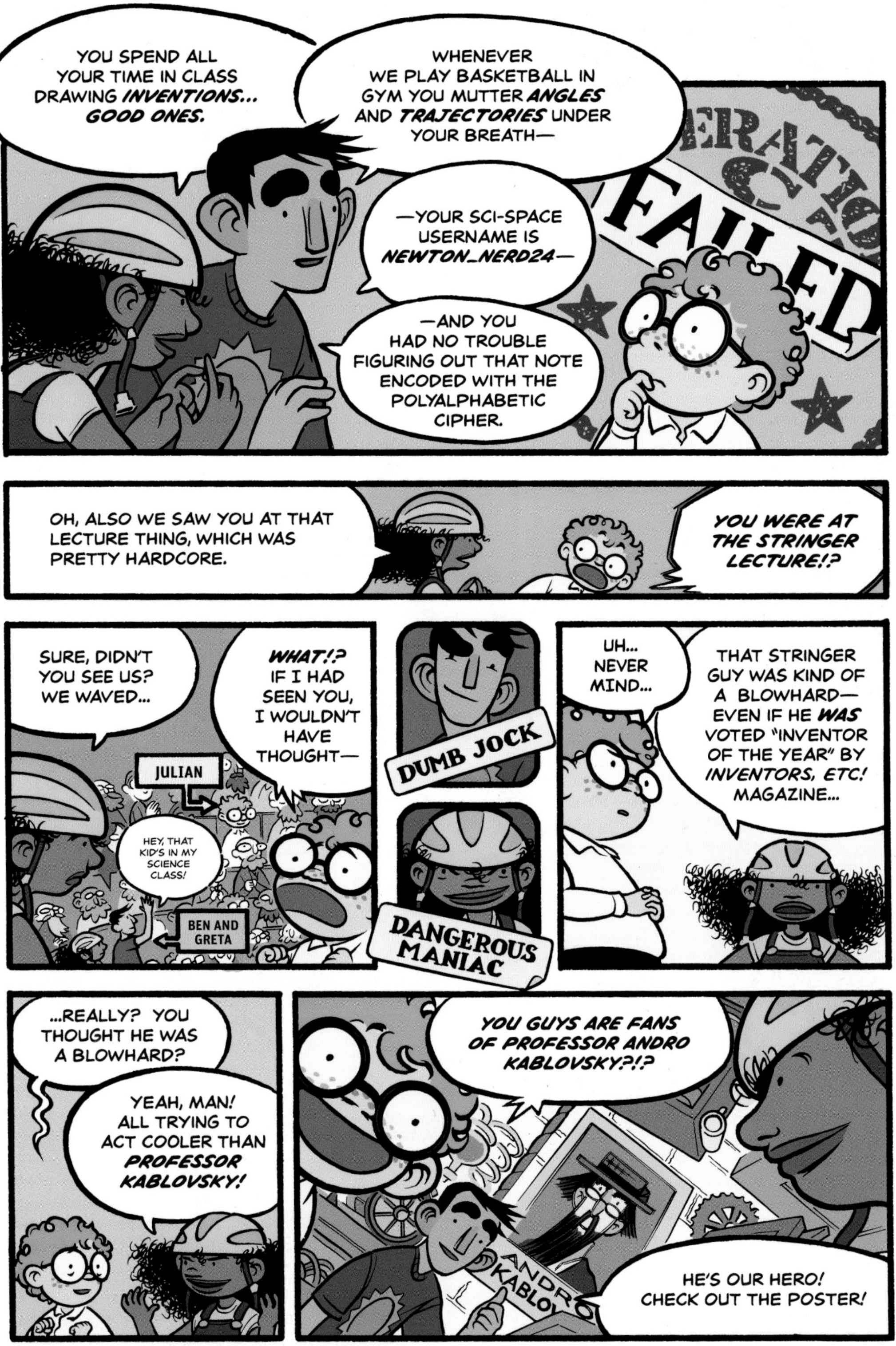

YOU SPEND ALL YOUR TIME IN CLASS DRAWING *INVENTIONS... GOOD ONES.*
WHENEVER WE PLAY BASKETBALL IN GYM YOU MUTTER *ANGLES* AND *TRAJECTORIES* UNDER YOUR BREATH—
—YOUR SCI-SPACE USERNAME IS *NEWTON_NERD24*—
—AND YOU HAD NO TROUBLE FIGURING OUT THAT NOTE ENCODED WITH THE POLYALPHABETIC CIPHER.
FAILED
OH, ALSO WE SAW YOU AT THAT LECTURE THING, WHICH WAS PRETTY HARDCORE.
YOU WERE AT THE STRINGER LECTURE!?
SURE, DIDN'T YOU SEE US? WE WAVED...
WHAT!? IF I HAD SEEN YOU, I WOULDN'T HAVE THOUGHT—
JULIAN
HEY, THAT KID'S IN MY SCIENCE CLASS!
BEN AND GRETA
DUMB JOCK
DANGEROUS MANIAC
UH... NEVER MIND...
THAT STRINGER GUY WAS KIND OF A BLOWHARD— EVEN IF HE *WAS* VOTED "INVENTOR OF THE YEAR" BY *INVENTORS, ETC!* MAGAZINE...
...REALLY? YOU THOUGHT HE WAS A BLOWHARD?
YEAH, MAN! ALL TRYING TO ACT COOLER THAN *PROFESSOR KABLOVSKY!*
YOU GUYS ARE FANS OF PROFESSOR ANDRO KABLOVSKY?!?
HE'S OUR HERO! CHECK OUT THE POSTER!

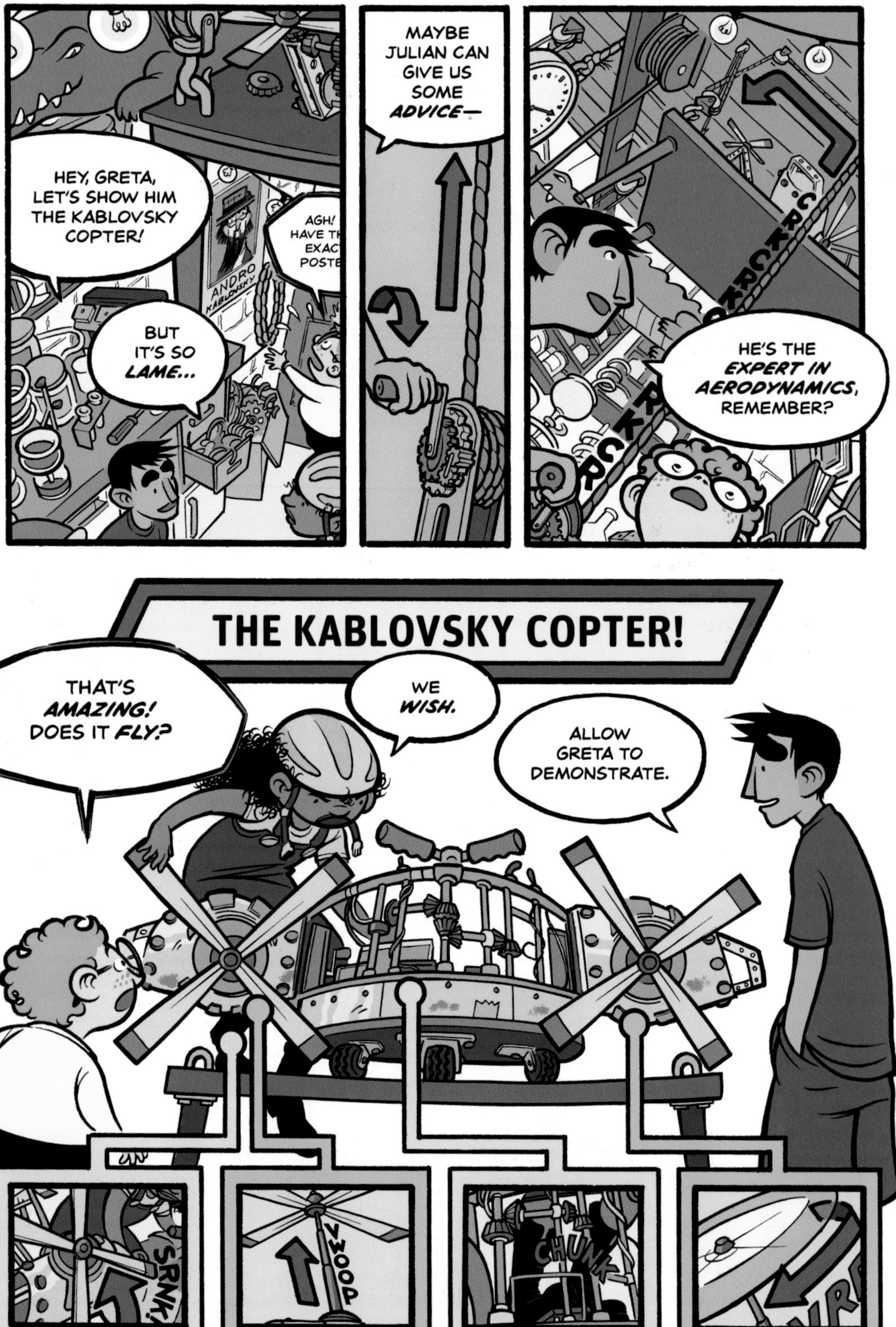
HEY, GRETA, LET'S SHOW HIM THE KABLOVSKY COPTER!
ANDRO KABLOVSKY
AGH!
BUT IT'S SO *LAME...*
MAYBE JULIAN CAN GIVE US SOME *ADVICE—*
HE'S THE *EXPERT IN AERODYNAMICS*, REMEMBER?
THE KABLOVSKY COPTER!
THAT'S *AMAZING!* DOES IT *FLY?*
WE *WISH.*
ALLOW GRETA TO DEMONSTRATE.
SRNK!
VWOOP
CHUNK

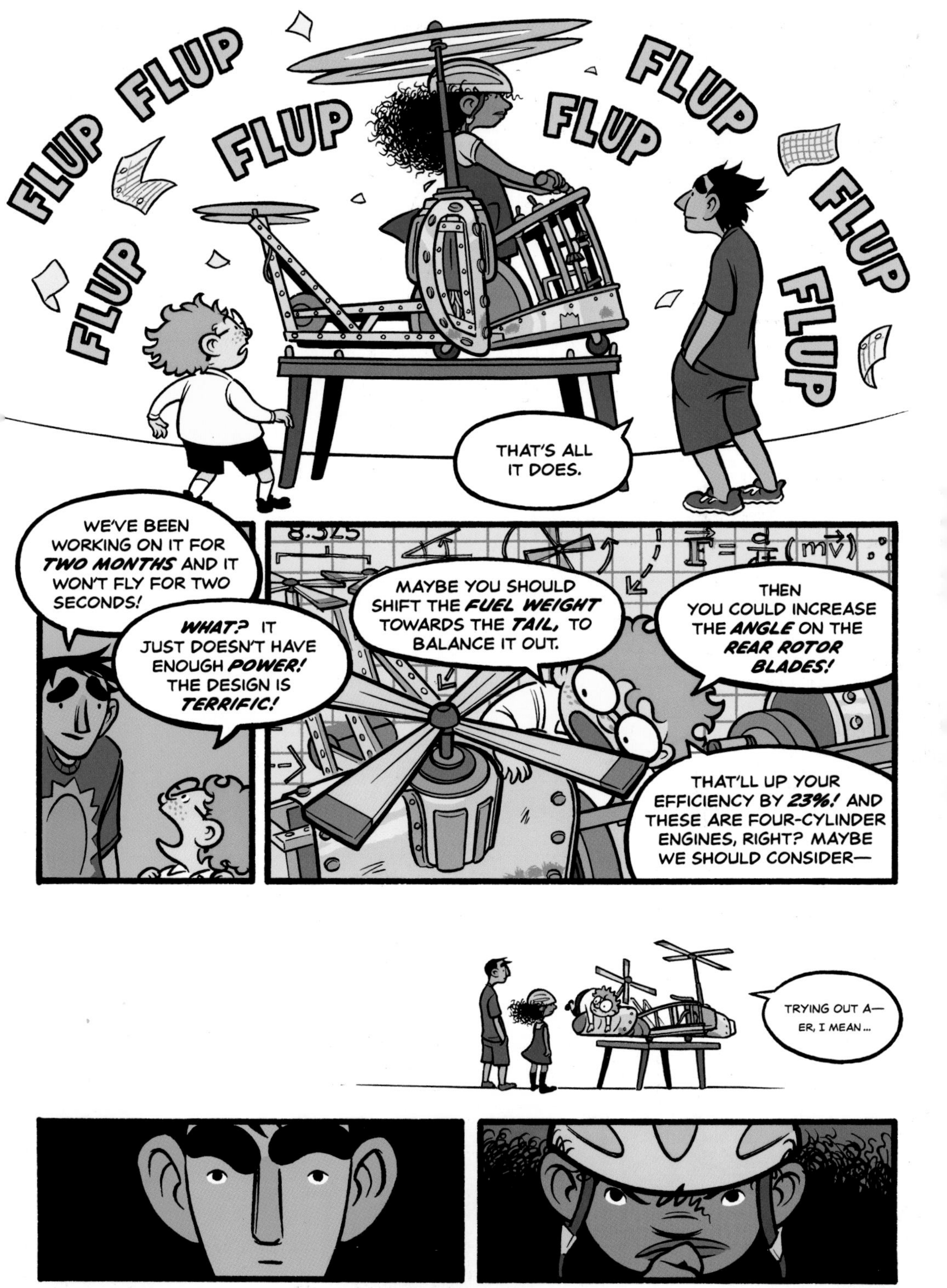
FLUP FLUP FLUP FLUP FLUP FLUP FLUP FLUP
THAT'S ALL IT DOES.
WE'VE BEEN WORKING ON IT FOR TWO MONTHS AND IT WON'T FLY FOR TWO SECONDS!
WHAT? IT JUST DOESN'T HAVE ENOUGH POWER! THE DESIGN IS TERRIFIC!
MAYBE YOU SHOULD SHIFT THE FUEL WEIGHT TOWARDS THE TAIL, TO BALANCE IT OUT.
THEN YOU COULD INCREASE THE ANGLE ON THE REAR ROTOR BLADES!
THAT'LL UP YOUR EFFICIENCY BY 23%! AND THESE ARE FOUR-CYLINDER ENGINES, RIGHT? MAYBE WE SHOULD CONSIDER—
TRYING OUT A— ER, I MEAN ...

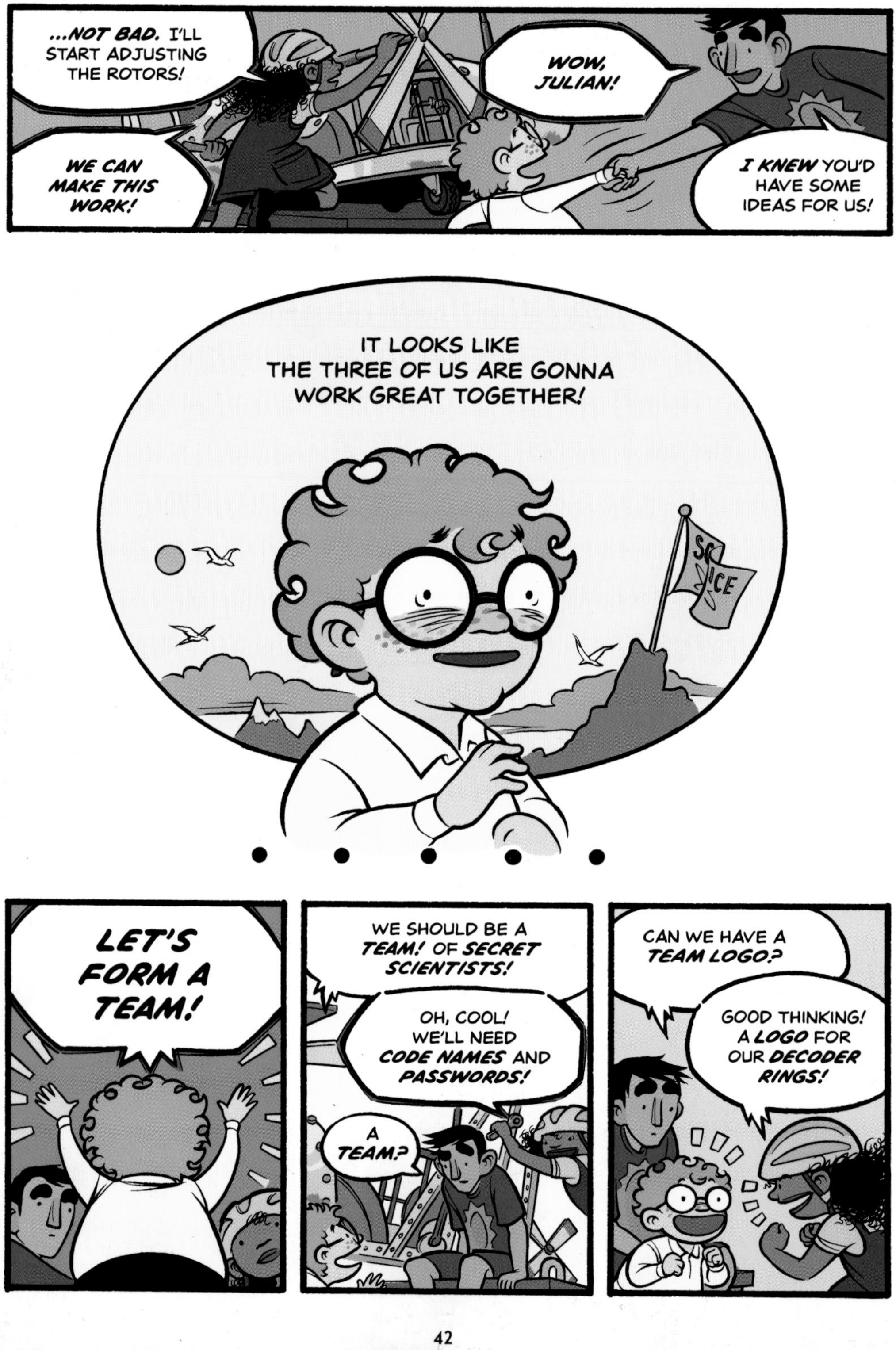
...NOT BAD. I'LL START ADJUSTING THE ROTORS!
WE CAN MAKE THIS WORK!
WOW, JULIAN!
I KNEW YOU'D HAVE SOME IDEAS FOR US!
IT LOOKS LIKE THE THREE OF US ARE GONNA WORK GREAT TOGETHER!
LET'S FORM A TEAM!
WE SHOULD BE A TEAM! OF SECRET SCIENTISTS!
A TEAM?
OH, COOL! WE'LL NEED CODE NAMES AND PASSWORDS!
CAN WE HAVE A TEAM LOGO?
GOOD THINKING! A LOGO FOR OUR DECODER RINGS!

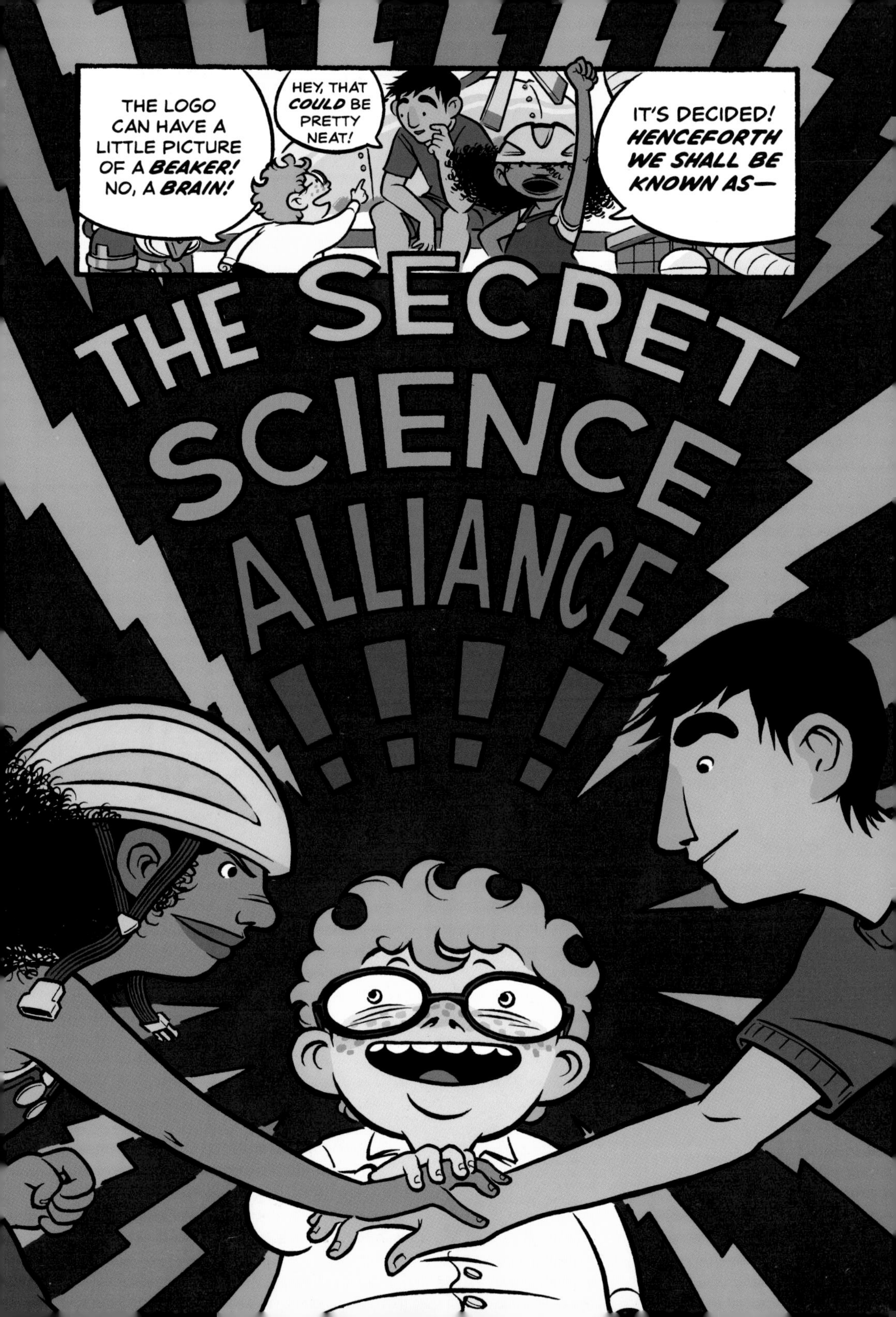
THE LOGO CAN HAVE A LITTLE PICTURE OF A BEAKER! NO, A BRAIN!
HEY, THAT COULD BE PRETTY NEAT!
IT'S DECIDED! HENCEFORTH WE SHALL BE KNOWN AS—
THE SECRET SCIENCE ALLIANCE!!!!

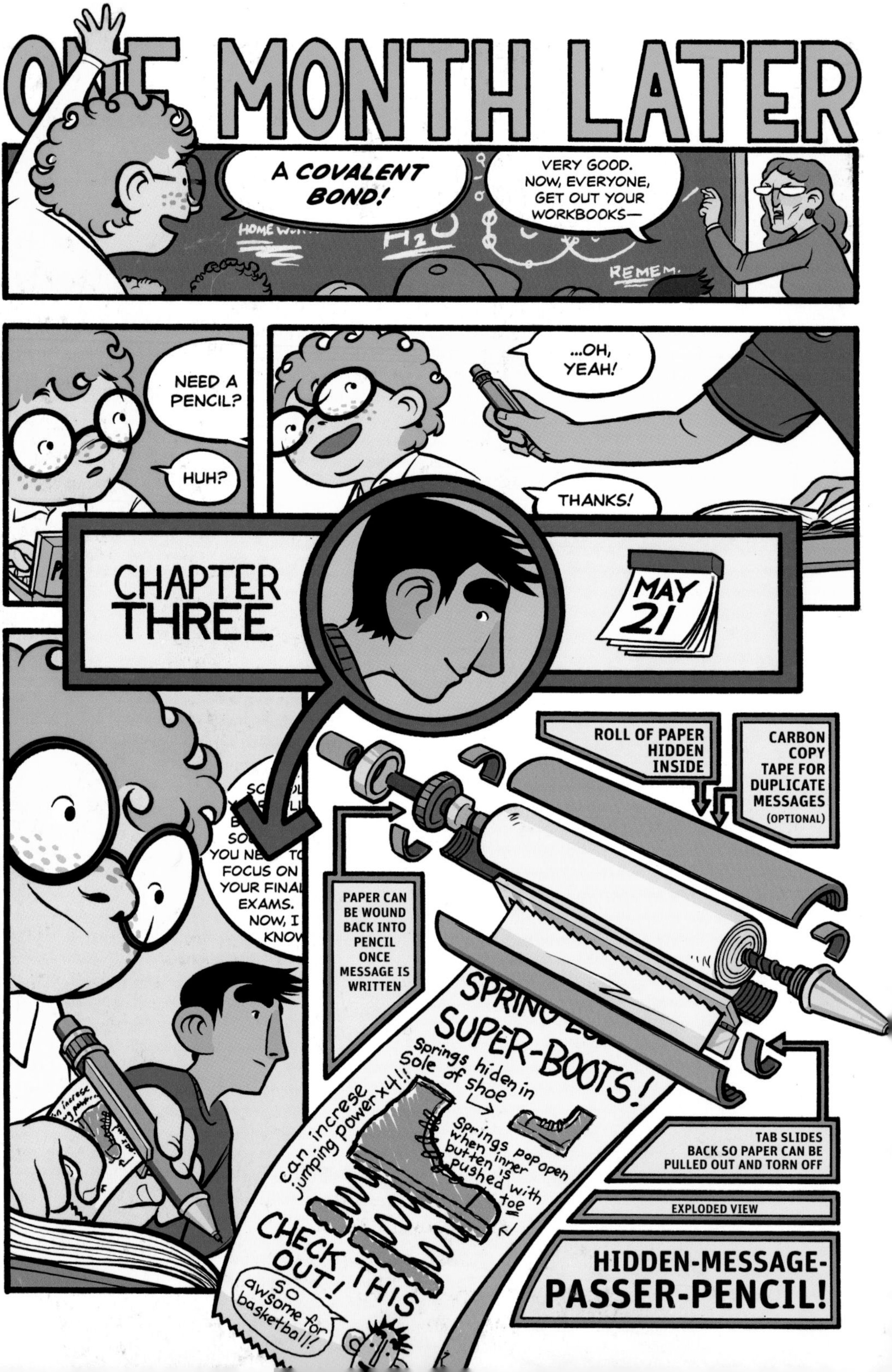

ONE MONTH LATER
A COVALENT BOND!
VERY GOOD. NOW, EVERYONE, GET OUT YOUR WORKBOOKS—
NEED A PENCIL?
HUH?
...OH, YEAH!
THANKS!
CHAPTER THREE
MAY 21
YOU NE TO FOCUS ON YOUR FINAL EXAMS. NOW, I KNOW
ROLL OF PAPER HIDDEN INSIDE
CARBON COPY TAPE FOR DUPLICATE MESSAGES (OPTIONAL)
PAPER CAN BE WOUND BACK INTO PENCIL ONCE MESSAGE IS WRITTEN
SUPER-BOOTS!
Springs hiden in Sole of shoe
can increse jumping power x4!!
Springs pop open when inner butten is pushed with toe
CHECK THIS OUT!
so awsome for basketball!!
TAB SLIDES BACK SO PAPER CAN BE PULLED OUT AND TORN OFF
EXPLODED VIEW
HIDDEN-MESSAGE-PASSER-PENCIL!

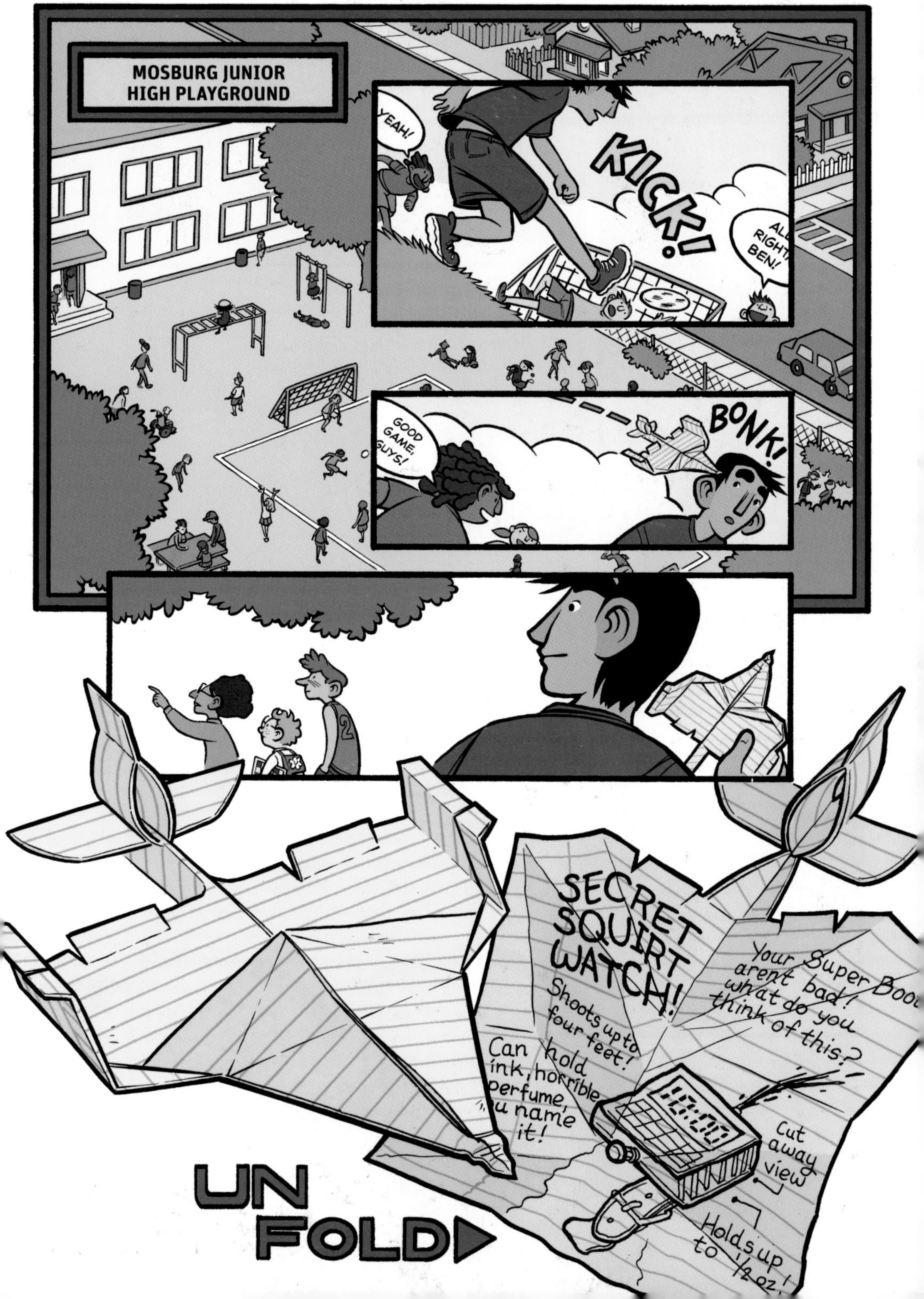
MOSBURG JUNIOR HIGH PLAYGROUND
YEAH!
KICK!
ALL RIGHT, BEN!
GOOD GAME, GUYS!
BONK!
SECRET SQUIRT WATCH!
Shoots up to four feet!
Can hold ink, horrible perfume, you name it!
Your Super Boo... arent bad! what do you think of this?
Cut away view
Holds up to 1/2 oz!
12:00
UN FOLD

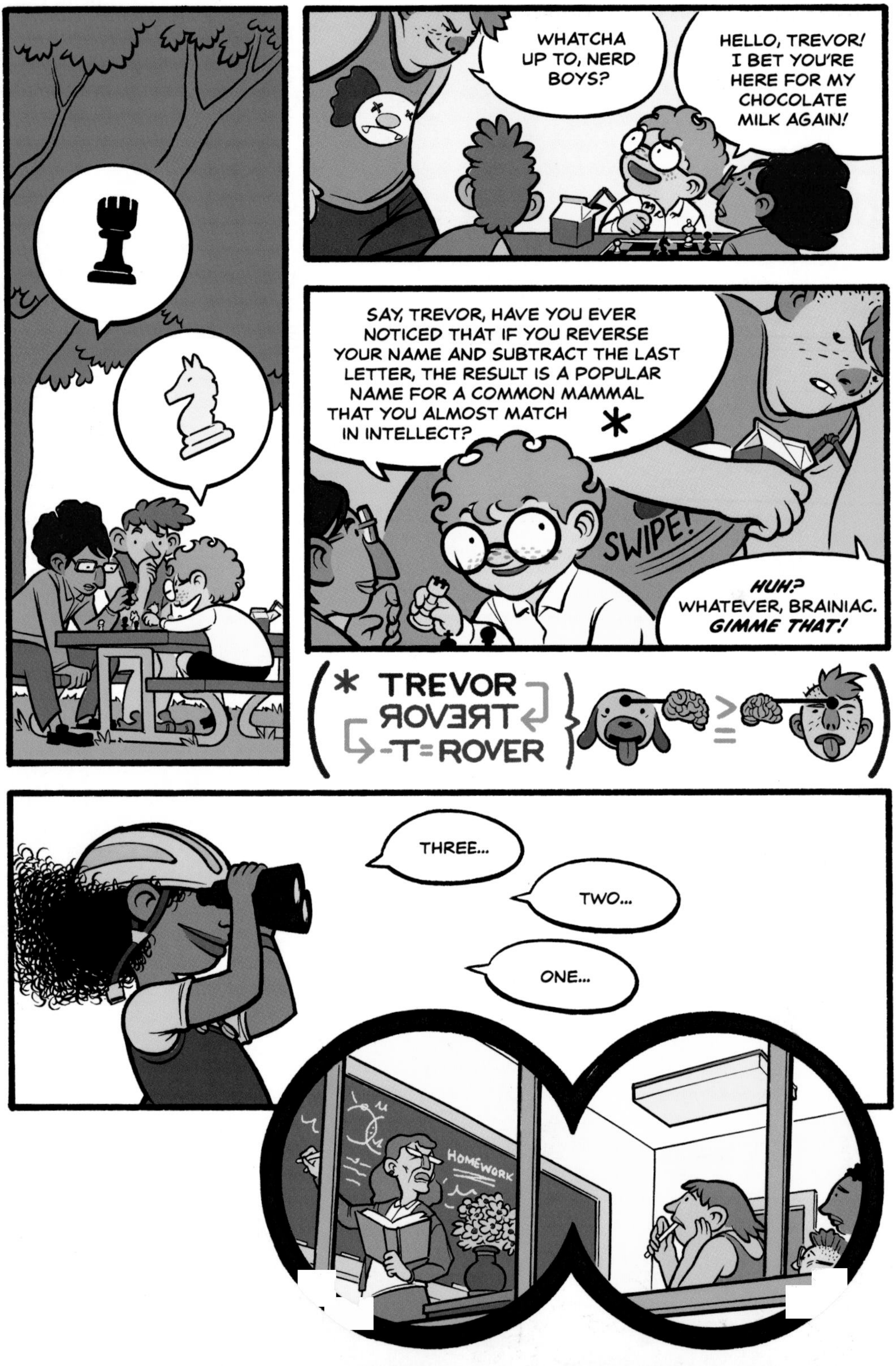
WHATCHA UP TO, NERD BOYS?
HELLO, TREVOR! I BET YOU'RE HERE FOR MY CHOCOLATE MILK AGAIN!
SAY, TREVOR, HAVE YOU EVER NOTICED THAT IF YOU REVERSE YOUR NAME AND SUBTRACT THE LAST LETTER, THE RESULT IS A POPULAR NAME FOR A COMMON MAMMAL THAT YOU ALMOST MATCH IN INTELLECT? *
SWIPE!
HUH? WHATEVER, BRAINIAC. GIMME THAT!
* TREVOR
ROVERT
-T=ROVER
THREE...
TWO...
ONE...
HOMEWORK

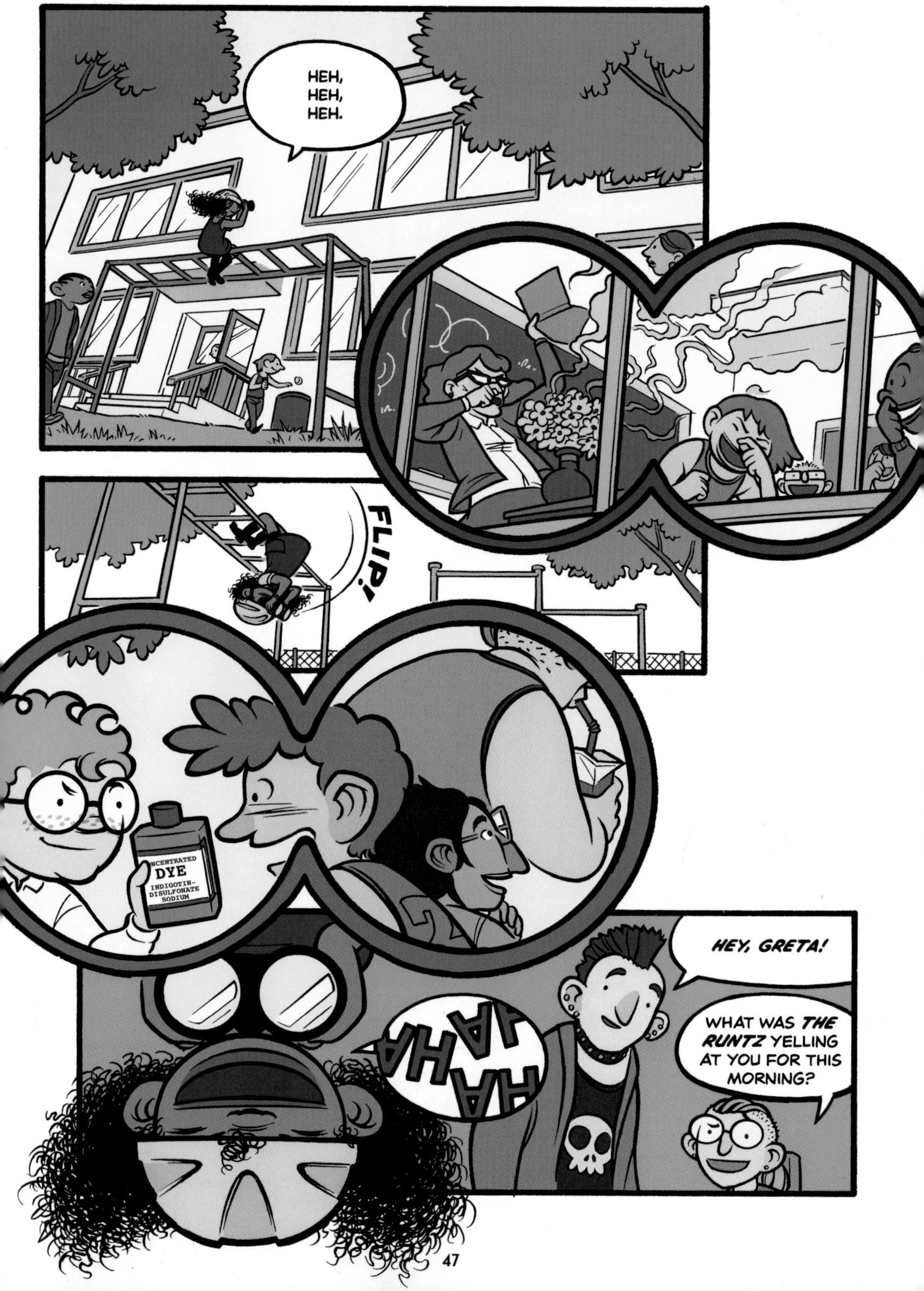
HEH,
HEH,
HEH.
FLIP!
CONCENTRATED
DYE
INDIGOTIN-
DISULFONATE
SODIUM
HEY, GRETA!
WHAT WAS *THE RUNTZ* YELLING AT YOU FOR THIS MORNING?
HAHAHA

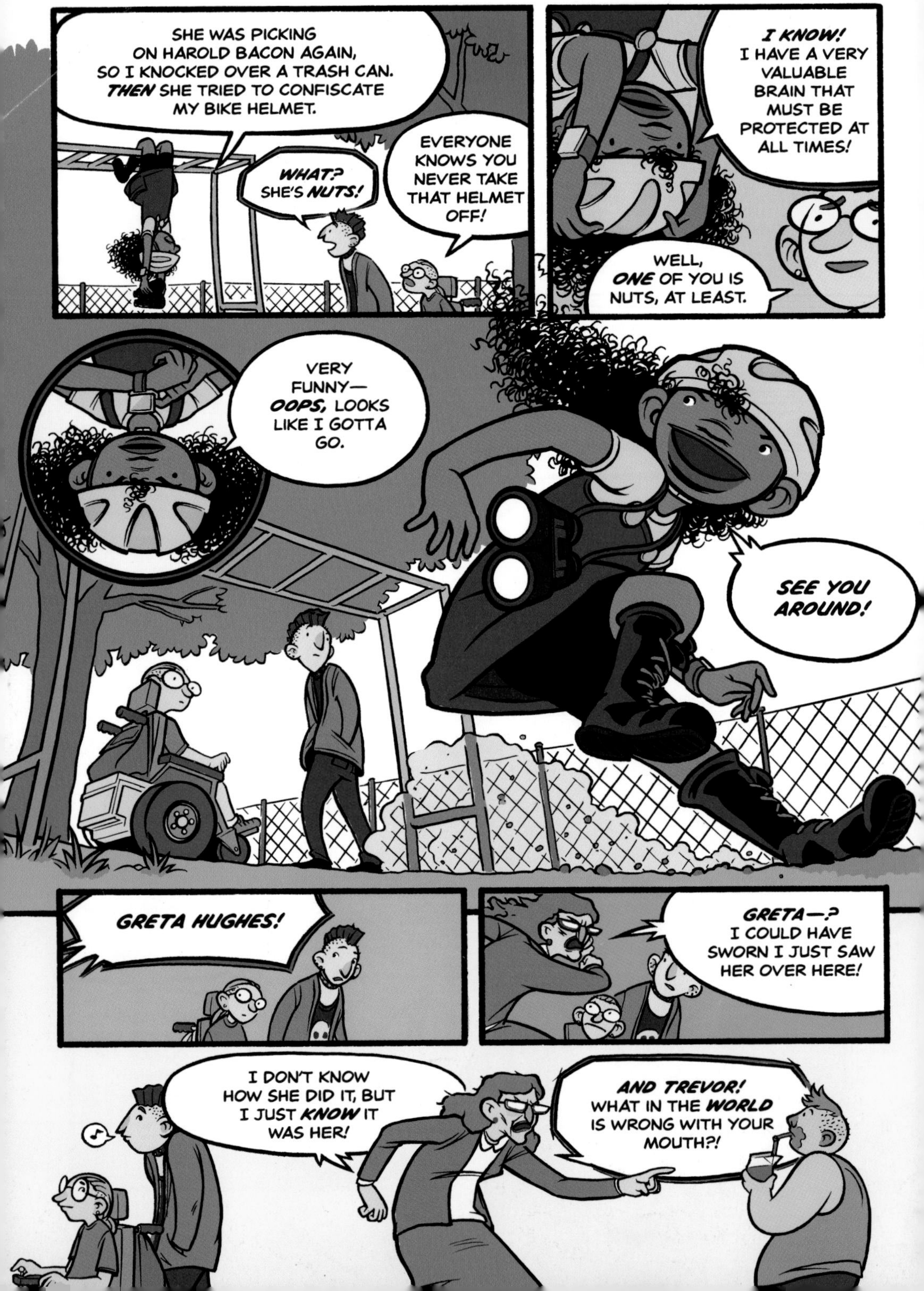
SHE WAS PICKING ON HAROLD BACON AGAIN, SO I KNOCKED OVER A TRASH CAN. THEN SHE TRIED TO CONFISCATE MY BIKE HELMET.
WHAT? SHE'S NUTS!
EVERYONE KNOWS YOU NEVER TAKE THAT HELMET OFF!
I KNOW! I HAVE A VERY VALUABLE BRAIN THAT MUST BE PROTECTED AT ALL TIMES!
WELL, ONE OF YOU IS NUTS, AT LEAST.
VERY FUNNY— OOPS, LOOKS LIKE I GOTTA GO.
SEE YOU AROUND!
GRETA HUGHES!
GRETA—? I COULD HAVE SWORN I JUST SAW HER OVER HERE!
I DON'T KNOW HOW SHE DID IT, BUT I JUST KNOW IT WAS HER!
AND TREVOR! WHAT IN THE WORLD IS WRONG WITH YOUR MOUTH?!

AFTER SCHOOL

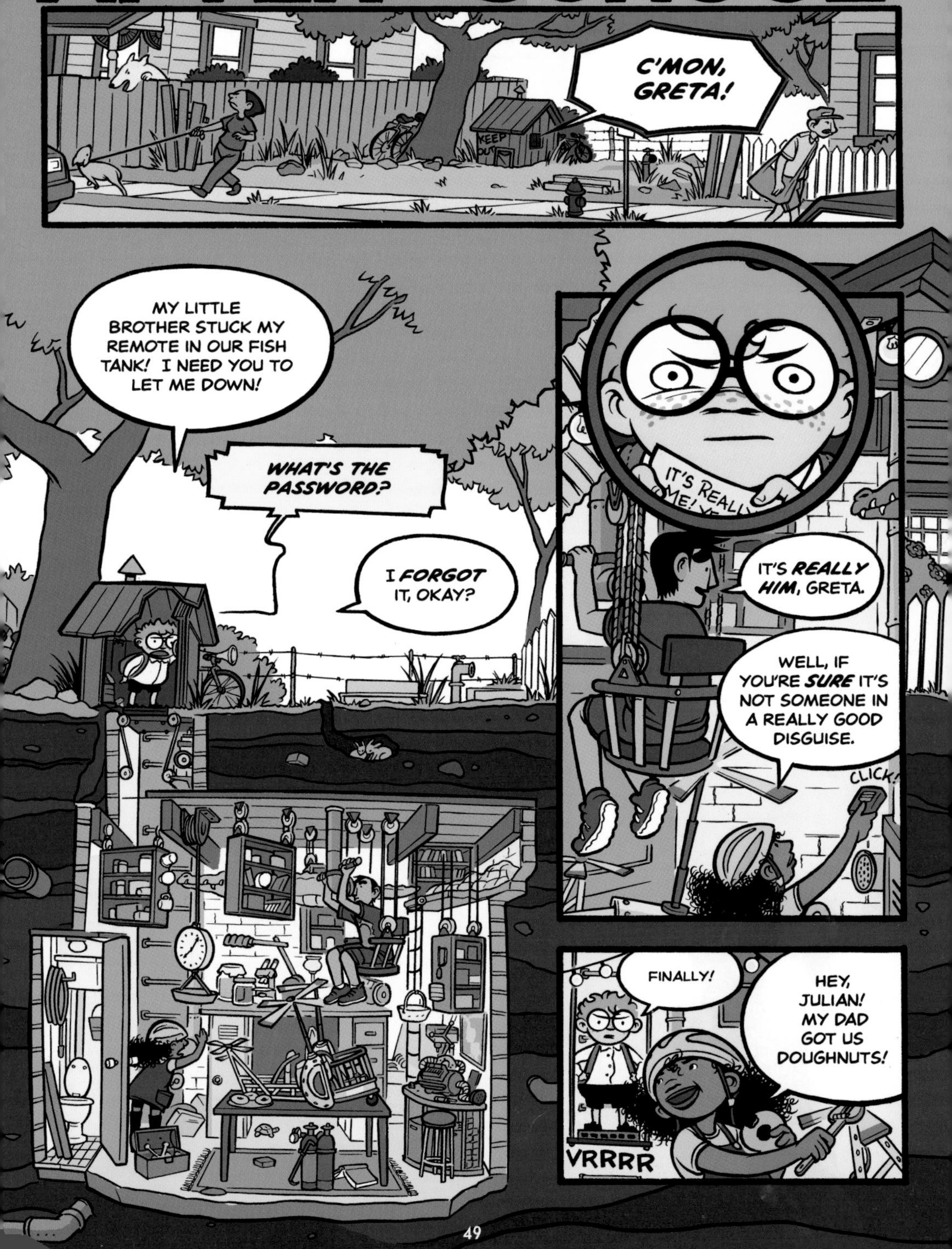
C'MON, GRETA!
KEEP OUT
MY LITTLE BROTHER STUCK MY REMOTE IN OUR FISH TANK! I NEED YOU TO LET ME DOWN!
WHAT'S THE PASSWORD?
I *FORGOT* IT, OKAY?
IT'S ***REALLY HIM***, GRETA.
WELL, IF YOU'RE ***SURE*** IT'S NOT SOMEONE IN A REALLY GOOD DISGUISE.
CLICK!
FINALLY!
HEY, JULIAN! MY DAD GOT US DOUGHNUTS!
VRRRR

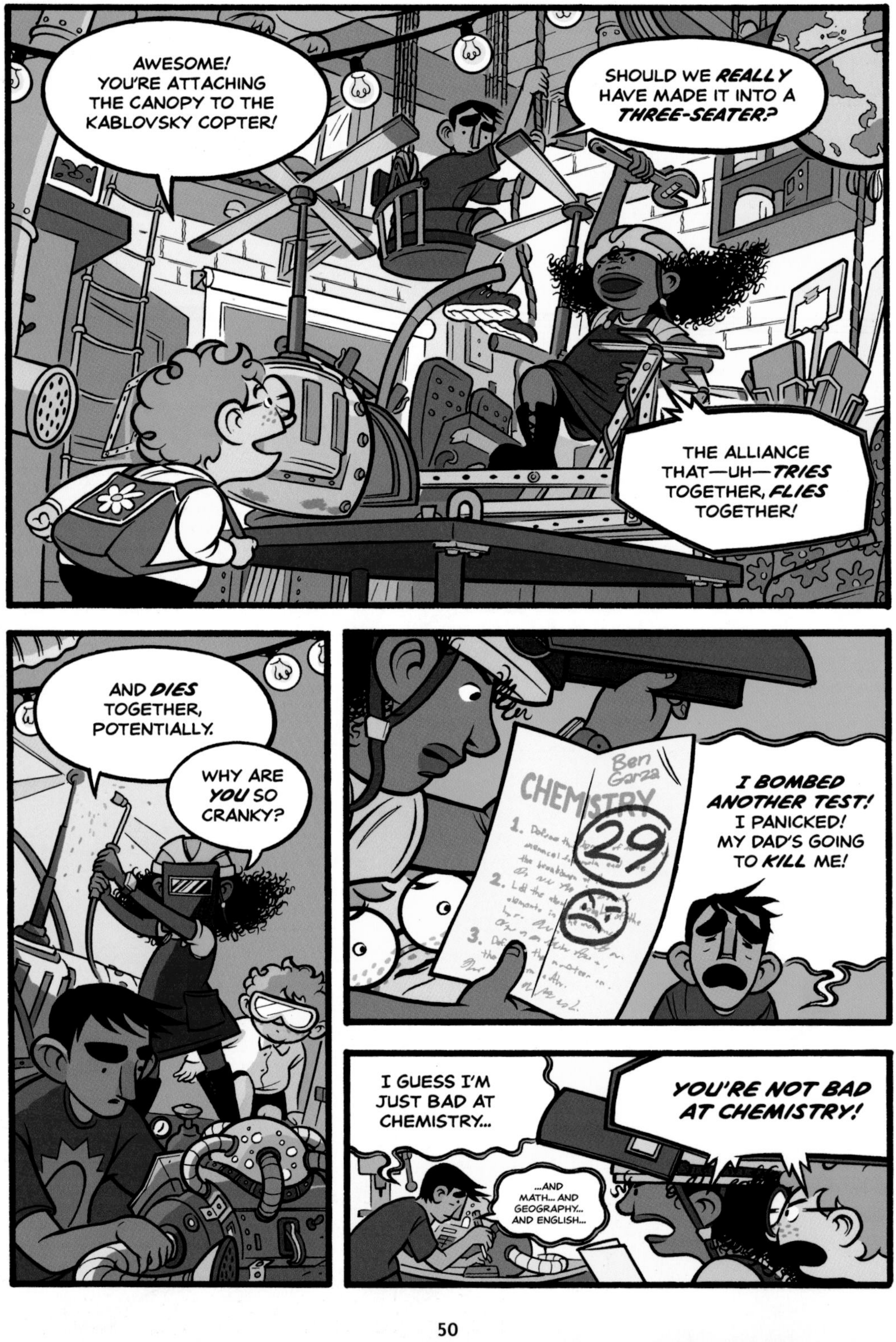
AWESOME! YOU'RE ATTACHING THE CANOPY TO THE KABLOVSKY COPTER!
SHOULD WE *REALLY* HAVE MADE IT INTO A *THREE-SEATER?*
THE ALLIANCE THAT—UH—*TRIES* TOGETHER, *FLIES* TOGETHER!
AND *DIES* TOGETHER, POTENTIALLY.
WHY ARE *YOU* SO CRANKY?
Ben Garza
CHEMISTRY
29
I BOMBED ANOTHER TEST! I PANICKED! MY DAD'S GOING TO *KILL* ME!
I GUESS I'M JUST BAD AT CHEMISTRY...
YOU'RE NOT BAD AT CHEMISTRY!
...AND MATH... AND GEOGRAPHY... AND ENGLISH...

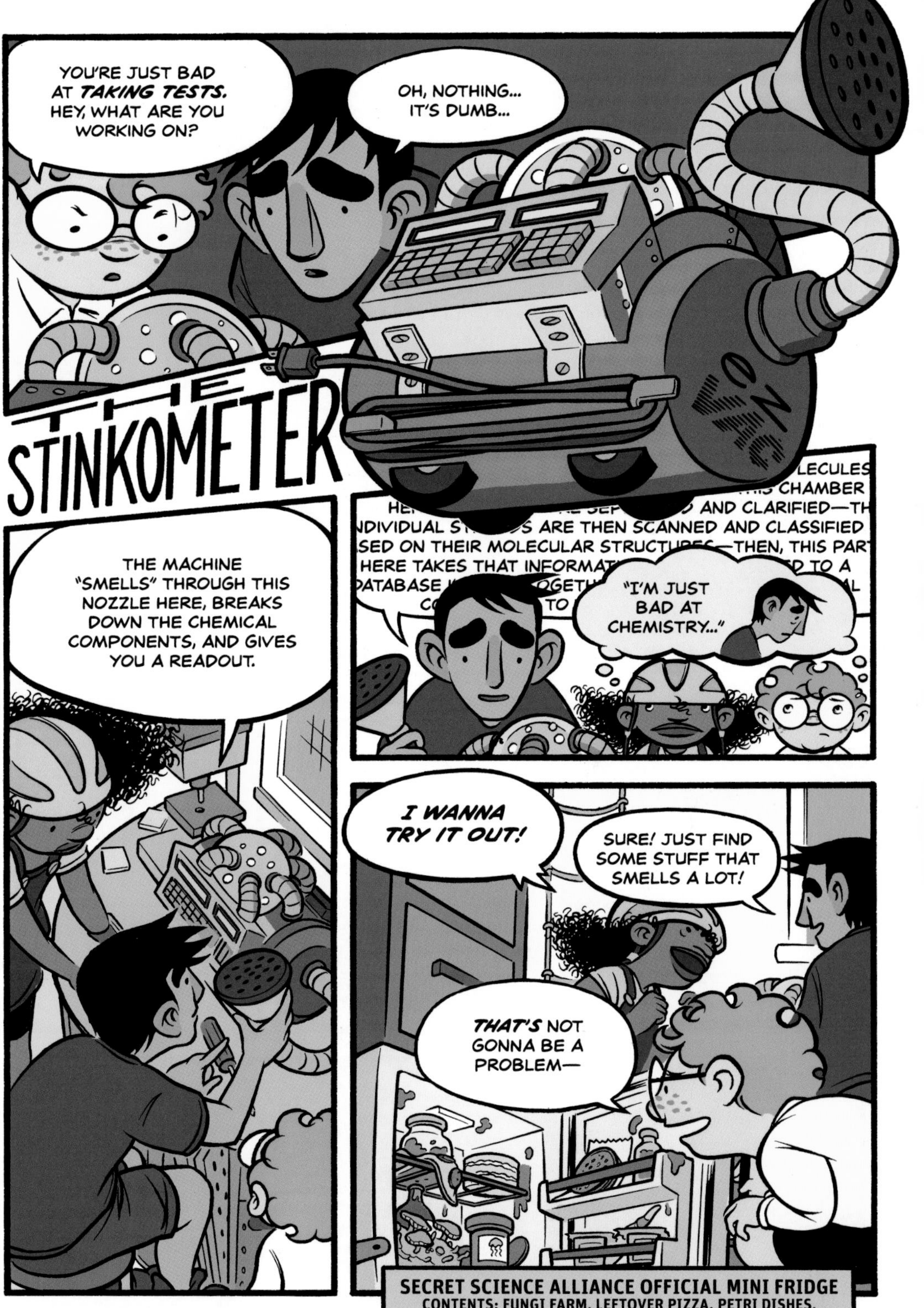

YOU'RE JUST BAD AT *TAKING TESTS.* HEY, WHAT ARE YOU WORKING ON?
OH, NOTHING... IT'S DUMB...
THE STINKOMETER
THE MACHINE "SMELLS" THROUGH THIS NOZZLE HERE, BREAKS DOWN THE CHEMICAL COMPONENTS, AND GIVES YOU A READOUT.
LECULES
THIS CHAMBER
D AND CLARIFIED—TH
NDIVIDUAL ST S ARE THEN SCANNED AND CLASSIFIED
SED ON THEIR MOLECULAR STRUCTURES—THEN, THIS PART
HERE TAKES THAT INFORMAT ED TO A
DATABASE
"I'M JUST BAD AT CHEMISTRY..."
I WANNA TRY IT OUT!
SURE! JUST FIND SOME STUFF THAT SMELLS A LOT!
THAT'S NOT GONNA BE A PROBLEM—
SECRET SCIENCE ALLIANCE OFFICIAL MINI FRIDGE
CONTENTS: FUNGI FARM, LEFTOVER PIZZA, PETRI DISHES, JELLYFISH FOOD, SODA, CHOCOLATE PUDDING, BOLOGNA, ETC.

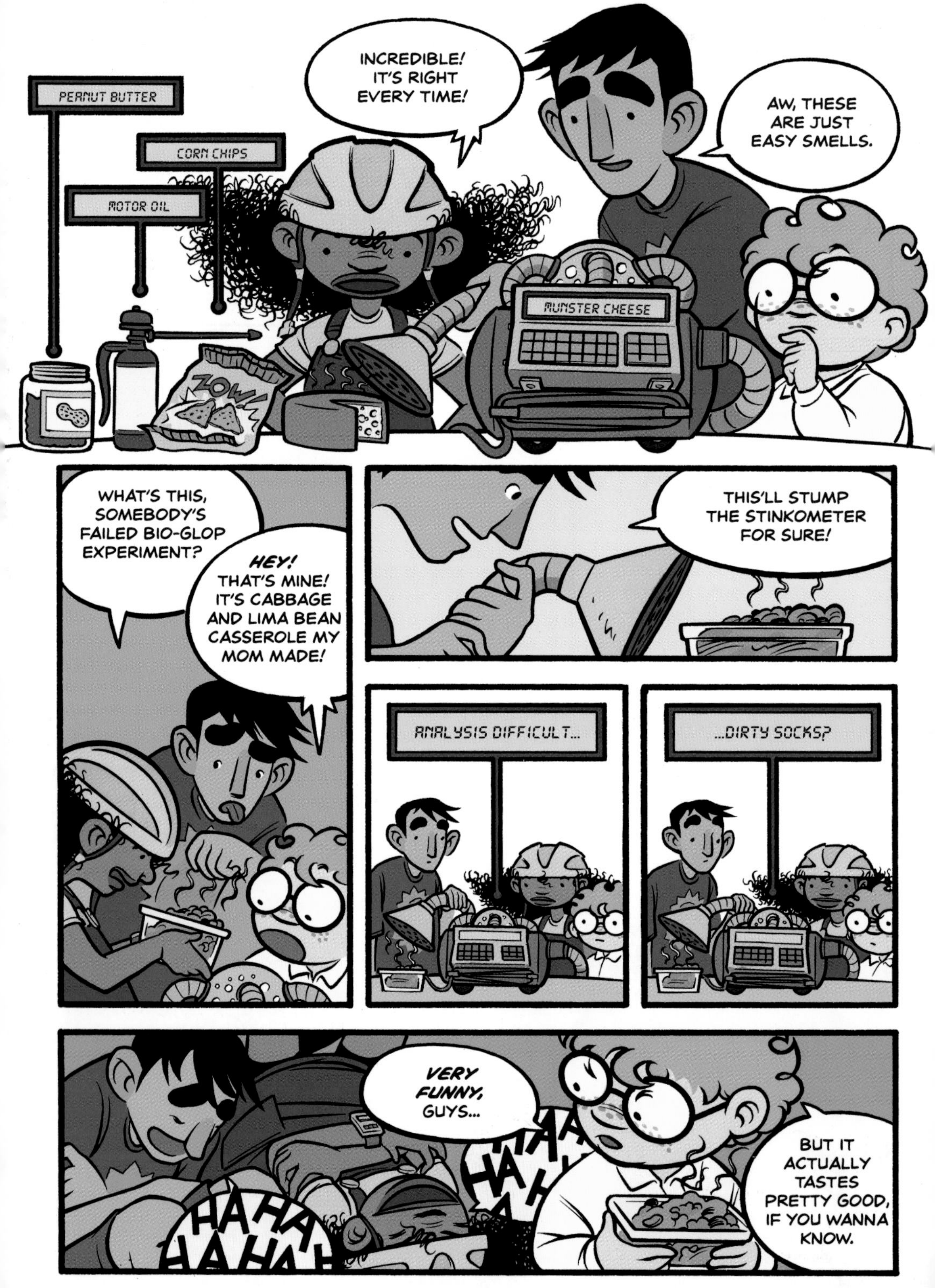
PEANUT BUTTER
CORN CHIPS
MOTOR OIL
ZOW!
MUNSTER CHEESE
INCREDIBLE! IT'S RIGHT EVERY TIME!
AW, THESE ARE JUST EASY SMELLS.
WHAT'S THIS, SOMEBODY'S FAILED BIO-GLOP EXPERIMENT?
HEY! THAT'S MINE! IT'S CABBAGE AND LIMA BEAN CASSEROLE MY MOM MADE!
THIS'LL STUMP THE STINKOMETER FOR SURE!
ANALYSIS DIFFICULT...
...DIRTY SOCKS?
VERY FUNNY, GUYS...
BUT IT ACTUALLY TASTES PRETTY GOOD, IF YOU WANNA KNOW.

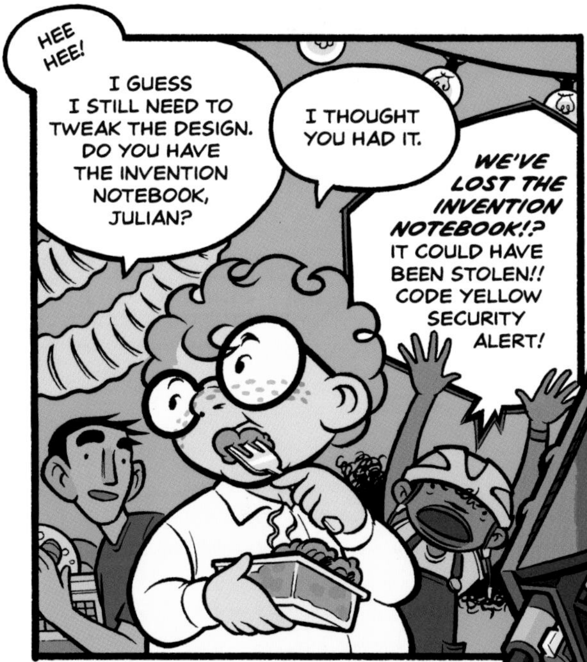
HEE HEE!
I GUESS I STILL NEED TO TWEAK THE DESIGN. DO YOU HAVE THE INVENTION NOTEBOOK, JULIAN?
I THOUGHT YOU HAD IT.
WE'VE LOST THE INVENTION NOTEBOOK!? IT COULD HAVE BEEN STOLEN!! CODE YELLOW SECURITY ALERT!

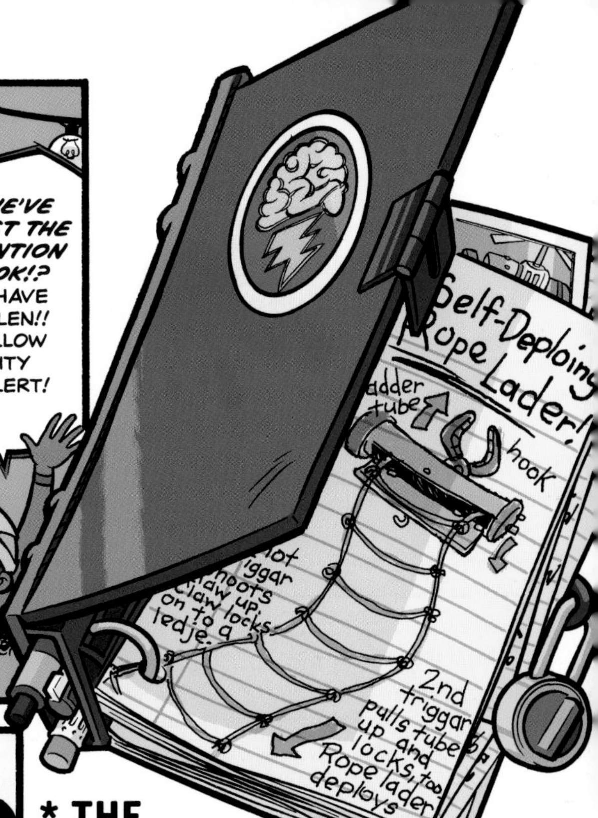
Self-Deploing Rope Lader!
ladder tube
hook
triggar
hoots
claw up,
claw locks
on to a
ledje.
2nd triggar pulls tube up and locks, too. Rope lader deploys

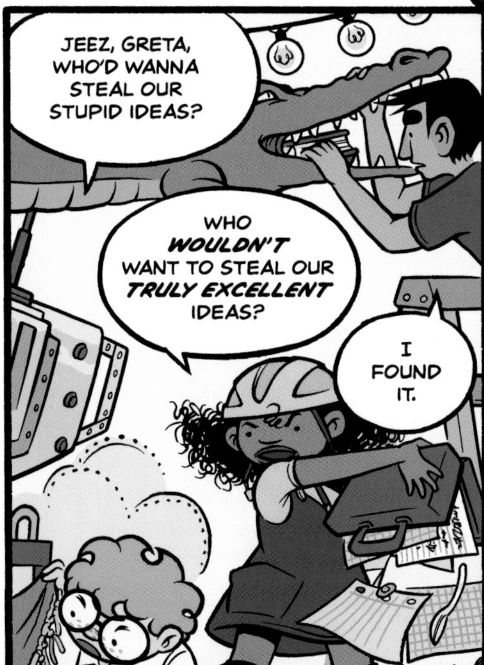
JEEZ, GRETA, WHO'D WANNA STEAL OUR STUPID IDEAS?
WHO *WOULDN'T* WANT TO STEAL OUR *TRULY EXCELLENT* IDEAS?
I FOUND IT.

* THE INVENTION NOTEBOOK!

THE NOTES AND DIAGRAMS FOR EVERY SCI-ALLI INVENTION ARE CONTAINED WITHIN THIS HIGHLY VALUABLE VOLUME. FOR THIS REASON THE INVENTION NOTEBOOK IS THE SECRET SCIENCE ALLIANCE'S MOST CLOSELY GUARDED POSSESSION!

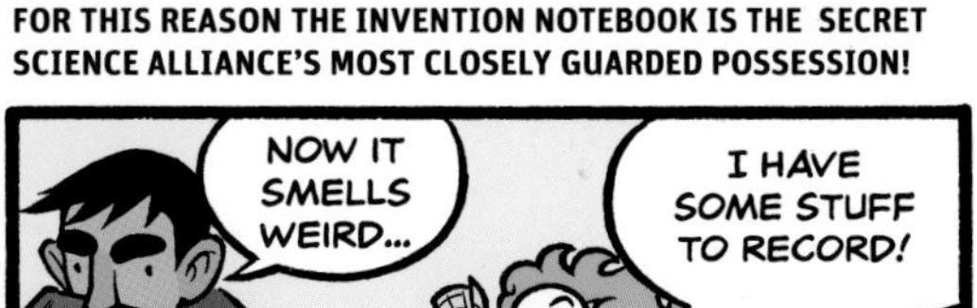
NOW IT SMELLS WEIRD...
I HAVE SOME STUFF TO RECORD!

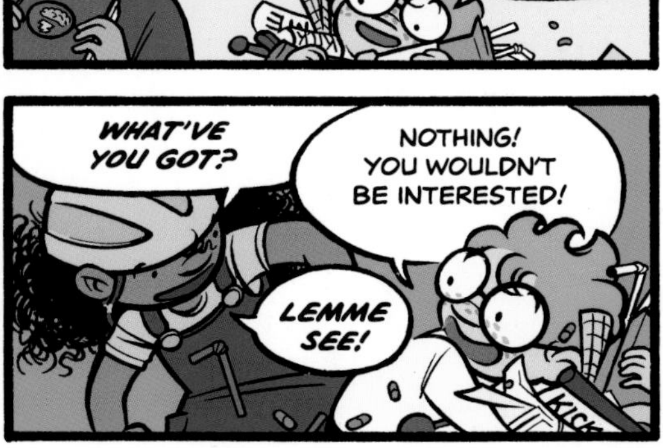
WHAT'VE YOU GOT?
NOTHING! YOU WOULDN'T BE INTERESTED!
LEMME SEE!

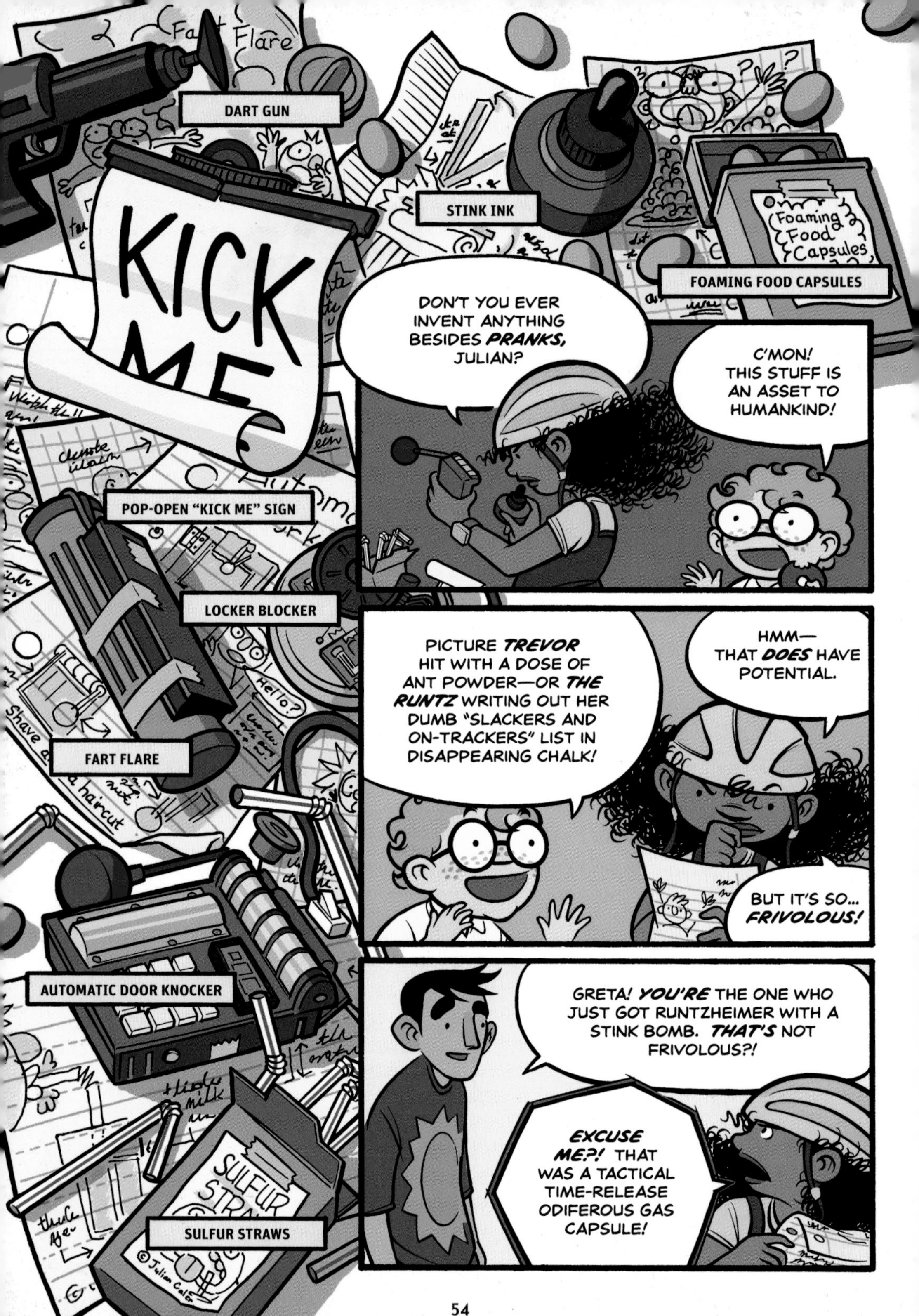
DART GUN
KICK ME
STINK INK
Foaming Food Capsules
FOAMING FOOD CAPSULES
POP-OPEN "KICK ME" SIGN
LOCKER BLOCKER
FART FLARE
AUTOMATIC DOOR KNOCKER
SULFUR STRAWS
SULFUR STRAWS
DON'T YOU EVER INVENT ANYTHING BESIDES *PRANKS,* JULIAN?
C'MON! THIS STUFF IS AN ASSET TO HUMANKIND!
PICTURE *TREVOR* HIT WITH A DOSE OF ANT POWDER—OR *THE RUNTZ* WRITING OUT HER DUMB "SLACKERS AND ON-TRACKERS" LIST IN DISAPPEARING CHALK!
HMM— THAT *DOES* HAVE POTENTIAL.
BUT IT'S SO... *FRIVOLOUS!*
GRETA! *YOU'RE* THE ONE WHO JUST GOT RUNTZHEIMER WITH A STINK BOMB. *THAT'S* NOT FRIVOLOUS?!
EXCUSE ME?! THAT WAS A TACTICAL TIME-RELEASE ODIFEROUS GAS CAPSULE!

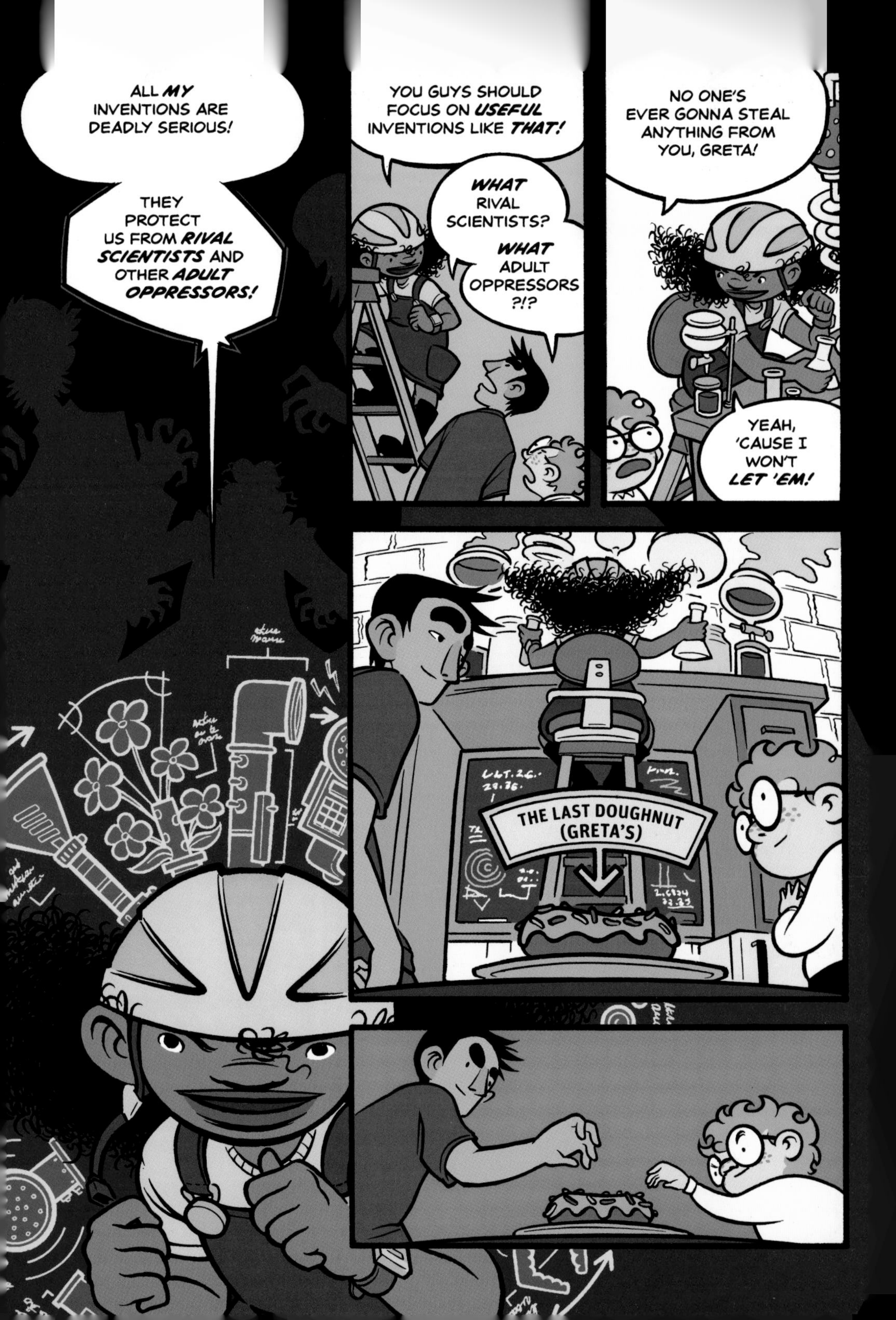
ALL MY INVENTIONS ARE DEADLY SERIOUS!
THEY PROTECT US FROM RIVAL SCIENTISTS AND OTHER ADULT OPPRESSORS!
YOU GUYS SHOULD FOCUS ON USEFUL INVENTIONS LIKE THAT!
WHAT RIVAL SCIENTISTS?
WHAT ADULT OPPRESSORS ?!?
NO ONE'S EVER GONNA STEAL ANYTHING FROM YOU, GRETA!
YEAH, 'CAUSE I WON'T LET 'EM!
THE LAST DOUGHNUT (GRETA'S)

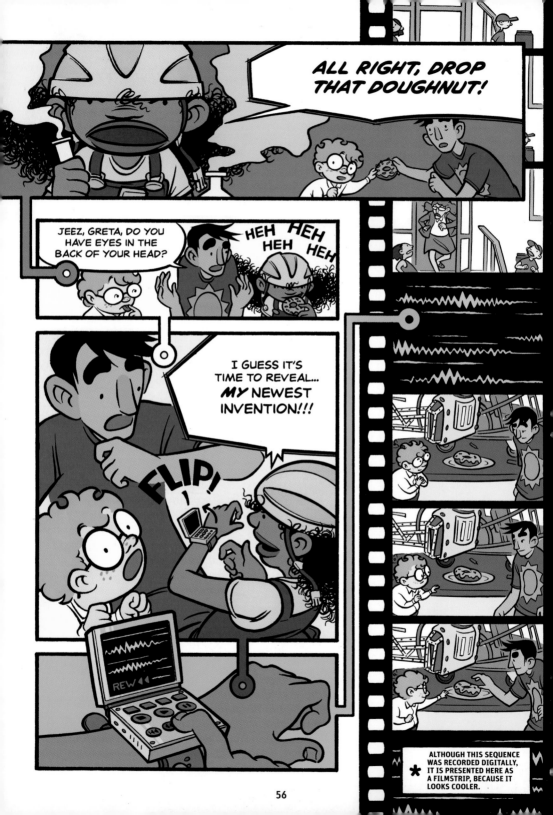

ALL RIGHT, DROP THAT DOUGHNUT!

JEEZ, GRETA, DO YOU HAVE EYES IN THE BACK OF YOUR HEAD?

HEH HEH HEH HEH

I GUESS IT'S TIME TO REVEAL... *MY* NEWEST INVENTION!!!

FLIP!

REW ◄◄

ALTHOUGH THIS SEQUENCE WAS RECORDED DIGITALLY, IT IS PRESENTED HERE AS A FILMSTRIP, BECAUSE IT LOOKS COOLER.

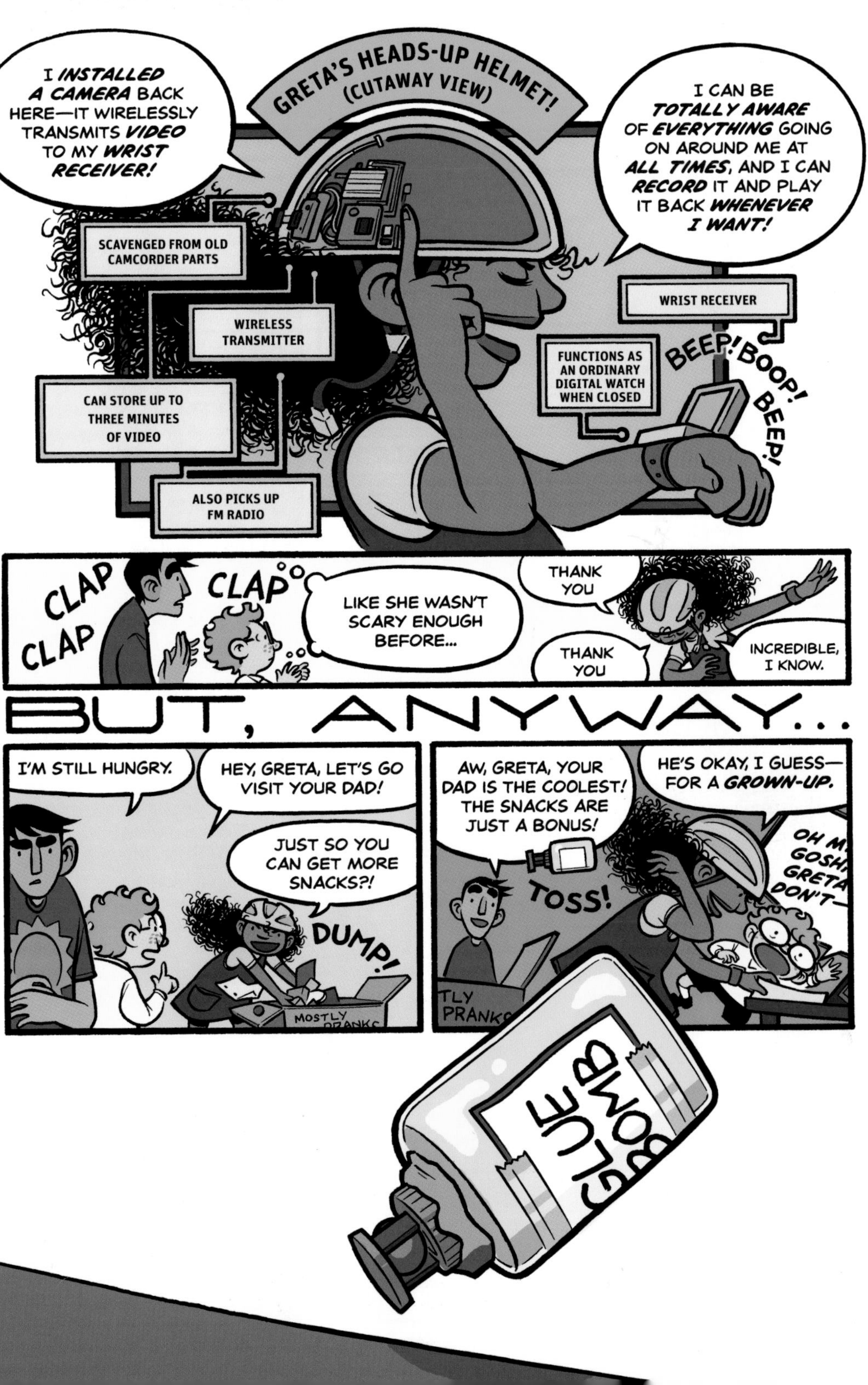
I INSTALLED A CAMERA BACK HERE—IT WIRELESSLY TRANSMITS VIDEO TO MY WRIST RECEIVER!
GRETA'S HEADS-UP HELMET! (CUTAWAY VIEW)
I CAN BE TOTALLY AWARE OF EVERYTHING GOING ON AROUND ME AT ALL TIMES, AND I CAN RECORD IT AND PLAY IT BACK WHENEVER I WANT!
SCAVENGED FROM OLD CAMCORDER PARTS
WIRELESS TRANSMITTER
CAN STORE UP TO THREE MINUTES OF VIDEO
ALSO PICKS UP FM RADIO
WRIST RECEIVER
FUNCTIONS AS AN ORDINARY DIGITAL WATCH WHEN CLOSED
BEEP! BOOP! BEEP!
CLAP CLAP
CLAP
LIKE SHE WASN'T SCARY ENOUGH BEFORE...
THANK YOU
THANK YOU
INCREDIBLE, I KNOW.
BUT, ANYWAY...
I'M STILL HUNGRY.
HEY, GRETA, LET'S GO VISIT YOUR DAD!
JUST SO YOU CAN GET MORE SNACKS?!
DUMP!
MOSTLY PRANKS
AW, GRETA, YOUR DAD IS THE COOLEST! THE SNACKS ARE JUST A BONUS!
HE'S OKAY, I GUESS—FOR A GROWN-UP.
TOSS!
OH MY GOSH! GRETA DON'T—
TLY PRANKS
GLUE BOMB

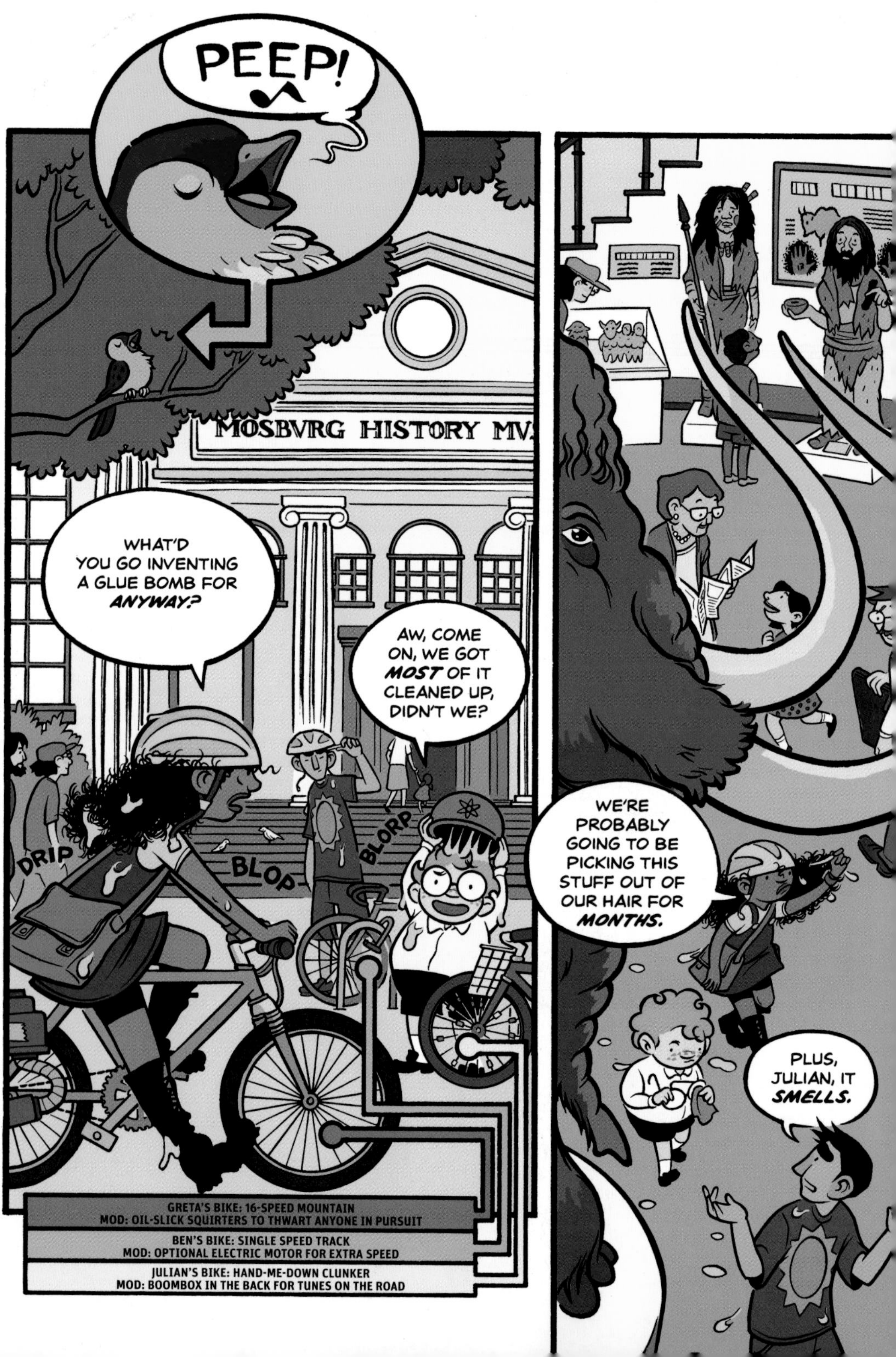
PEEP!
MOSBVRG HISTORY MV
WHAT'D YOU GO INVENTING A GLUE BOMB FOR *ANYWAY?*
AW, COME ON, WE GOT *MOST* OF IT CLEANED UP, DIDN'T WE?
DRIP
BLOP
BLORP
GRETA'S BIKE: 16-SPEED MOUNTAIN
MOD: OIL-SLICK SQUIRTERS TO THWART ANYONE IN PURSUIT
BEN'S BIKE: SINGLE SPEED TRACK
MOD: OPTIONAL ELECTRIC MOTOR FOR EXTRA SPEED
JULIAN'S BIKE: HAND-ME-DOWN CLUNKER
MOD: BOOMBOX IN THE BACK FOR TUNES ON THE ROAD
WE'RE PROBABLY GOING TO BE PICKING THIS STUFF OUT OF OUR HAIR FOR *MONTHS.*
PLUS, JULIAN, IT *SMELLS.*

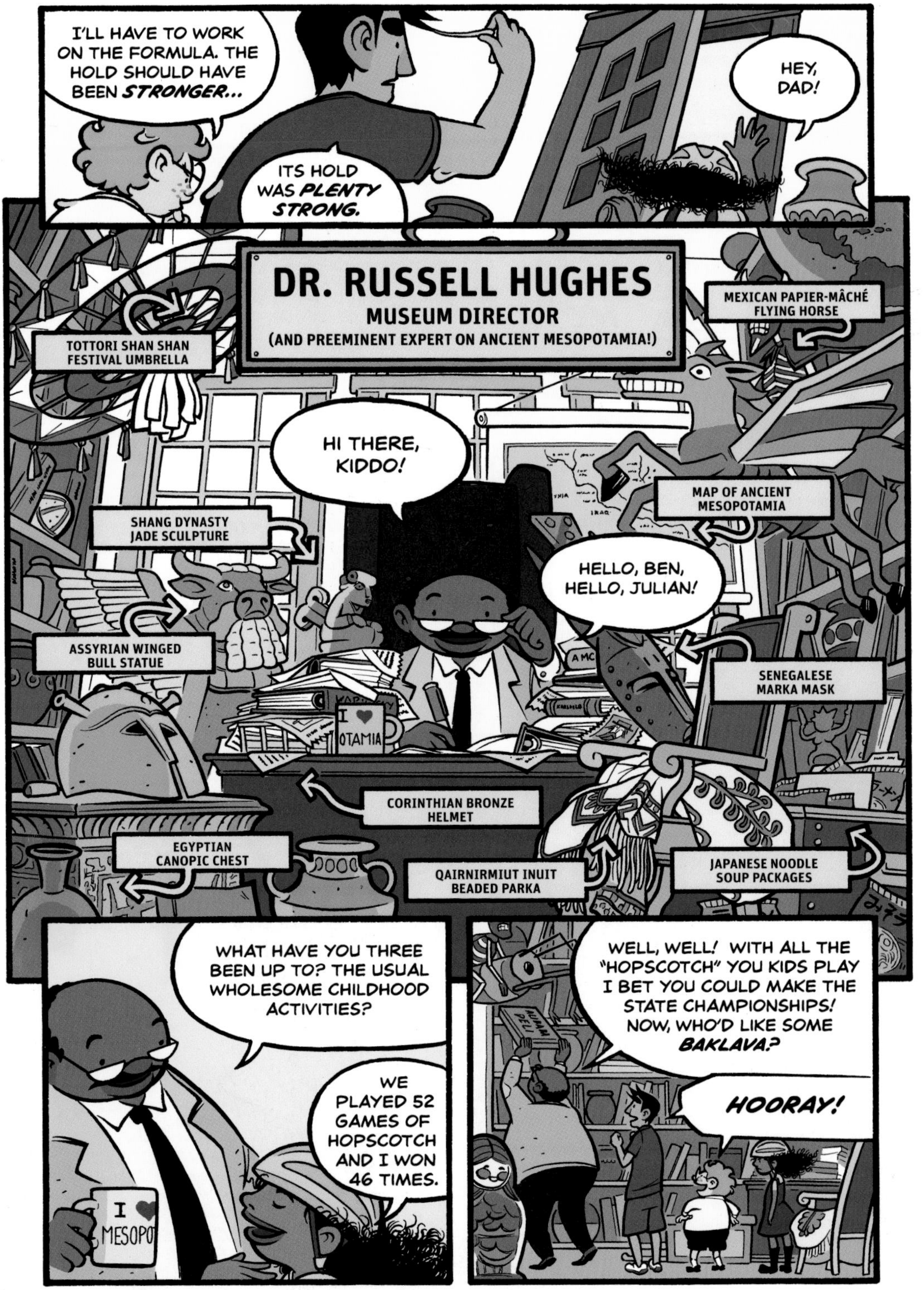

I'LL HAVE TO WORK ON THE FORMULA. THE HOLD SHOULD HAVE BEEN STRONGER...
ITS HOLD WAS PLENTY STRONG.
HEY, DAD!
DR. RUSSELL HUGHES
MUSEUM DIRECTOR
(AND PREEMINENT EXPERT ON ANCIENT MESOPOTAMIA!)
TOTTORI SHAN SHAN FESTIVAL UMBRELLA
MEXICAN PAPIER-MÂCHÉ FLYING HORSE
HI THERE, KIDDO!
MAP OF ANCIENT MESOPOTAMIA
SHANG DYNASTY JADE SCULPTURE
HELLO, BEN, HELLO, JULIAN!
ASSYRIAN WINGED BULL STATUE
SENEGALESE MARKA MASK
I ♥ OTAMIA
CORINTHIAN BRONZE HELMET
EGYPTIAN CANOPIC CHEST
QAIRNIRMIUT INUIT BEADED PARKA
JAPANESE NOODLE SOUP PACKAGES
WHAT HAVE YOU THREE BEEN UP TO? THE USUAL WHOLESOME CHILDHOOD ACTIVITIES?
WE PLAYED 52 GAMES OF HOPSCOTCH AND I WON 46 TIMES.
I ♥ MESOPO
WELL, WELL! WITH ALL THE "HOPSCOTCH" YOU KIDS PLAY I BET YOU COULD MAKE THE STATE CHAMPIONSHIPS! NOW, WHO'D LIKE SOME BAKLAVA?
HOORAY!

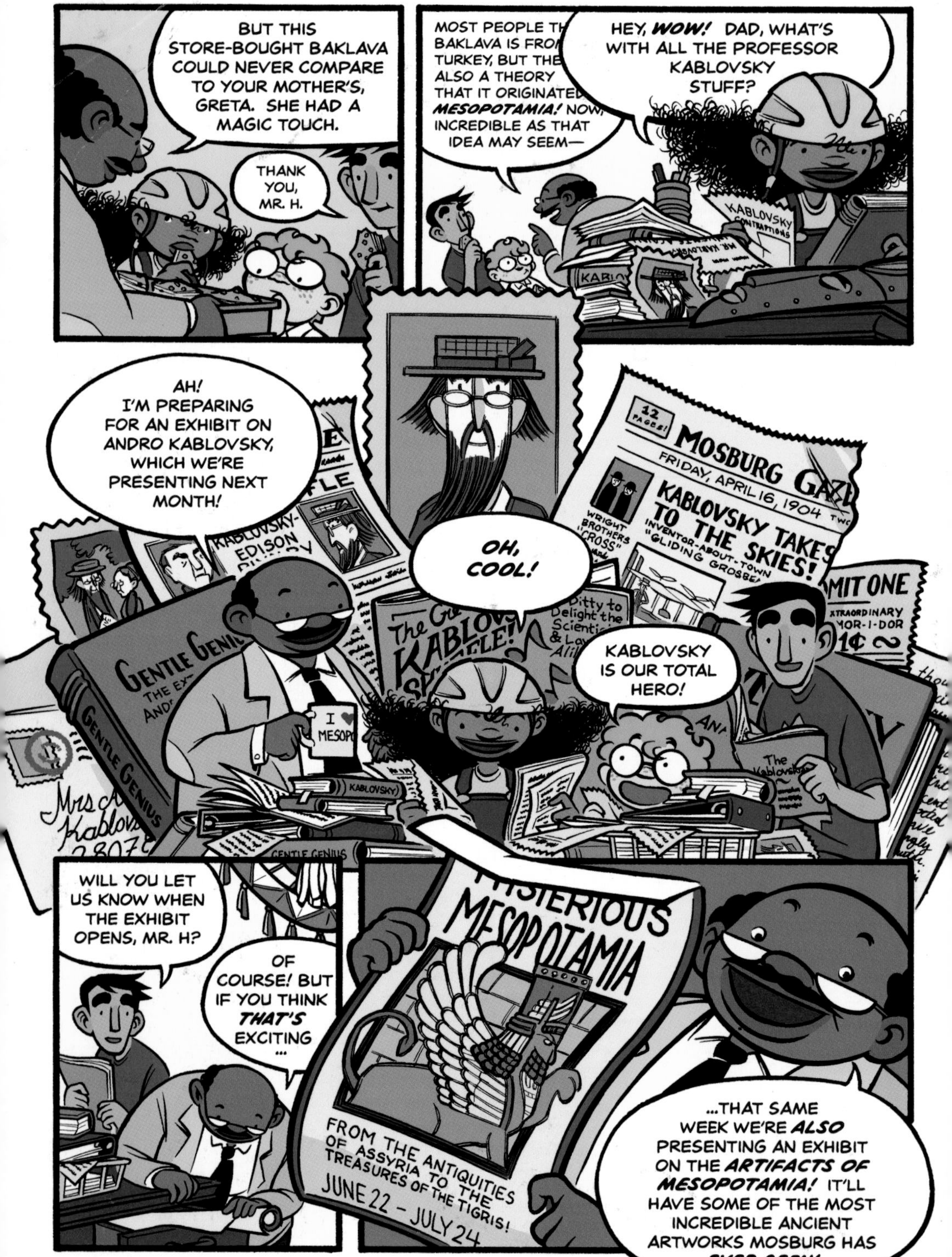
BUT THIS STORE-BOUGHT BAKLAVA COULD NEVER COMPARE TO YOUR MOTHER'S, GRETA. SHE HAD A MAGIC TOUCH.
THANK YOU, MR. H.
MOST PEOPLE TH BAKLAVA IS FROM TURKEY, BUT THE ALSO A THEORY THAT IT ORIGINATED MESOPOTAMIA! NOW, INCREDIBLE AS THAT IDEA MAY SEEM—
HEY, WOW! DAD, WHAT'S WITH ALL THE PROFESSOR KABLOVSKY STUFF?
KABLOVSKY CONTRAPTIONS
AH! I'M PREPARING FOR AN EXHIBIT ON ANDRO KABLOVSKY, WHICH WE'RE PRESENTING NEXT MONTH!
MOSBURG GAZ
FRIDAY, APRIL 16, 1904
KABLOVSKY TAKES TO THE SKIES!
INVENTOR-ABOUT-TOWN "GLIDING GROSBE
WRIGHT BROTHERS "CROSS"
KABLOVSKY-EDISON
OH, COOL!
GENTLE GENIUS
KABLOVSKY IS OUR TOTAL HERO!
MIT ONE
XTRAORDINARY
1¢
I ♥ MESOPO
KABLOVSKY
WILL YOU LET US KNOW WHEN THE EXHIBIT OPENS, MR. H?
OF COURSE! BUT IF YOU THINK THAT'S EXCITING ...
MESOPOTAMIA
FROM THE ANTIQUITIES OF ASSYRIA TO THE TREASURES OF THE TIGRIS!
JUNE 22 – JULY 24
...THAT SAME WEEK WE'RE ALSO PRESENTING AN EXHIBIT ON THE ARTIFACTS OF MESOPOTAMIA! IT'LL HAVE SOME OF THE MOST INCREDIBLE ANCIENT ARTWORKS MOSBURG HAS EVER SEEN!

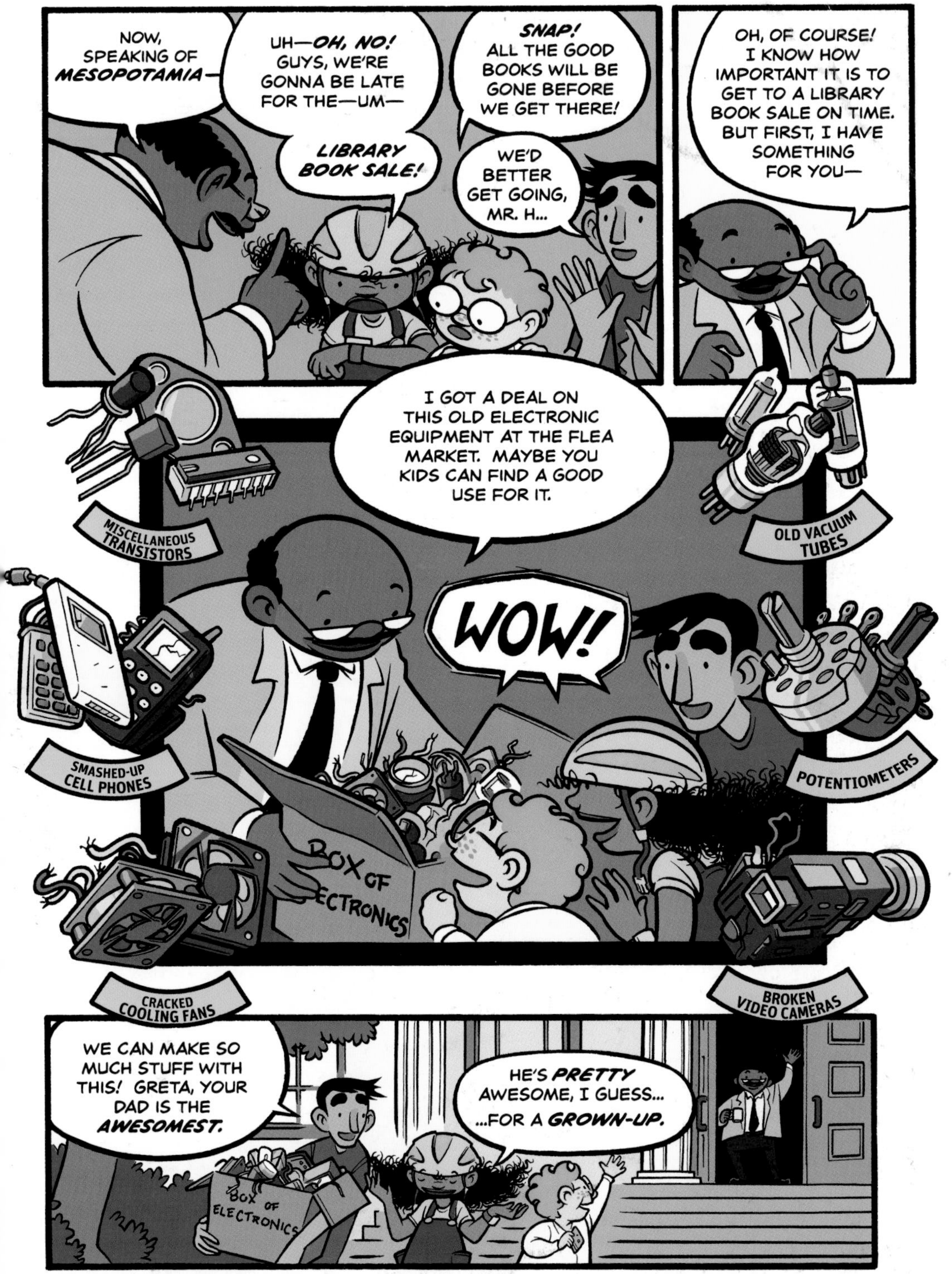
NOW, SPEAKING OF MESOPOTAMIA—
UH—OH, NO! GUYS, WE'RE GONNA BE LATE FOR THE—UM—
LIBRARY BOOK SALE!
SNAP! ALL THE GOOD BOOKS WILL BE GONE BEFORE WE GET THERE!
WE'D BETTER GET GOING, MR. H...
OH, OF COURSE! I KNOW HOW IMPORTANT IT IS TO GET TO A LIBRARY BOOK SALE ON TIME. BUT FIRST, I HAVE SOMETHING FOR YOU—
I GOT A DEAL ON THIS OLD ELECTRONIC EQUIPMENT AT THE FLEA MARKET. MAYBE YOU KIDS CAN FIND A GOOD USE FOR IT.
MISCELLANEOUS TRANSISTORS
OLD VACUUM TUBES
WOW!
SMASHED-UP CELL PHONES
POTENTIOMETERS
BOX OF ELECTRONICS
CRACKED COOLING FANS
BROKEN VIDEO CAMERAS
WE CAN MAKE SO MUCH STUFF WITH THIS! GRETA, YOUR DAD IS THE AWESOMEST.
HE'S PRETTY AWESOME, I GUESS... ...FOR A GROWN-UP.
BOX OF ELECTRONICS

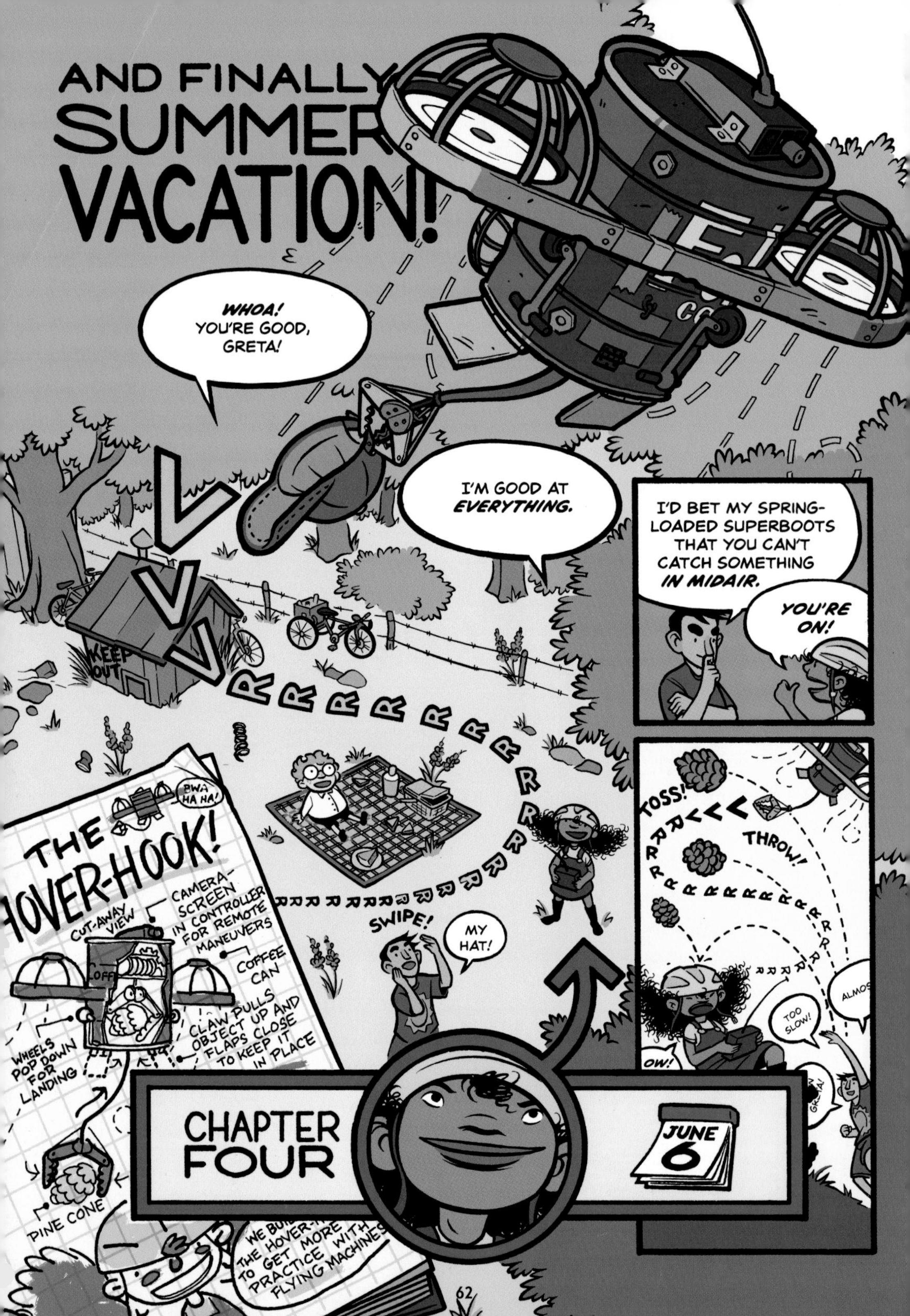
AND FINALLY SUMMER VACATION!
WHOA! YOU'RE GOOD, GRETA!
I'M GOOD AT EVERYTHING.
I'D BET MY SPRING-LOADED SUPERBOOTS THAT YOU CAN'T CATCH SOMETHING IN MIDAIR.
YOU'RE ON!
KEEP OUT
SWIPE!
MY HAT!
THE HOVER-HOOK!
BWA HA HA!
CUT-AWAY VIEW
CAMERA-SCREEN IN CONTROLLER FOR REMOTE MANEUVERS
COFFEE CAN
CLAW PULLS OBJECT UP AND FLAPS CLOSE TO KEEP IT IN PLACE
WHEELS POP DOWN FOR LANDING
PINE CONE
TOSS!
THROW!
TOO SLOW!
ALMOS
OW!
CHAPTER FOUR
JUNE 6

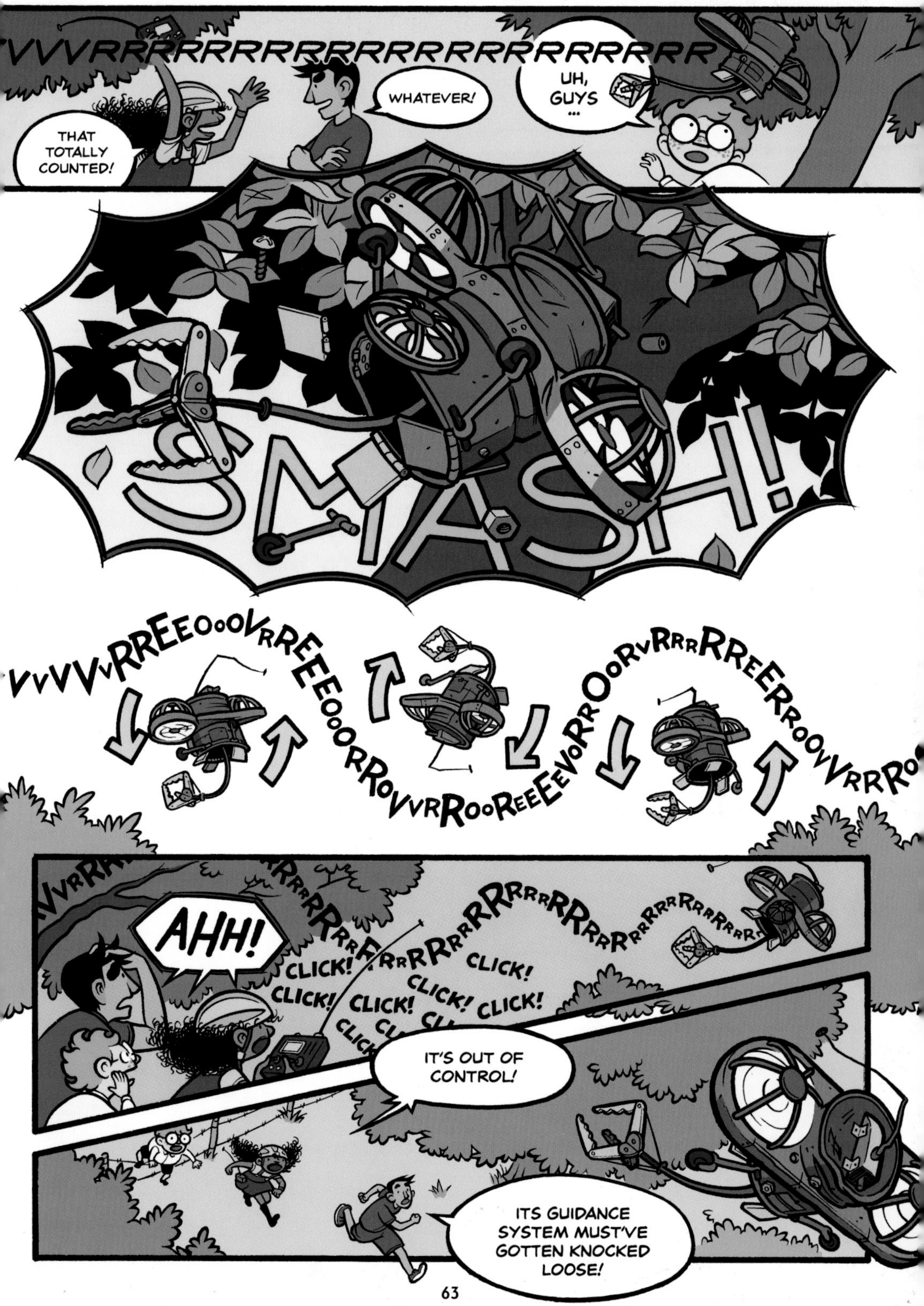
VVVVRRRRRRRRRRRRRRRRRRRRRRRRR
THAT TOTALLY COUNTED!
WHATEVER!
UH, GUYS ...
SMASH!
VVVVVRREEOOOVRREEEOOOORROVVRROOREEEEVORROORVRRRRREERROOVVRRRO
AHH!
CLICK! CLICK! CLICK! CLICK! CLICK!
IT'S OUT OF CONTROL!
ITS GUIDANCE SYSTEM MUST'VE GOTTEN KNOCKED LOOSE!

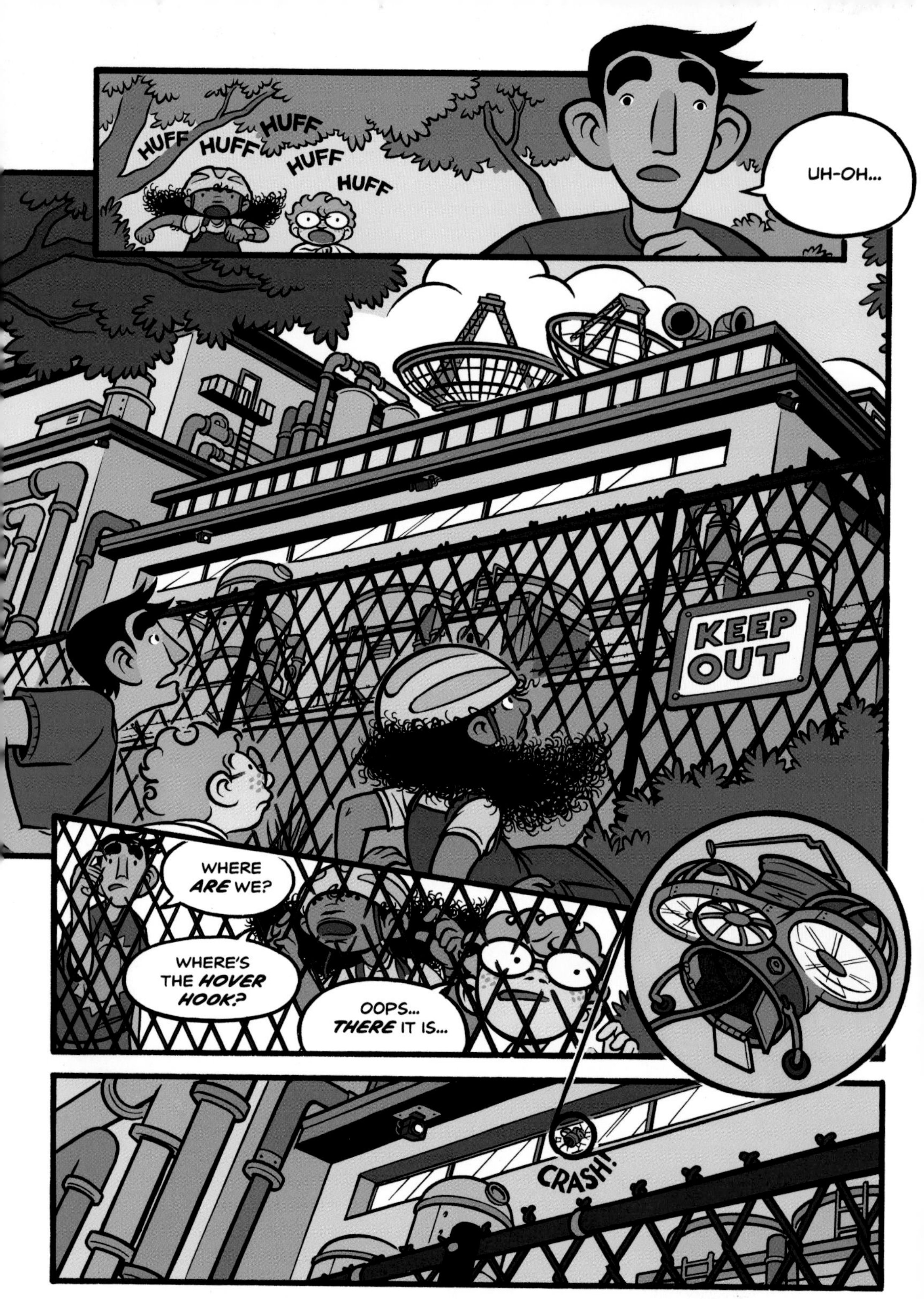
HUFF HUFF HUFF HUFF HUFF
UH-OH...
KEEP OUT
WHERE *ARE* WE?
WHERE'S THE *HOVER HOOK?*
OOPS... *THERE* IT IS...
CRASH!

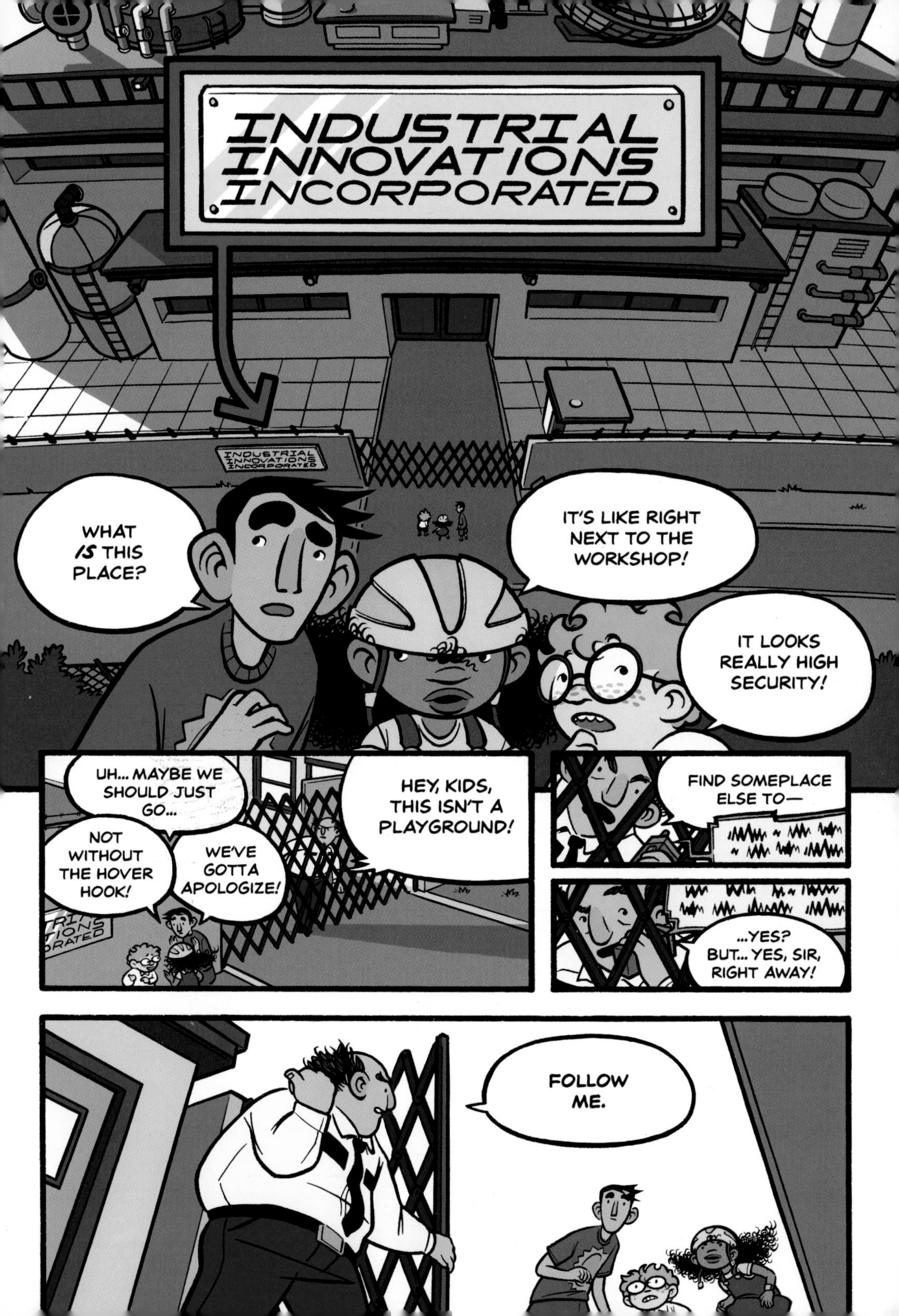
INDUSTRIAL INNOVATIONS INCORPORATED
INDUSTRIAL INNOVATIONS INCORPORATED
WHAT *IS* THIS PLACE?
IT'S LIKE RIGHT NEXT TO THE WORKSHOP!
IT LOOKS REALLY HIGH SECURITY!
UH... MAYBE WE SHOULD JUST GO...
NOT WITHOUT THE HOVER HOOK!
WE'VE GOTTA APOLOGIZE!
HEY, KIDS, THIS ISN'T A PLAYGROUND!
FIND SOMEPLACE ELSE TO—
...YES? BUT... YES, SIR, RIGHT AWAY!
FOLLOW ME.

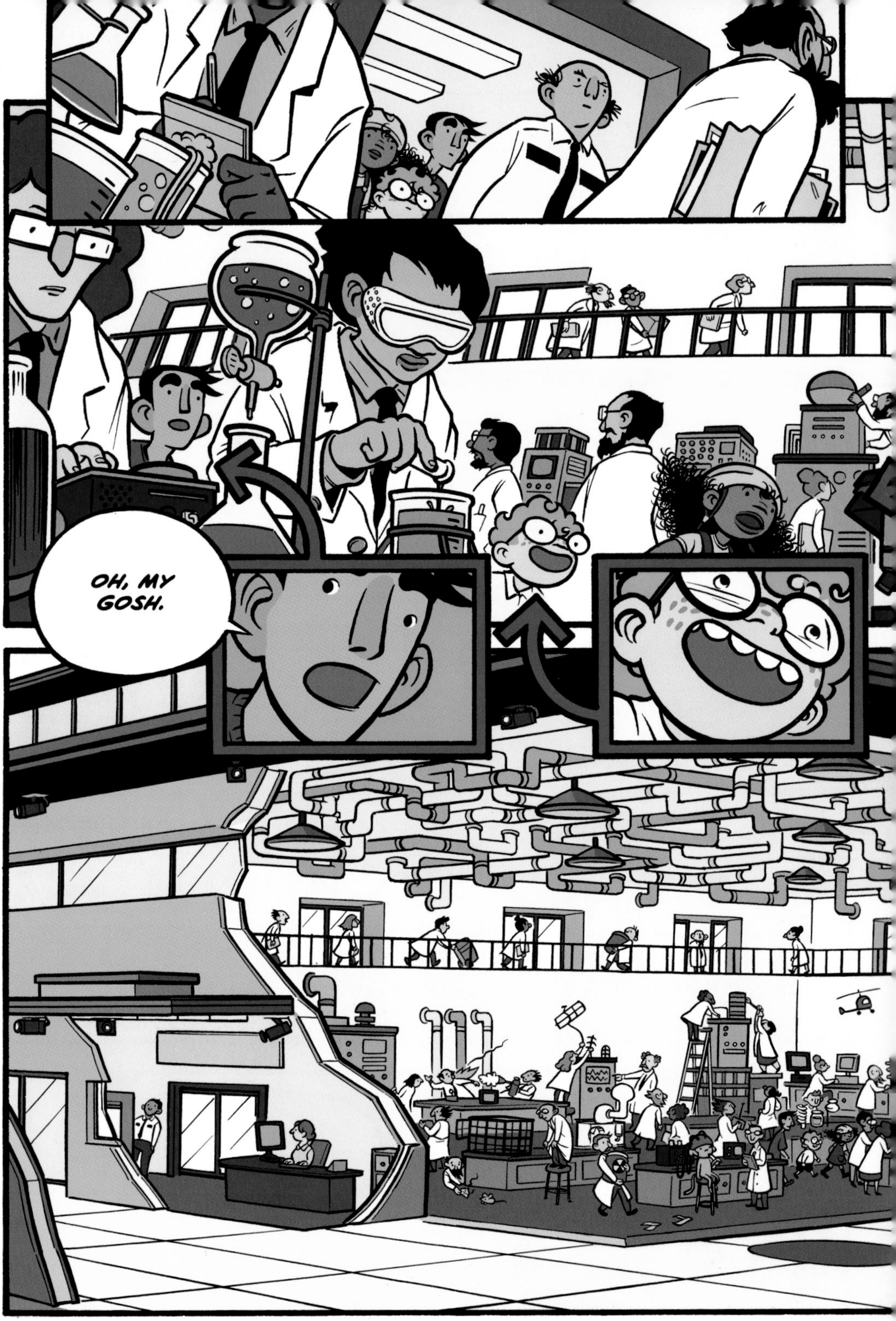
OH, MY GOSH.

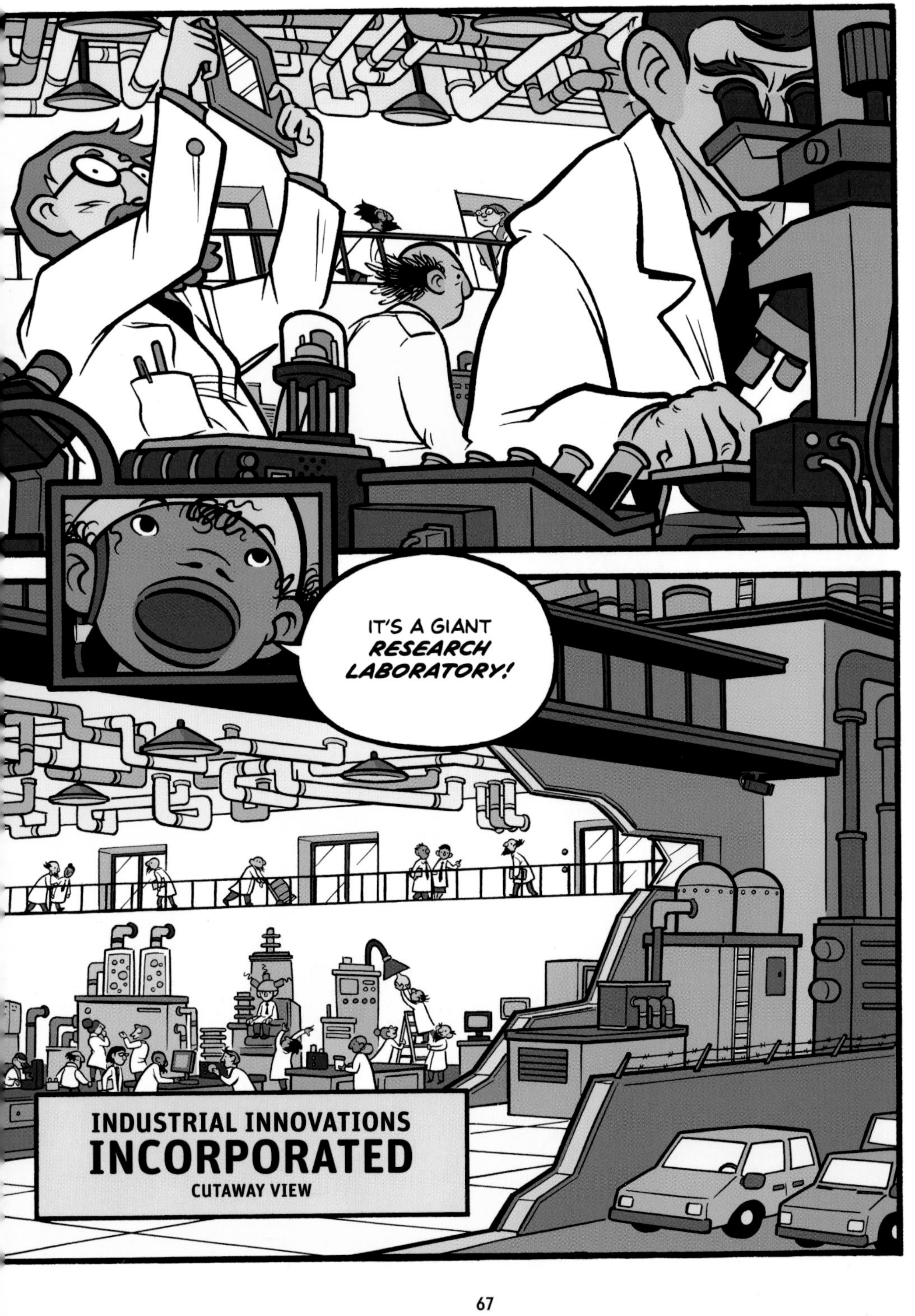
IT'S A GIANT *RESEARCH LABORATORY!*
INDUSTRIAL INNOVATIONS
INCORPORATED
CUTAWAY VIEW

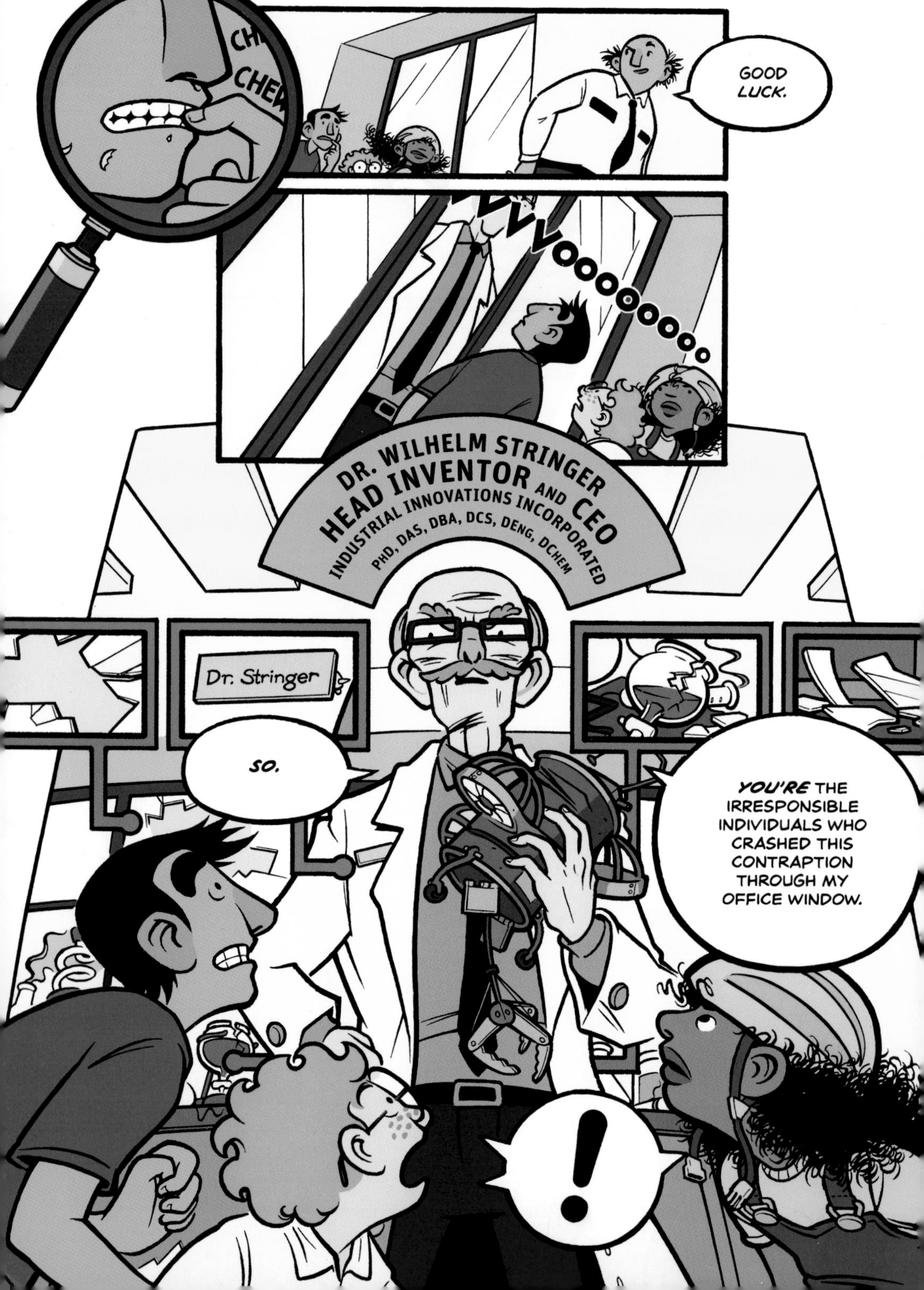
CHEW
CHEW
GOOD LUCK.
VVVOOOOOOOOOOOO
DR. WILHELM STRINGER
HEAD INVENTOR AND CEO
INDUSTRIAL INNOVATIONS INCORPORATED
PHD, DAS, DBA, DCS, DENG, DCHEM
Dr. Stringer
SO.
YOU'RE THE IRRESPONSIBLE INDIVIDUALS WHO CRASHED THIS CONTRAPTION THROUGH MY OFFICE WINDOW.
!

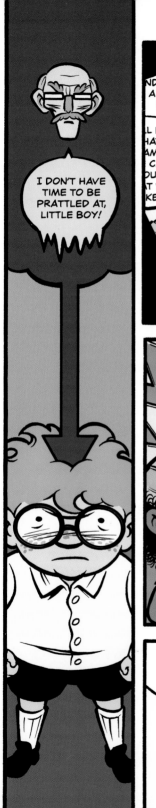

I DON'T HAVE TIME TO BE PRATTLED AT, LITTLE BOY!

...LY SORRY. ...E WERE FLYING IT ...ND AND IT CRASHED ...A TREE AND WENT HAYWIRE!

...L PAY ...HATEVER ...AMAGES ...CAUSED ...OU'LL TELL ...T WAS ...KEN—

HMPH. A LIKELY STORY. ...AS FOR THIS... PIECE OF WORK...

WHERE DID YOU CHILDREN ACQUIRE SUCH AN—AH— ODD-LOOKING TOY?

W-WE MADE IT OURSELVES!

WELL! IT'S THE EXCITABLE BOY FROM MY LECTURE!

YOU LIKE TO PLAY AT INVENTOR, YOU SAID?

THIS IS YOUR HANDIWORK?

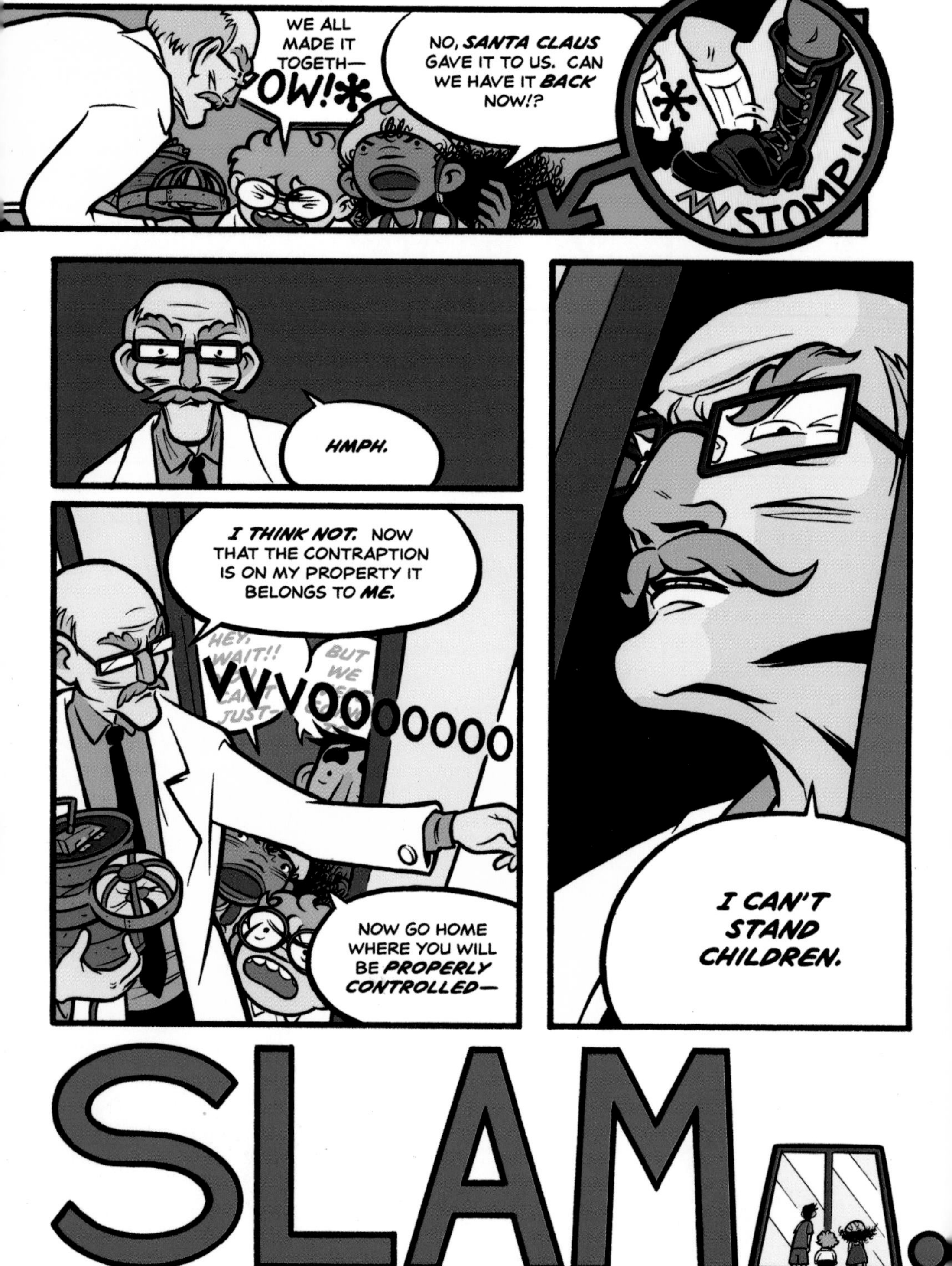
WE ALL MADE IT TOGETH—
OW!*
NO, SANTA CLAUS GAVE IT TO US. CAN WE HAVE IT BACK NOW!?
*
STOMP!
HMPH.
I THINK NOT. NOW THAT THE CONTRAPTION IS ON MY PROPERTY IT BELONGS TO ME.
HEY, WAIT!!
BUT WE
VVVOOOOOOO
NOW GO HOME WHERE YOU WILL BE PROPERLY CONTROLLED—
I CAN'T STAND CHILDREN.
SLAM.

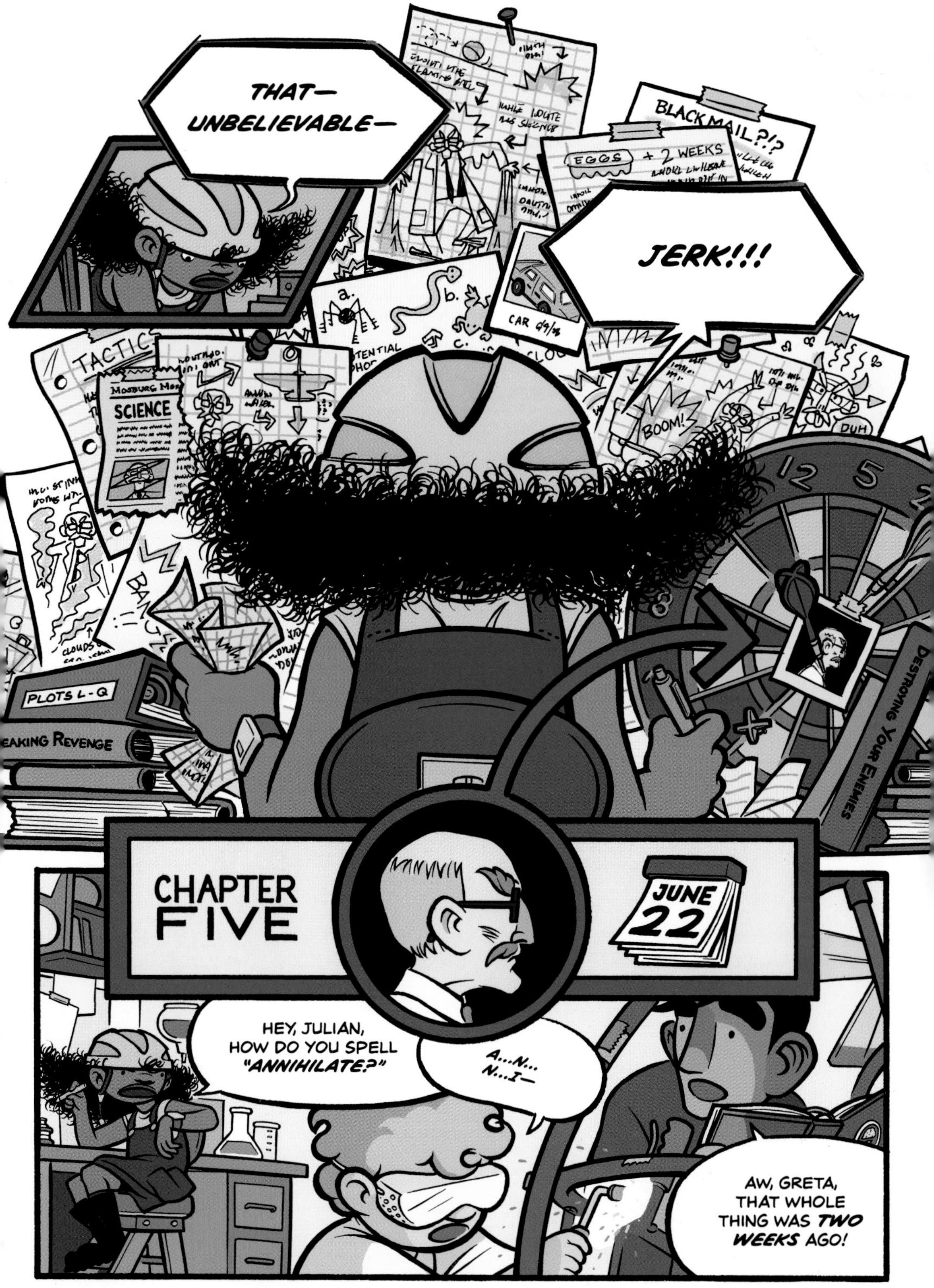
THAT—
UNBELIEVABLE—
JERK!!!
BLACKMAIL?!?
EGGS
+ 2 WEEKS
TACTIC
SCIENCE
BOOM!
DUH
PLOTS L-Q
EAKING REVENGE
DESTROYING YOUR ENEMIES
CHAPTER FIVE
JUNE 22
HEY, JULIAN, HOW DO YOU SPELL "ANNIHILATE?"
A...N... N...I—
AW, GRETA, THAT WHOLE THING WAS TWO WEEKS AGO!

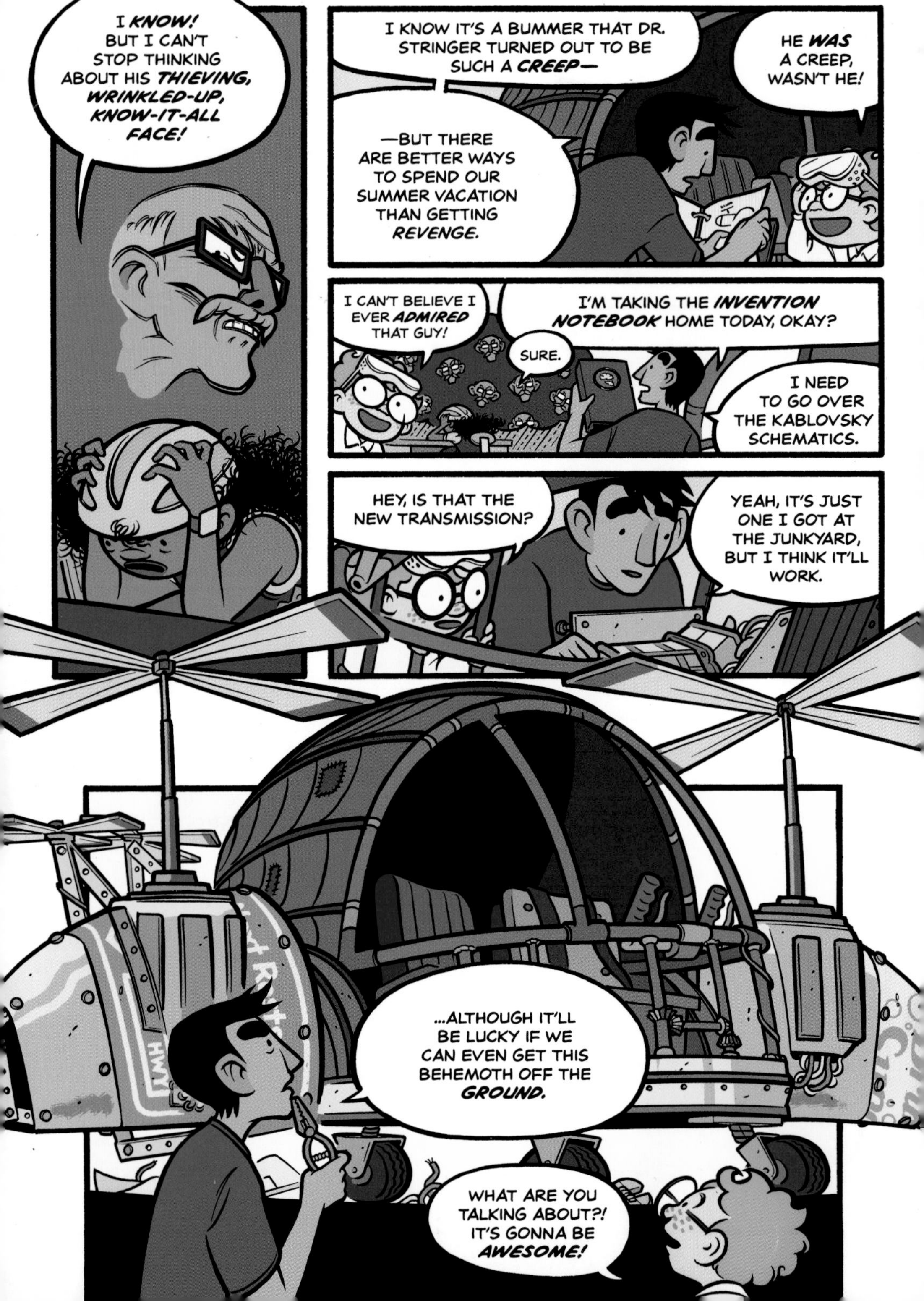

I *KNOW!* BUT I CAN'T STOP THINKING ABOUT HIS *THIEVING, WRINKLED-UP, KNOW-IT-ALL FACE!*
I KNOW IT'S A BUMMER THAT DR. STRINGER TURNED OUT TO BE SUCH A *CREEP*—
HE *WAS* A CREEP, WASN'T HE!
—BUT THERE ARE BETTER WAYS TO SPEND OUR SUMMER VACATION THAN GETTING *REVENGE.*
I CAN'T BELIEVE I EVER *ADMIRED* THAT GUY!
I'M TAKING THE *INVENTION NOTEBOOK* HOME TODAY, OKAY?
SURE.
I NEED TO GO OVER THE KABLOVSKY SCHEMATICS.
HEY, IS THAT THE NEW TRANSMISSION?
YEAH, IT'S JUST ONE I GOT AT THE JUNKYARD, BUT I THINK IT'LL WORK.
...ALTHOUGH IT'LL BE LUCKY IF WE CAN EVEN GET THIS BEHEMOTH OFF THE *GROUND.*
WHAT ARE YOU TALKING ABOUT?! IT'S GONNA BE *AWESOME!*

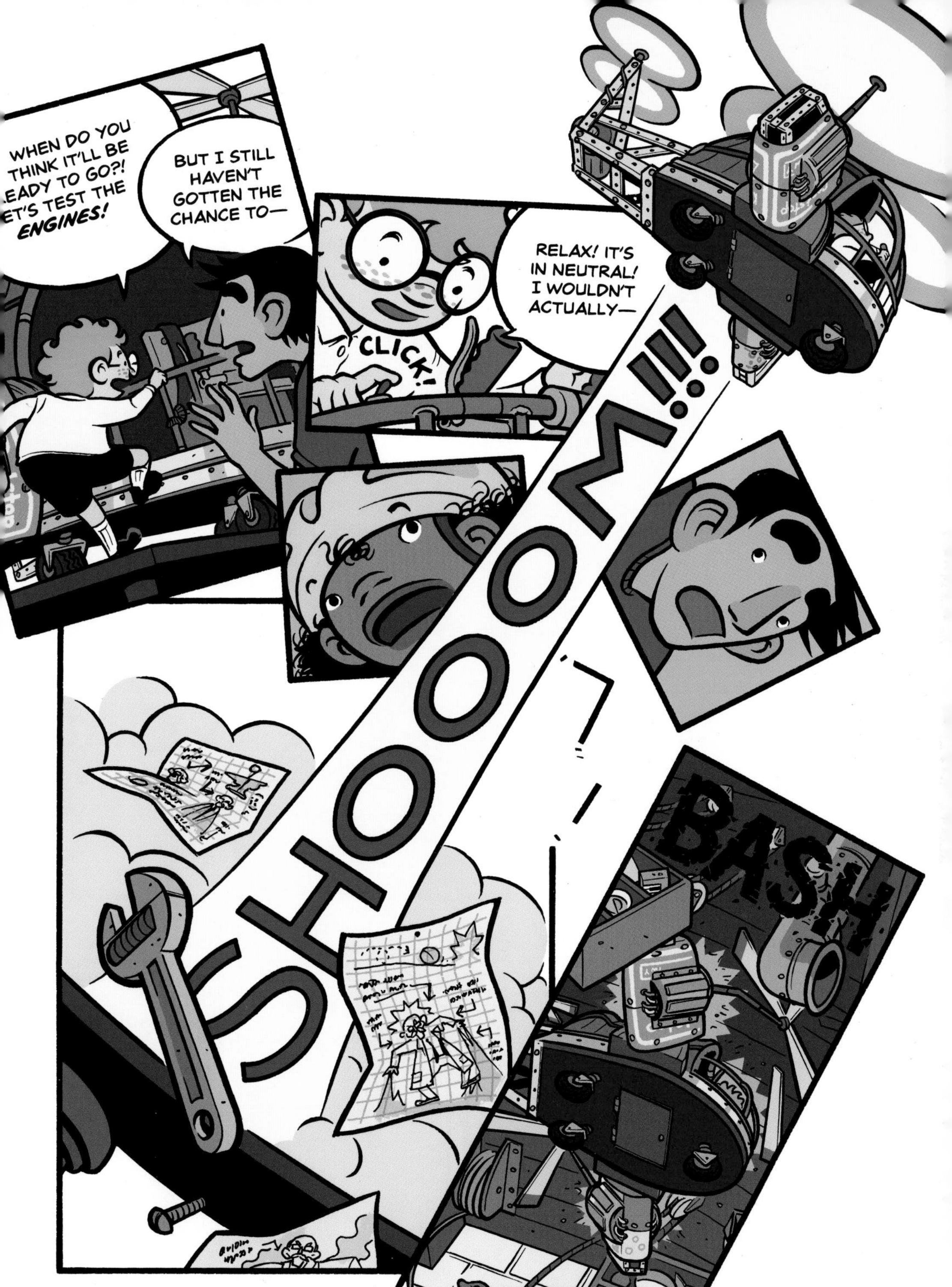

WHEN DO YOU THINK IT'LL BE READY TO GO?! LET'S TEST THE *ENGINES!*
BUT I STILL HAVEN'T GOTTEN THE CHANCE TO—
CLICK!
RELAX! IT'S IN NEUTRAL! I WOULDN'T ACTUALLY—
SHOOOOM!!!
BASH

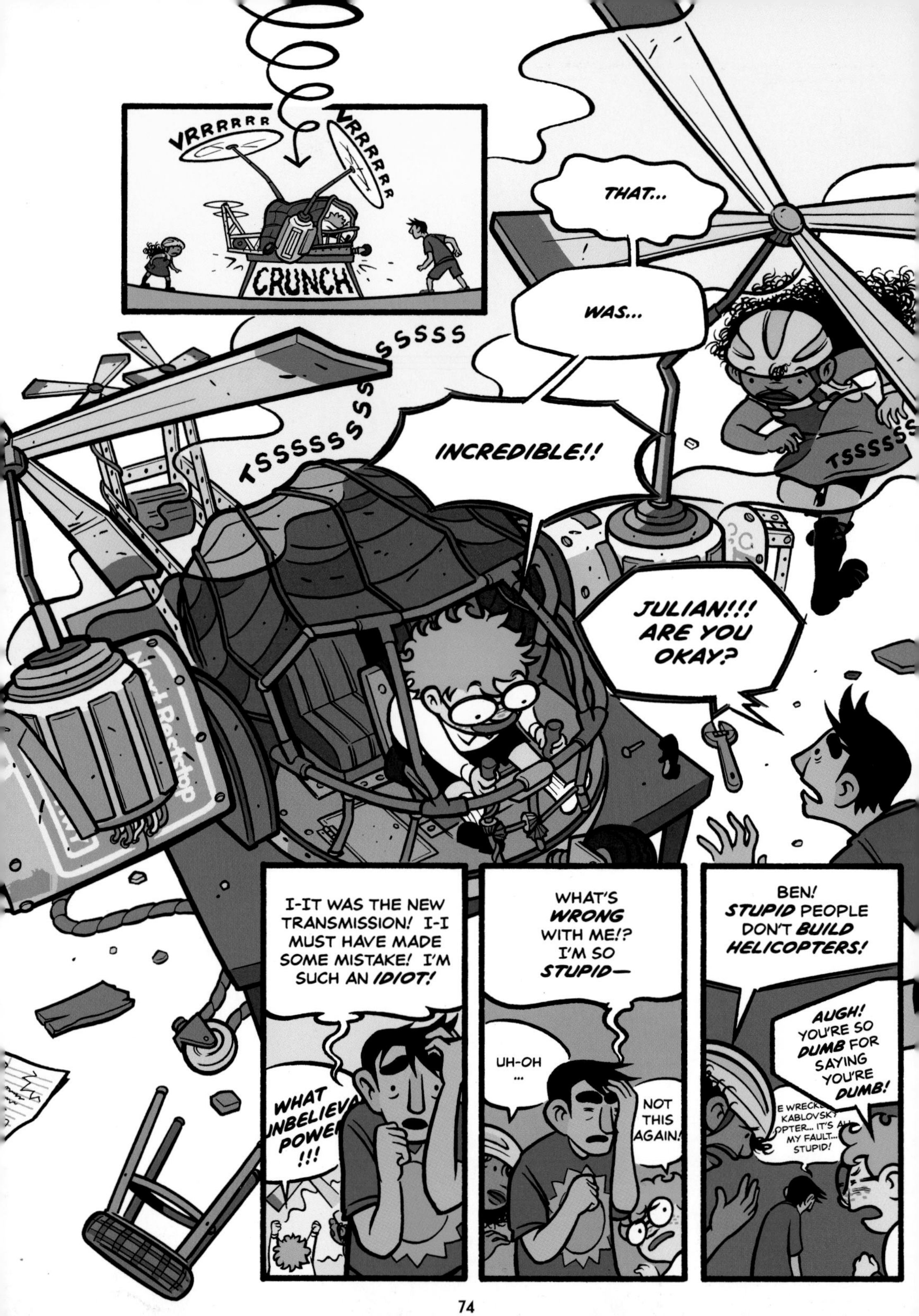
VRRRRRR
VRRRRRRR
CRUNCH
THAT...
WAS...
INCREDIBLE!!
TSSSSSSSSSSSSSSS
TSSSSSS
JULIAN!!! ARE YOU OKAY?
I-IT WAS THE NEW TRANSMISSION! I-I MUST HAVE MADE SOME MISTAKE! I'M SUCH AN *IDIOT!*
WHAT UNBELIEVA POWE !!!
WHAT'S *WRONG* WITH ME!? I'M SO *STUPID—*
UH-OH ...
NOT THIS AGAIN!
BEN! *STUPID* PEOPLE DON'T *BUILD HELICOPTERS!*
AUGH! YOU'RE SO *DUMB* FOR SAYING YOU'RE *DUMB!*
MY FAULT... STUPID!

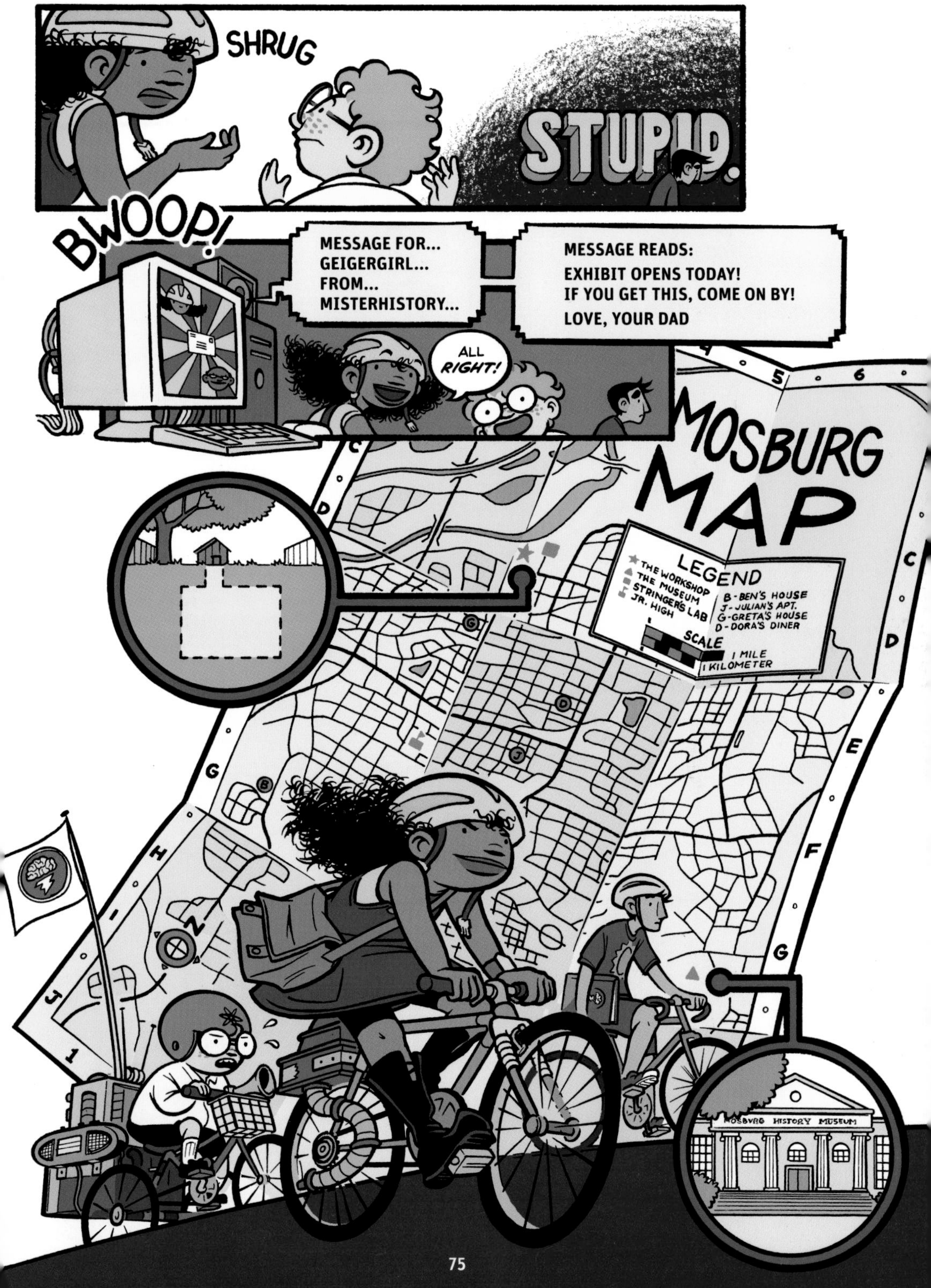
SHRUG
STUPID.
BWOOP!
MESSAGE FOR... GEIGERGIRL... FROM... MISTERHISTORY...
MESSAGE READS:
EXHIBIT OPENS TODAY!
IF YOU GET THIS, COME ON BY!
LOVE, YOUR DAD
ALL RIGHT!
MOSBURG MAP
LEGEND
THE WORKSHOP
THE MUSEUM
STRINGER'S LAB
JR. HIGH
B-BEN'S HOUSE
J-JULIAN'S APT.
G-GRETA'S HOUSE
D-DORA'S DINER
SCALE
1 MILE
1 KILOMETER
MOSBURG HISTORY MUSEUM

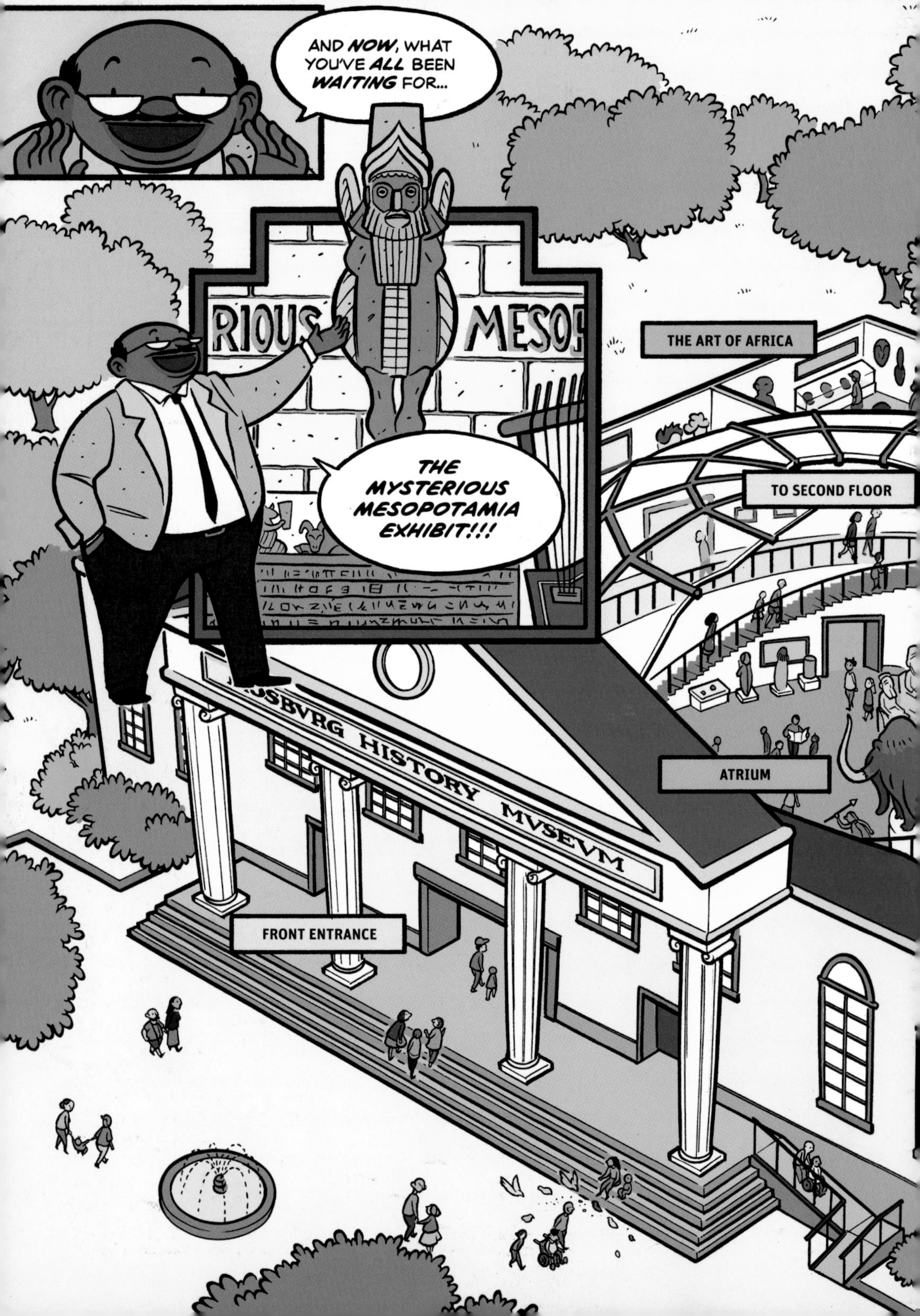
AND NOW, WHAT YOU'VE ALL BEEN WAITING FOR...
RIOUS MESOP
THE MYSTERIOUS MESOPOTAMIA EXHIBIT!!!
THE ART OF AFRICA
TO SECOND FLOOR
ATRIUM
SBVRG HISTORY MVSEVM
FRONT ENTRANCE

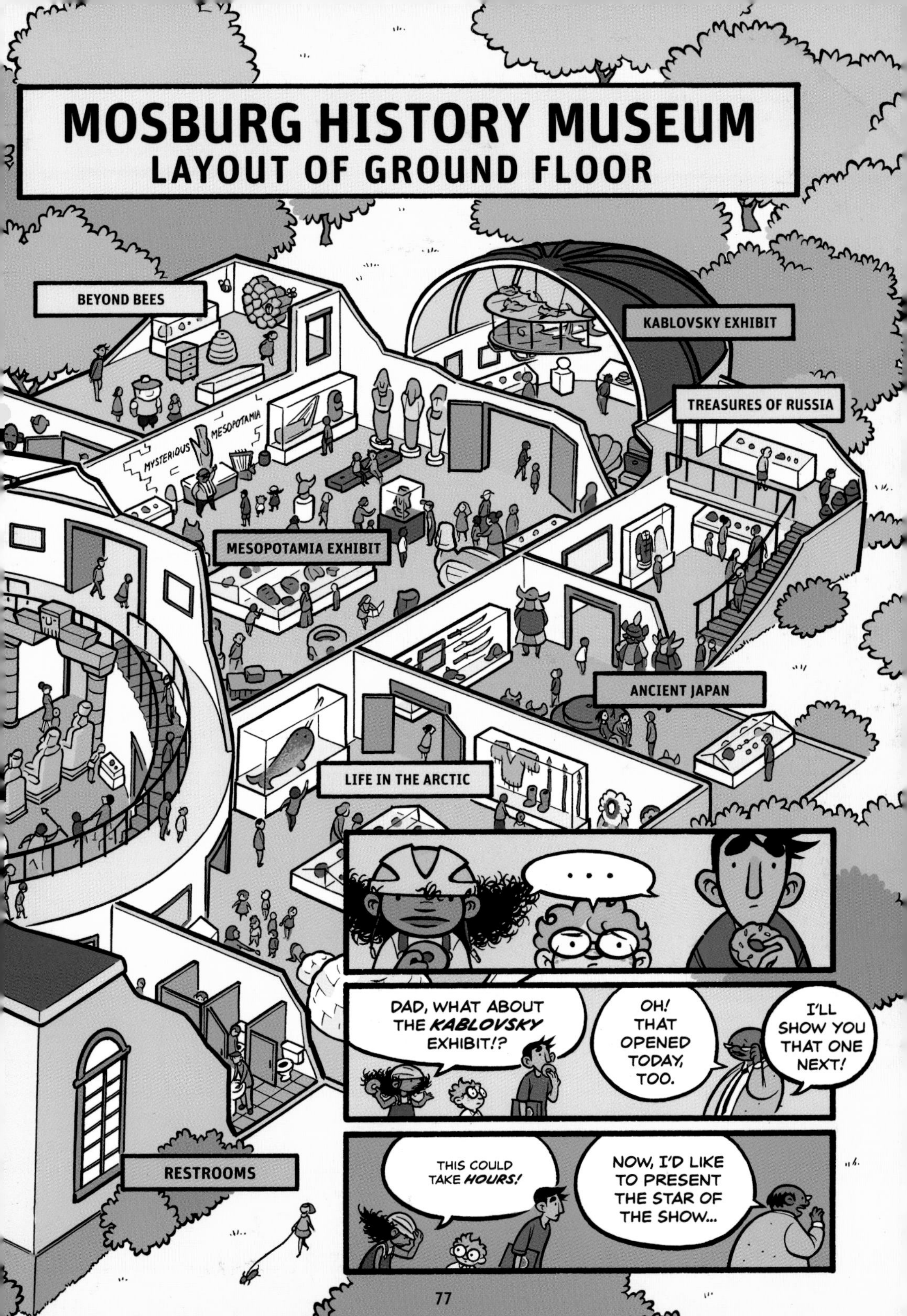
MOSBURG HISTORY MUSEUM
LAYOUT OF GROUND FLOOR
BEYOND BEES
KABLOVSKY EXHIBIT
TREASURES OF RUSSIA
MYSTERIOUS MESOPOTAMIA
MESOPOTAMIA EXHIBIT
ANCIENT JAPAN
LIFE IN THE ARCTIC
RESTROOMS
. . .
DAD, WHAT ABOUT THE *KABLOVSKY* EXHIBIT!?
OH! THAT OPENED TODAY, TOO.
I'LL SHOW YOU THAT ONE NEXT!
THIS COULD TAKE *HOURS!*
NOW, I'D LIKE TO PRESENT THE STAR OF THE SHOW...

...*THE GOLDEN BUST OF ASHURBANIPAL*, ON LOAN FROM THE SMITHSONIAN!!!

MADE OF HAMMERED GOLD AND INSET WITH SHELL AND LAPIS LAZULI, THIS BUST IS THE MOST *PRICELESS* THING IN THE WHOLE MUSEUM!

SNIFF!

PRESENTING MOSBURG WITH SUCH AN ASTONISHING PIECE OF ANCIENT ART HAS BEEN ONE OF THE PROUDEST ACHIEVEMENTS OF MY CAREER.

ISN'T THE MUSEUM KIND OF *LOW SECURITY* FOR SOMETHING SO VALUABLE??

OF COURSE *YOU'D* ASK ABOUT THAT, GRETA! DON'T WORRY—WE HAD A SPECIAL LASER ALARM INSTALLED TO PROTECT THIS ENTIRE ROOM.

I DON'T THINK THAT AN ADEQUATE AMOUNT SECURITY DAD!

NOW, THIS SHELL HERE IS NOT NATIVE TO THE PERSIAN GULF. HOW DID IT MAKE ITS WAY TO NINEVEH, YOU ASK? WELL, COMPLEX TRADE ROUTES WERE ESTABLISHED BETWEEN

1 HOUR 45 MINUTES LATER

DID WE GO OVER THE SMELTING METHODS THEY USED? THERE IS SOME CONTROVERSY AS TO EXACTLY HOW THEY WOULD HAVE

YES. YES. YES.

HOW ABOUT THE ENGRAVING RECENTLY THE WAS A FASCINA DISCUSSION AB WHETHER THE OULD HAVE U HE METHODS

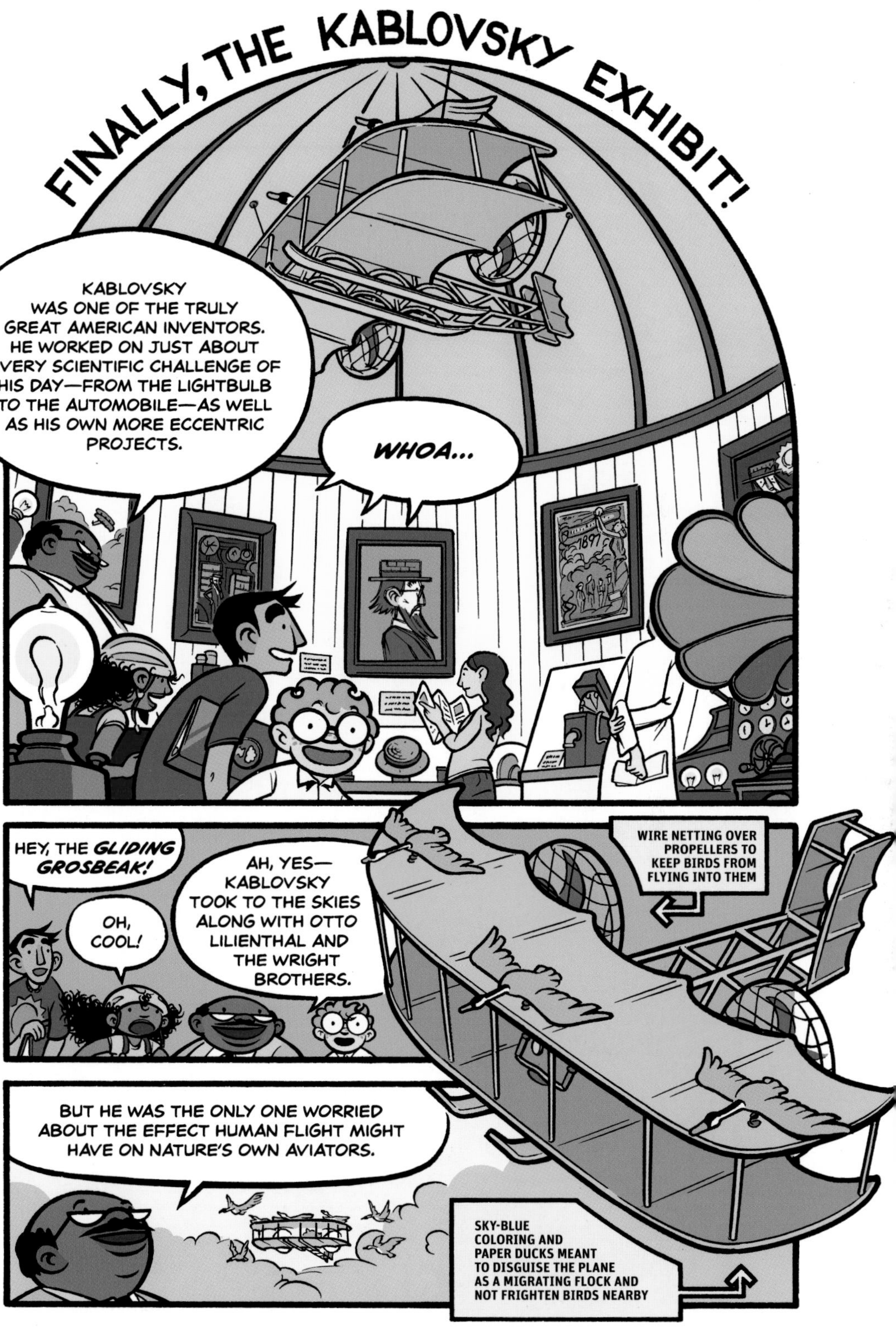
FINALLY, THE KABLOVSKY EXHIBIT!
KABLOVSKY WAS ONE OF THE TRULY GREAT AMERICAN INVENTORS. HE WORKED ON JUST ABOUT EVERY SCIENTIFIC CHALLENGE OF HIS DAY—FROM THE LIGHTBULB TO THE AUTOMOBILE—AS WELL AS HIS OWN MORE ECCENTRIC PROJECTS.
WHOA...
1897
HEY, THE GLIDING GROSBEAK!
OH, COOL!
AH, YES—KABLOVSKY TOOK TO THE SKIES ALONG WITH OTTO LILIENTHAL AND THE WRIGHT BROTHERS.
WIRE NETTING OVER PROPELLERS TO KEEP BIRDS FROM FLYING INTO THEM
BUT HE WAS THE ONLY ONE WORRIED ABOUT THE EFFECT HUMAN FLIGHT MIGHT HAVE ON NATURE'S OWN AVIATORS.
SKY-BLUE COLORING AND PAPER DUCKS MEANT TO DISGUISE THE PLANE AS A MIGRATING FLOCK AND NOT FRIGHTEN BIRDS NEARBY

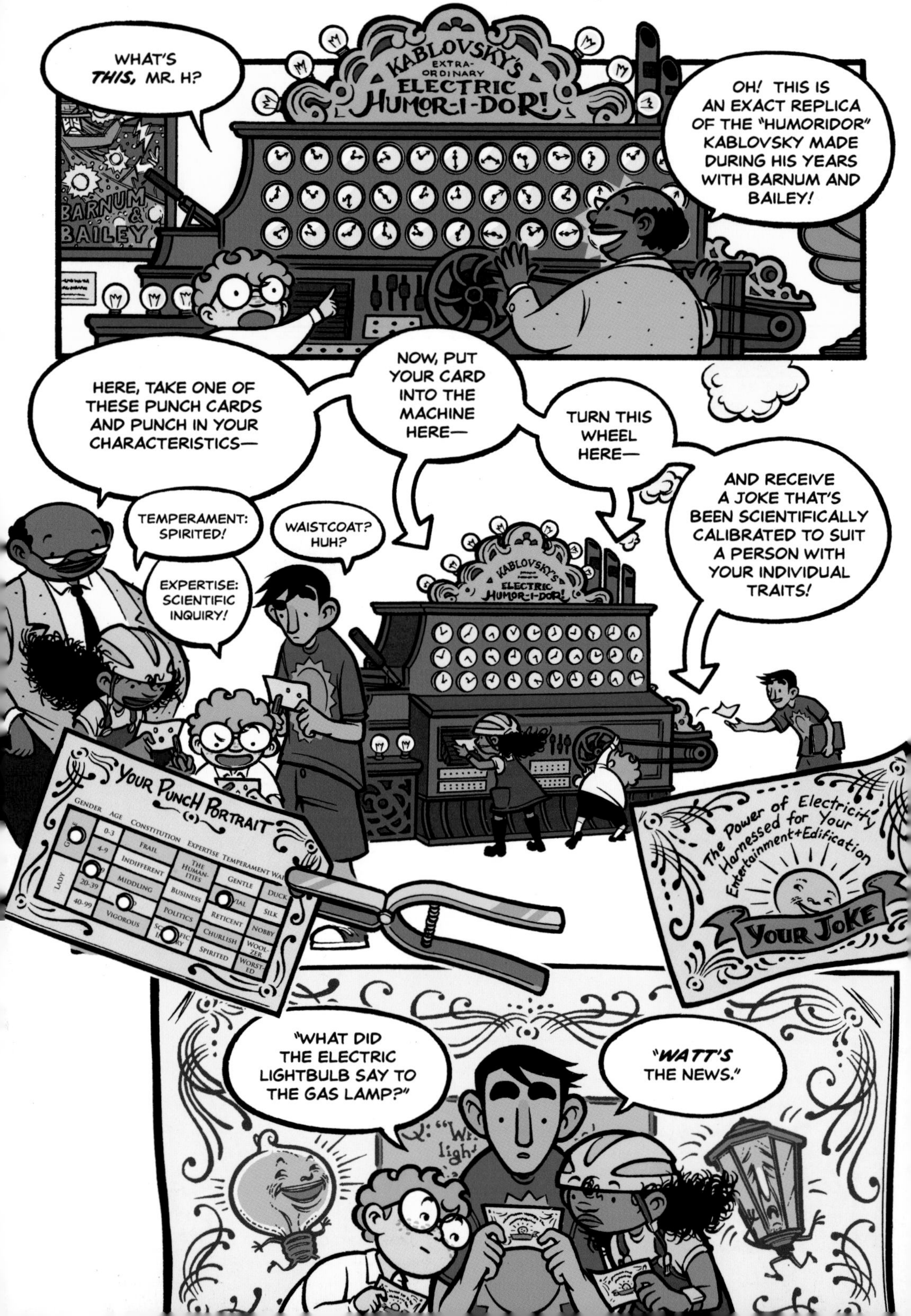
KABLOVSKY'S EXTRA-ORDINARY ELECTRIC HUMOR-I-DOR!
WHAT'S *THIS,* MR. H?
BARNUM & BAILEY
OH! THIS IS AN EXACT REPLICA OF THE "HUMORIDOR" KABLOVSKY MADE DURING HIS YEARS WITH BARNUM AND BAILEY!
HERE, TAKE ONE OF THESE PUNCH CARDS AND PUNCH IN YOUR CHARACTERISTICS—
NOW, PUT YOUR CARD INTO THE MACHINE HERE—
TURN THIS WHEEL HERE—
AND RECEIVE A JOKE THAT'S BEEN SCIENTIFICALLY CALIBRATED TO SUIT A PERSON WITH YOUR INDIVIDUAL TRAITS!
TEMPERAMENT: SPIRITED!
EXPERTISE: SCIENTIFIC INQUIRY!
WAISTCOAT? HUH?
KABLOVSKY'S ELECTRIC HUMOR-I-DOR!
YOUR PUNCH PORTRAIT
GENDER AGE CONSTITUTION EXPERTISE TEMPERAMENT
0-3
4-9 FRAIL
LADY INDIFFERENT THE HUMANITIES GENTLE DUCK
20-39 MIDDLING BUSINESS SILK
40-99 POLITICS RETICENT NOBBY
VIGOROUS CHURLISH WOOLZER
SPIRITED WORSTED
The Power of Electricity Harnessed for Your Entertainment+Edification
YOUR JOKE
"WHAT DID THE ELECTRIC LIGHTBULB SAY TO THE GAS LAMP?"
"*WATT'S* THE NEWS."

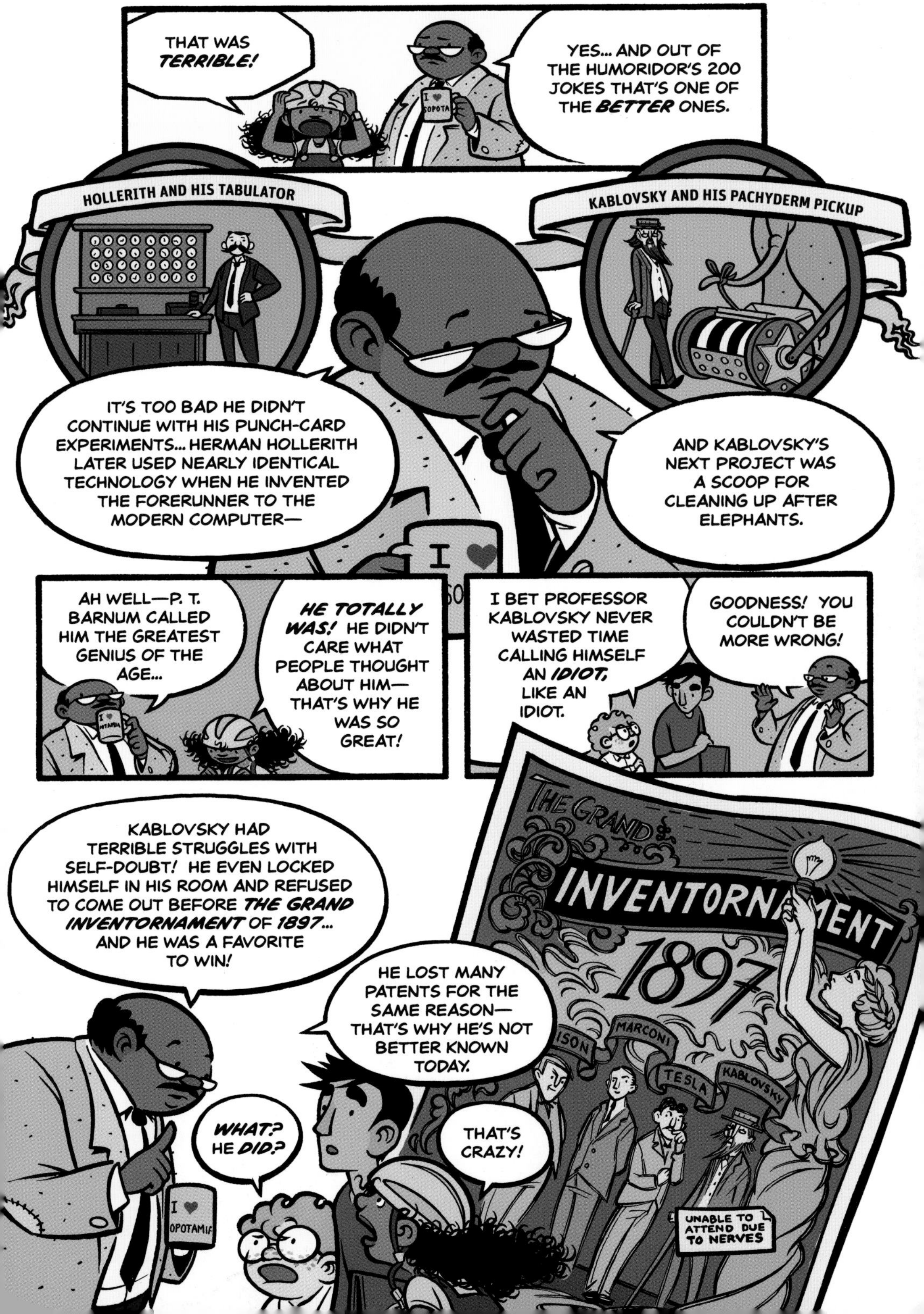
THAT WAS *TERRIBLE!*
YES... AND OUT OF THE HUMORIDOR'S 200 JOKES THAT'S ONE OF THE *BETTER* ONES.
I ♥ SOPOTA
HOLLERITH AND HIS TABULATOR
KABLOVSKY AND HIS PACHYDERM PICKUP
IT'S TOO BAD HE DIDN'T CONTINUE WITH HIS PUNCH-CARD EXPERIMENTS... HERMAN HOLLERITH LATER USED NEARLY IDENTICAL TECHNOLOGY WHEN HE INVENTED THE FORERUNNER TO THE MODERN COMPUTER—
AND KABLOVSKY'S NEXT PROJECT WAS A SCOOP FOR CLEANING UP AFTER ELEPHANTS.
AH WELL—P. T. BARNUM CALLED HIM THE GREATEST GENIUS OF THE AGE...
HE TOTALLY WAS! HE DIDN'T CARE WHAT PEOPLE THOUGHT ABOUT HIM—THAT'S WHY HE WAS SO GREAT!
I BET PROFESSOR KABLOVSKY NEVER WASTED TIME CALLING HIMSELF AN *IDIOT,* LIKE AN IDIOT.
GOODNESS! YOU COULDN'T BE MORE WRONG!
KABLOVSKY HAD TERRIBLE STRUGGLES WITH SELF-DOUBT! HE EVEN LOCKED HIMSELF IN HIS ROOM AND REFUSED TO COME OUT BEFORE *THE GRAND INVENTORNAMENT* OF 1897... AND HE WAS A FAVORITE TO WIN!
THE GRAND INVENTORNAMENT 1897
MARCONI
TESLA
KABLOVSKY
UNABLE TO ATTEND DUE TO NERVES
HE LOST MANY PATENTS FOR THE SAME REASON—THAT'S WHY HE'S NOT BETTER KNOWN TODAY.
WHAT? HE DID?
THAT'S CRAZY!

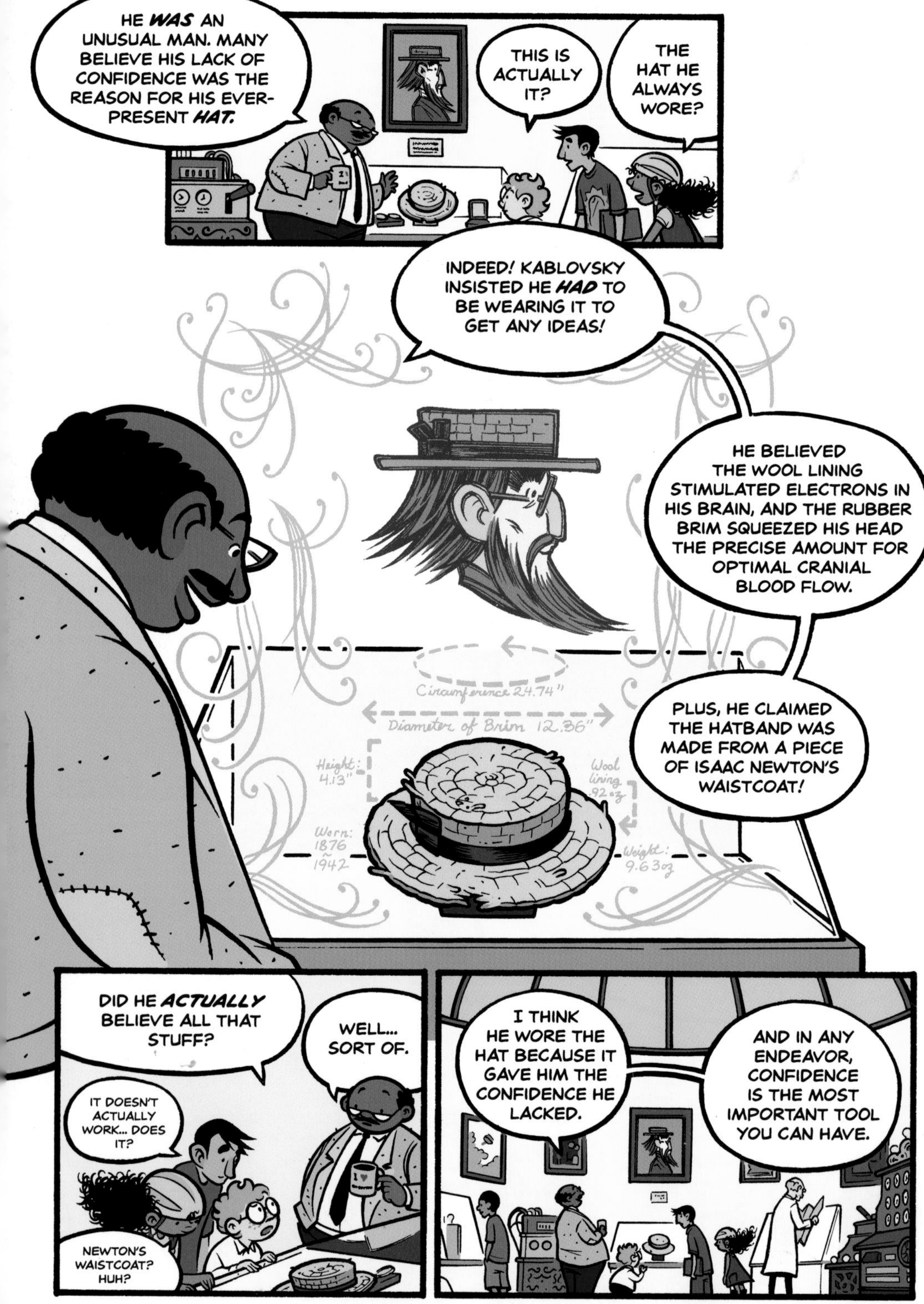
HE *WAS* AN UNUSUAL MAN. MANY BELIEVE HIS LACK OF CONFIDENCE WAS THE REASON FOR HIS EVER-PRESENT *HAT.*
THIS IS ACTUALLY IT?
THE HAT HE ALWAYS WORE?
INDEED! KABLOVSKY INSISTED HE *HAD* TO BE WEARING IT TO GET ANY IDEAS!
HE BELIEVED THE WOOL LINING STIMULATED ELECTRONS IN HIS BRAIN, AND THE RUBBER BRIM SQUEEZED HIS HEAD THE PRECISE AMOUNT FOR OPTIMAL CRANIAL BLOOD FLOW.
PLUS, HE CLAIMED THE HATBAND WAS MADE FROM A PIECE OF ISAAC NEWTON'S WAISTCOAT!
Circumference 24.74"
Diameter of Brim 12.36"
Height: 4.13"
Wool lining .92 oz
Worn: 1876 ~ 1942
Weight: 9.63 oz
DID HE *ACTUALLY* BELIEVE ALL THAT STUFF?
WELL... SORT OF.
IT DOESN'T ACTUALLY WORK... DOES IT?
NEWTON'S WAISTCOAT? HUH?
I THINK HE WORE THE HAT BECAUSE IT GAVE HIM THE CONFIDENCE HE LACKED.
AND IN ANY ENDEAVOR, CONFIDENCE IS THE MOST IMPORTANT TOOL YOU CAN HAVE.

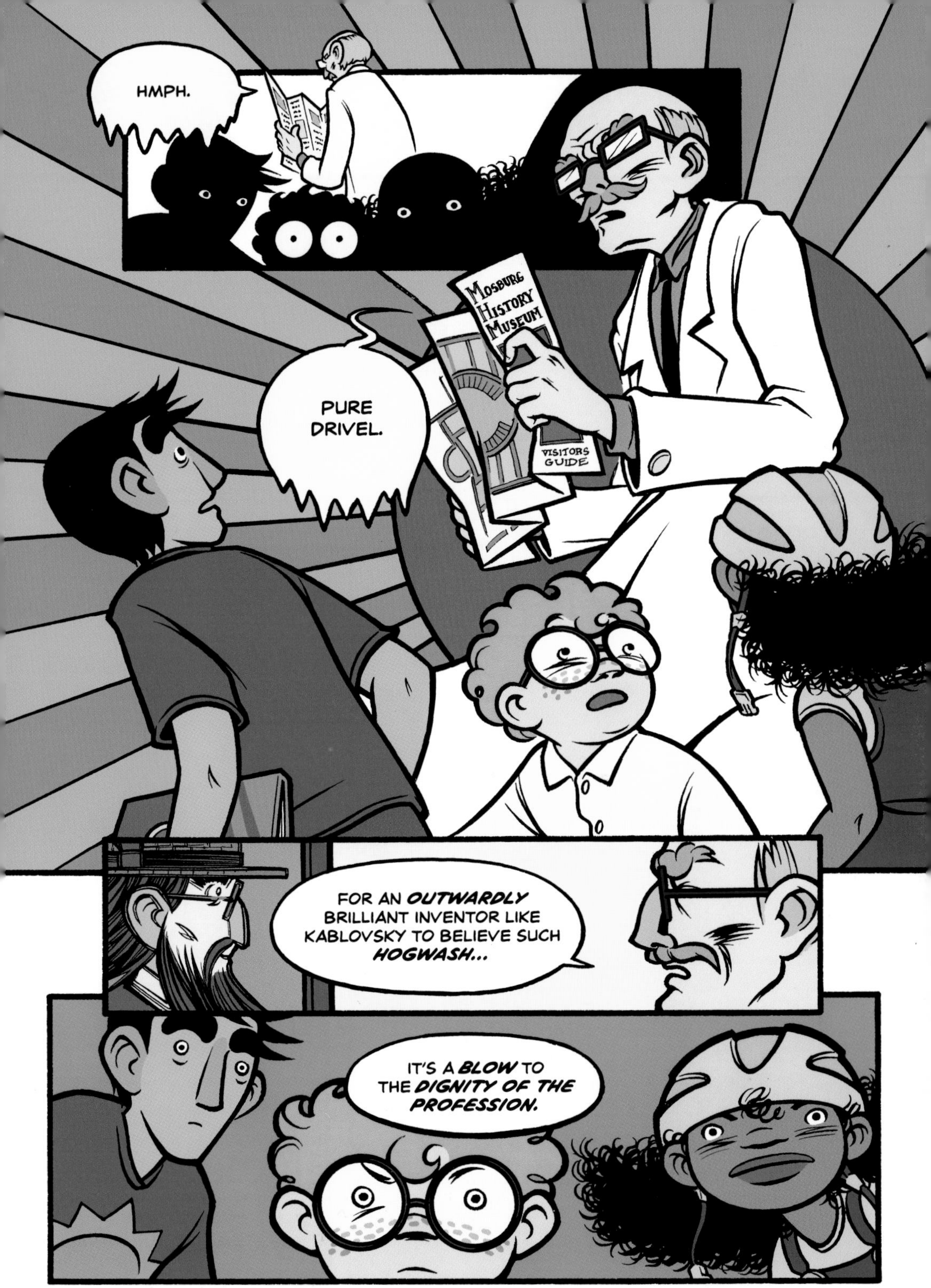
HMPH.
PURE DRIVEL.
MOSBURG HISTORY MUSEUM
VISITORS GUIDE
FOR AN *OUTWARDLY* BRILLIANT INVENTOR LIKE KABLOVSKY TO BELIEVE SUCH *HOGWASH...*
IT'S A *BLOW* TO THE *DIGNITY OF THE PROFESSION.*

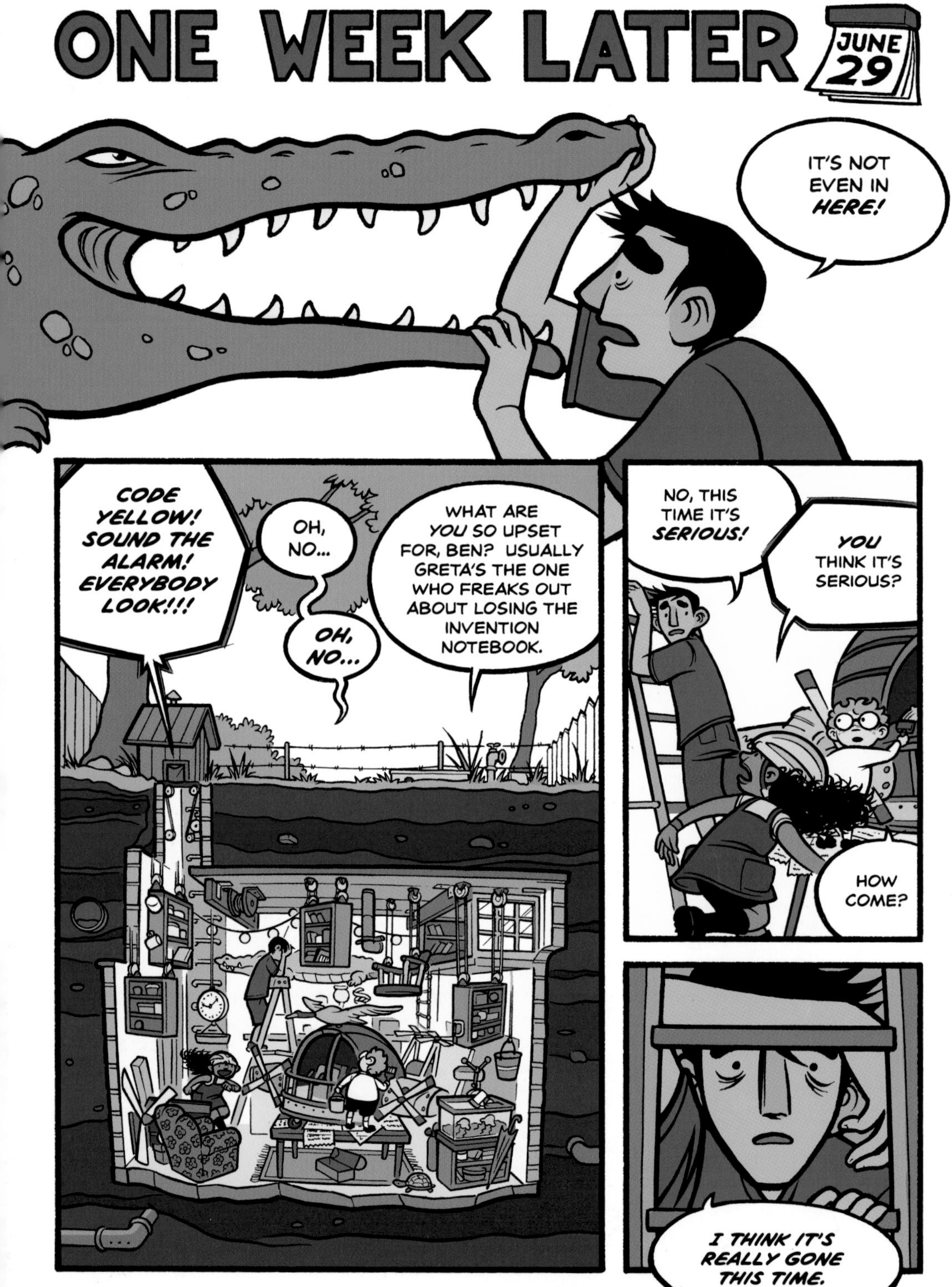

ONE WEEK LATER
JUNE 29
IT'S NOT EVEN IN *HERE!*
CODE YELLOW! SOUND THE ALARM! EVERYBODY LOOK!!!
OH, NO...
OH, NO...
WHAT ARE *YOU* SO UPSET FOR, BEN? USUALLY GRETA'S THE ONE WHO FREAKS OUT ABOUT LOSING THE INVENTION NOTEBOOK.
NO, THIS TIME IT'S *SERIOUS!*
YOU THINK IT'S SERIOUS?
HOW COME?
I THINK IT'S REALLY GONE THIS TIME.

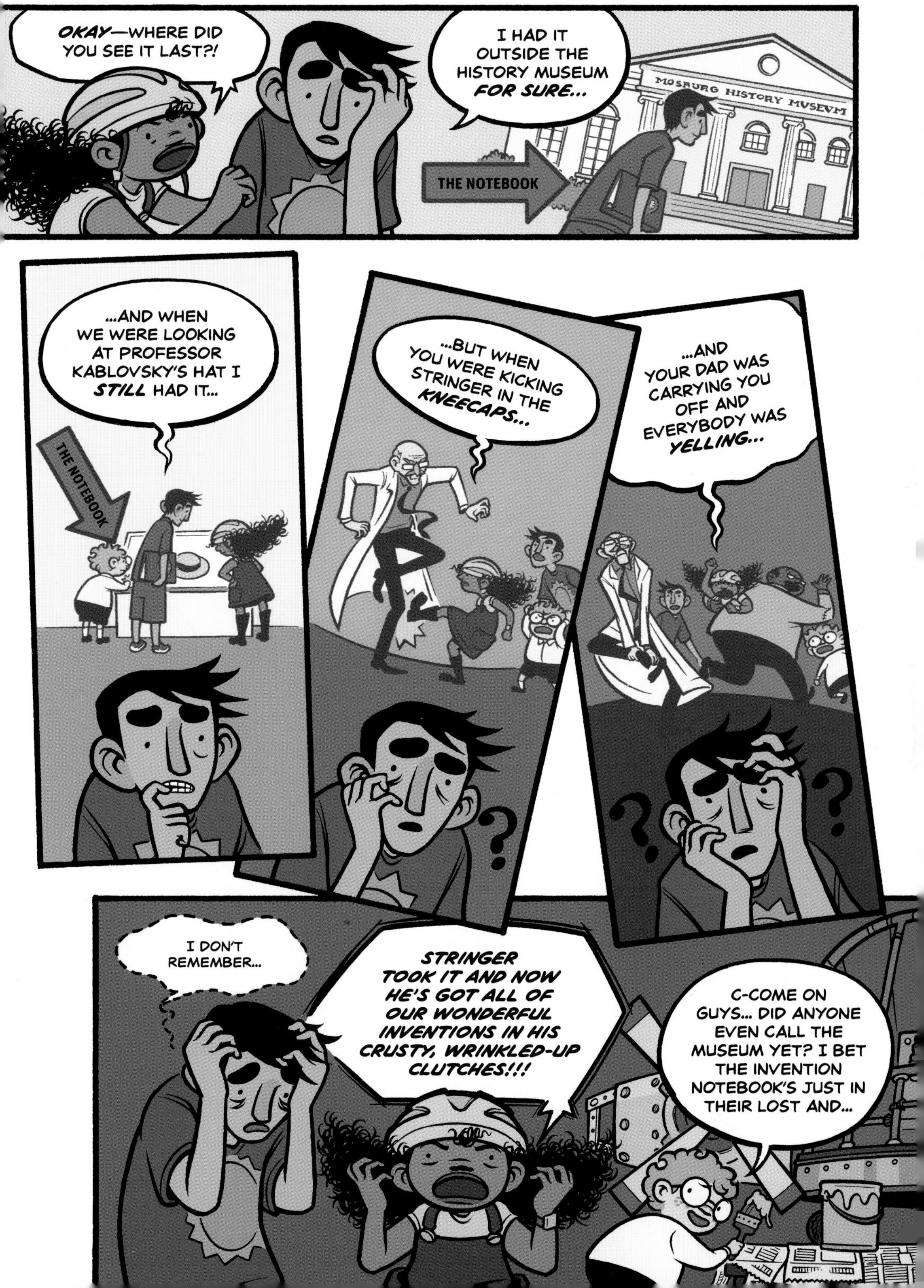

OKAY—WHERE DID YOU SEE IT LAST?!
I HAD IT OUTSIDE THE HISTORY MUSEUM FOR SURE...
MOSBURG HISTORY MUSEVM
THE NOTEBOOK
...AND WHEN WE WERE LOOKING AT PROFESSOR KABLOVSKY'S HAT I STILL HAD IT...
THE NOTEBOOK
...BUT WHEN YOU WERE KICKING STRINGER IN THE KNEECAPS...
...AND YOUR DAD WAS CARRYING YOU OFF AND EVERYBODY WAS YELLING...
I DON'T REMEMBER...
STRINGER TOOK IT AND NOW HE'S GOT ALL OF OUR WONDERFUL INVENTIONS IN HIS CRUSTY, WRINKLED-UP CLUTCHES!!!
C-COME ON GUYS... DID ANYONE EVEN CALL THE MUSEUM YET? I BET THE INVENTION NOTEBOOK'S JUST IN THEIR LOST AND...

...FOUND.

MOSBURG MORNING

STRINGER INVENTS STELLAR SMELLER!

NATION AGOG AT BRILLIANT BREAKTHROUGH!

ODORS OUTED!

Mosburg's own Genius Inventor Dr. Wilhelm Stringer has done it again! His latest invention, the Smell-O-Tron 2000, can identify anything from peanut butter to corn chips by its odor alone. This new technology will be invaluable to researchers of all kinds, as well as aiding the

MIGHTY MIND MODEST

We asked Dr. Stringer about his inventive process. "As Thomas Edison said, 'Invention is 10 percent inspiration and 90 percent perspiration.' The Smell-O-Tron took me years of intensive work. it was quite a challen

86

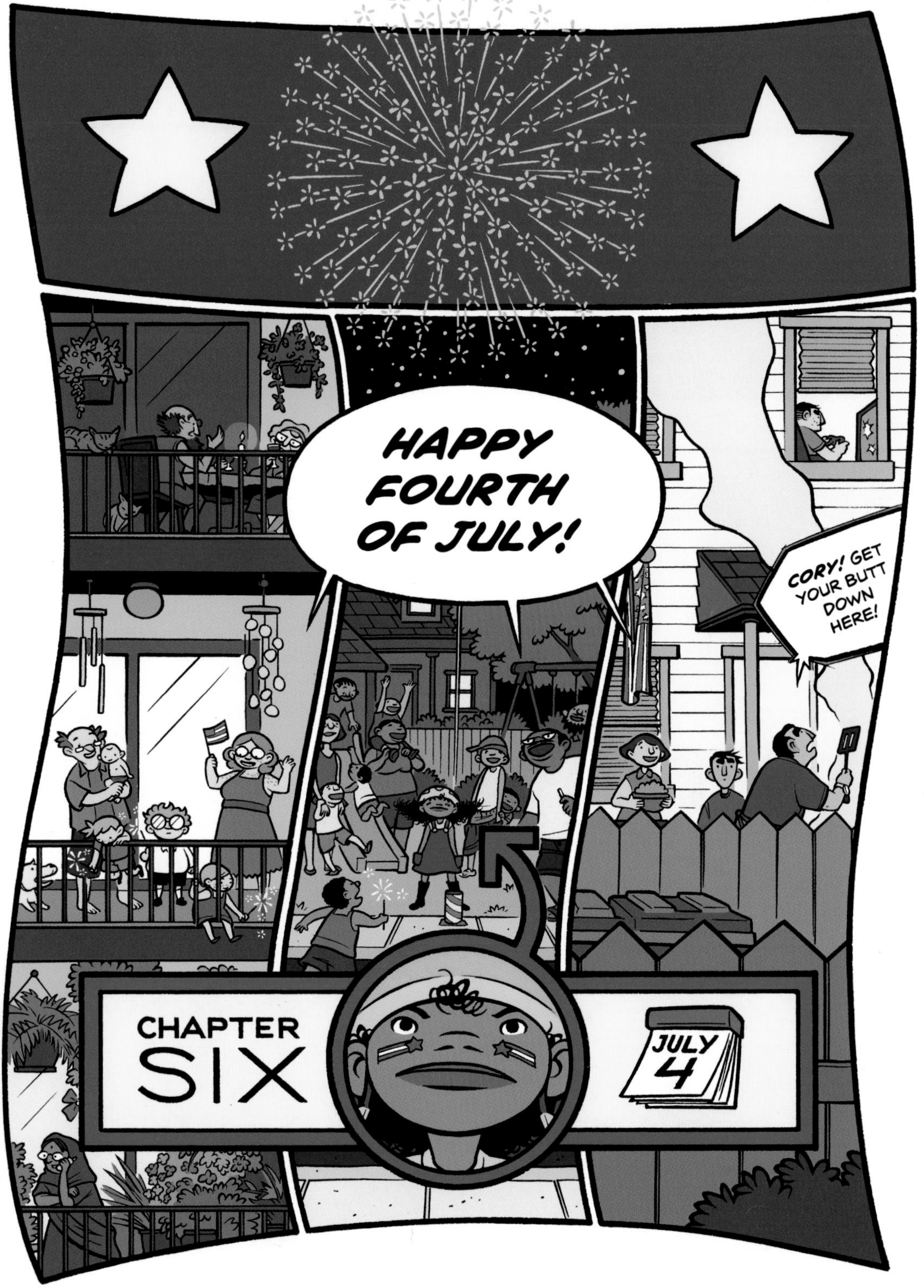
HAPPY FOURTH OF JULY!
CORY! GET YOUR BUTT DOWN HERE!
CHAPTER SIX
JULY 4

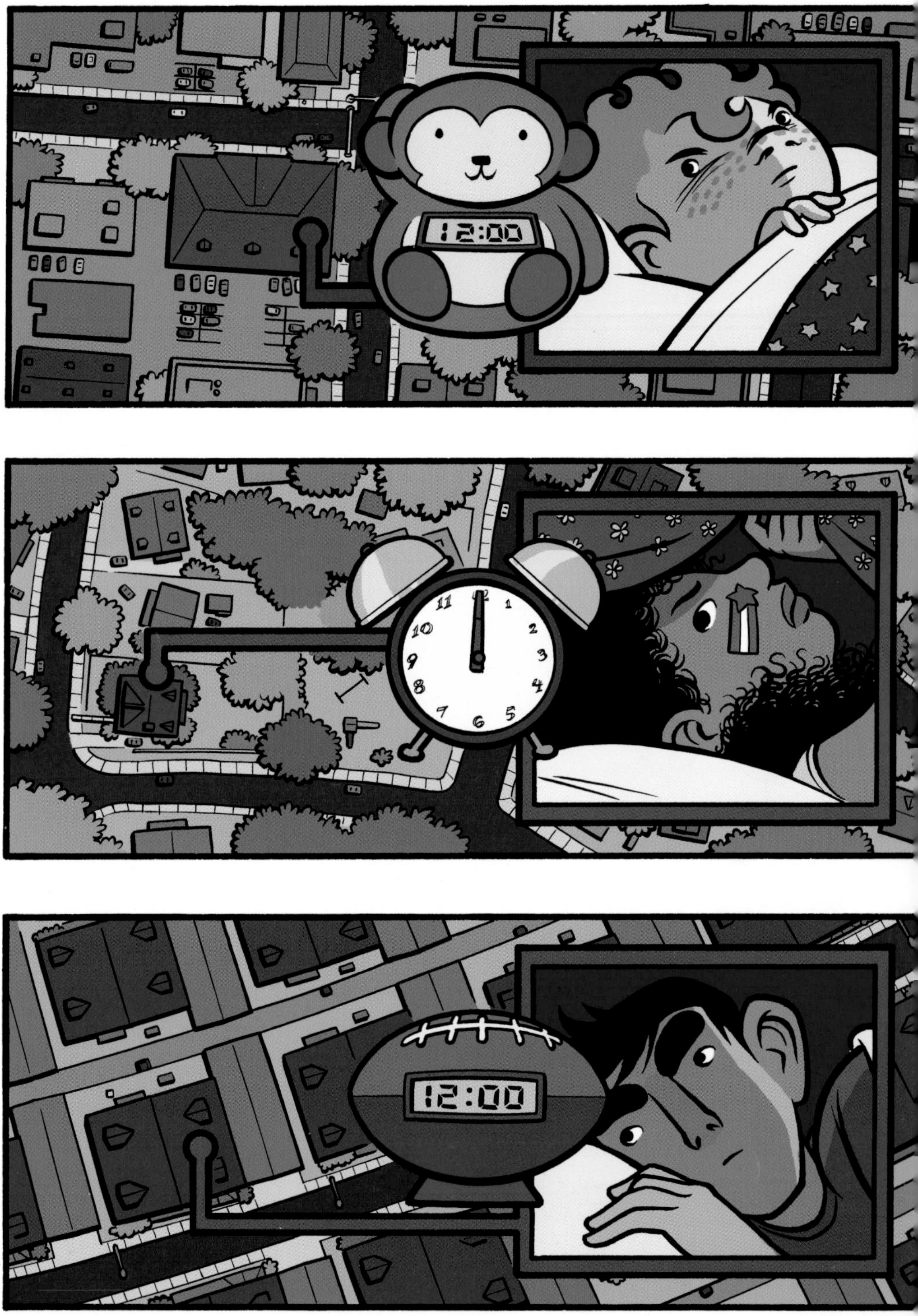
12:00
12:00

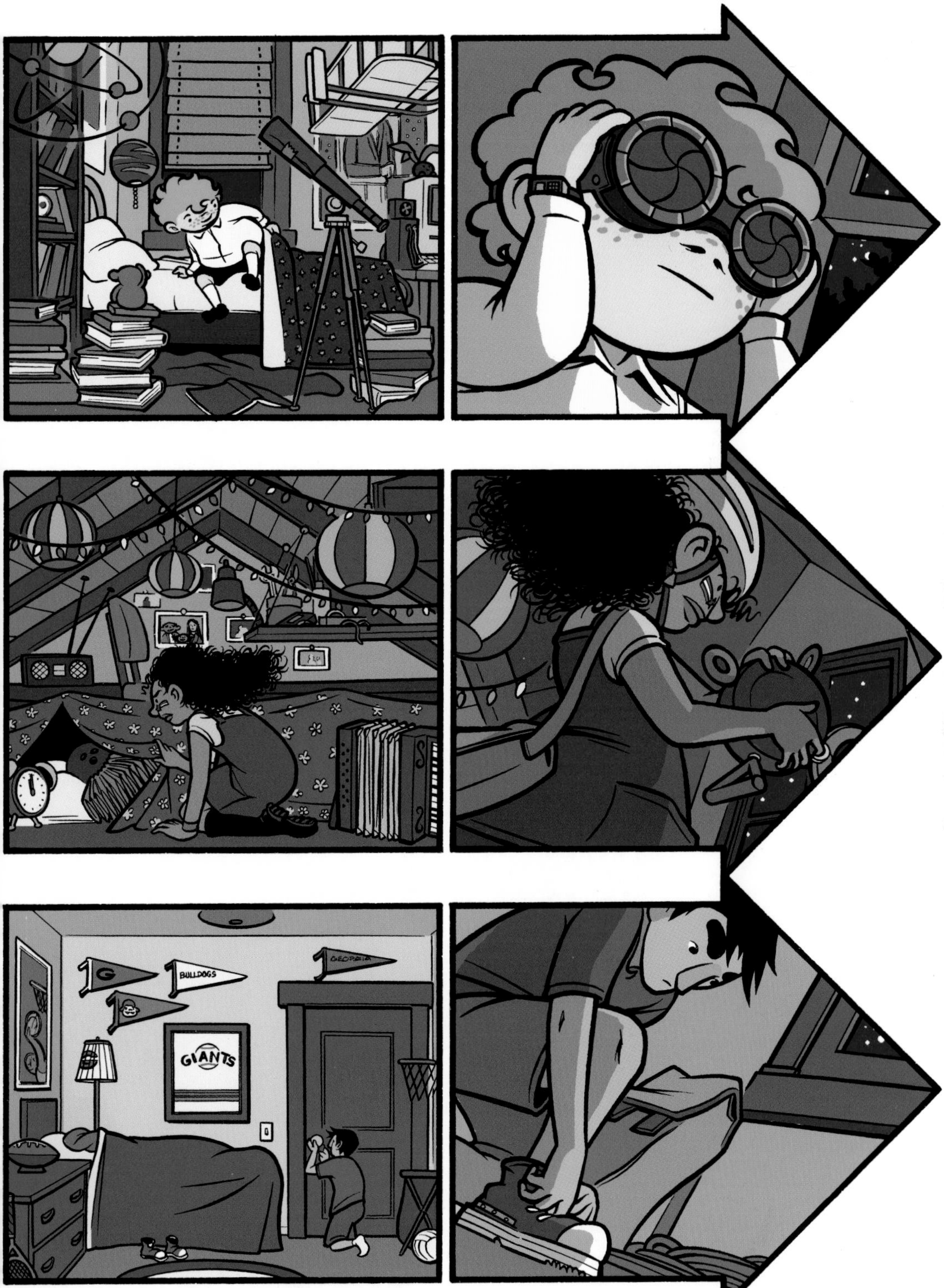
BULLDOGS
GIANTS

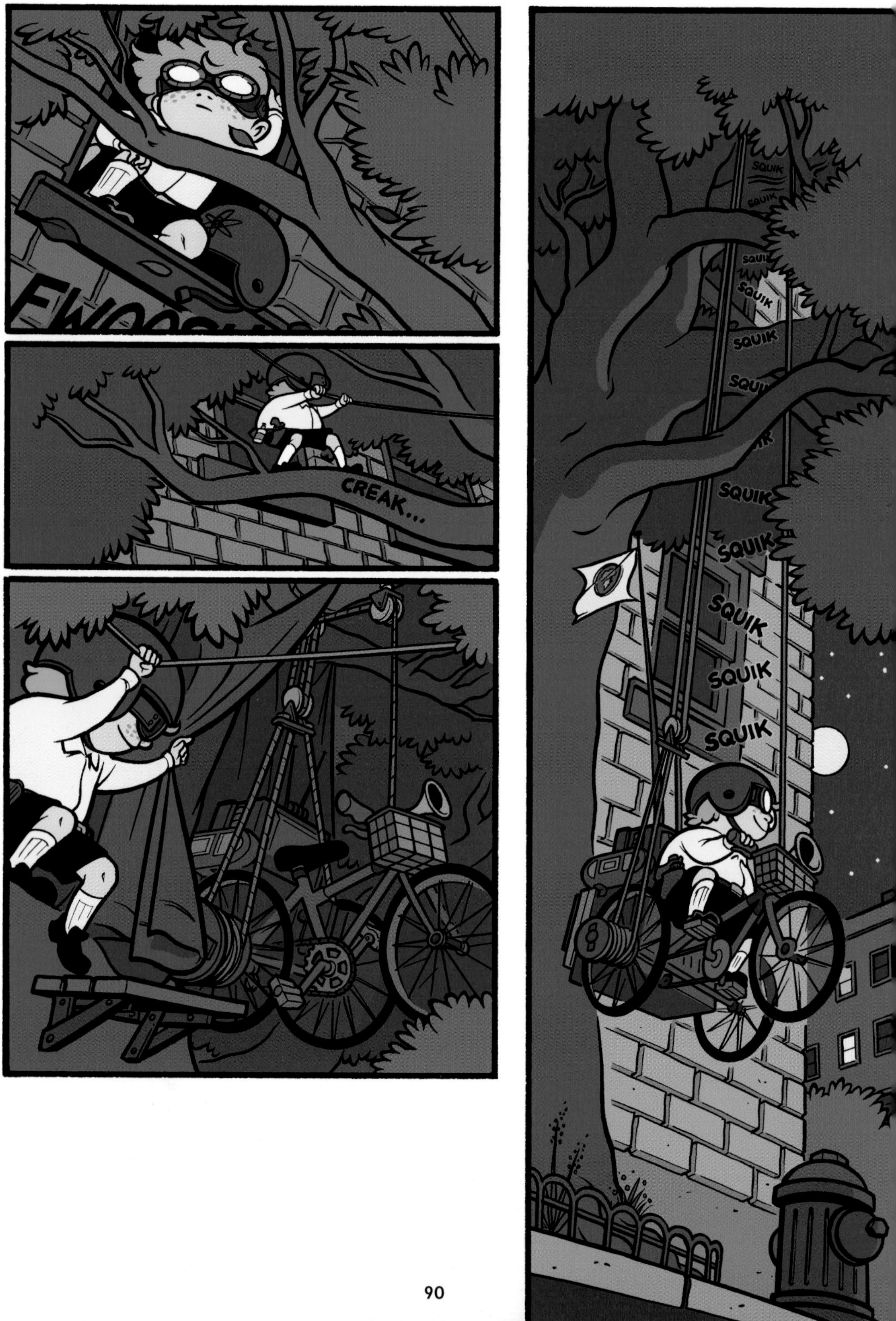
FWOOSH
CREAK...
SQUIK
SQUIK
SQUIK
SQUIK
SQUIK
SQUIK
SQUIK
SQUIK
SQUIK
SQUIK
SQUIK

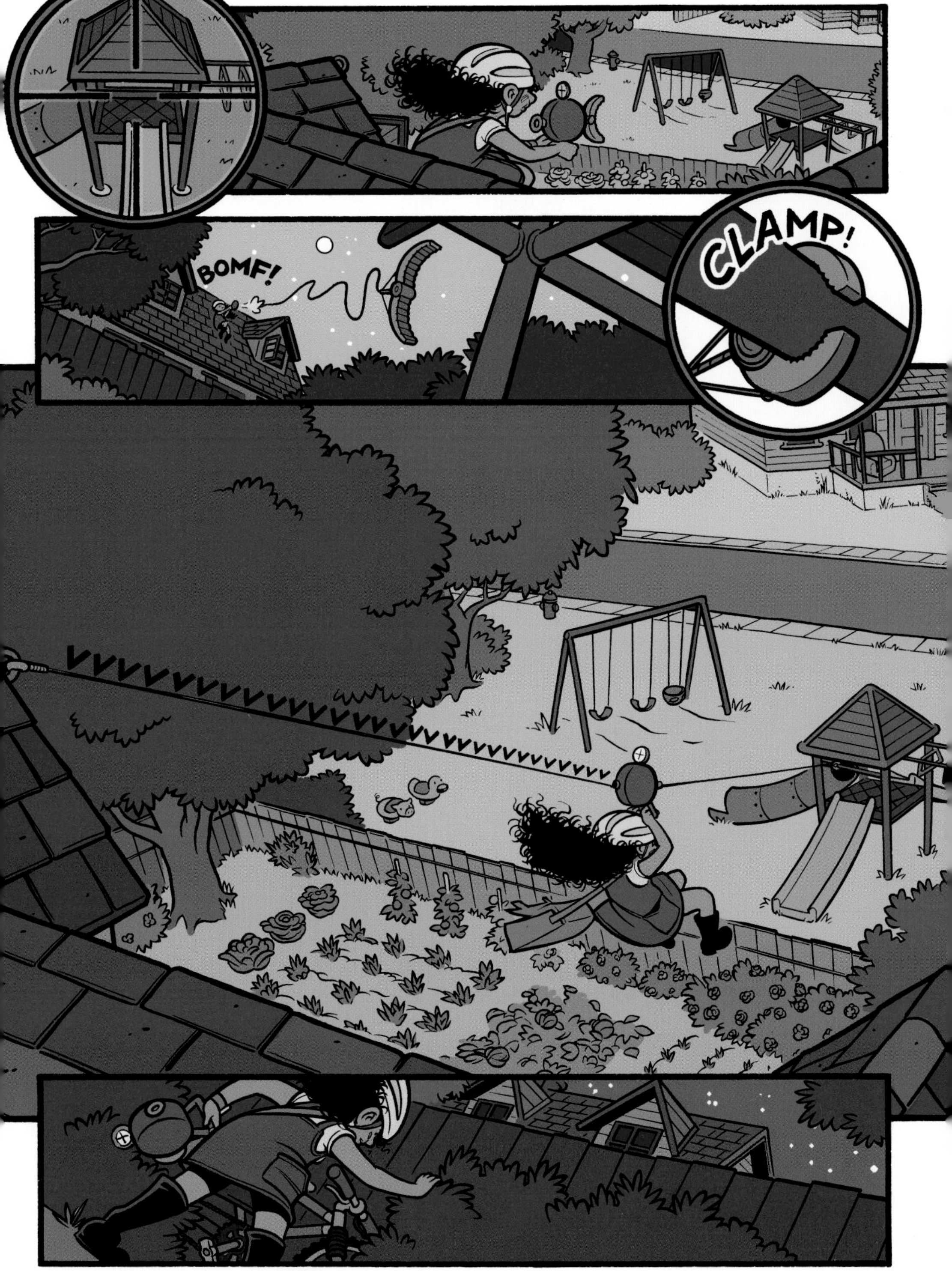
BOMF!
CLAMP!

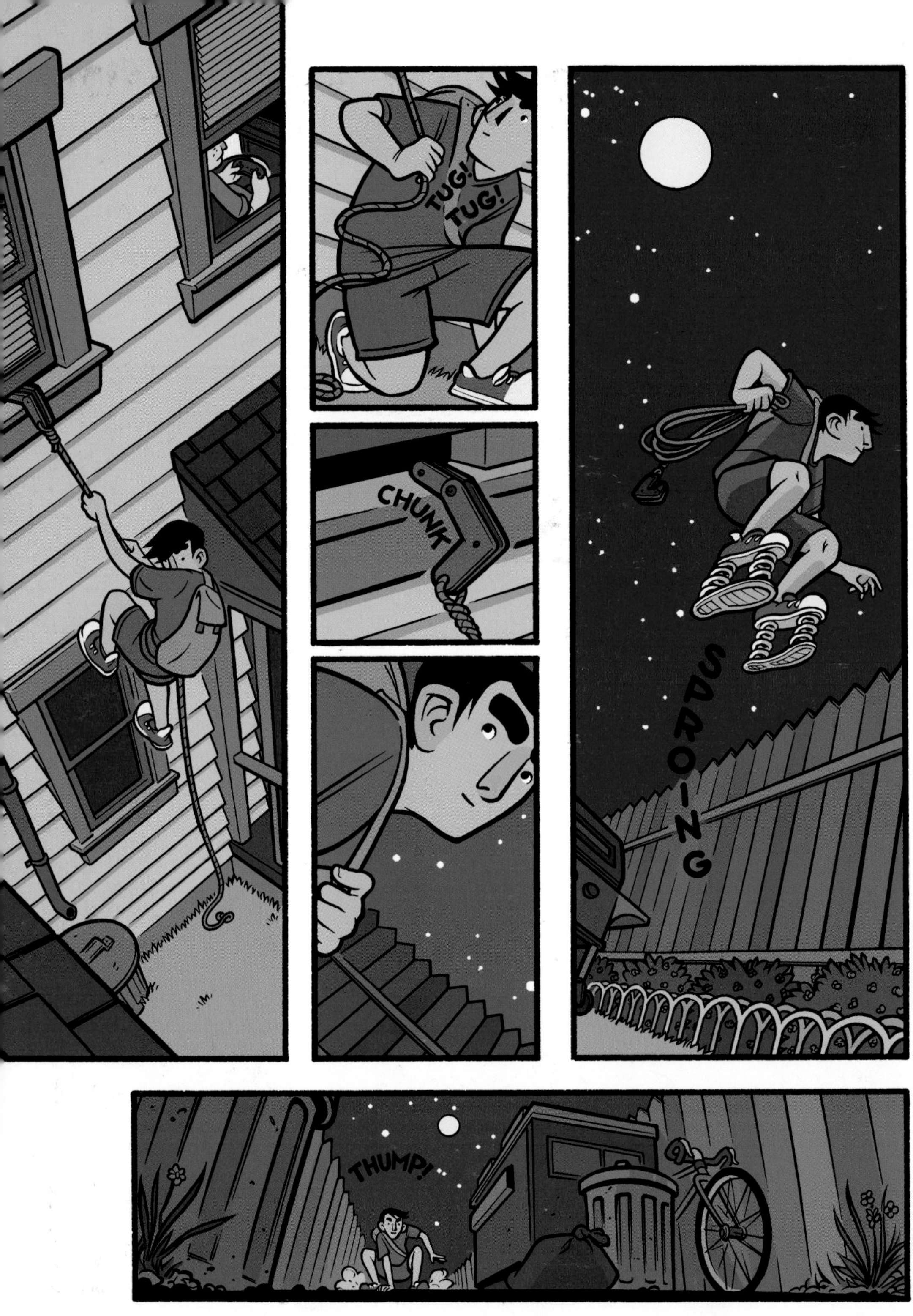
TUG!
TUG!
CHUNK
SPROING
THUMP!

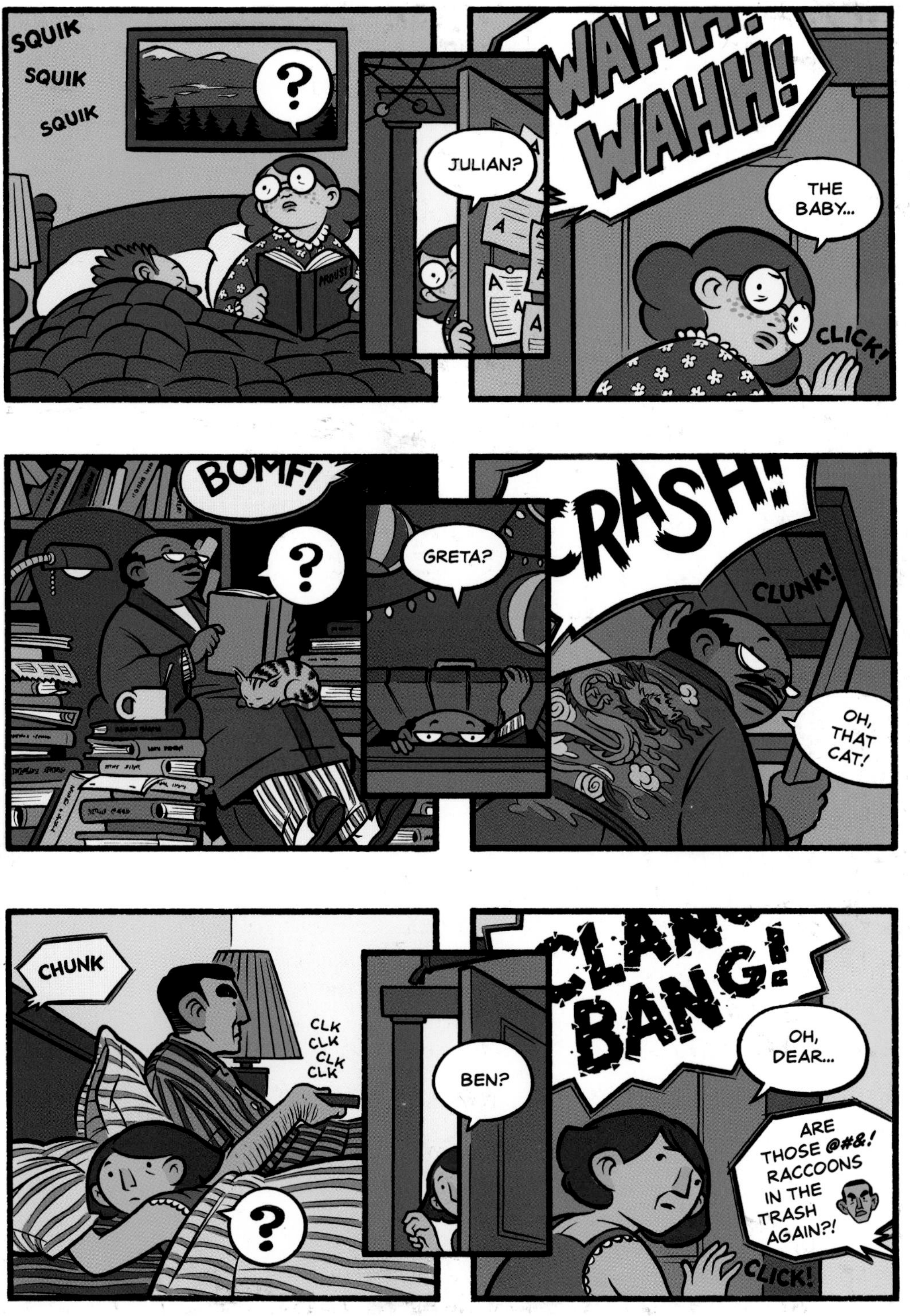
SQUIK
SQUIK
SQUIK
?
PROUST
JULIAN?
WAHH! WAHH!
THE BABY...
CLICK!
BOMF!
?
GRETA?
CRASH!
CLUNK!
OH, THAT CAT!
CHUNK
CLK CLK CLK CLK
?
BEN?
CLANG BANG!
OH, DEAR...
ARE THOSE @#&! RACCOONS IN THE TRASH AGAIN?!
CLICK!

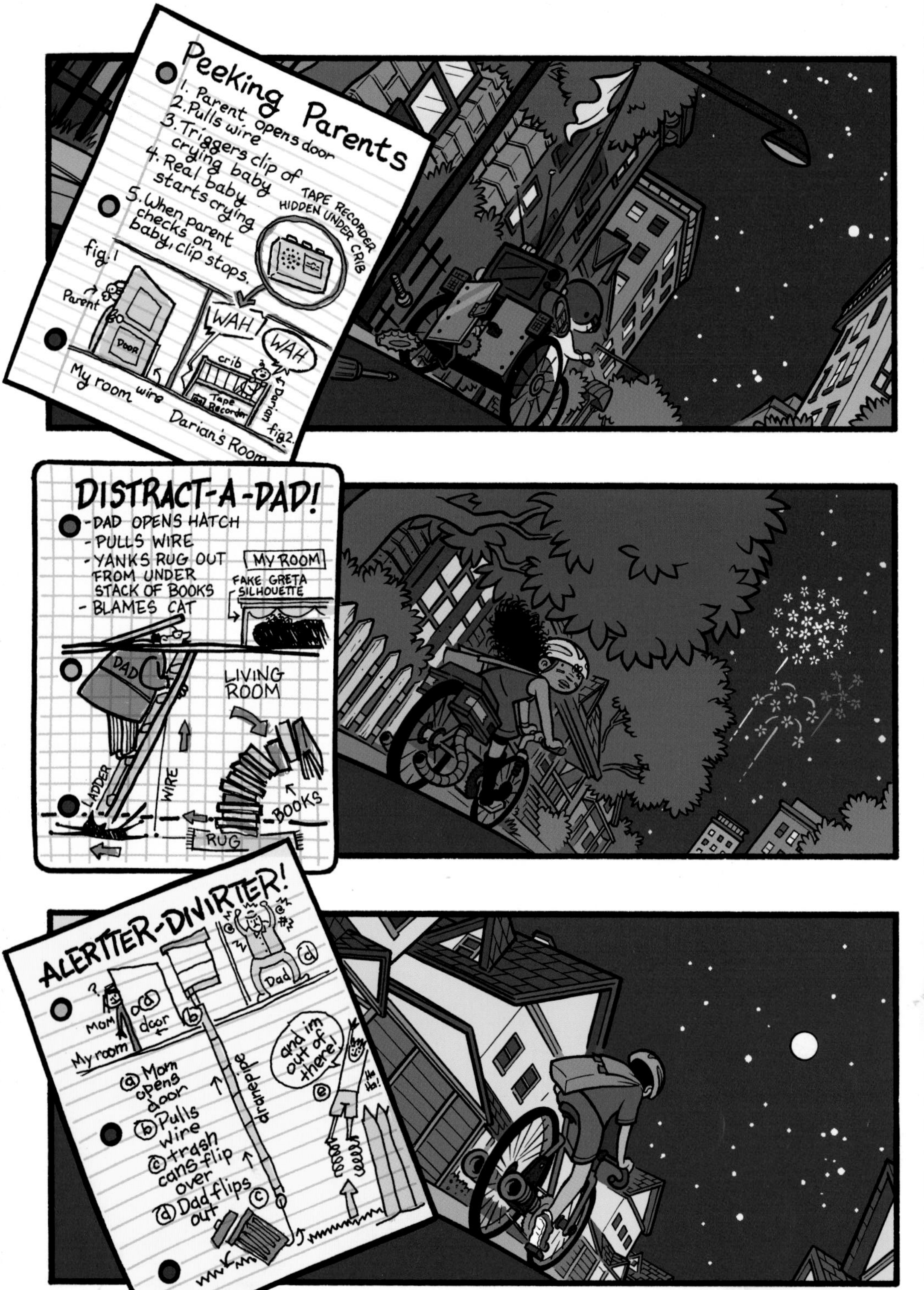
Peeking Parents
1. Parent opens door
2. Pulls wire
3. Triggers clip of crying baby
4. Real baby starts crying
5. When parent checks on baby, clip stops.
TAPE RECORDER HIDDEN UNDER CRIB
fig.1
Parent
DOOR
WAH
WAH
crib
Tape Recorder
Darian
My room
wire
Darian's Room
fig2.
DISTRACT-A-DAD!
-DAD OPENS HATCH
-PULLS WIRE
-YANKS RUG OUT FROM UNDER STACK OF BOOKS
- BLAMES CAT
MY ROOM
FAKE GRETA SILHOUETTE
DAD
LIVING ROOM
LADDER
WIRE
BOOKS
RUG
ALERTTER-DIVIRTER!
Dad
MOM
door
My room
ⓐ Mom opens door
ⓑ Pulls wire
ⓒ trash cans flip over
ⓓ Dad flips out
dranepipe
and im out of there!
Ha Ha!

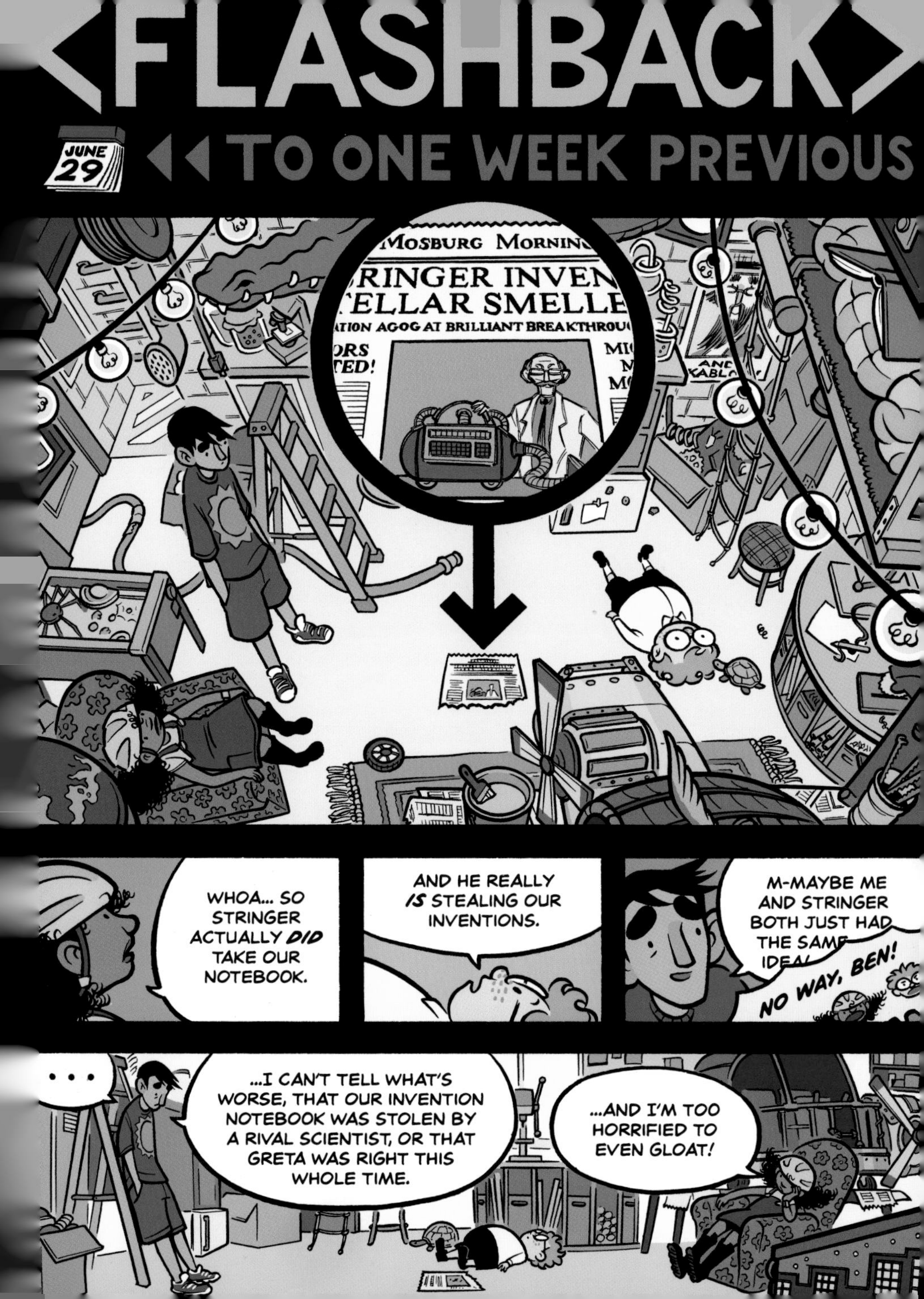
FLASHBACK
JUNE 29
TO ONE WEEK PREVIOUS
WHOA... SO STRINGER ACTUALLY *DID* TAKE OUR NOTEBOOK.
AND HE REALLY *IS* STEALING OUR INVENTIONS.
M-MAYBE ME AND STRINGER BOTH JUST HAD THE SAME IDEA
NO WAY, BEN!
. . .
...I CAN'T TELL WHAT'S WORSE, THAT OUR INVENTION NOTEBOOK WAS STOLEN BY A RIVAL SCIENTIST, OR THAT GRETA WAS RIGHT THIS WHOLE TIME.
...AND I'M TOO HORRIFIED TO EVEN GLOAT!

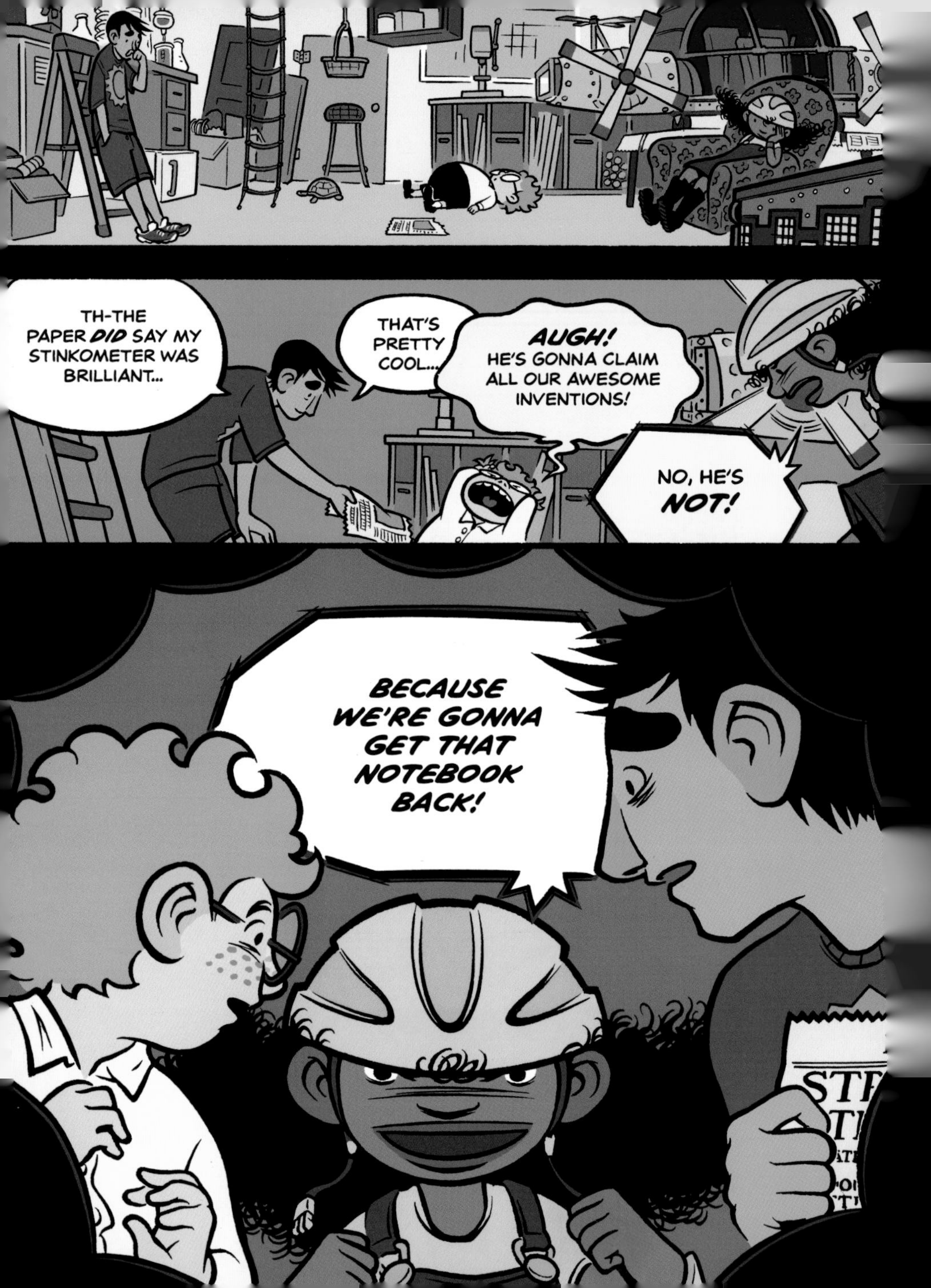

TH-THE PAPER *DID* SAY MY STINKOMETER WAS BRILLIANT...
THAT'S PRETTY COOL...
AUGH! HE'S GONNA CLAIM ALL OUR AWESOME INVENTIONS!
NO, HE'S *NOT!*
BECAUSE WE'RE GONNA GET THAT NOTEBOOK BACK!

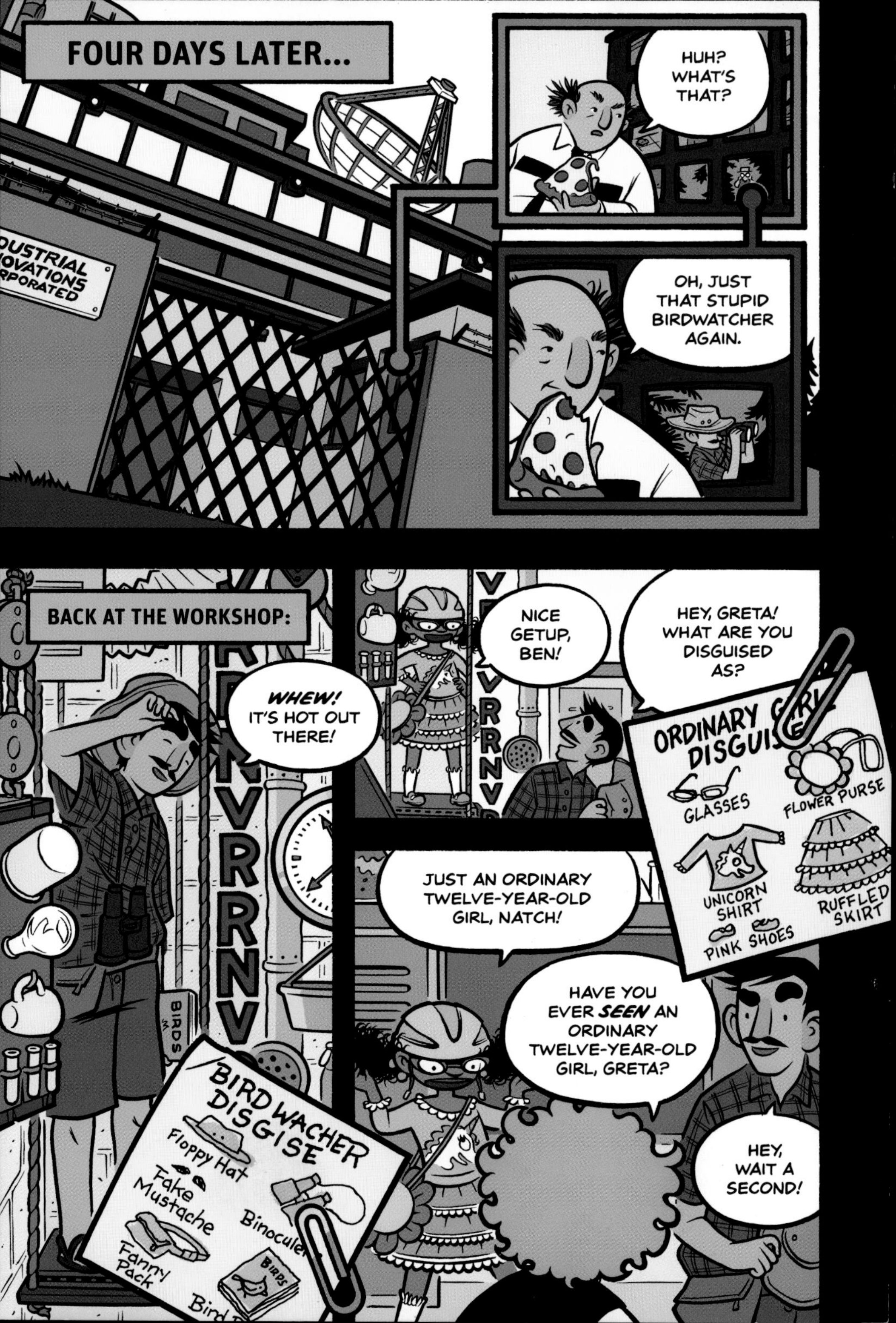
FOUR DAYS LATER...
HUH? WHAT'S THAT?
OUSTRIAL
NOVATIONS
RPORATED
OH, JUST THAT STUPID BIRDWATCHER AGAIN.
BACK AT THE WORKSHOP:
WHEW! IT'S HOT OUT THERE!
NICE GETUP, BEN!
HEY, GRETA! WHAT ARE YOU DISGUISED AS?
ORDINARY GIRL DISGUISE
GLASSES
FLOWER PURSE
UNICORN SHIRT
RUFFLED SKIRT
PINK SHOES
JUST AN ORDINARY TWELVE-YEAR-OLD GIRL, NATCH!
HAVE YOU EVER SEEN AN ORDINARY TWELVE-YEAR-OLD GIRL, GRETA?
HEY, WAIT A SECOND!
BIRD WACHER DISGISE
Floppy Hat
Fake Mustache
Binoculers
Fanny Pack
BIRDS

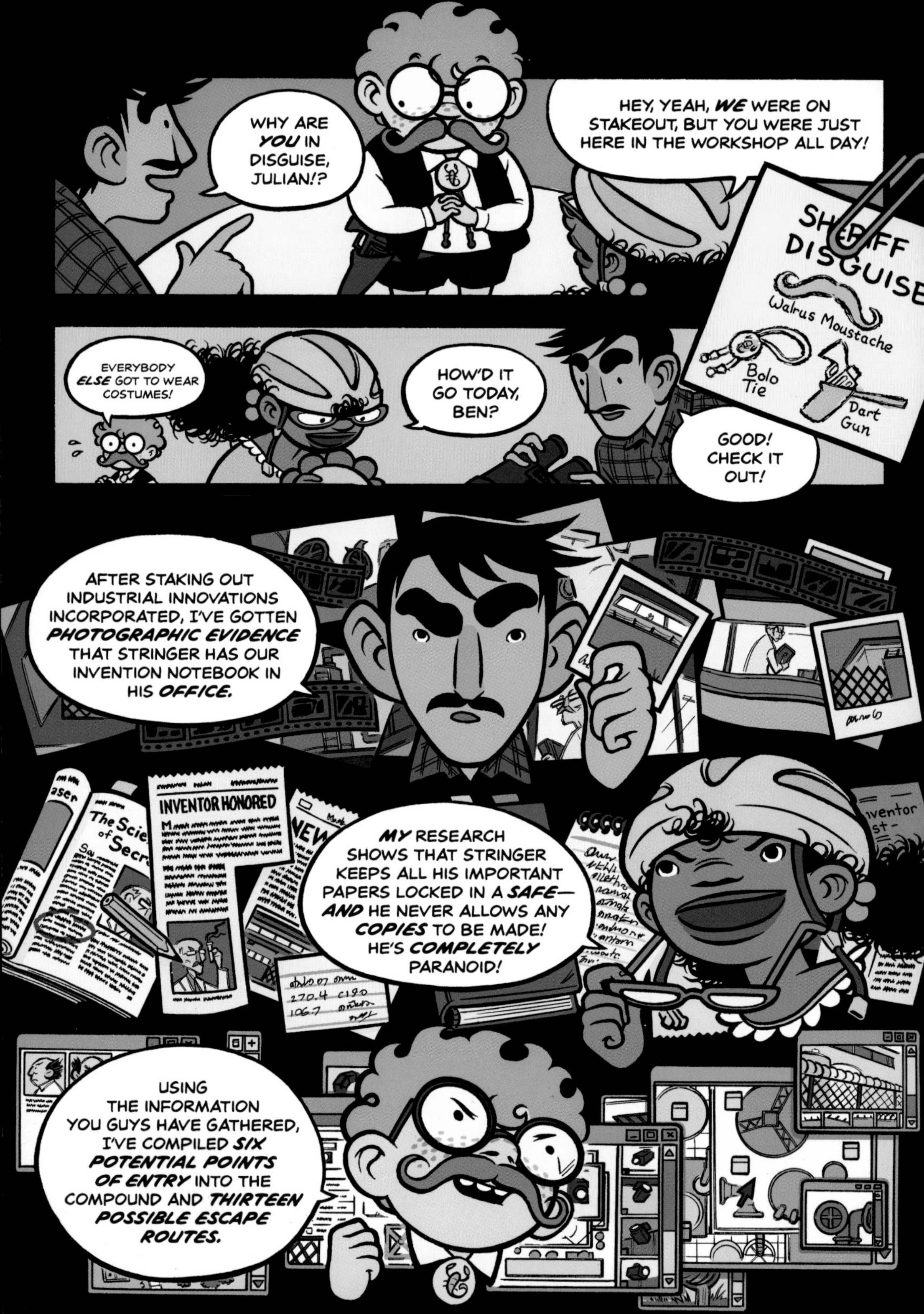
WHY ARE YOU IN DISGUISE, JULIAN!?
HEY, YEAH, WE WERE ON STAKEOUT, BUT YOU WERE JUST HERE IN THE WORKSHOP ALL DAY!
SHERIFF DISGUISE
Walrus Moustache
Bolo Tie
Dart Gun
EVERYBODY ELSE GOT TO WEAR COSTUMES!
HOW'D IT GO TODAY, BEN?
GOOD! CHECK IT OUT!
AFTER STAKING OUT INDUSTRIAL INNOVATIONS INCORPORATED, I'VE GOTTEN PHOTOGRAPHIC EVIDENCE THAT STRINGER HAS OUR INVENTION NOTEBOOK IN HIS OFFICE.
INVENTOR HONORED
MY RESEARCH SHOWS THAT STRINGER KEEPS ALL HIS IMPORTANT PAPERS LOCKED IN A SAFE—AND HE NEVER ALLOWS ANY COPIES TO BE MADE! HE'S COMPLETELY PARANOID!
USING THE INFORMATION YOU GUYS HAVE GATHERED, I'VE COMPILED SIX POTENTIAL POINTS OF ENTRY INTO THE COMPOUND AND THIRTEEN POSSIBLE ESCAPE ROUTES.

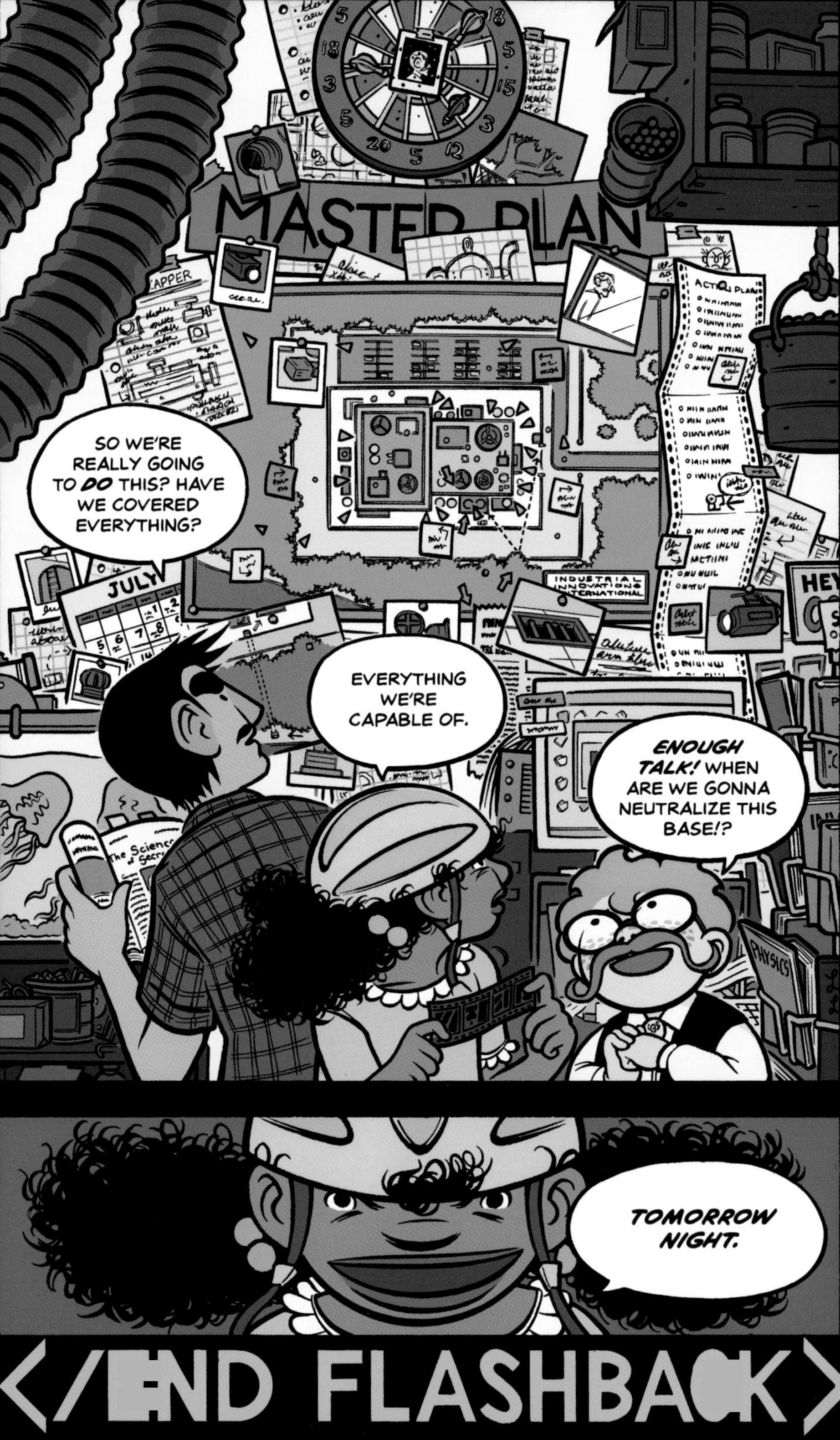
MASTER PLAN
ACTION PLAN
INDUSTRIAL INNOVATIONS INTERNATIONAL
JULY
SO WE'RE REALLY GOING TO *DO* THIS? HAVE WE COVERED EVERYTHING?
EVERYTHING WE'RE CAPABLE OF.
ENOUGH TALK! WHEN ARE WE GONNA NEUTRALIZE THIS BASE!?
PHYSICS
TOMORROW NIGHT.
</END FLASHBACK>

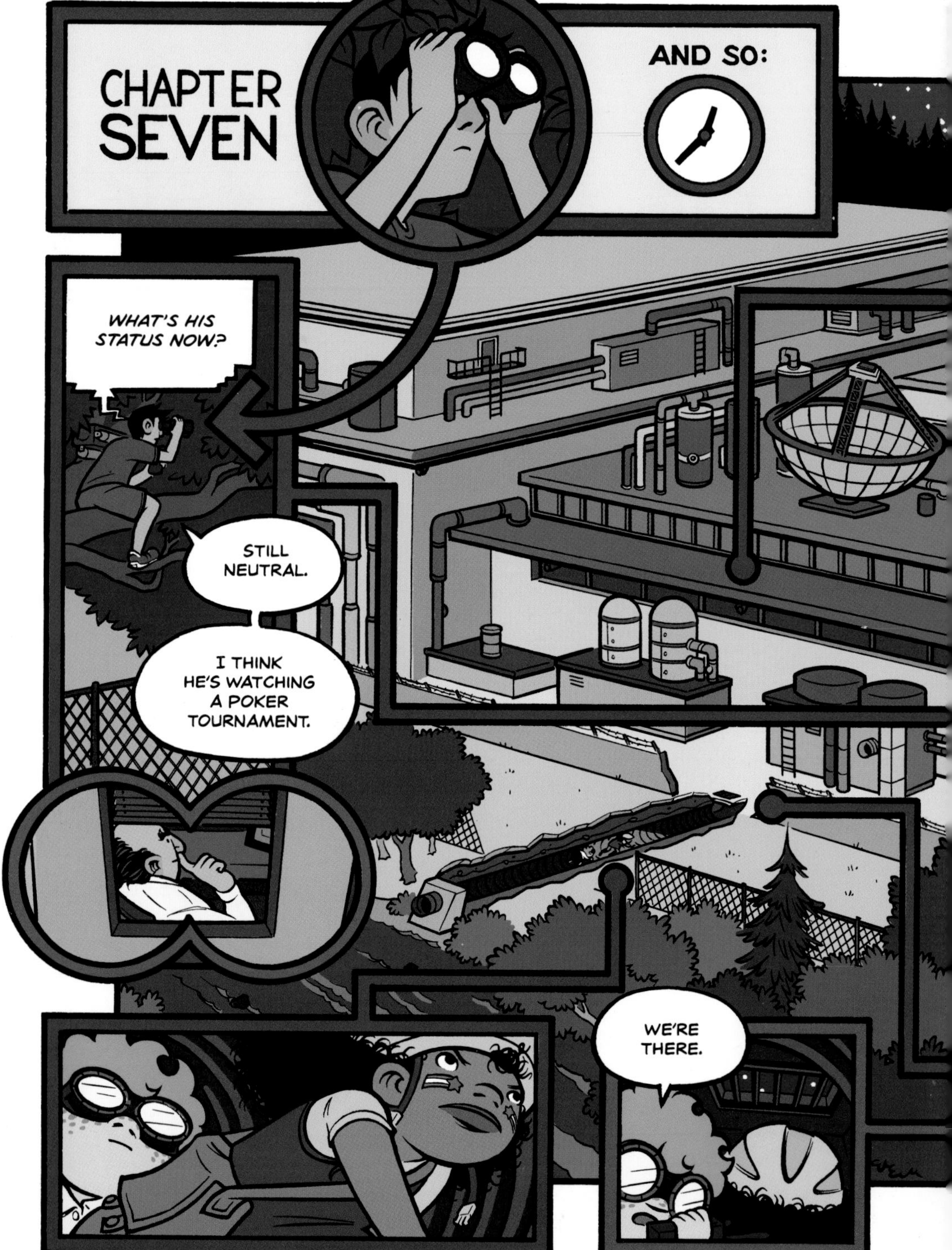
CHAPTER SEVEN
AND SO:
WHAT'S HIS STATUS NOW?
STILL NEUTRAL.
I THINK HE'S WATCHING A POKER TOURNAMENT.
WE'RE THERE.

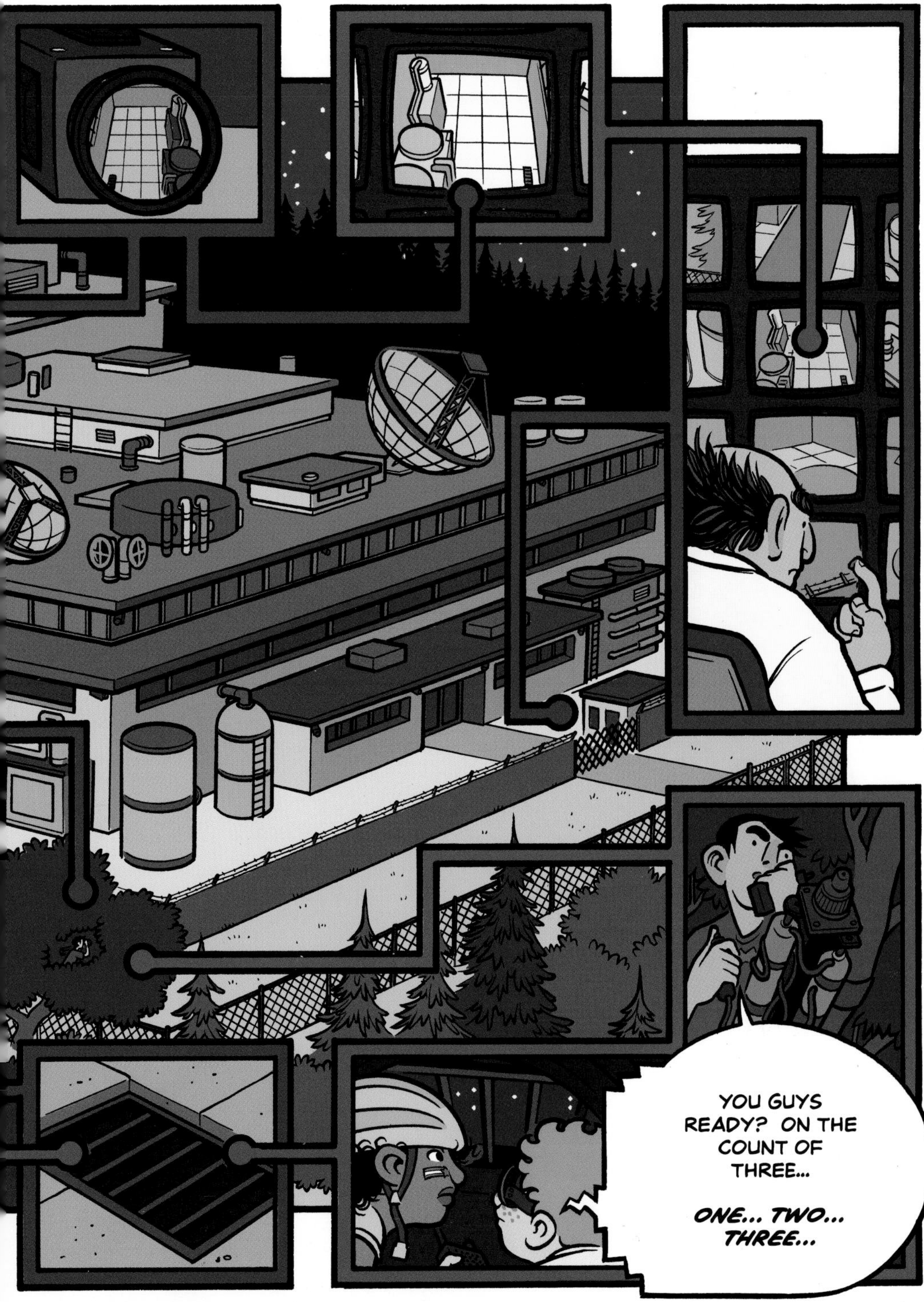
YOU GUYS READY? ON THE COUNT OF THREE...
ONE... TWO... THREE...

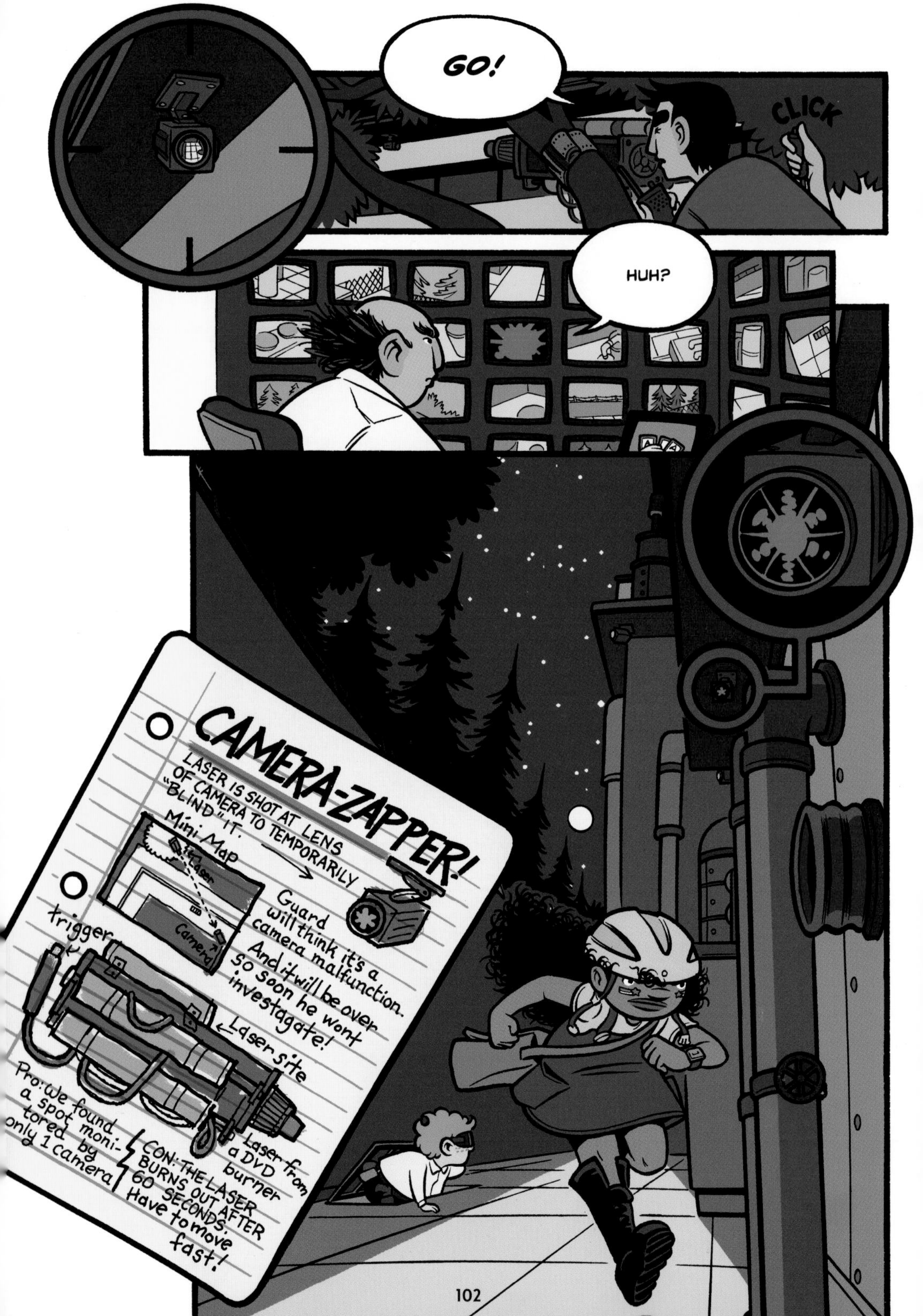
GO!
CLICK
HUH?
CAMERA-ZAPPER!
LASER IS SHOT AT LENS OF CAMERA TO TEMPORARILY "BLIND" IT.
Mini Map
Laser
Camera
Guard will think it's a camera malfunction. And it will be over so soon he wont investagate!
trigger
Laser site
Laser from a DVD burner
Pro: We found a spot moni-tored by only 1 camera
CON: THE LASER BURNS OUT AFTER 60 SECONDS. Have to move fast!

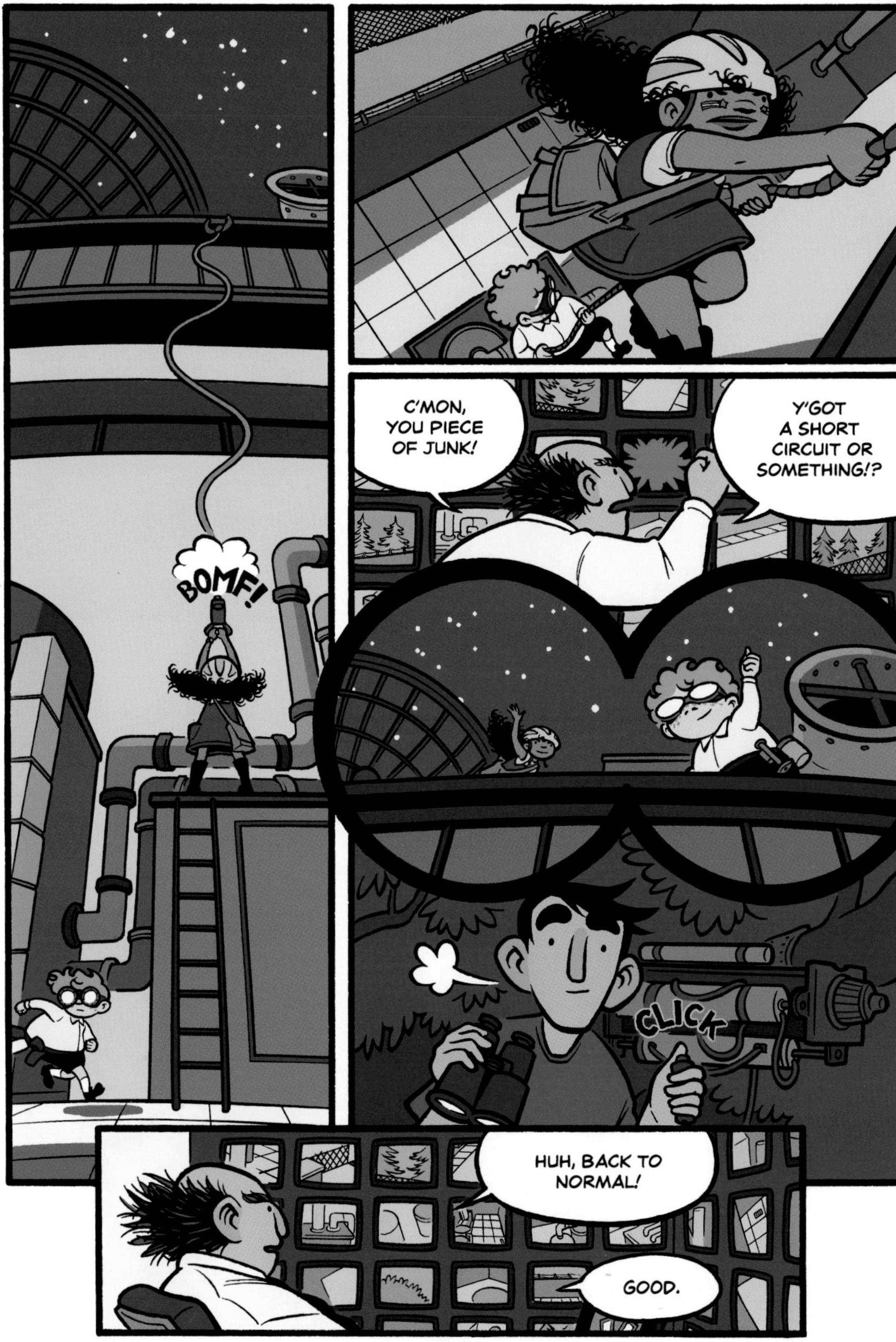
BOMF!
C'MON, YOU PIECE OF JUNK!
Y'GOT A SHORT CIRCUIT OR SOMETHING!?
CLICK
HUH, BACK TO NORMAL!
GOOD.

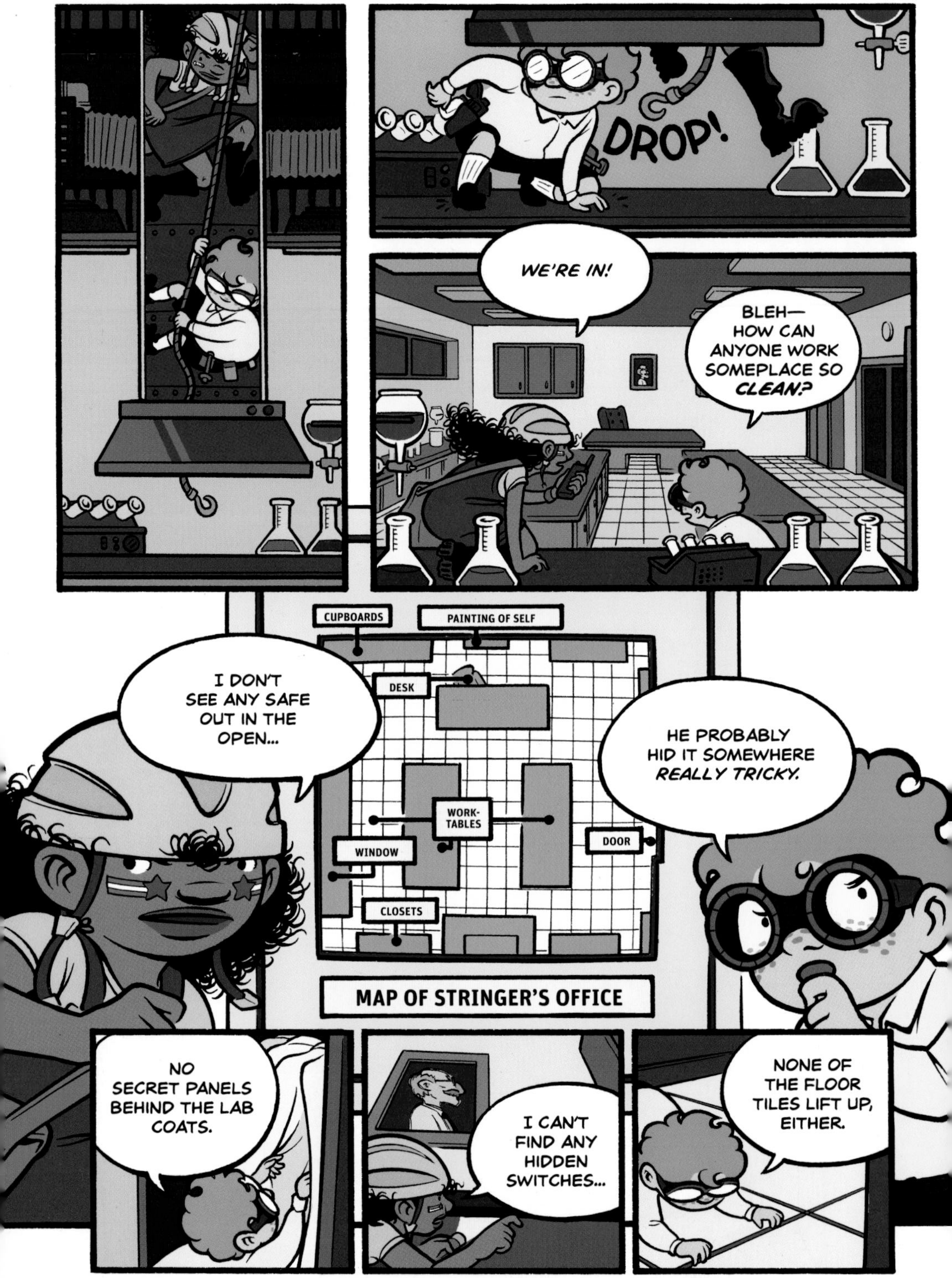
DROP!
WE'RE IN!
BLEH—
HOW CAN
ANYONE WORK
SOMEPLACE SO
CLEAN?
CUPBOARDS
PAINTING OF SELF
DESK
WORK-
TABLES
WINDOW
DOOR
CLOSETS
MAP OF STRINGER'S OFFICE
I DON'T
SEE ANY SAFE
OUT IN THE
OPEN...
HE PROBABLY
HID IT SOMEWHERE
REALLY TRICKY.
NO
SECRET PANELS
BEHIND THE LAB
COATS.
I CAN'T
FIND ANY
HIDDEN
SWITCHES...
NONE OF
THE FLOOR
TILES LIFT UP,
EITHER.

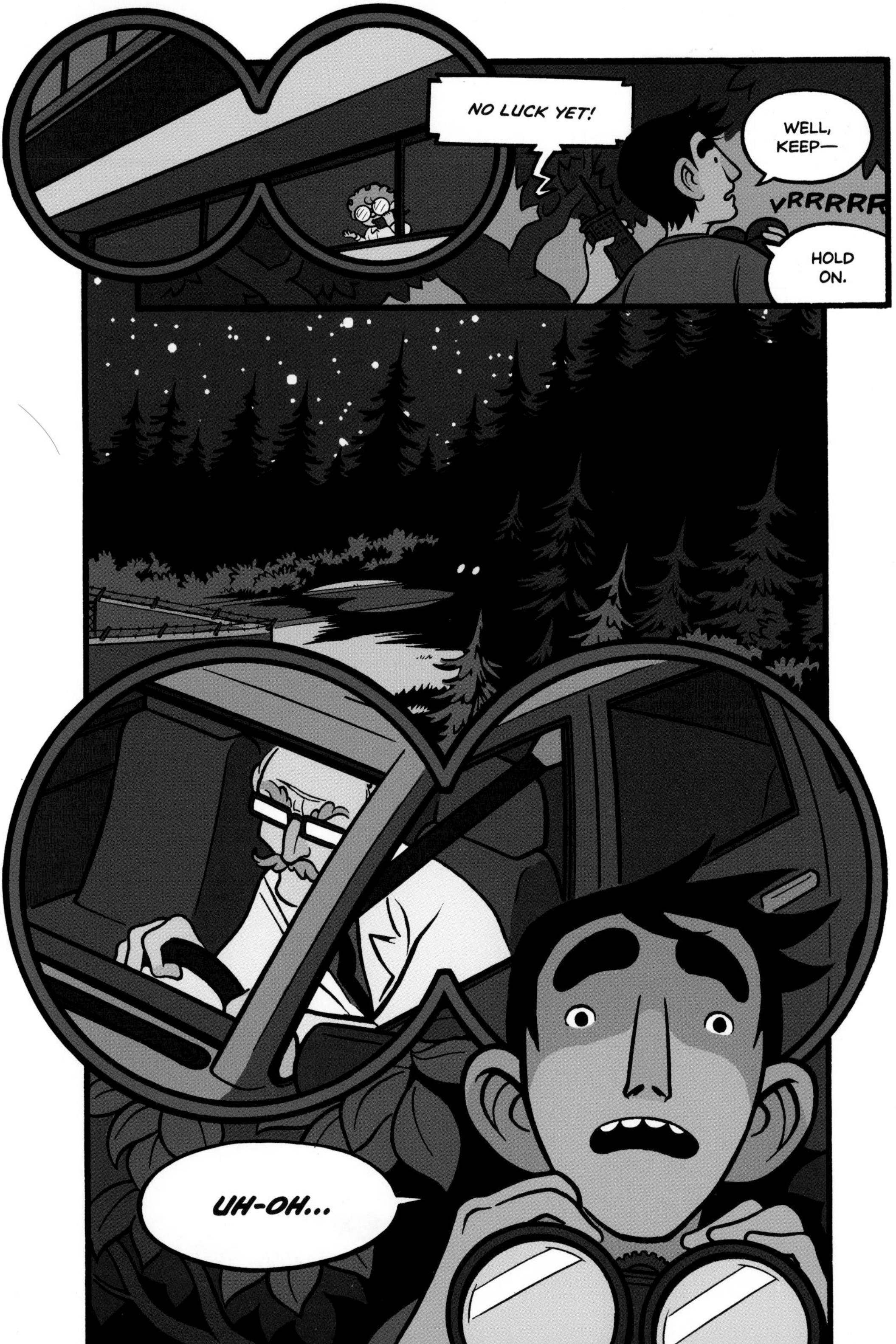
NO LUCK YET!
WELL, KEEP—
VRRRRR
HOLD ON.
UH-OH...

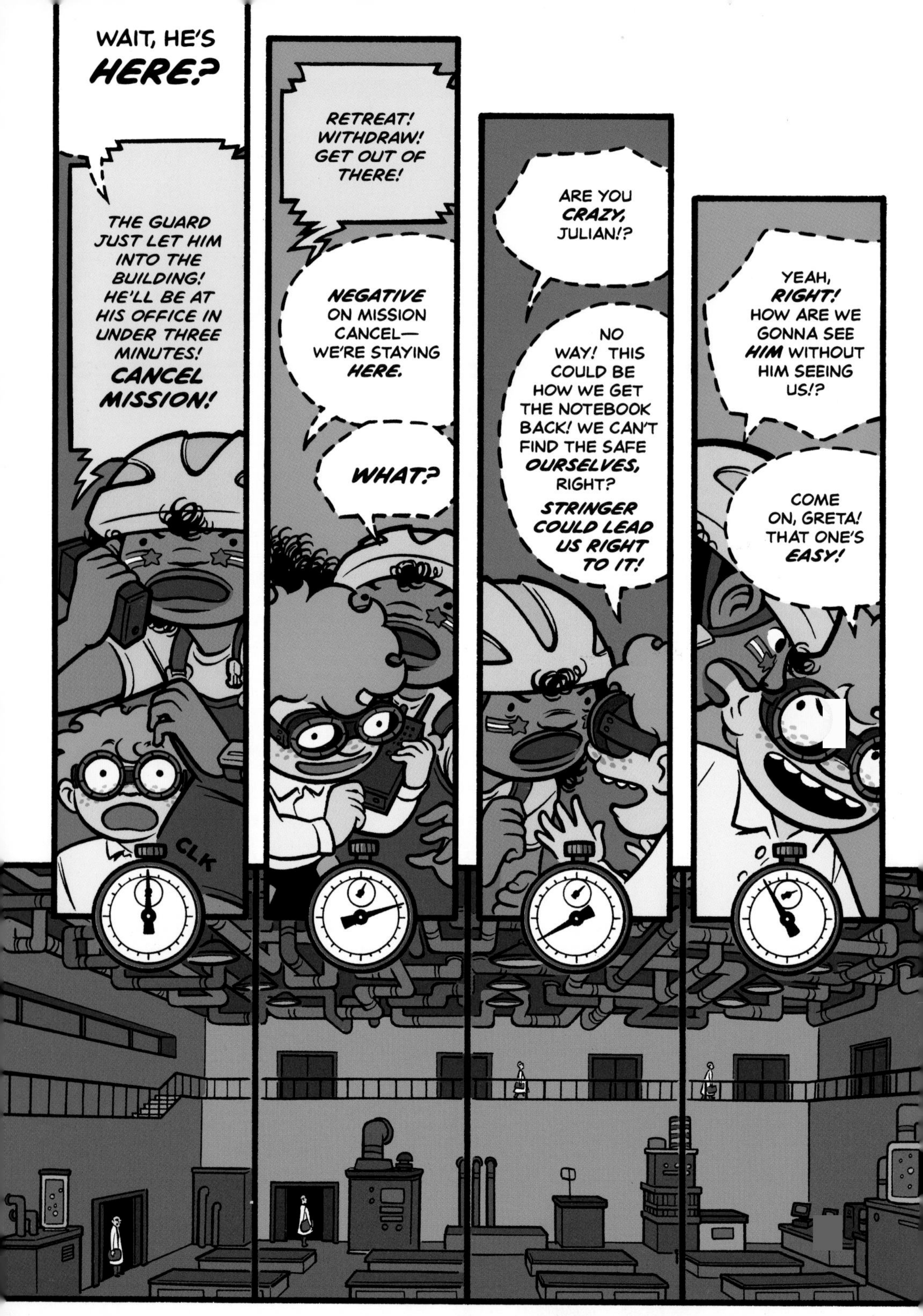

WAIT, HE'S HERE?
THE GUARD JUST LET HIM INTO THE BUILDING! HE'LL BE AT HIS OFFICE IN UNDER THREE MINUTES! CANCEL MISSION!
CLK
RETREAT! WITHDRAW! GET OUT OF THERE!
NEGATIVE ON MISSION CANCEL— WE'RE STAYING HERE.
WHAT?
ARE YOU CRAZY, JULIAN!?
NO WAY! THIS COULD BE HOW WE GET THE NOTEBOOK BACK! WE CAN'T FIND THE SAFE OURSELVES, RIGHT? STRINGER COULD LEAD US RIGHT TO IT!
YEAH, RIGHT! HOW ARE WE GONNA SEE HIM WITHOUT HIM SEEING US!?
COME ON, GRETA! THAT ONE'S EASY!

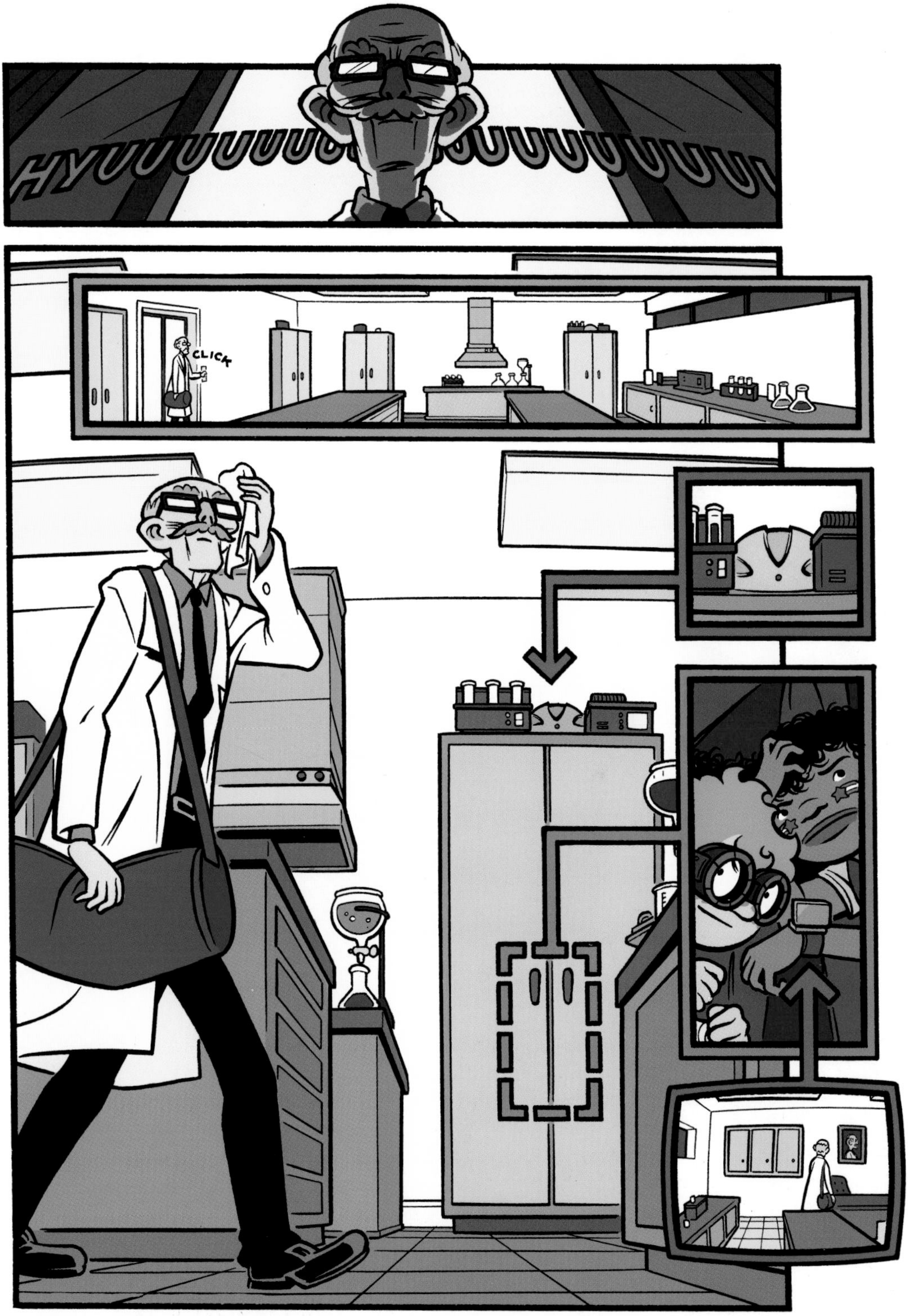

HYUUUUUUUUUUUUUUUUU
CLICK

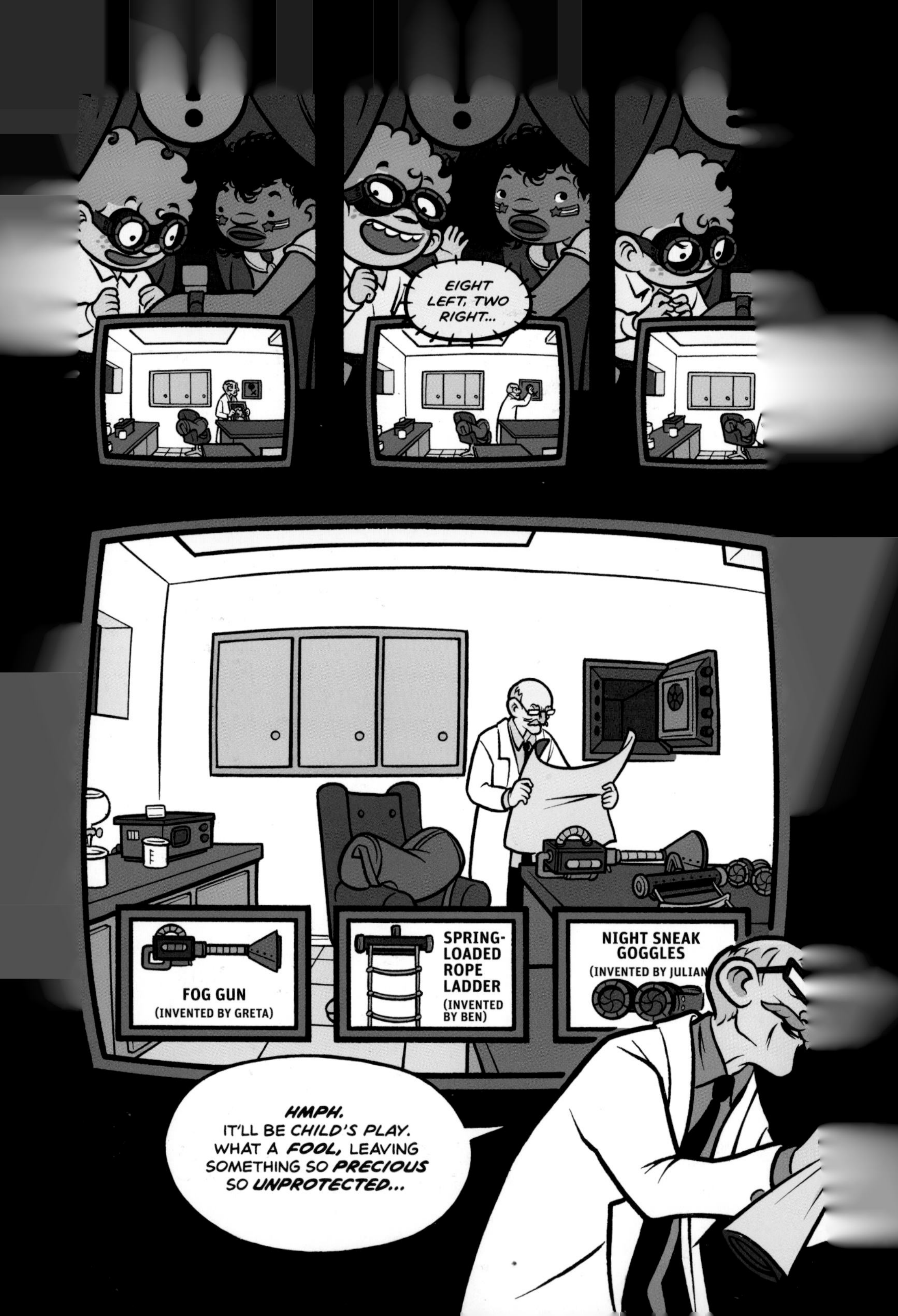
EIGHT LEFT, TWO RIGHT...
FOG GUN
(INVENTED BY GRETA)
SPRING-LOADED ROPE LADDER
(INVENTED BY BEN)
NIGHT SNEAK GOGGLES
(INVENTED BY JULIAN
HMPH.
IT'LL BE CHILD'S PLAY.
WHAT A FOOL, LEAVING SOMETHING SO PRECIOUS SO UNPROTECTED...

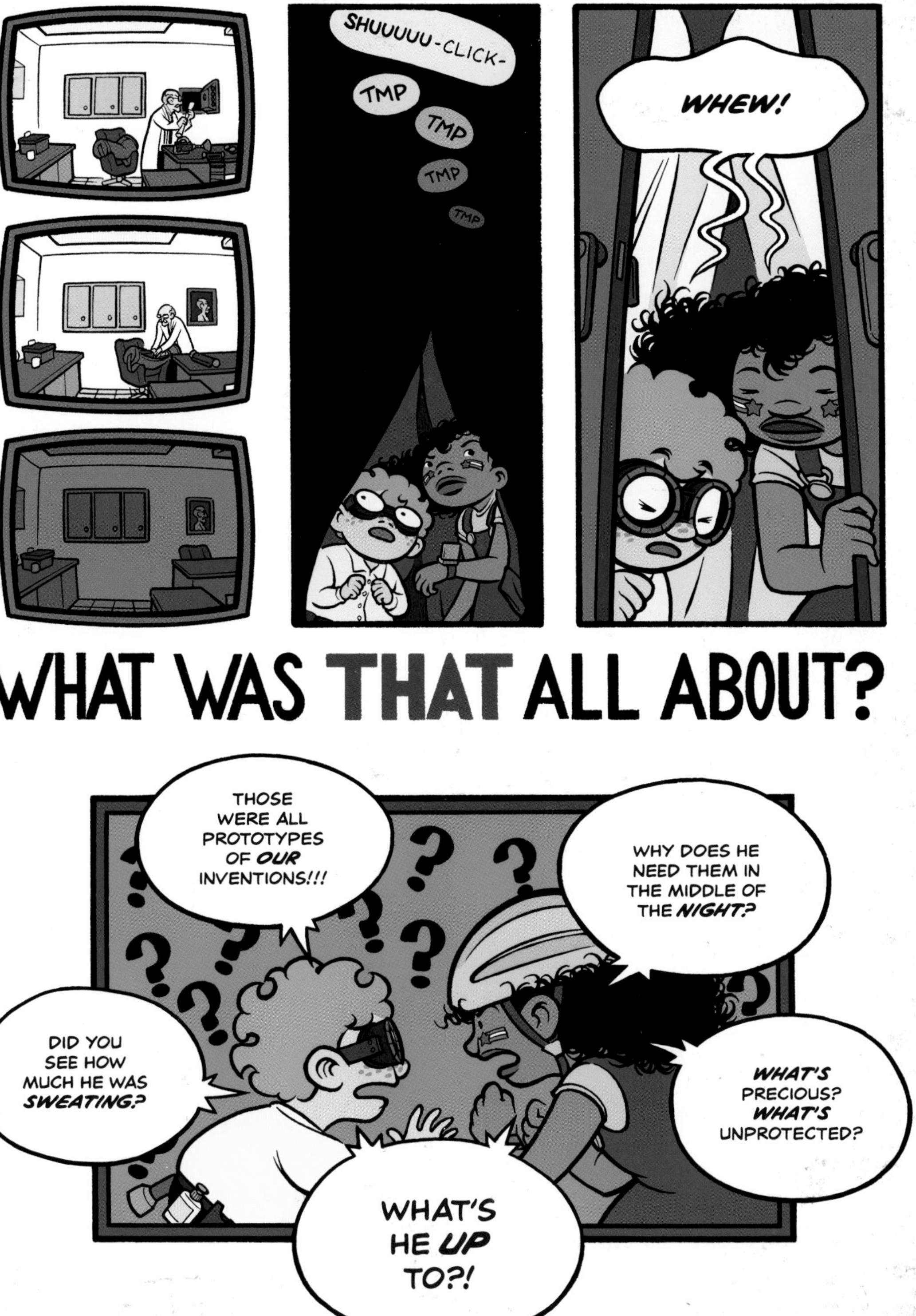
SHUUUUU-CLICK-
TMP
TMP
TMP
TMP
WHEW!
WHAT WAS THAT ALL ABOUT?
THOSE WERE ALL PROTOTYPES OF OUR INVENTIONS!!!
WHY DOES HE NEED THEM IN THE MIDDLE OF THE NIGHT?
DID YOU SEE HOW MUCH HE WAS SWEATING?
WHAT'S PRECIOUS? WHAT'S UNPROTECTED?
WHAT'S HE UP TO?!

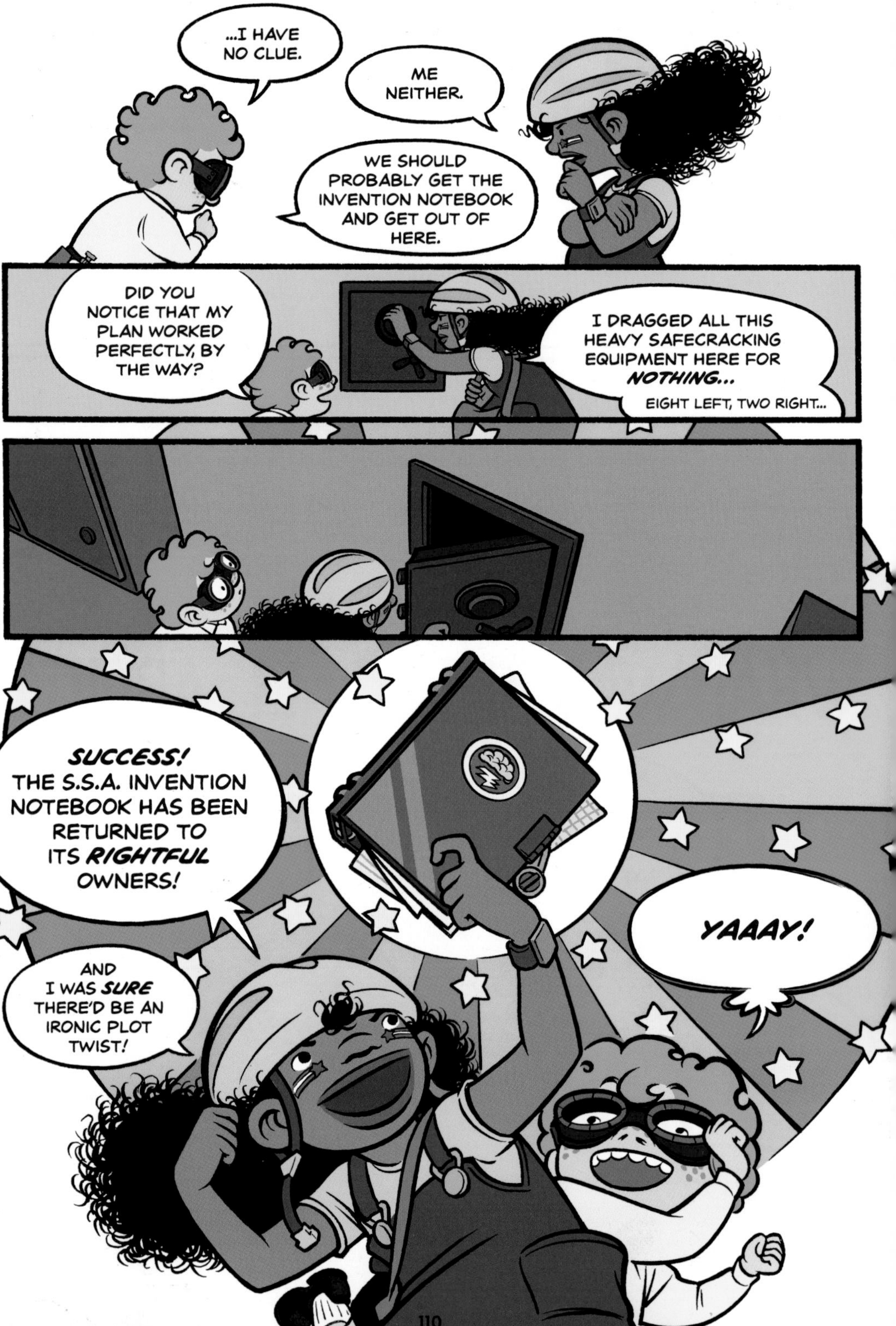

...I HAVE NO CLUE.
ME NEITHER.
WE SHOULD PROBABLY GET THE INVENTION NOTEBOOK AND GET OUT OF HERE.
DID YOU NOTICE THAT MY PLAN WORKED PERFECTLY, BY THE WAY?
I DRAGGED ALL THIS HEAVY SAFECRACKING EQUIPMENT HERE FOR *NOTHING...*
EIGHT LEFT, TWO RIGHT...
SUCCESS! THE S.S.A. INVENTION NOTEBOOK HAS BEEN RETURNED TO ITS *RIGHTFUL* OWNERS!
AND I WAS *SURE* THERE'D BE AN IRONIC PLOT TWIST!
YAAAY!

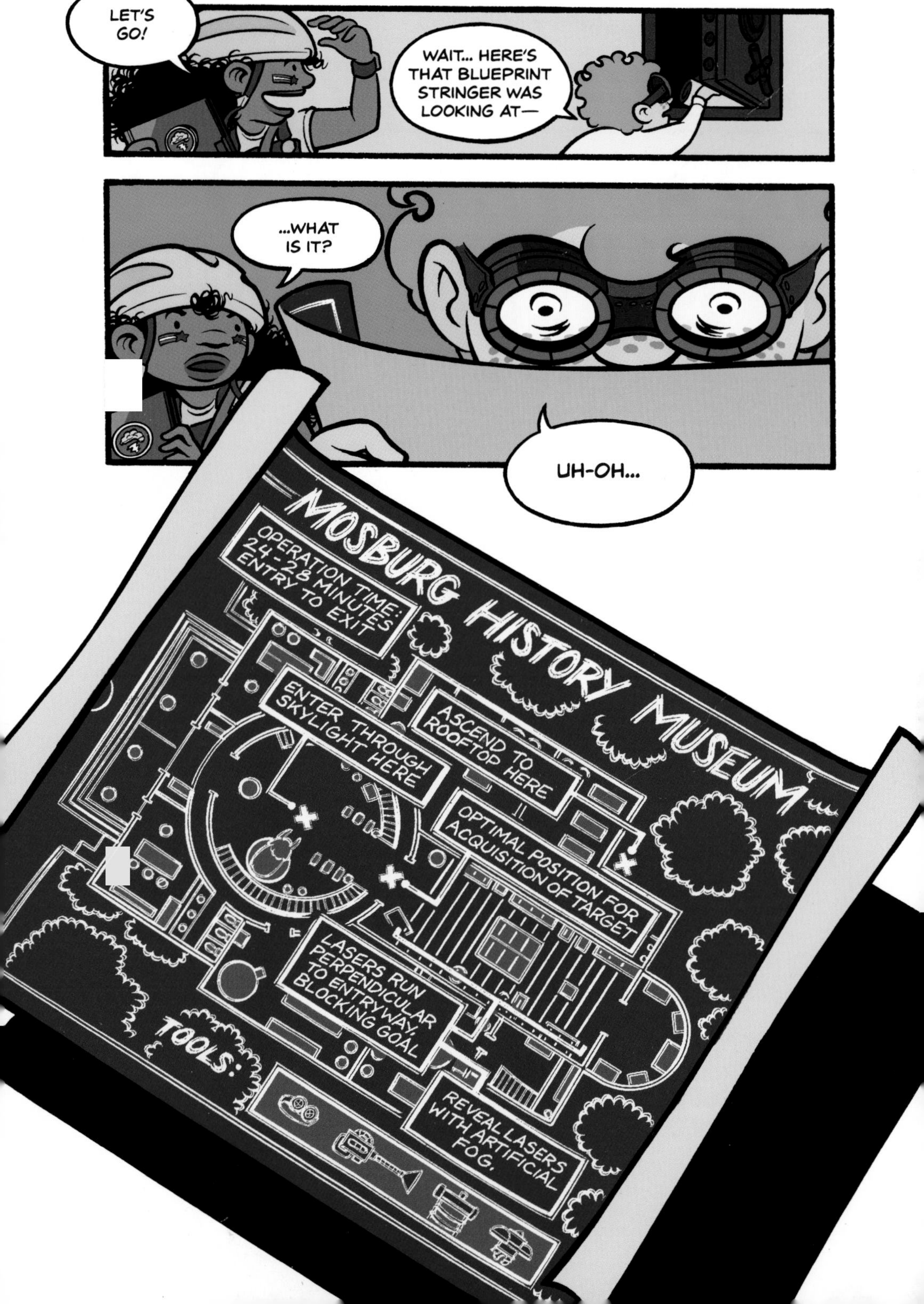
LET'S GO!
WAIT... HERE'S THAT BLUEPRINT STRINGER WAS LOOKING AT—
...WHAT IS IT?
UH-OH...
MOSBURG HISTORY MUSEUM
OPERATION TIME: 24-28 MINUTES ENTRY TO EXIT
ENTER THROUGH SKYLIGHT HERE
ASCEND TO ROOFTOP HERE
OPTIMAL POSITION FOR ACQUISITION OF TARGET
LASERS RUN PERPENDICULAR TO ENTRYWAY, BLOCKING GOAL
TOOLS:
REVEAL LASERS WITH ARTIFICIAL FOG.

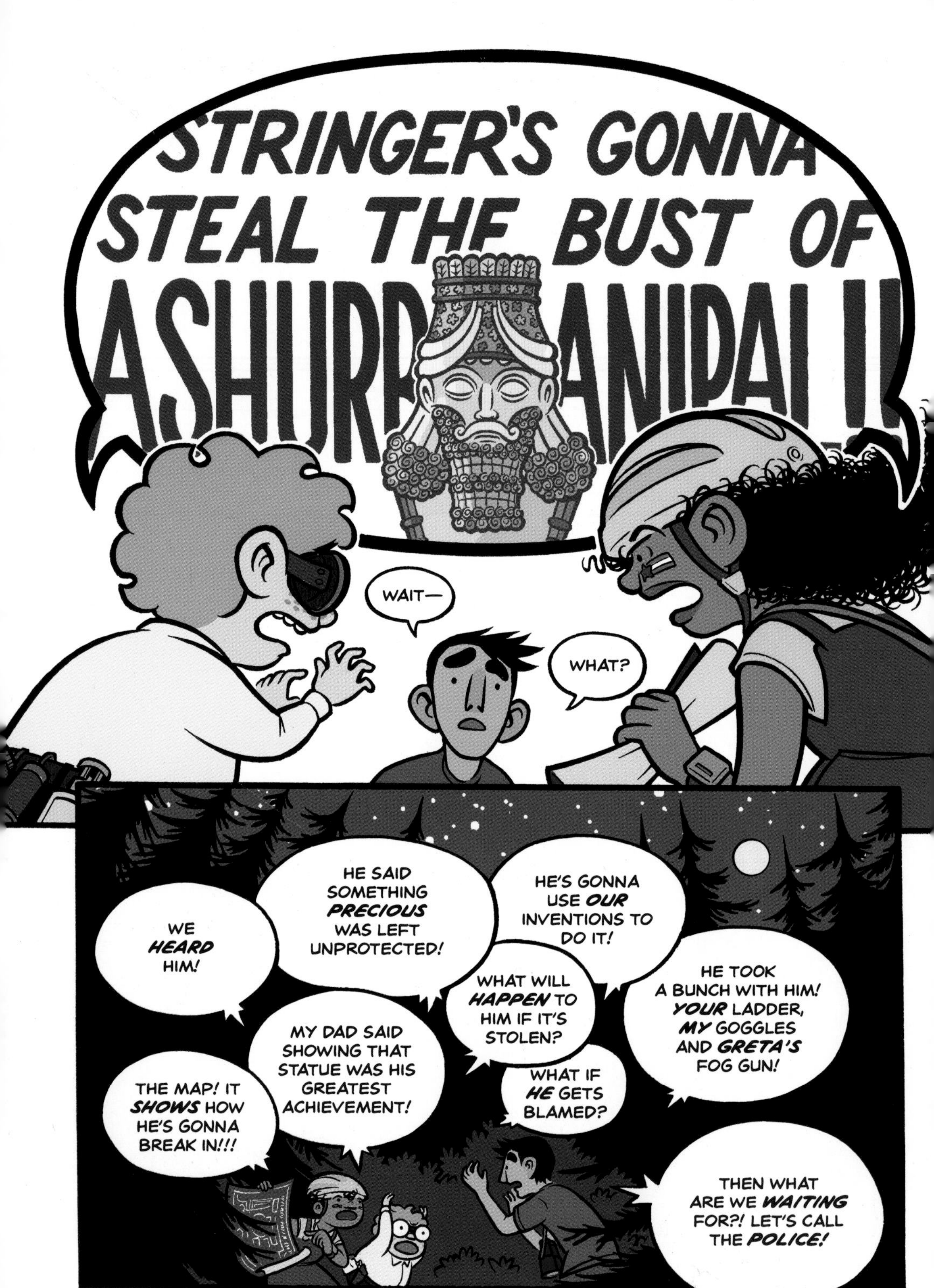
STRINGER'S GONNA STEAL THE BUST OF ASHURBANIPAL!!
WAIT—
WHAT?
WE *HEARD* HIM!
HE SAID SOMETHING *PRECIOUS* WAS LEFT UNPROTECTED!
HE'S GONNA USE *OUR* INVENTIONS TO DO IT!
WHAT WILL *HAPPEN* TO HIM IF IT'S STOLEN?
HE TOOK A BUNCH WITH HIM! *YOUR* LADDER, *MY* GOGGLES AND *GRETA'S* FOG GUN!
MY DAD SAID SHOWING THAT STATUE WAS HIS GREATEST ACHIEVEMENT!
WHAT IF *HE* GETS BLAMED?
THE MAP! IT *SHOWS* HOW HE'S GONNA BREAK IN!!!
THEN WHAT ARE WE *WAITING* FOR?! LET'S CALL THE *POLICE!*

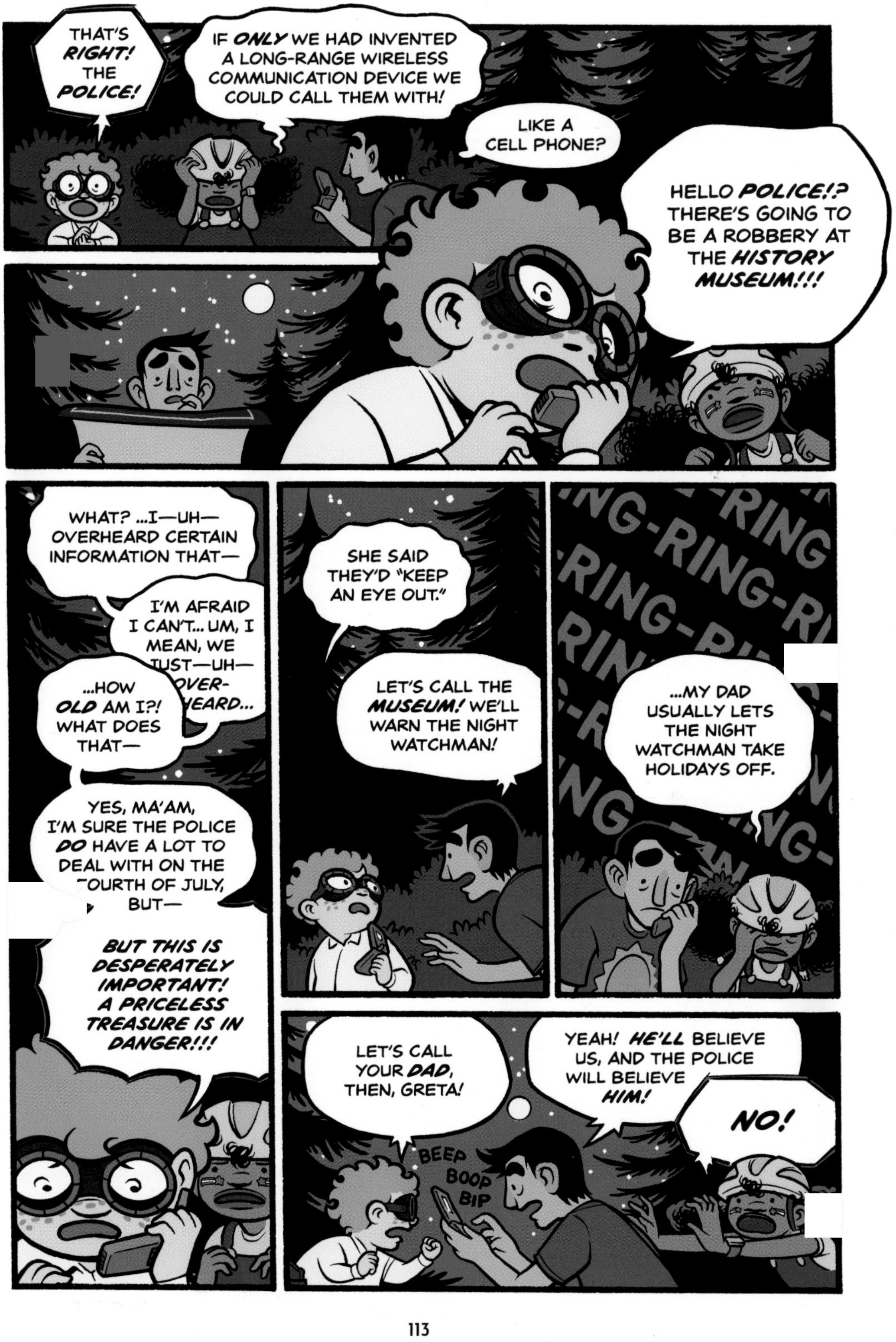
THAT'S RIGHT! THE POLICE!
IF ONLY WE HAD INVENTED A LONG-RANGE WIRELESS COMMUNICATION DEVICE WE COULD CALL THEM WITH!
LIKE A CELL PHONE?
HELLO POLICE!? THERE'S GOING TO BE A ROBBERY AT THE HISTORY MUSEUM!!!
WHAT? ...I—UH— OVERHEARD CERTAIN INFORMATION THAT—
I'M AFRAID I CAN'T... UM, I MEAN, WE JUST—UH— OVER-HEARD...
...HOW OLD AM I?! WHAT DOES THAT—
YES, MA'AM, I'M SURE THE POLICE DO HAVE A LOT TO DEAL WITH ON THE FOURTH OF JULY, BUT—
BUT THIS IS DESPERATELY IMPORTANT! A PRICELESS TREASURE IS IN DANGER!!!
SHE SAID THEY'D "KEEP AN EYE OUT."
LET'S CALL THE MUSEUM! WE'LL WARN THE NIGHT WATCHMAN!
RING-RING-RING-RING-RING-RING
...MY DAD USUALLY LETS THE NIGHT WATCHMAN TAKE HOLIDAYS OFF.
LET'S CALL YOUR DAD, THEN, GRETA!
YEAH! HE'LL BELIEVE US, AND THE POLICE WILL BELIEVE HIM!
NO!
BEEP BOOP BIP

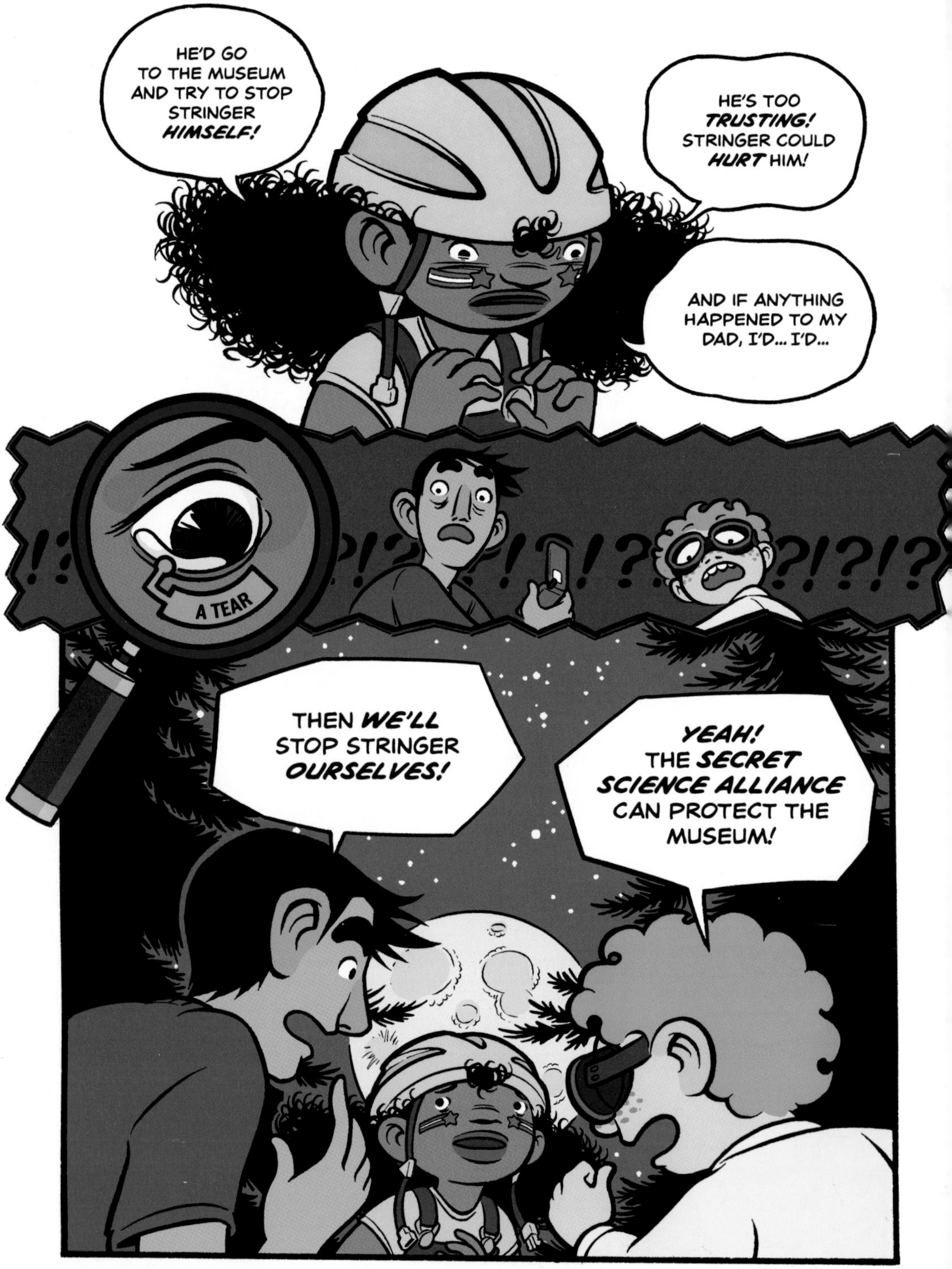
HE'D GO TO THE MUSEUM AND TRY TO STOP STRINGER HIMSELF!
HE'S TOO TRUSTING! STRINGER COULD HURT HIM!
AND IF ANYTHING HAPPENED TO MY DAD, I'D... I'D...
A TEAR
!?!?!?!?!?!?!?!?
THEN WE'LL STOP STRINGER OURSELVES!
YEAH! THE SECRET SCIENCE ALLIANCE CAN PROTECT THE MUSEUM!

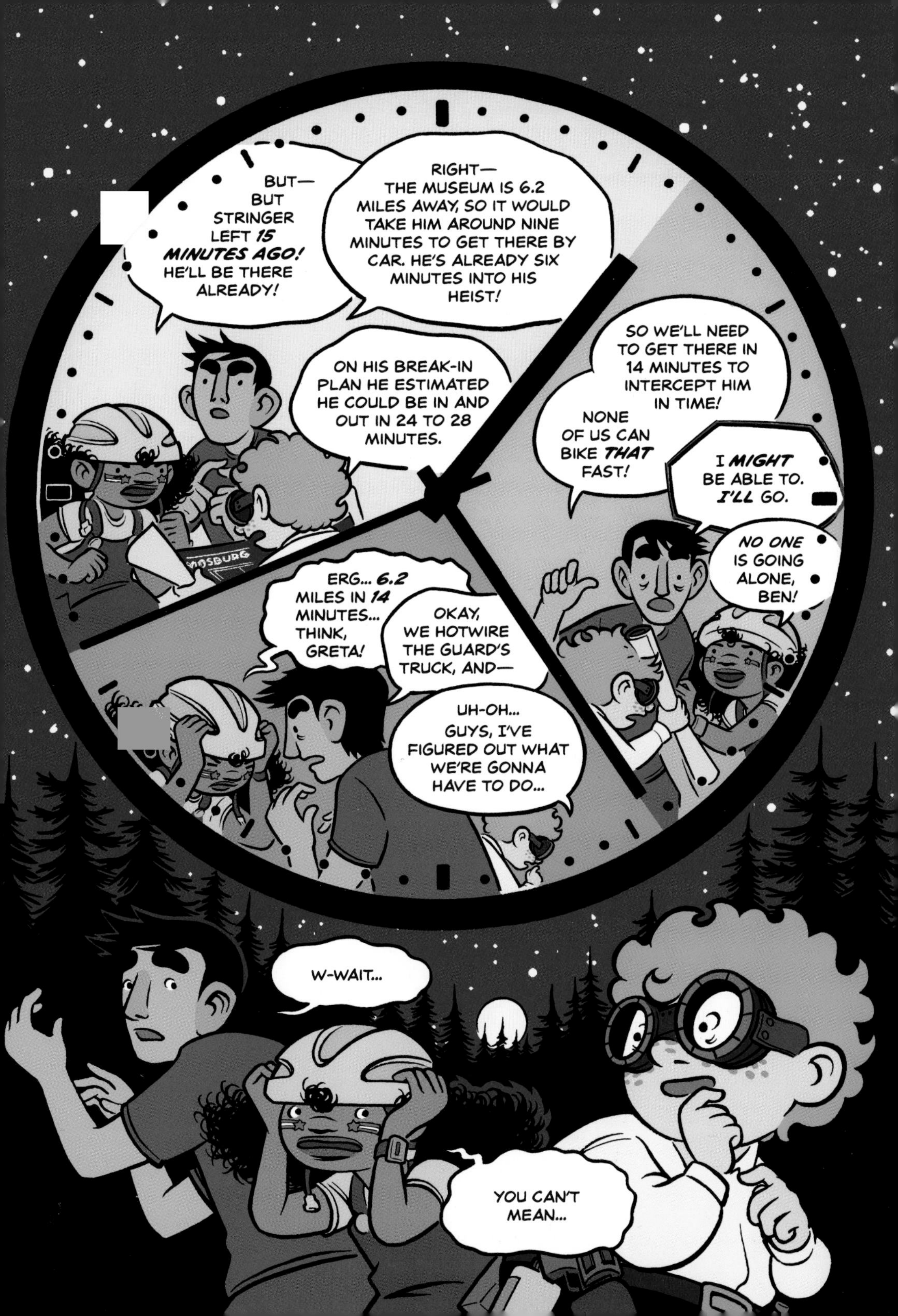
BUT— BUT STRINGER LEFT 15 MINUTES AGO! HE'LL BE THERE ALREADY!
RIGHT— THE MUSEUM IS 6.2 MILES AWAY, SO IT WOULD TAKE HIM AROUND NINE MINUTES TO GET THERE BY CAR. HE'S ALREADY SIX MINUTES INTO HIS HEIST!
ON HIS BREAK-IN PLAN HE ESTIMATED HE COULD BE IN AND OUT IN 24 TO 28 MINUTES.
SO WE'LL NEED TO GET THERE IN 14 MINUTES TO INTERCEPT HIM IN TIME!
NONE OF US CAN BIKE THAT FAST!
I MIGHT BE ABLE TO. I'LL GO.
NO ONE IS GOING ALONE, BEN!
ERG... 6.2 MILES IN 14 MINUTES... THINK, GRETA!
OKAY, WE HOTWIRE THE GUARD'S TRUCK, AND—
UH-OH... GUYS, I'VE FIGURED OUT WHAT WE'RE GONNA HAVE TO DO...
W-WAIT...
YOU CAN'T MEAN...

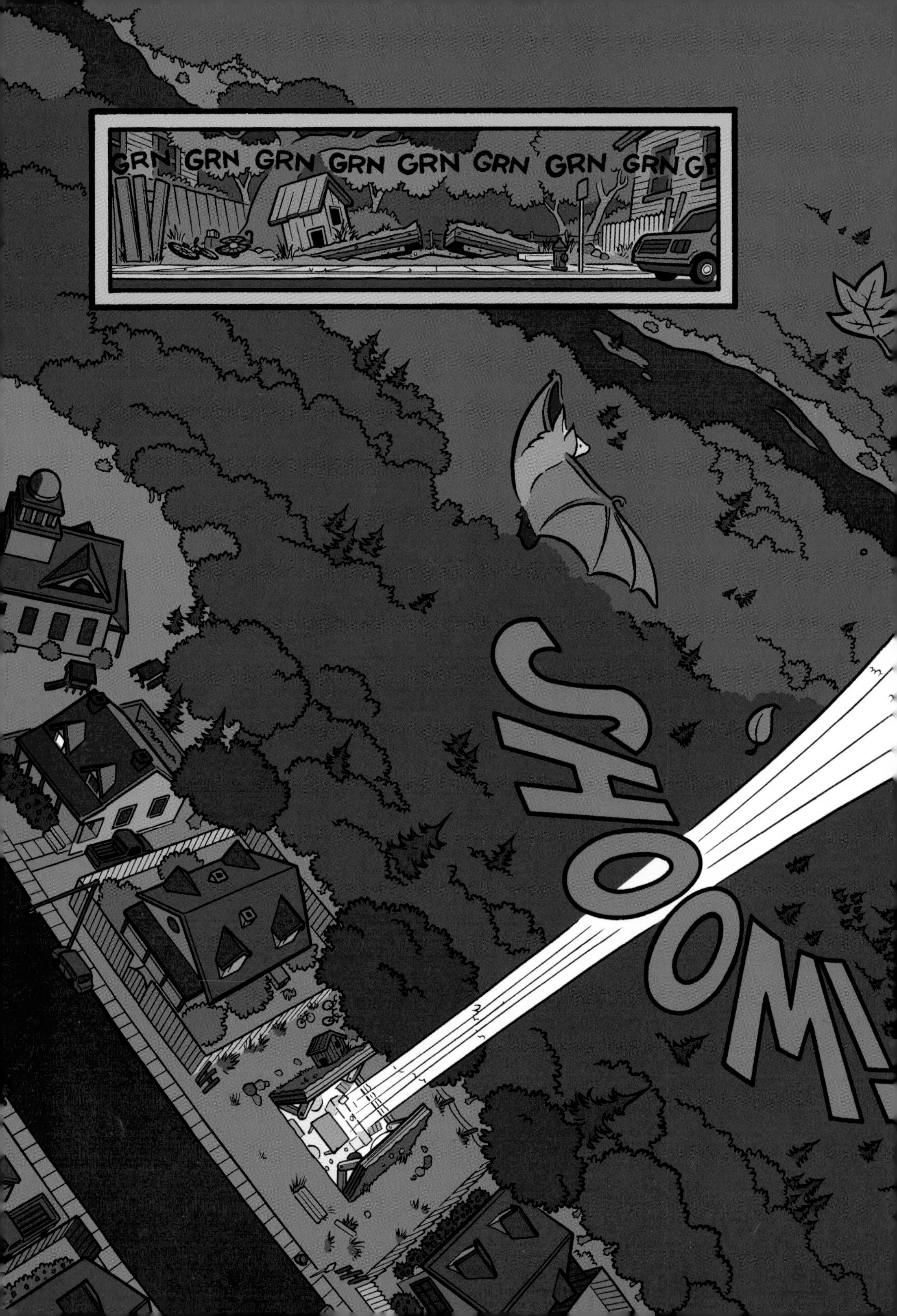
GRN GRN GRN GRN GRN GRN GRN GRN
SHOOM!

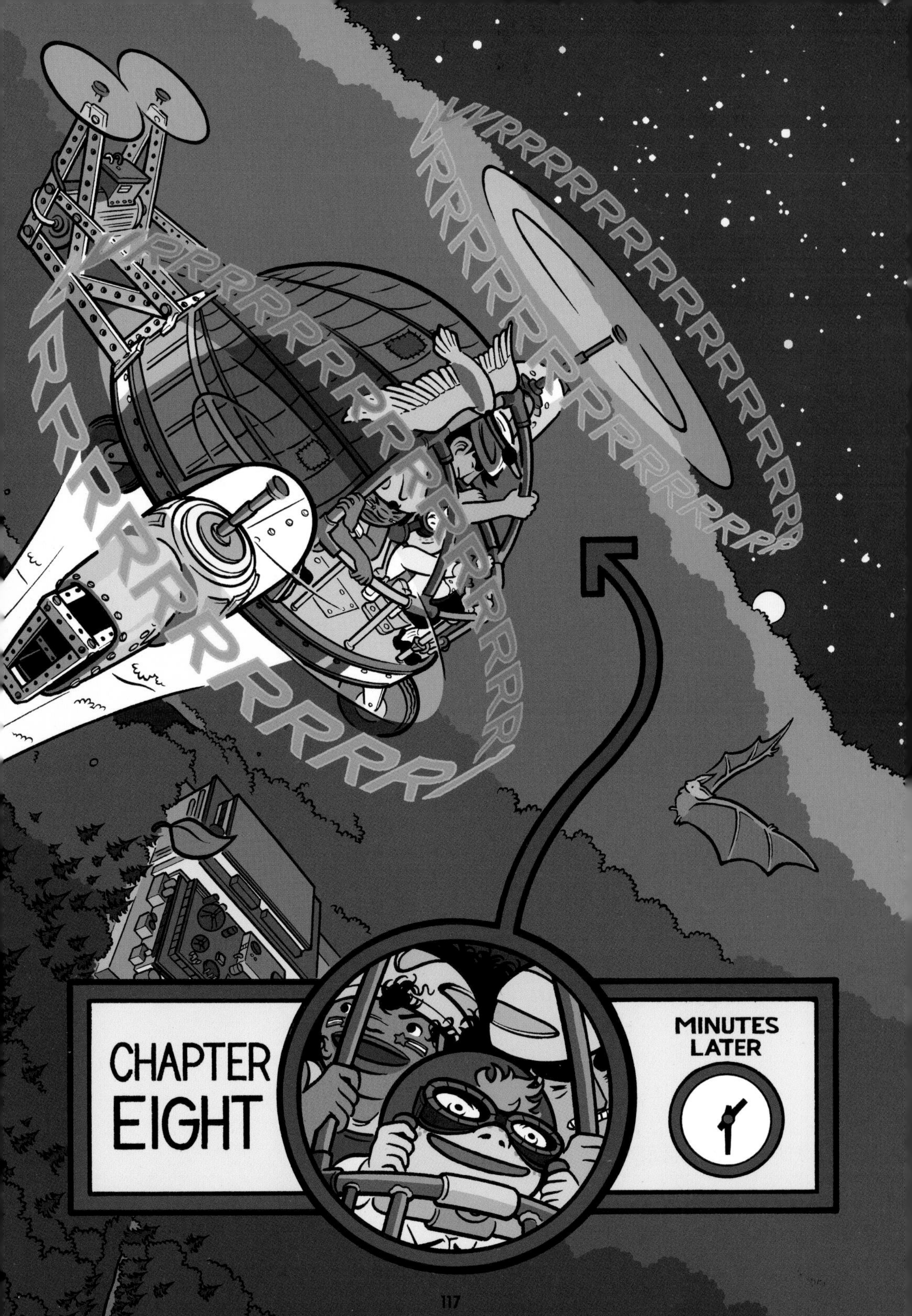
VVRRRRRRRRRRRRRRRRRRRR
VRRRRRRRRRRRRRRRRRRRRRRR!
CHAPTER EIGHT
MINUTES LATER

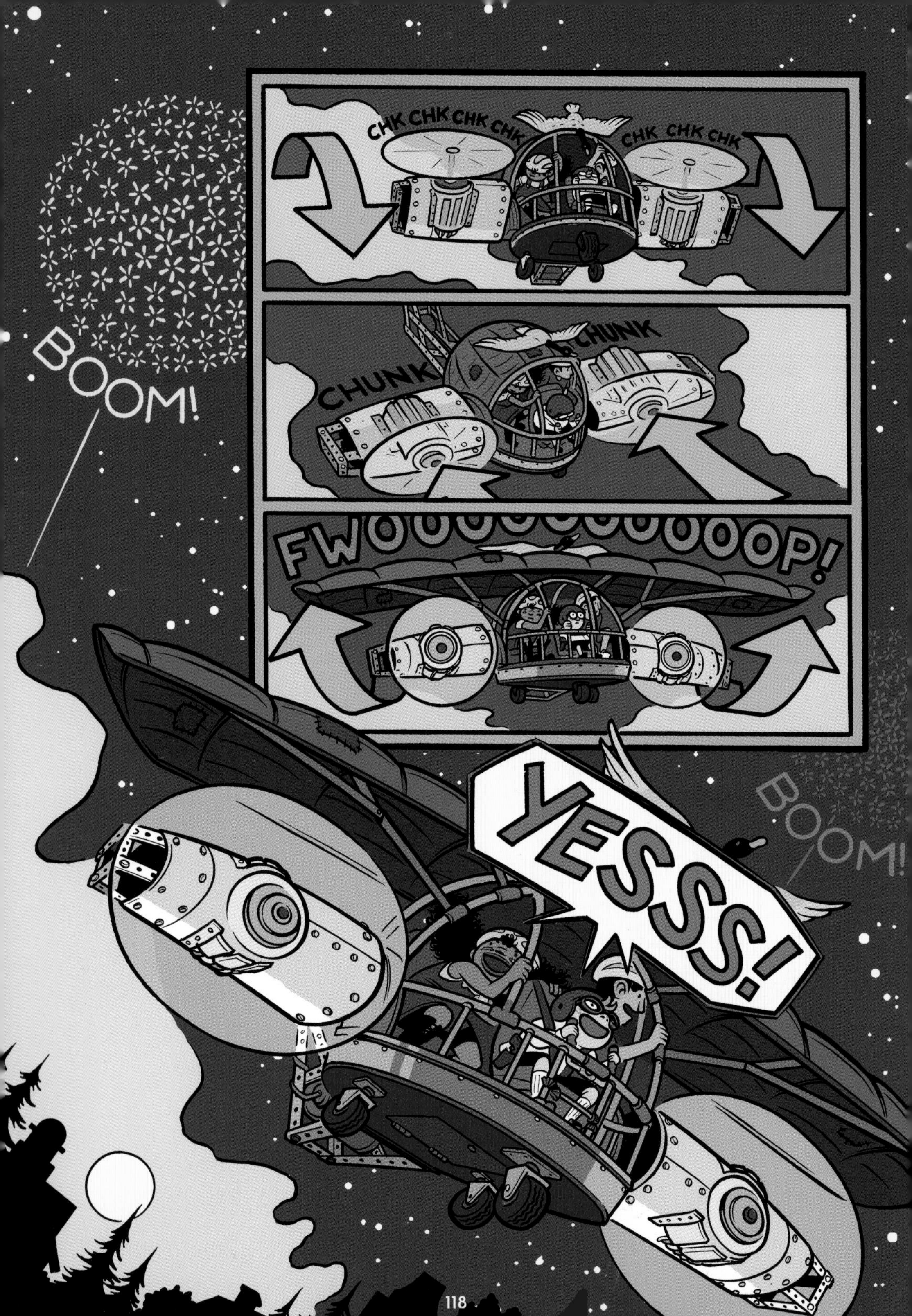
CHK CHK CHK CHK
CHK CHK CHK
CHUNK
CHUNK
FWOOOOOOOOOOOP!
BOOM!
YESSS!
BOOM!

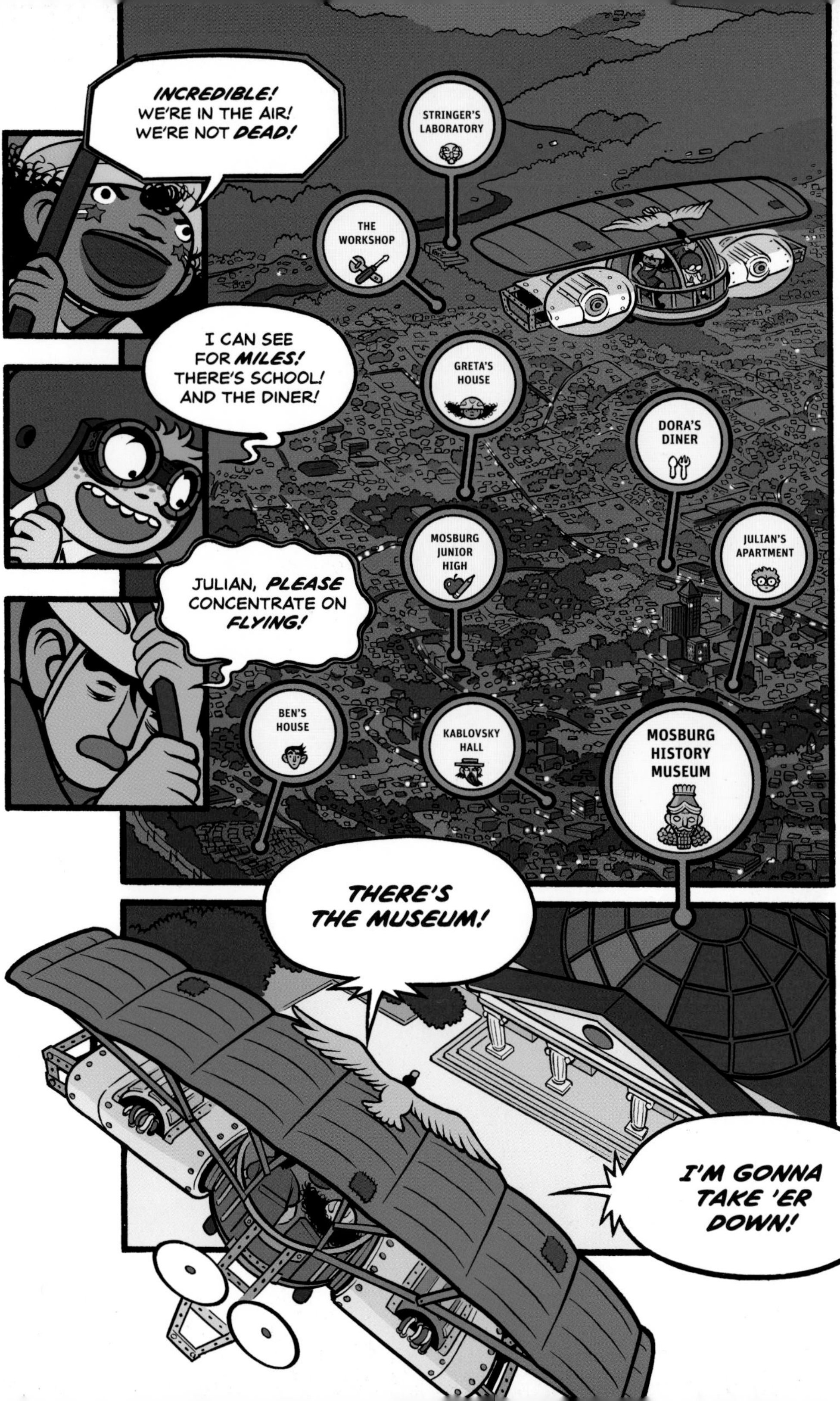
INCREDIBLE! WE'RE IN THE AIR! WE'RE NOT DEAD!
STRINGER'S LABORATORY
THE WORKSHOP
I CAN SEE FOR MILES! THERE'S SCHOOL! AND THE DINER!
GRETA'S HOUSE
DORA'S DINER
MOSBURG JUNIOR HIGH
JULIAN'S APARTMENT
JULIAN, PLEASE CONCENTRATE ON FLYING!
BEN'S HOUSE
KABLOVSKY HALL
MOSBURG HISTORY MUSEUM
THERE'S THE MUSEUM!
I'M GONNA TAKE 'ER DOWN!

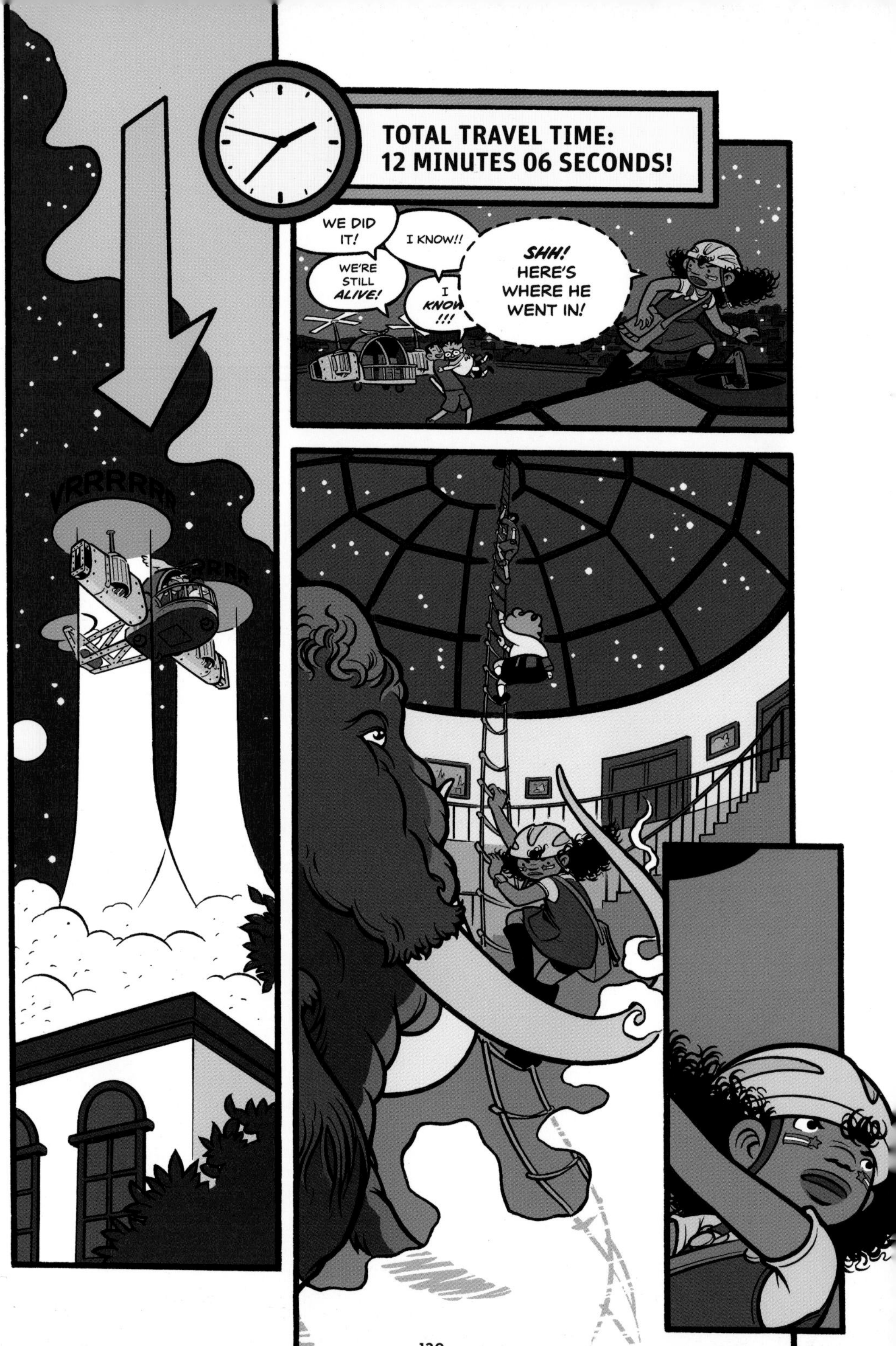

VRRRRRRR
TOTAL TRAVEL TIME:
12 MINUTES 06 SECONDS!
WE DID IT!
I KNOW!!
WE'RE STILL ALIVE!
I KNOW!!!
SHH! HERE'S WHERE HE WENT IN!

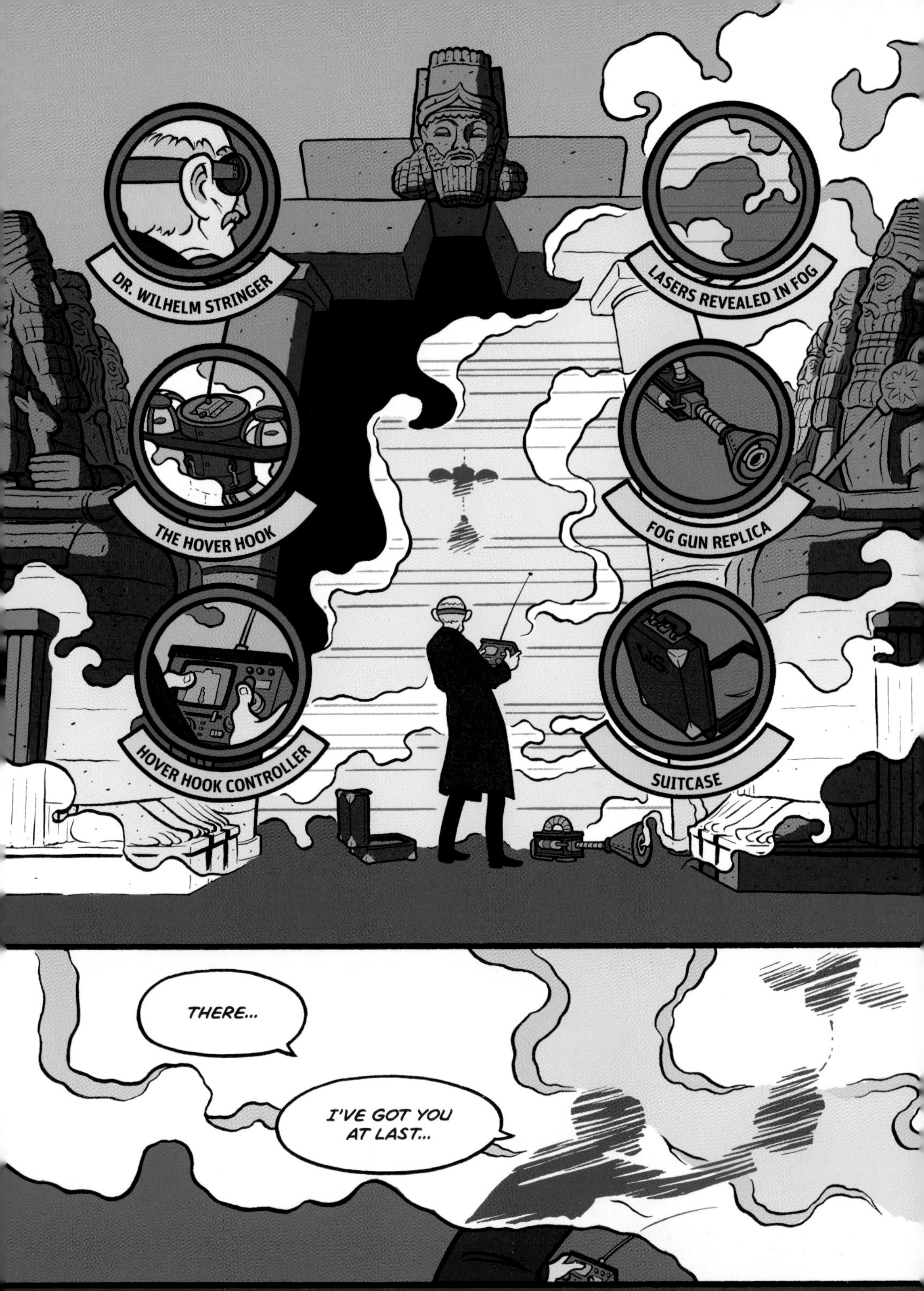
DR. WILHELM STRINGER
LASERS REVEALED IN FOG
THE HOVER HOOK
FOG GUN REPLICA
HOVER HOOK CONTROLLER
SUITCASE
W.S.
THERE...
I'VE GOT YOU AT LAST...

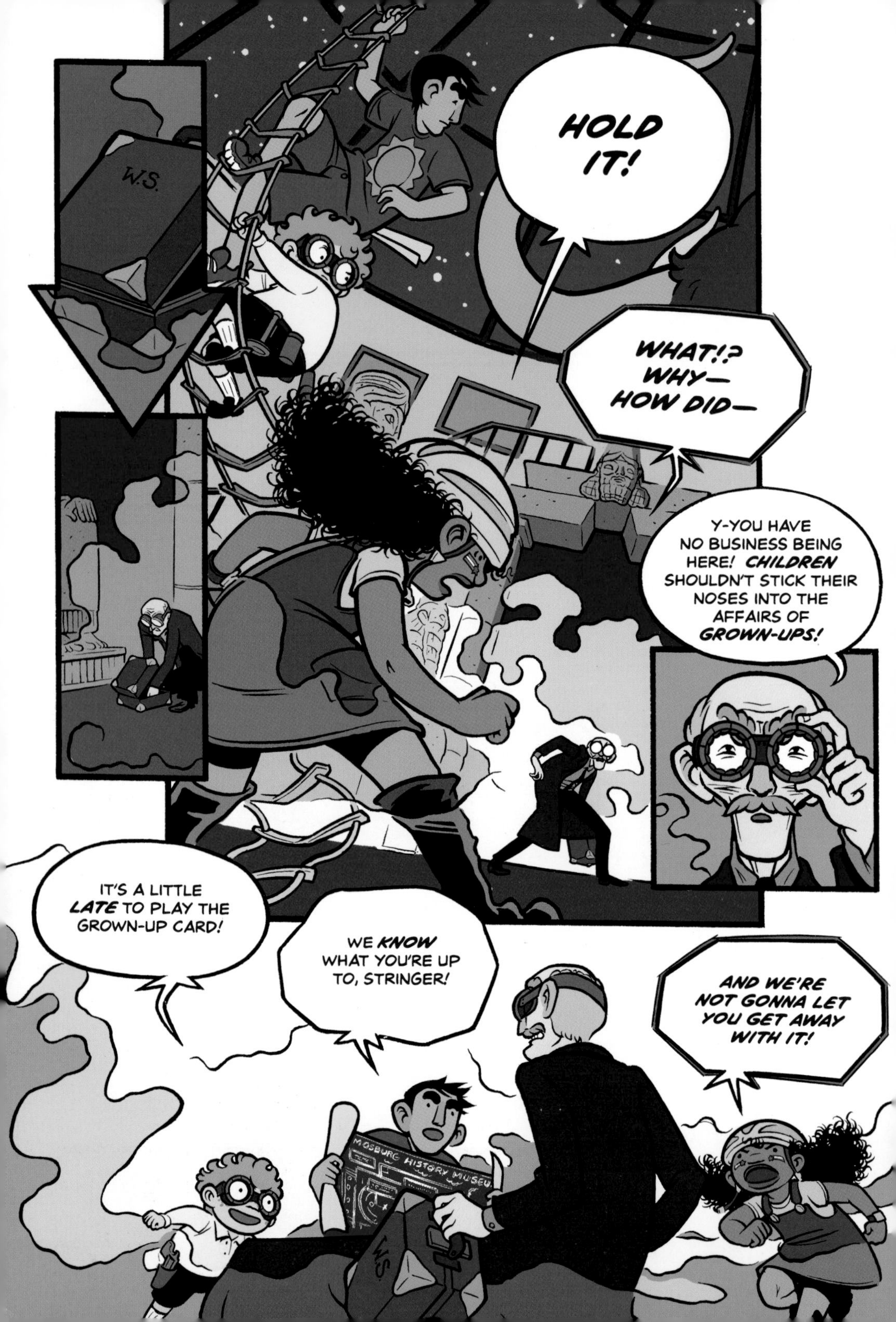
W.S.
HOLD IT!
WHAT!? WHY— HOW DID—
Y-YOU HAVE NO BUSINESS BEING HERE! CHILDREN SHOULDN'T STICK THEIR NOSES INTO THE AFFAIRS OF GROWN-UPS!
IT'S A LITTLE LATE TO PLAY THE GROWN-UP CARD!
WE KNOW WHAT YOU'RE UP TO, STRINGER!
AND WE'RE NOT GONNA LET YOU GET AWAY WITH IT!
MOSBURG HISTORY MUSEUM
W.S.

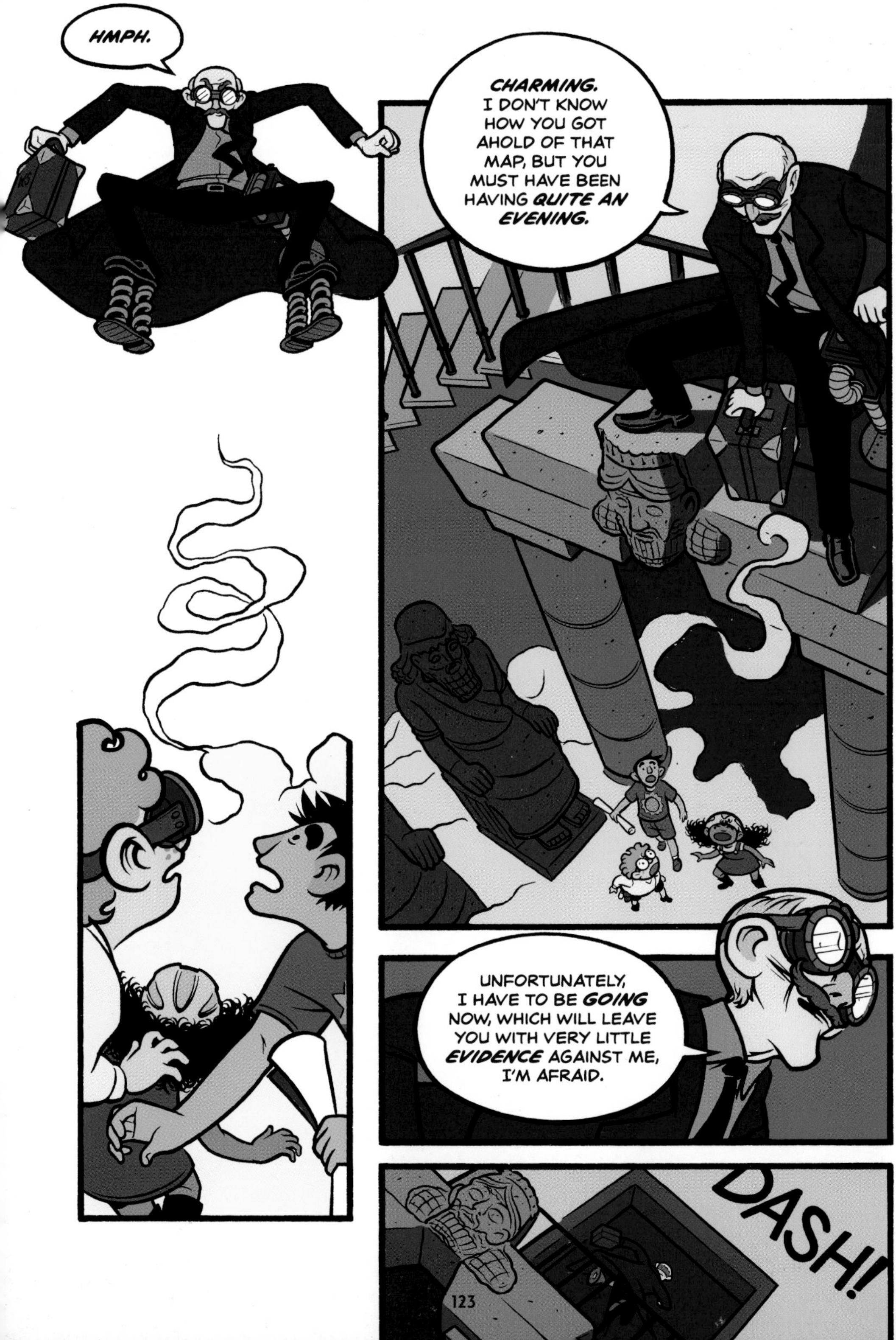
HMPH.
CHARMING. I DON'T KNOW HOW YOU GOT AHOLD OF THAT MAP, BUT YOU MUST HAVE BEEN HAVING QUITE AN EVENING.
UNFORTUNATELY, I HAVE TO BE GOING NOW, WHICH WILL LEAVE YOU WITH VERY LITTLE EVIDENCE AGAINST ME, I'M AFRAID.
DASH!

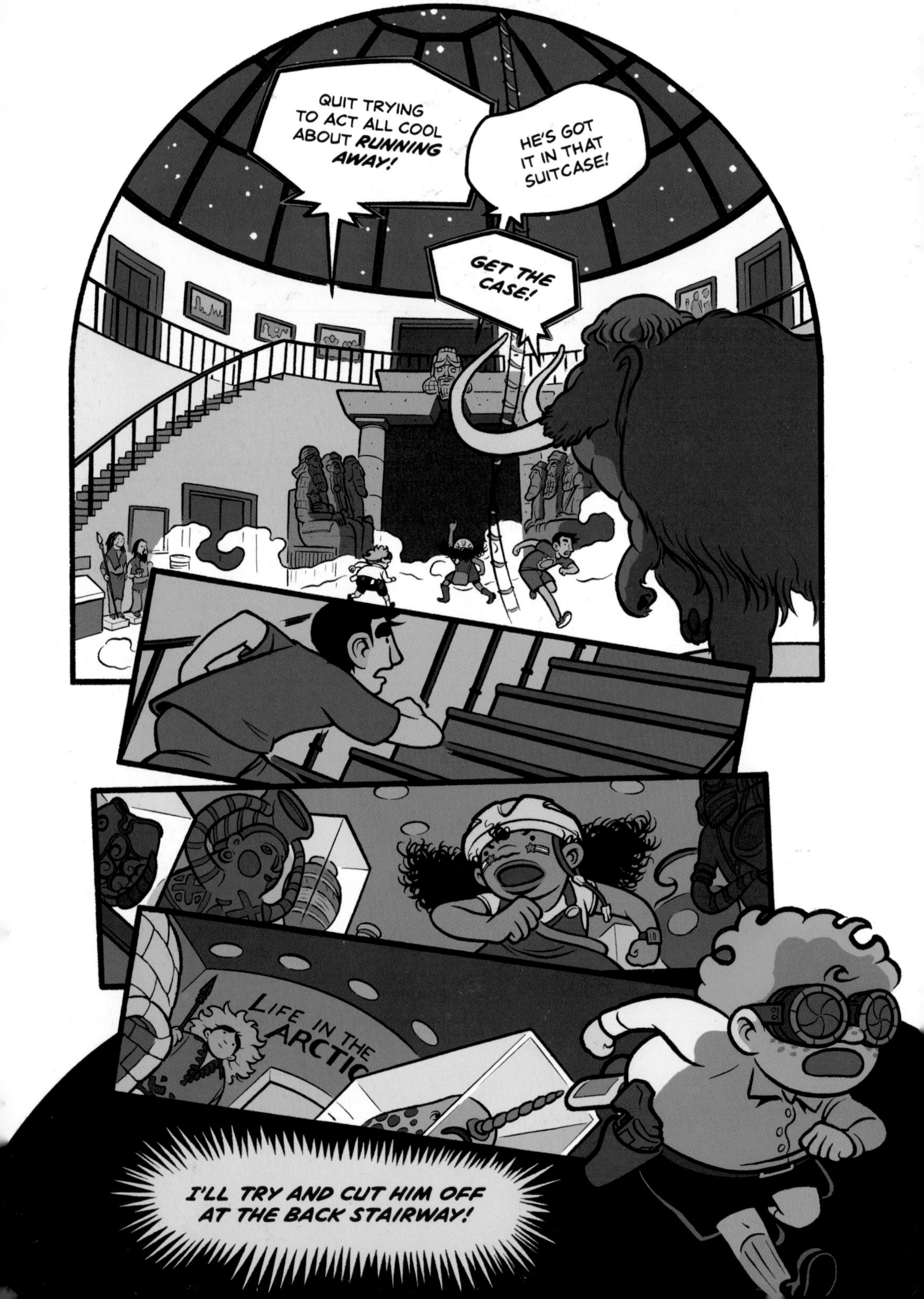

QUIT TRYING TO ACT ALL COOL ABOUT *RUNNING AWAY!*
HE'S GOT IT IN THAT SUITCASE!
GET THE CASE!
LIFE IN THE ARCTIC
I'LL TRY AND CUT HIM OFF AT THE BACK STAIRWAY!

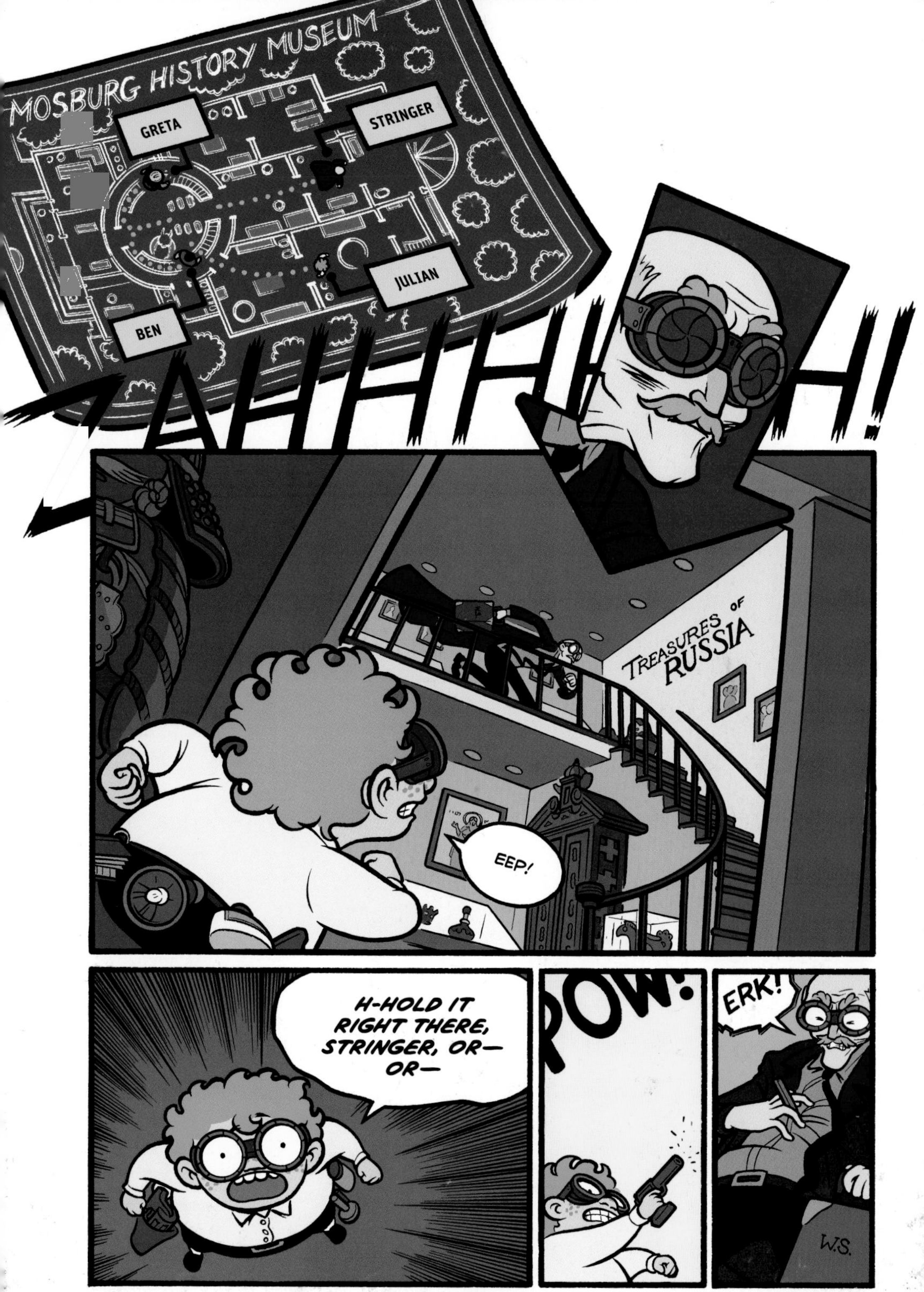
MOSBURG HISTORY MUSEUM
GRETA
STRINGER
JULIAN
BEN
AHHHHHHH!
TREASURES OF RUSSIA
EEP!
H-HOLD IT RIGHT THERE, STRINGER, OR— OR—
POW!
ERK!
W.S.

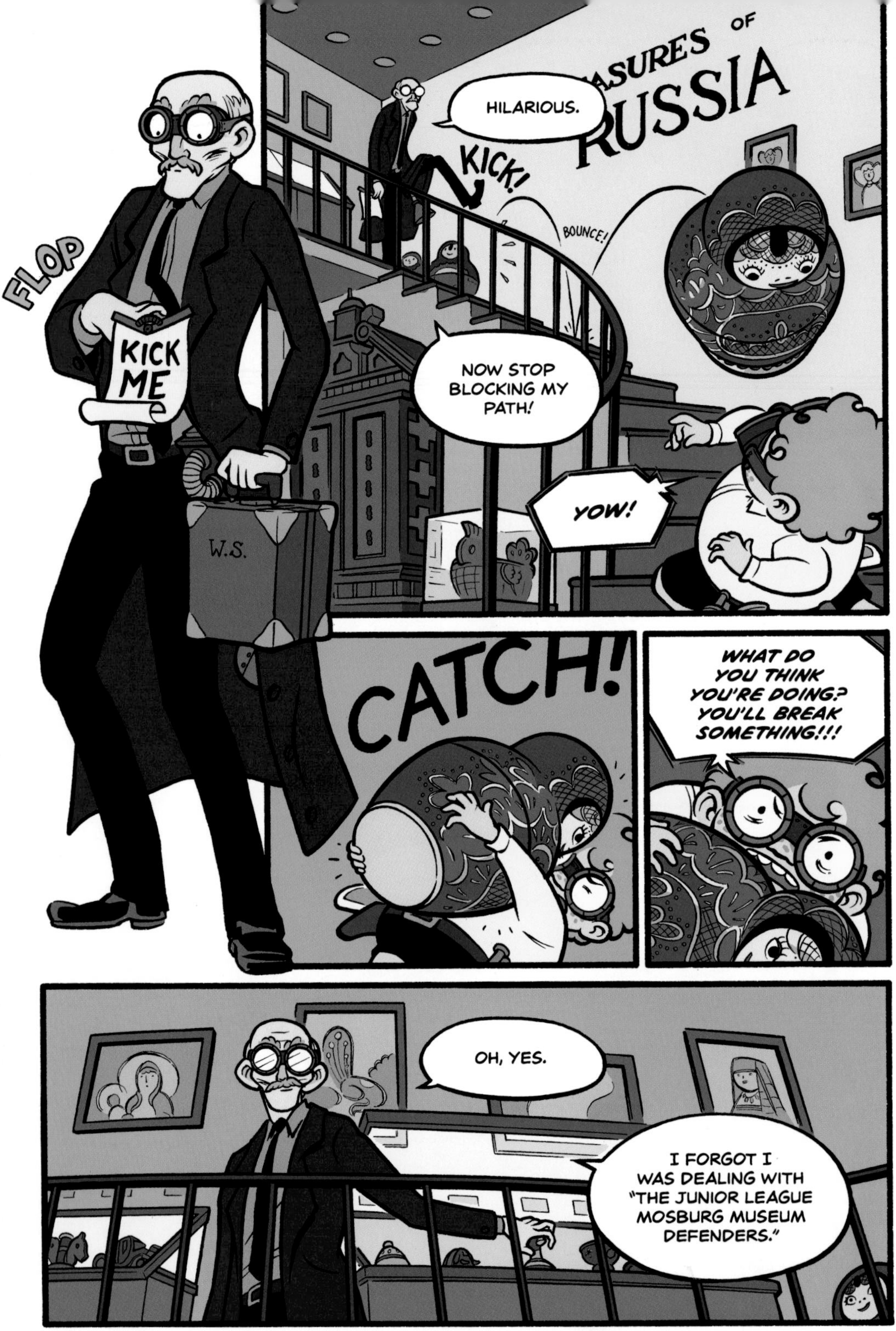

ASURES OF
RUSSIA
HILARIOUS.
KICK!
BOUNCE!
FLOP
KICK ME
NOW STOP BLOCKING MY PATH!
YOW!
W.S.
CATCH!
WHAT DO YOU THINK YOU'RE DOING? YOU'LL BREAK SOMETHING!!!
OH, YES.
I FORGOT I WAS DEALING WITH "THE JUNIOR LEAGUE MOSBURG MUSEUM DEFENDERS."

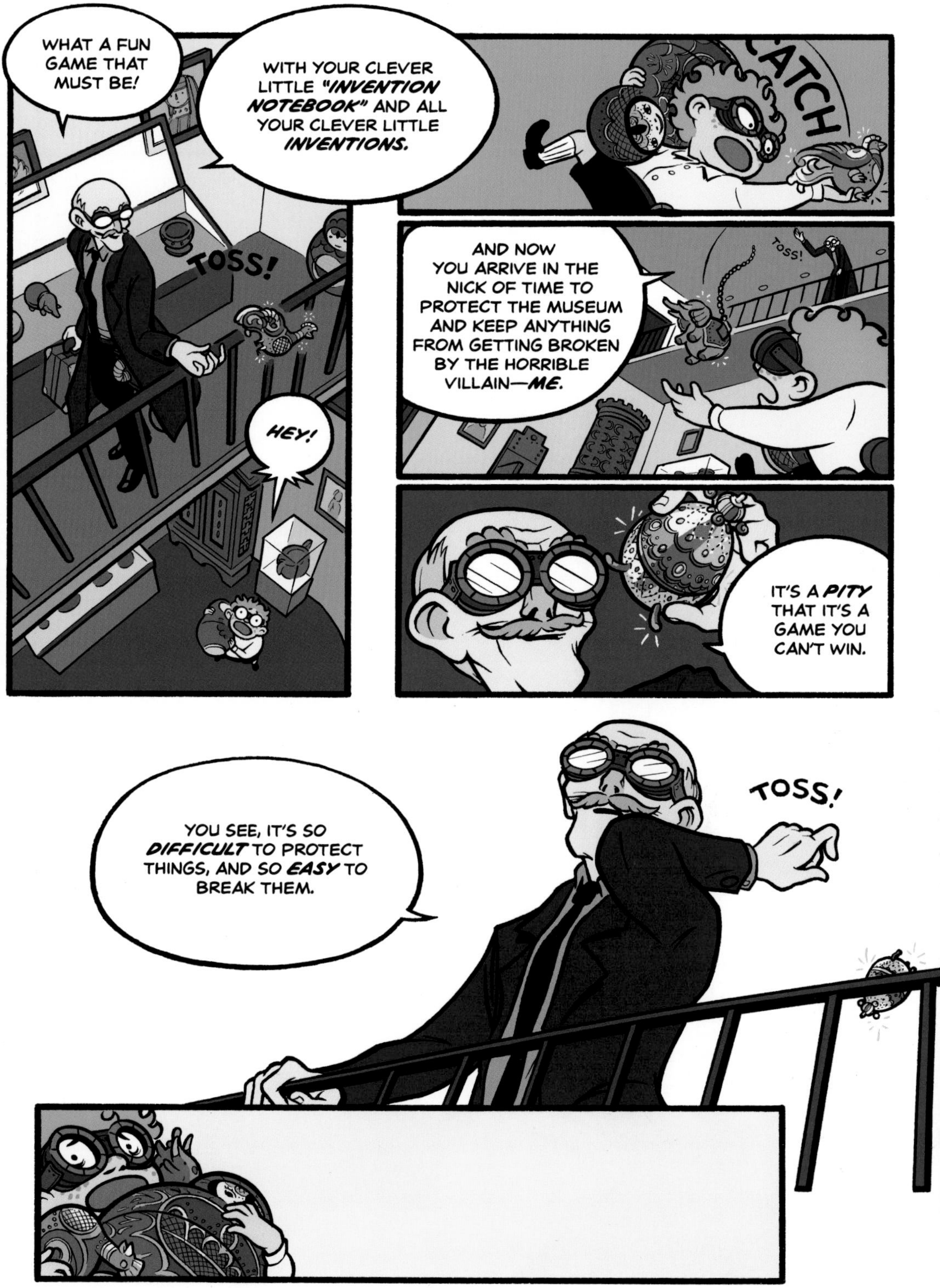
WHAT A FUN GAME THAT MUST BE!
WITH YOUR CLEVER LITTLE "INVENTION NOTEBOOK" AND ALL YOUR CLEVER LITTLE INVENTIONS.
TOSS!
HEY!
CATCH
AND NOW YOU ARRIVE IN THE NICK OF TIME TO PROTECT THE MUSEUM AND KEEP ANYTHING FROM GETTING BROKEN BY THE HORRIBLE VILLAIN—ME.
TOSS!
IT'S A PITY THAT IT'S A GAME YOU CAN'T WIN.
YOU SEE, IT'S SO DIFFICULT TO PROTECT THINGS, AND SO EASY TO BREAK THEM.
TOSS!

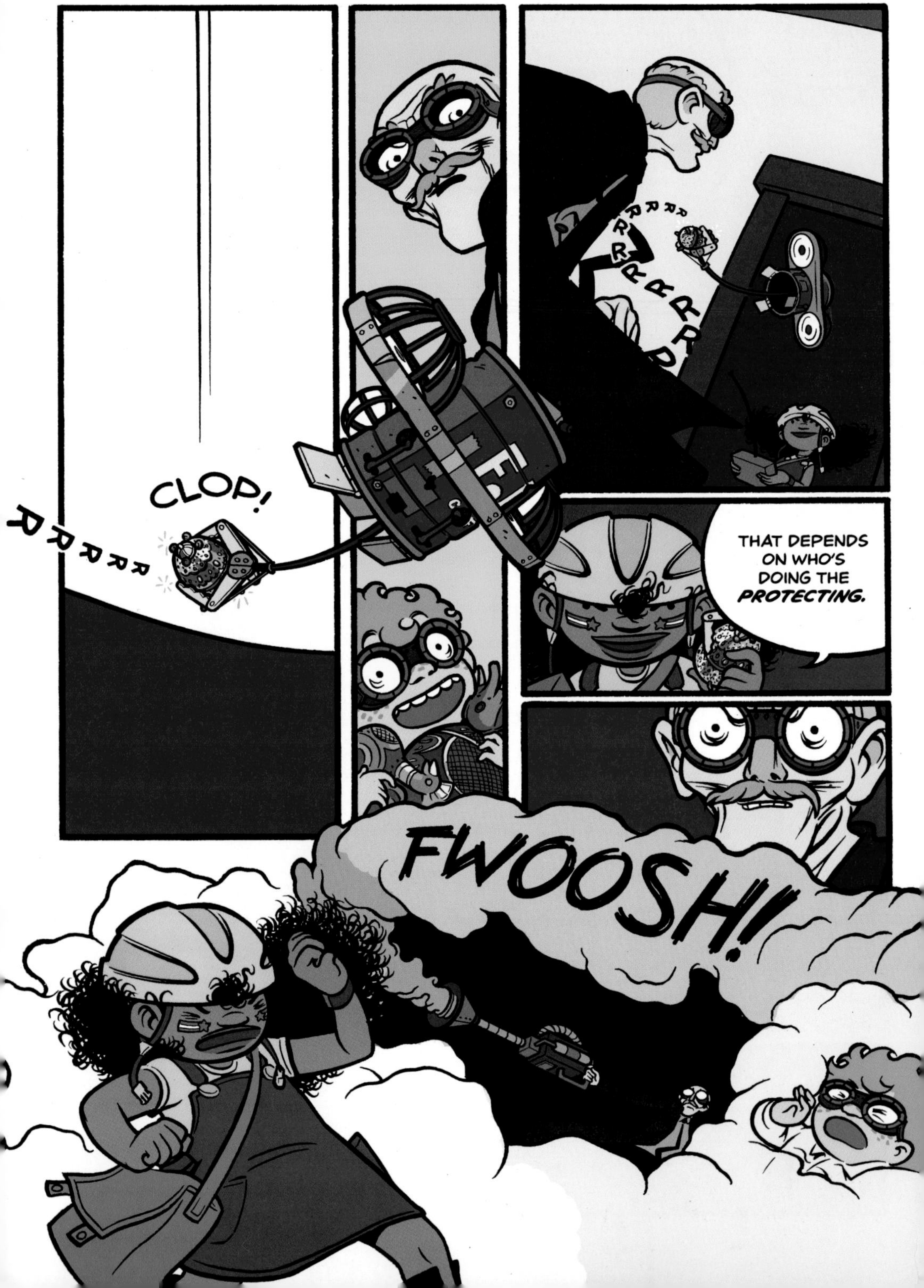
RRRRRRRRRR
CLOP!
RRRRRR
THAT DEPENDS ON WHO'S DOING THE *PROTECTING.*
FWOOSH!!

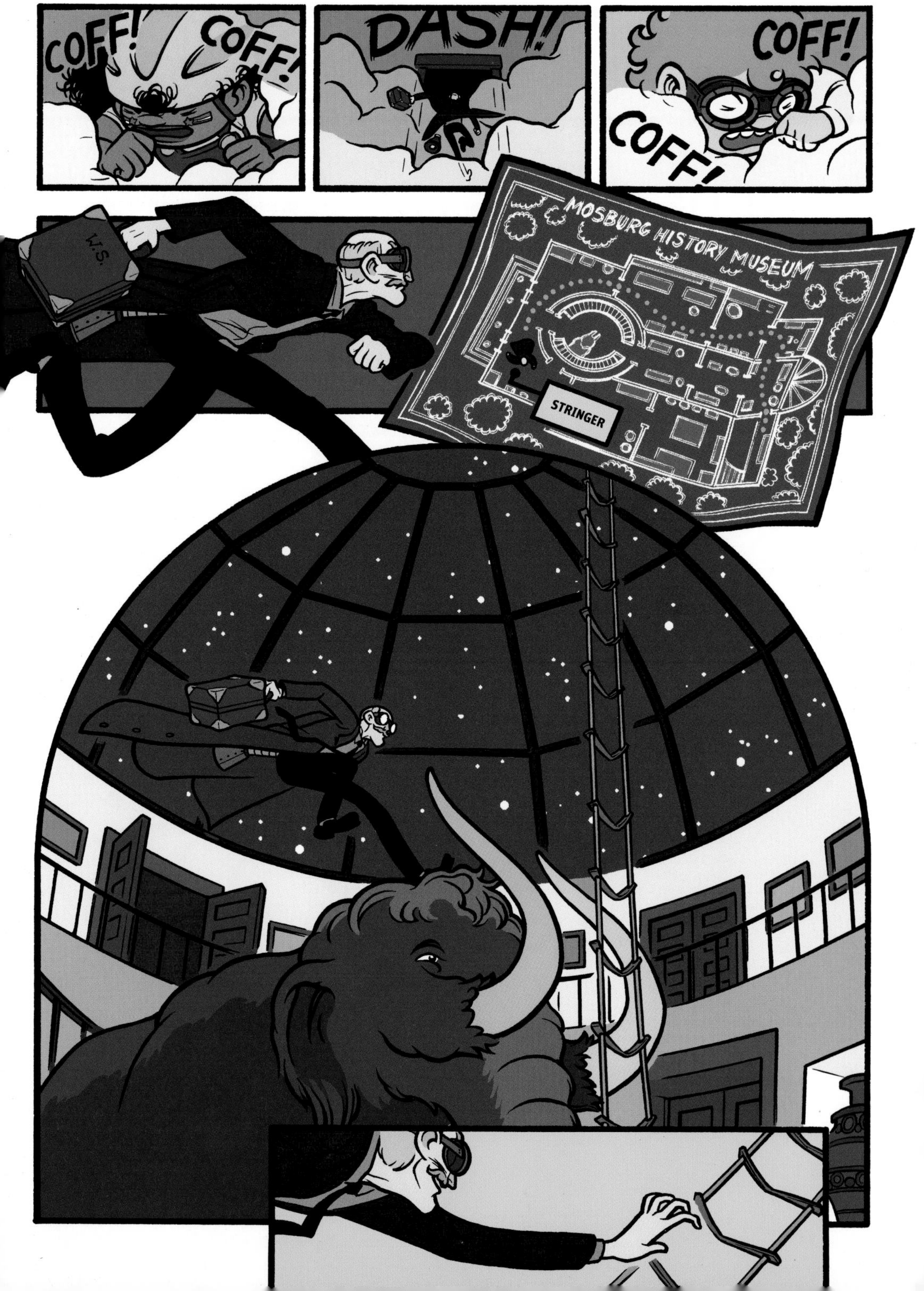
COFF! COFF!
DASH!
COFF!
COFF!
MOSBURG HISTORY MUSEUM
STRINGER
W.S.

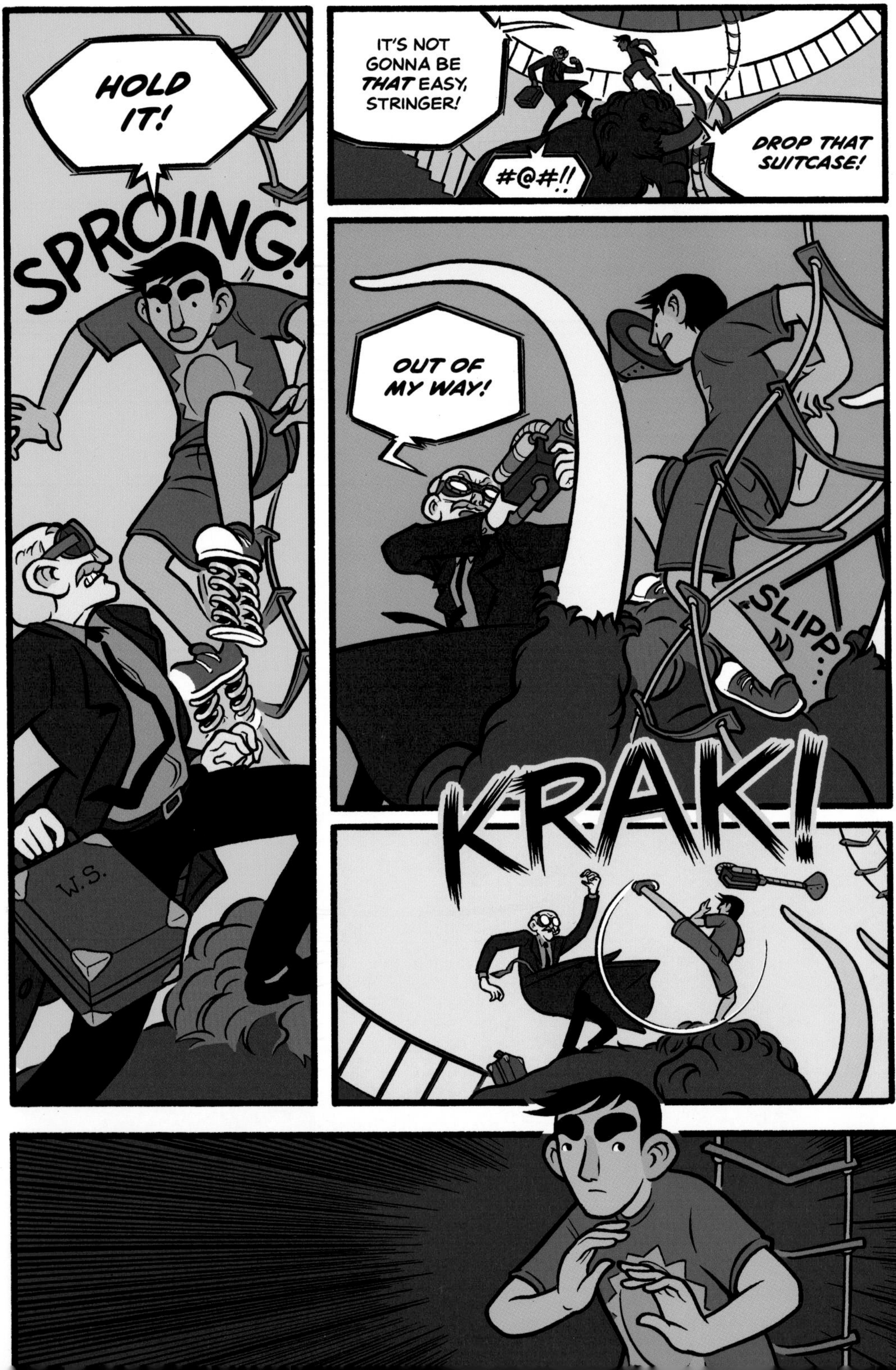
HOLD IT!
SPROING!
IT'S NOT GONNA BE *THAT* EASY, STRINGER!
#@#!!
DROP THAT SUITCASE!
W.S.
OUT OF MY WAY!
SLIPP...
KRAK!

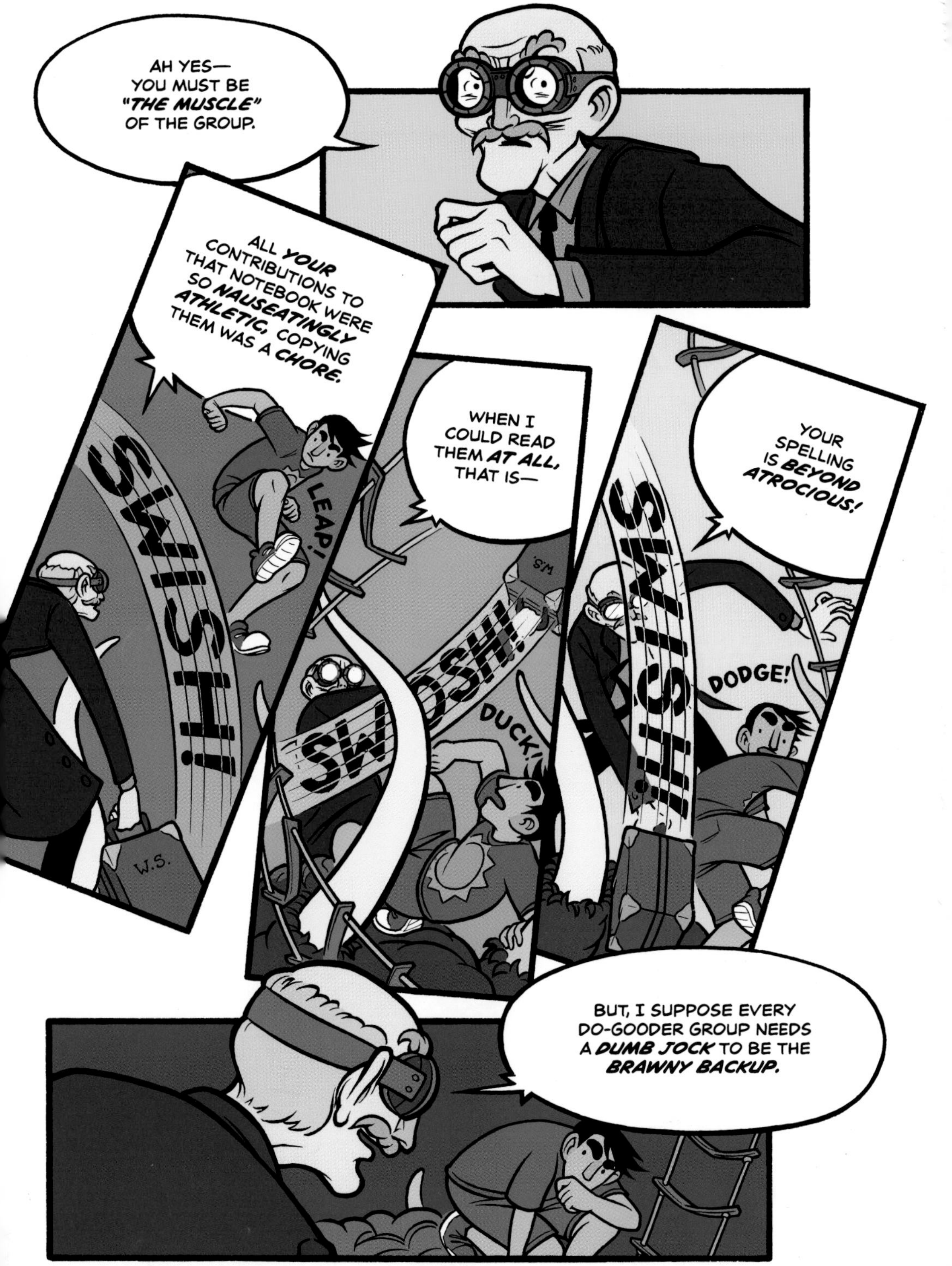
AH YES— YOU MUST BE "THE MUSCLE" OF THE GROUP.
ALL YOUR CONTRIBUTIONS TO THAT NOTEBOOK WERE SO NAUSEATINGLY ATHLETIC, COPYING THEM WAS A CHORE.
SWISH!
LEAP!
W.S.
WHEN I COULD READ THEM AT ALL, THAT IS—
SWOOSH!
DUCK!
W.S.
YOUR SPELLING IS BEYOND ATROCIOUS!
SWISH!
DODGE!
BUT, I SUPPOSE EVERY DO-GOODER GROUP NEEDS A DUMB JOCK TO BE THE BRAWNY BACKUP.

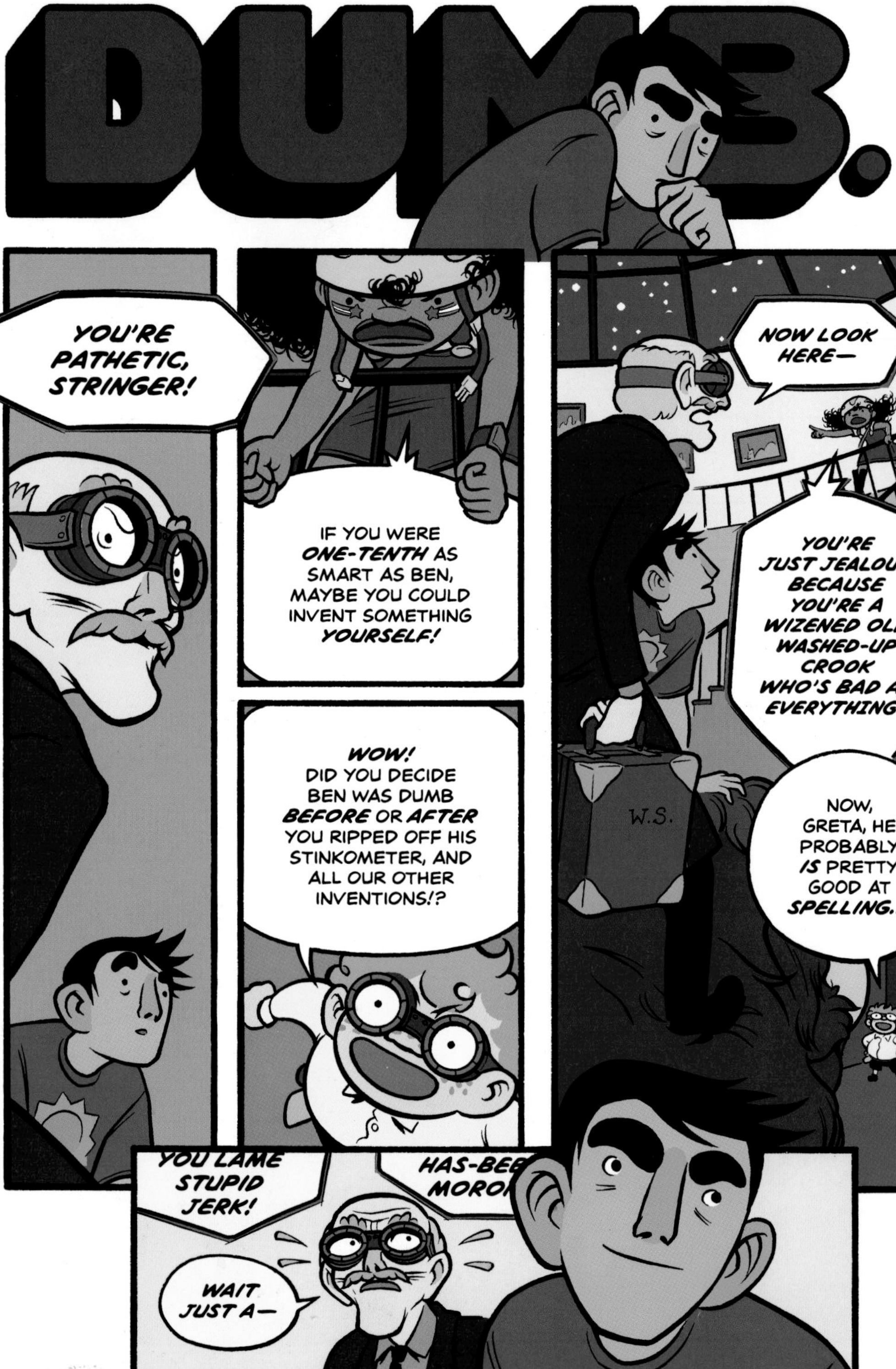
DUMB.
YOU'RE PATHETIC, STRINGER!
IF YOU WERE ONE-TENTH AS SMART AS BEN, MAYBE YOU COULD INVENT SOMETHING YOURSELF!
WOW! DID YOU DECIDE BEN WAS DUMB BEFORE OR AFTER YOU RIPPED OFF HIS STINKOMETER, AND ALL OUR OTHER INVENTIONS!?
NOW LOOK HERE—
YOU'RE JUST JEALOUS BECAUSE YOU'RE A WIZENED OLD WASHED-UP CROOK WHO'S BAD AT EVERYTHING!
W.S.
NOW, GRETA, HE PROBABLY IS PRETTY GOOD AT SPELLING...
YOU LAME STUPID JERK!
WAIT JUST A—

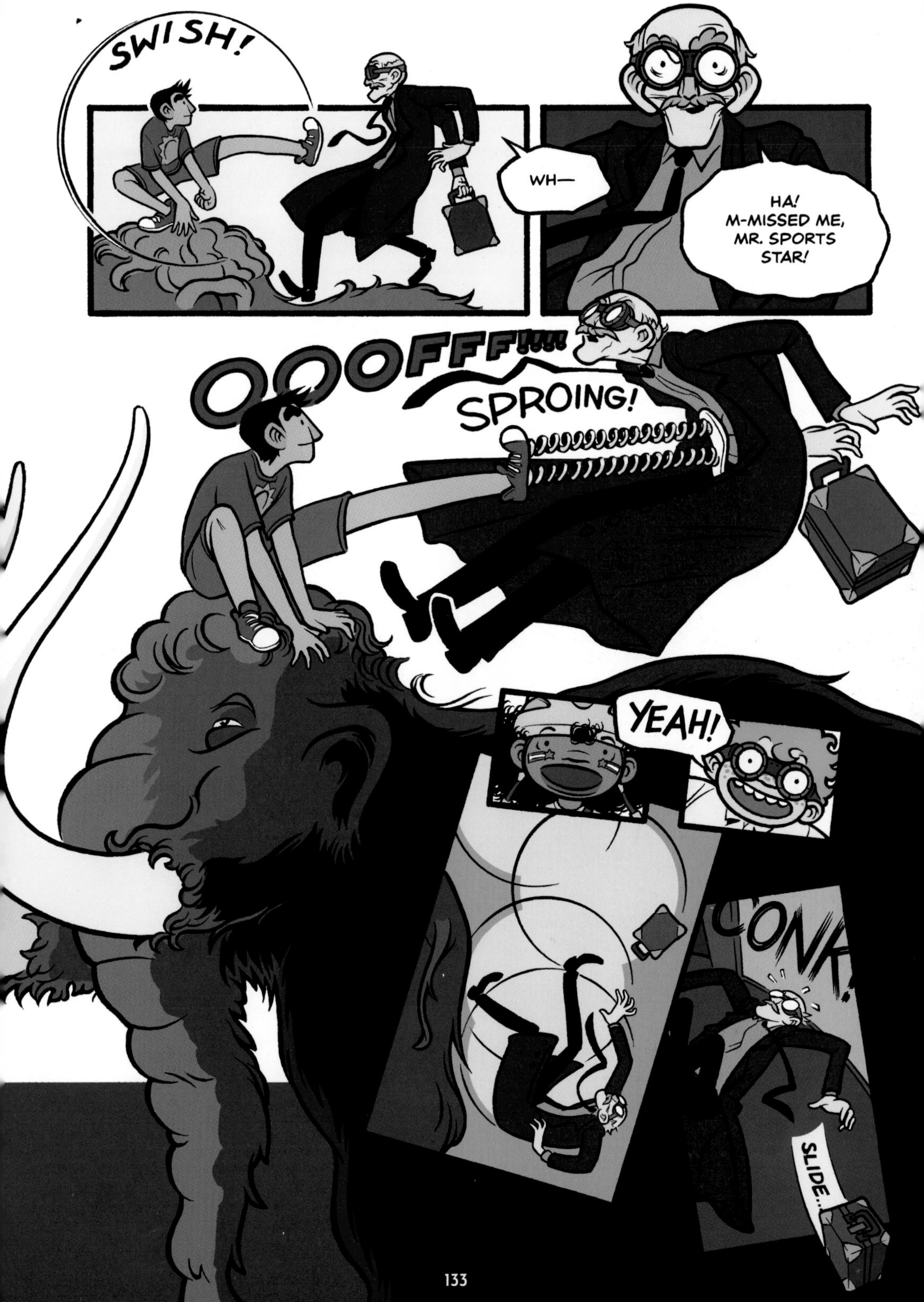
SWISH!
WH—
HA! M-MISSED ME, MR. SPORTS STAR!
OOOFFF!!!!
SPROING!
YEAH!
CONK!
SLIDE...

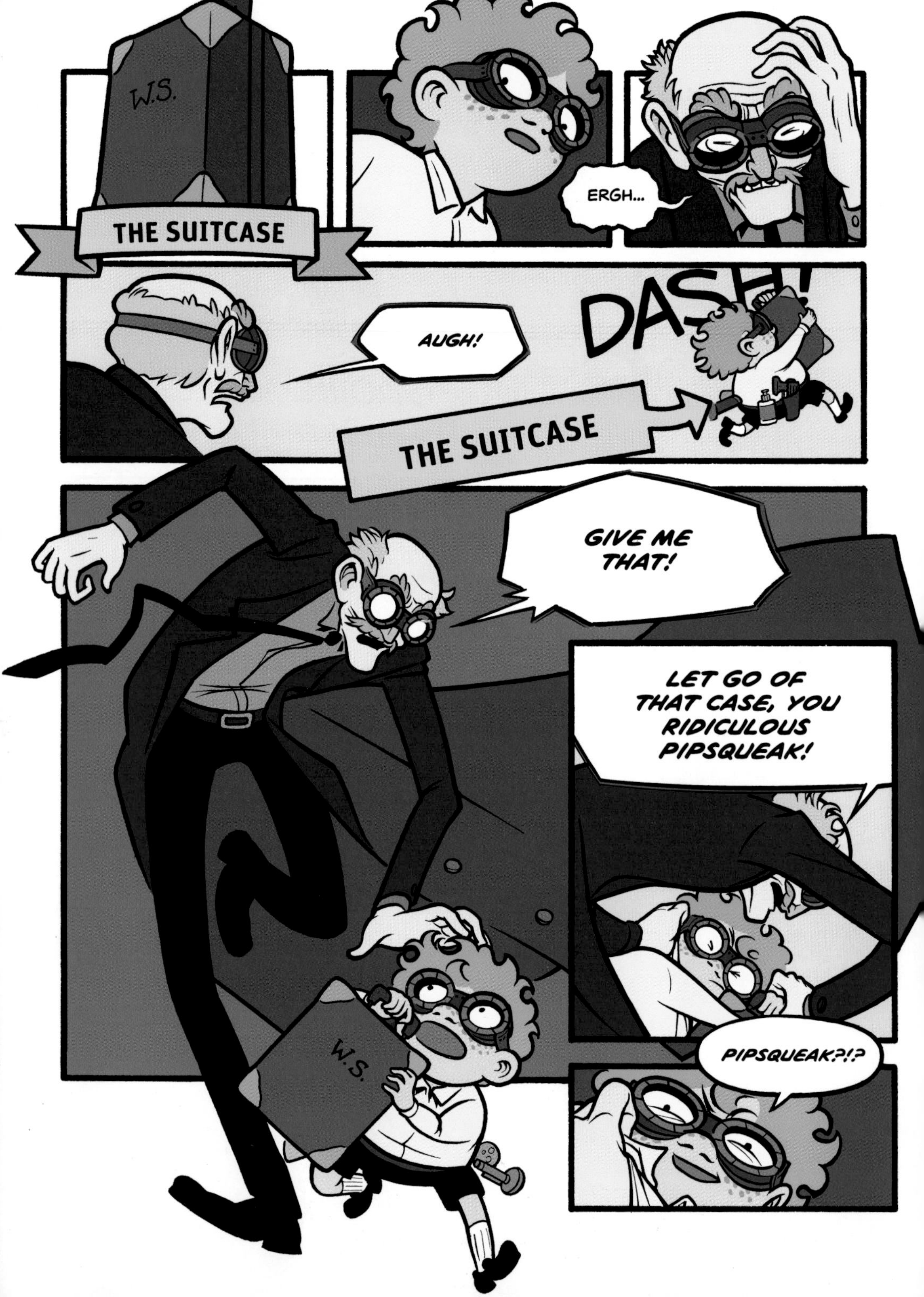

W.S.
THE SUITCASE
ERGH...
AUGH!
DASH!
THE SUITCASE
GIVE ME THAT!
W.S.
LET GO OF THAT CASE, YOU RIDICULOUS PIPSQUEAK!
PIPSQUEAK?!?

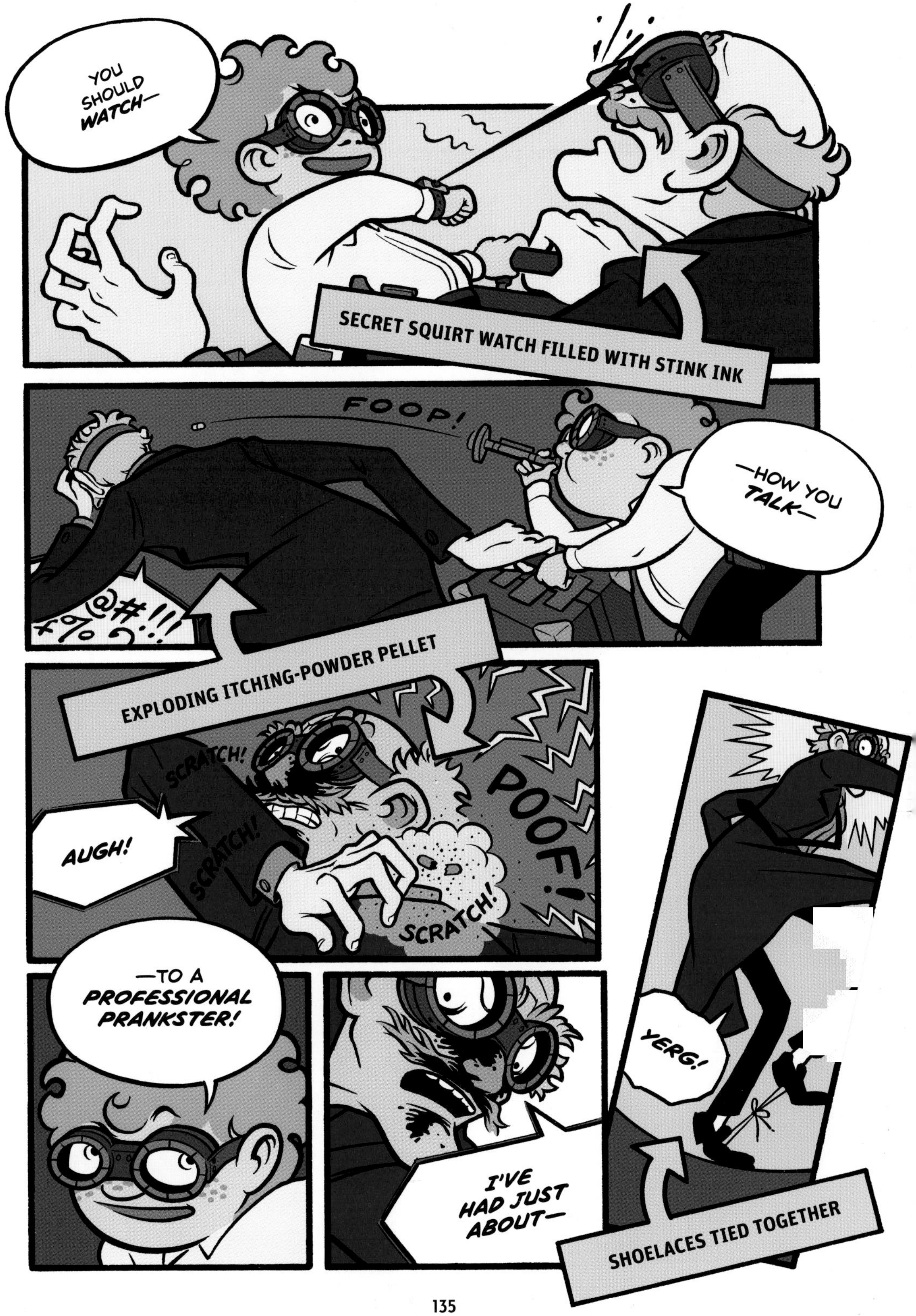
YOU SHOULD WATCH—
SECRET SQUIRT WATCH FILLED WITH STINK INK
FOOP!
—HOW YOU TALK—
*%@#!!!
EXPLODING ITCHING-POWDER PELLET
SCRATCH!
SCRATCH!
AUGH!
POOOF!!
SCRATCH!
—TO A PROFESSIONAL PRANKSTER!
I'VE HAD JUST ABOUT—
YERG!
SHOELACES TIED TOGETHER

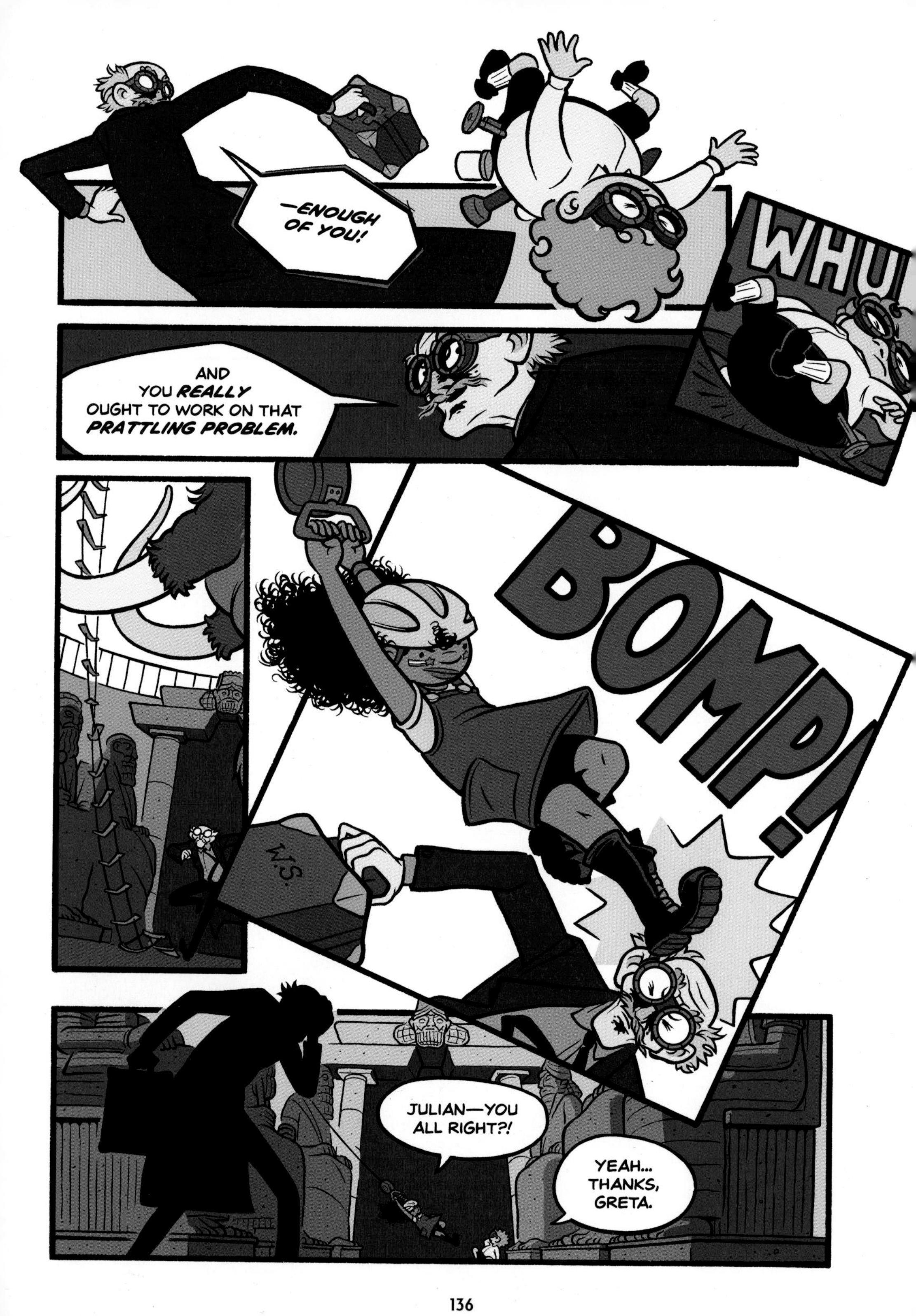
—ENOUGH OF YOU!
WHU
AND YOU REALLY OUGHT TO WORK ON THAT PRATTLING PROBLEM.
BOMP!
W.S.
JULIAN—YOU ALL RIGHT?!
YEAH... THANKS, GRETA.

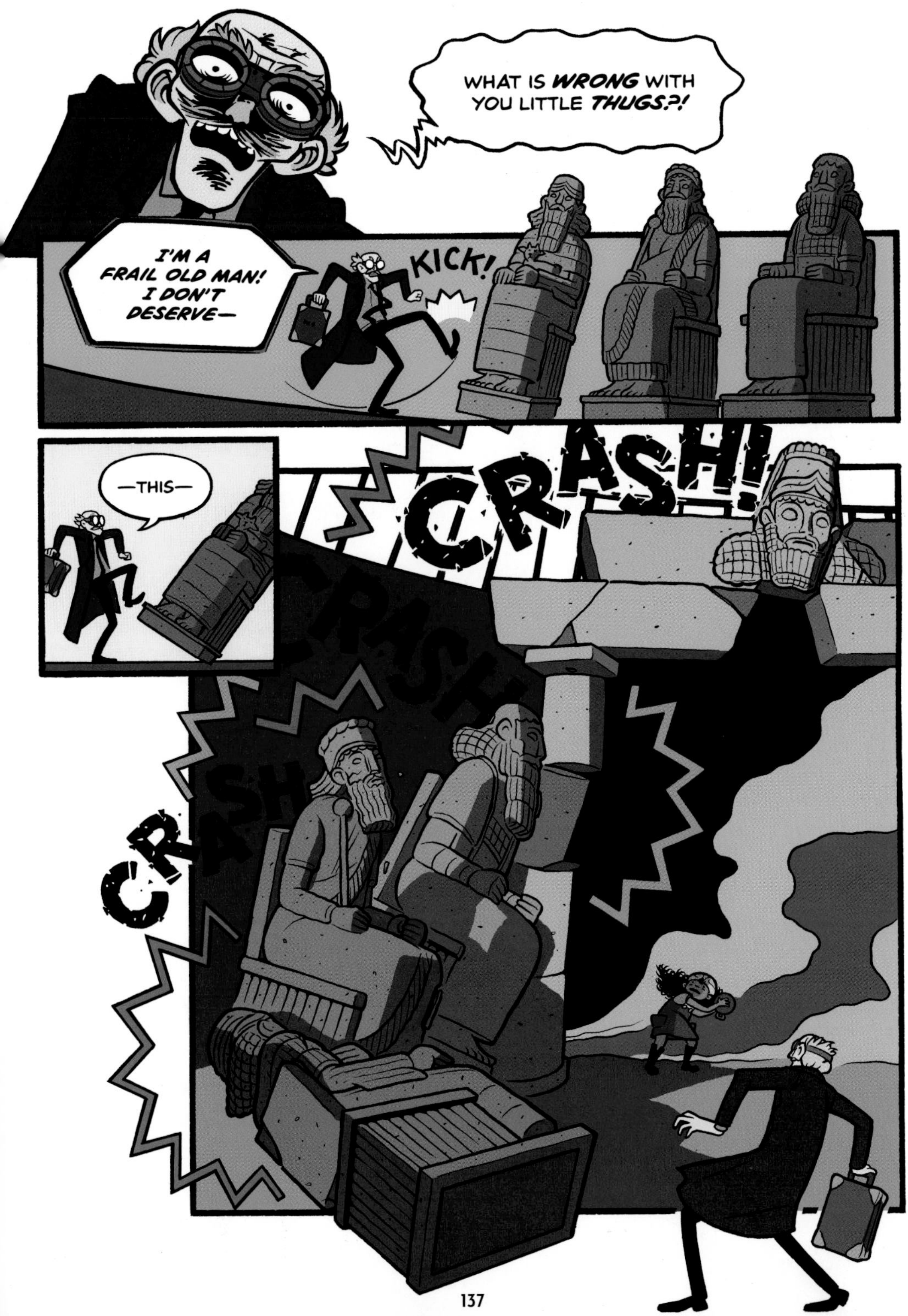
WHAT IS WRONG WITH YOU LITTLE THUGS?!
I'M A FRAIL OLD MAN! I DON'T DESERVE—
KICK!
—THIS—
CRASH!
CRASH
CRASH

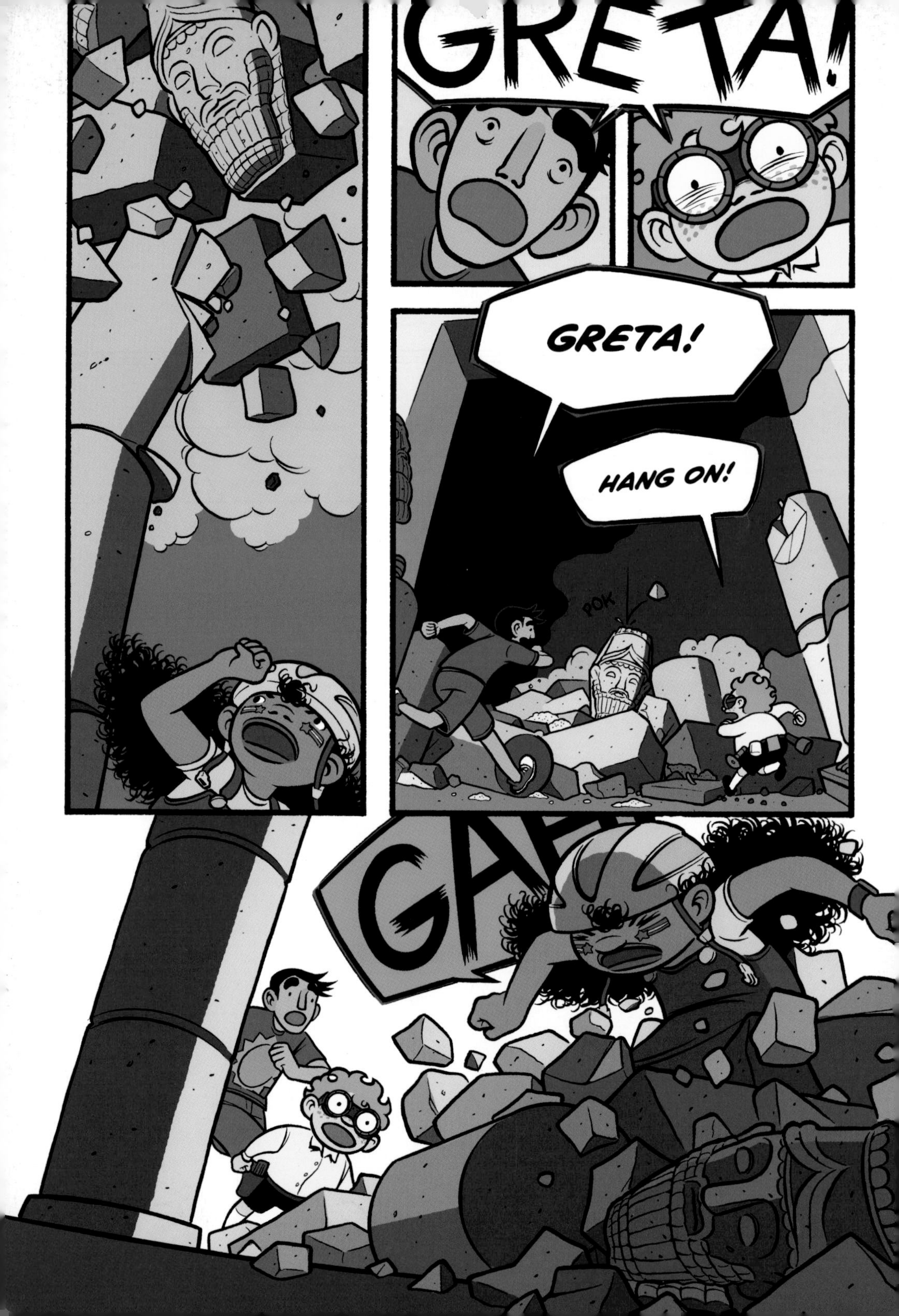
GRETA!
GRETA!
HANG ON!
POK
GA

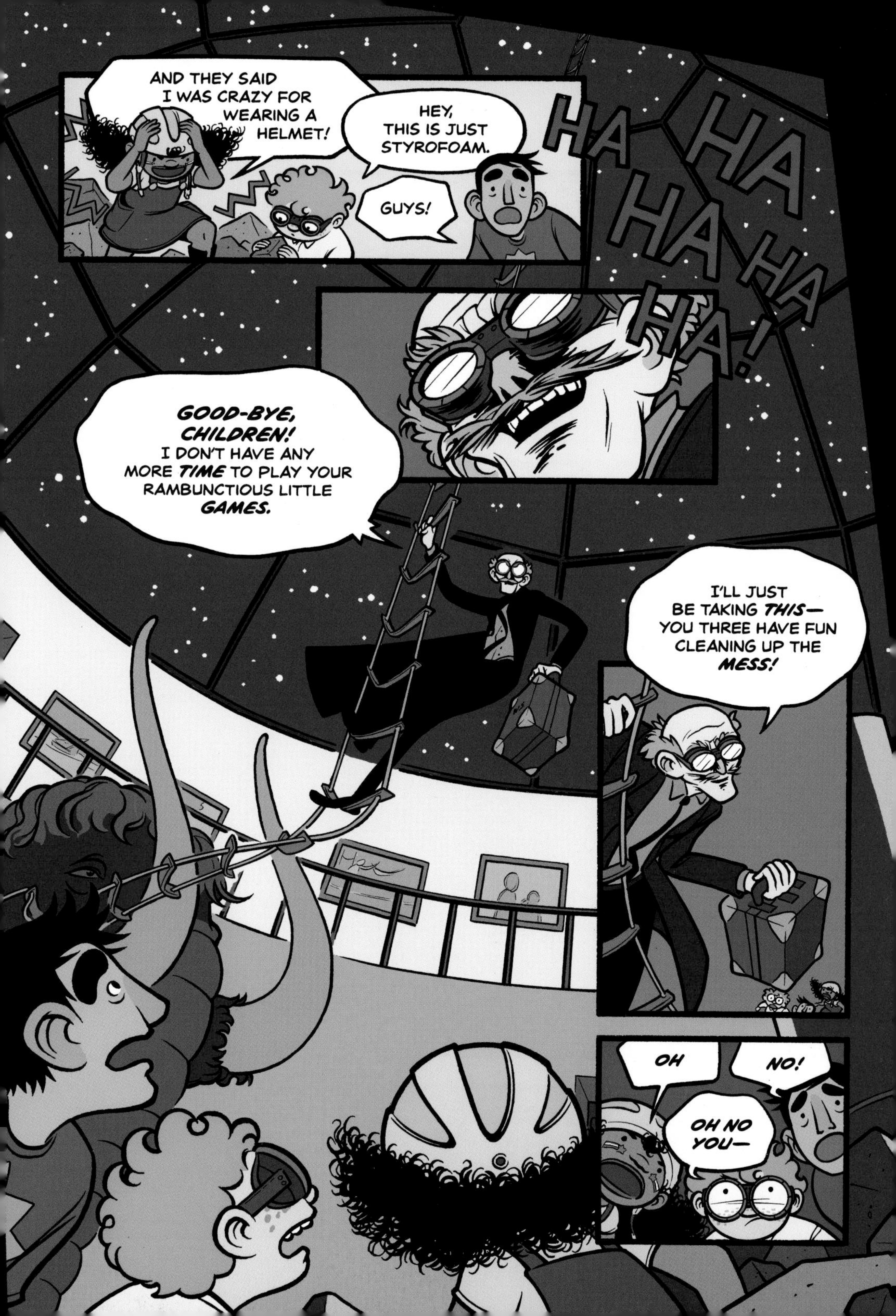

AND THEY SAID I WAS CRAZY FOR WEARING A HELMET!
HEY, THIS IS JUST STYROFOAM.
GUYS!
HA HA HA HA HA HA!
GOOD-BYE, CHILDREN! I DON'T HAVE ANY MORE TIME TO PLAY YOUR RAMBUNCTIOUS LITTLE GAMES.
I'LL JUST BE TAKING THIS— YOU THREE HAVE FUN CLEANING UP THE MESS!
OH
NO!
OH NO YOU—

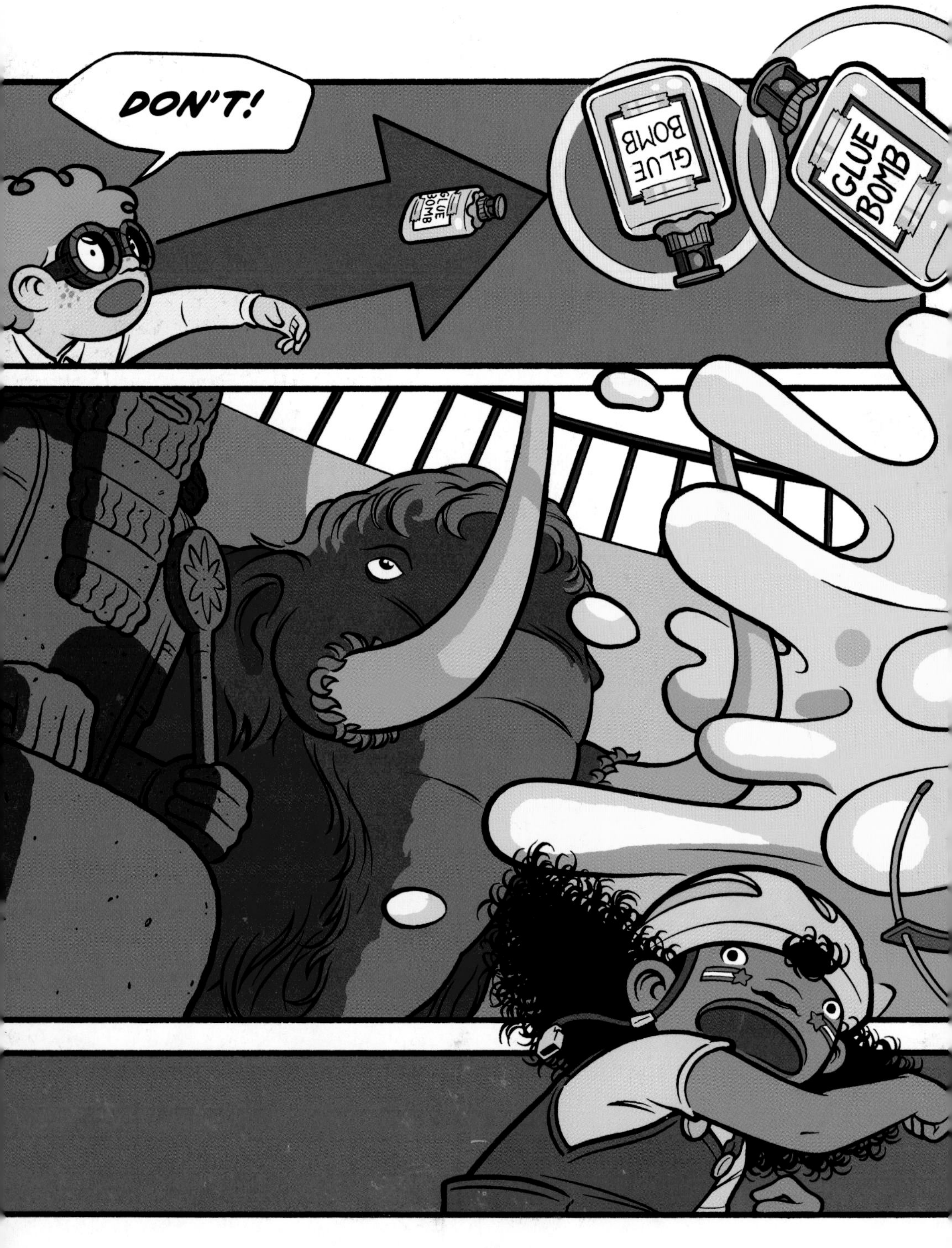
DON'T!
GLUE BOMB
GLUE BOMB
GLUE BOMB

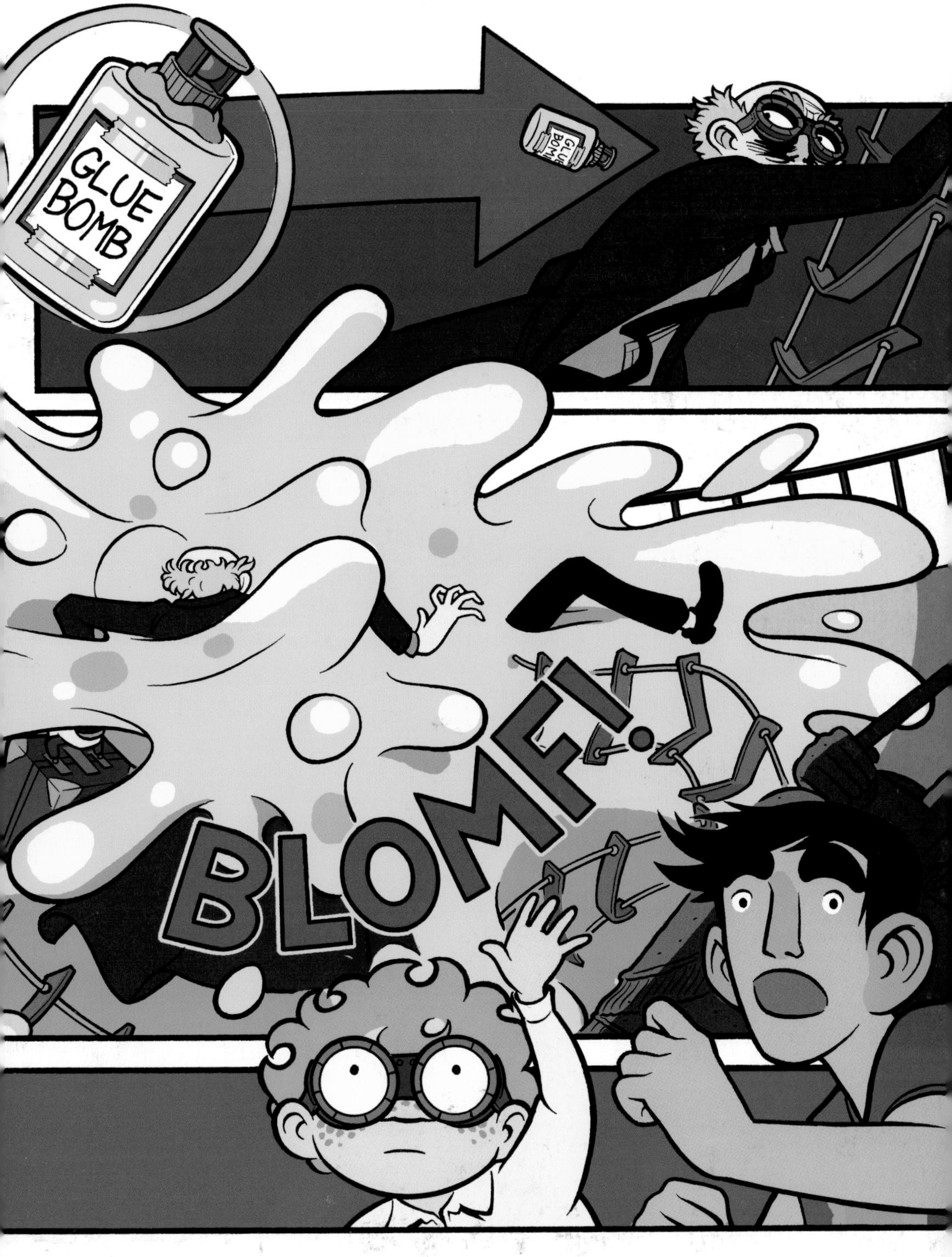
GLUE BOMB
GLUE BOMB
BLOMF!

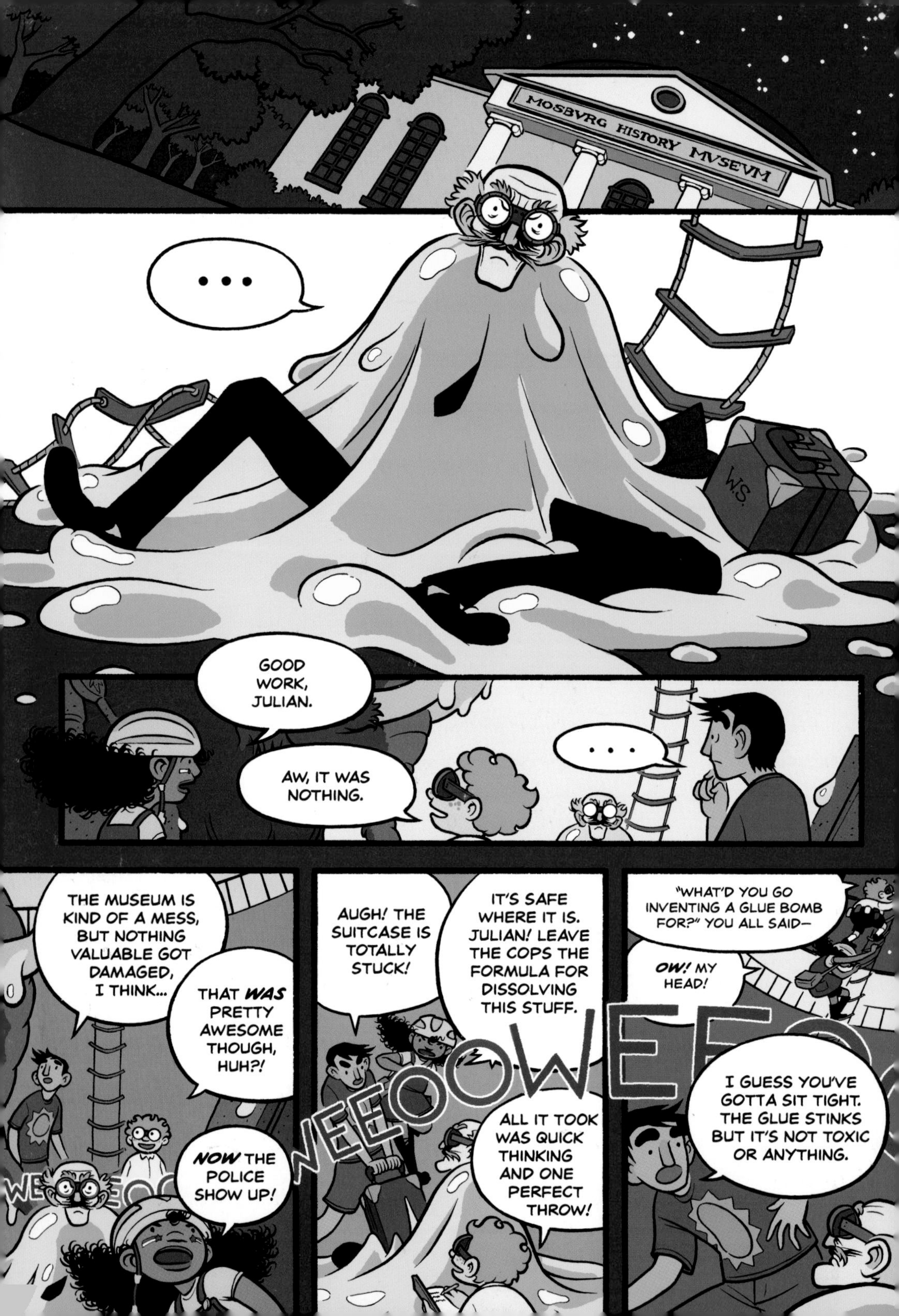
MOSBVRG HISTORY MVSEVM
...
W.S.
GOOD WORK, JULIAN.
AW, IT WAS NOTHING.
...
THE MUSEUM IS KIND OF A MESS, BUT NOTHING VALUABLE GOT DAMAGED, I THINK...
THAT WAS PRETTY AWESOME THOUGH, HUH?!
NOW THE POLICE SHOW UP!
AUGH! THE SUITCASE IS TOTALLY STUCK!
IT'S SAFE WHERE IT IS. JULIAN! LEAVE THE COPS THE FORMULA FOR DISSOLVING THIS STUFF.
ALL IT TOOK WAS QUICK THINKING AND ONE PERFECT THROW!
WEEOOWEEOOWEE
"WHAT'D YOU GO INVENTING A GLUE BOMB FOR?" YOU ALL SAID—
OW! MY HEAD!
I GUESS YOU'VE GOTTA SIT TIGHT. THE GLUE STINKS BUT IT'S NOT TOXIC OR ANYTHING.

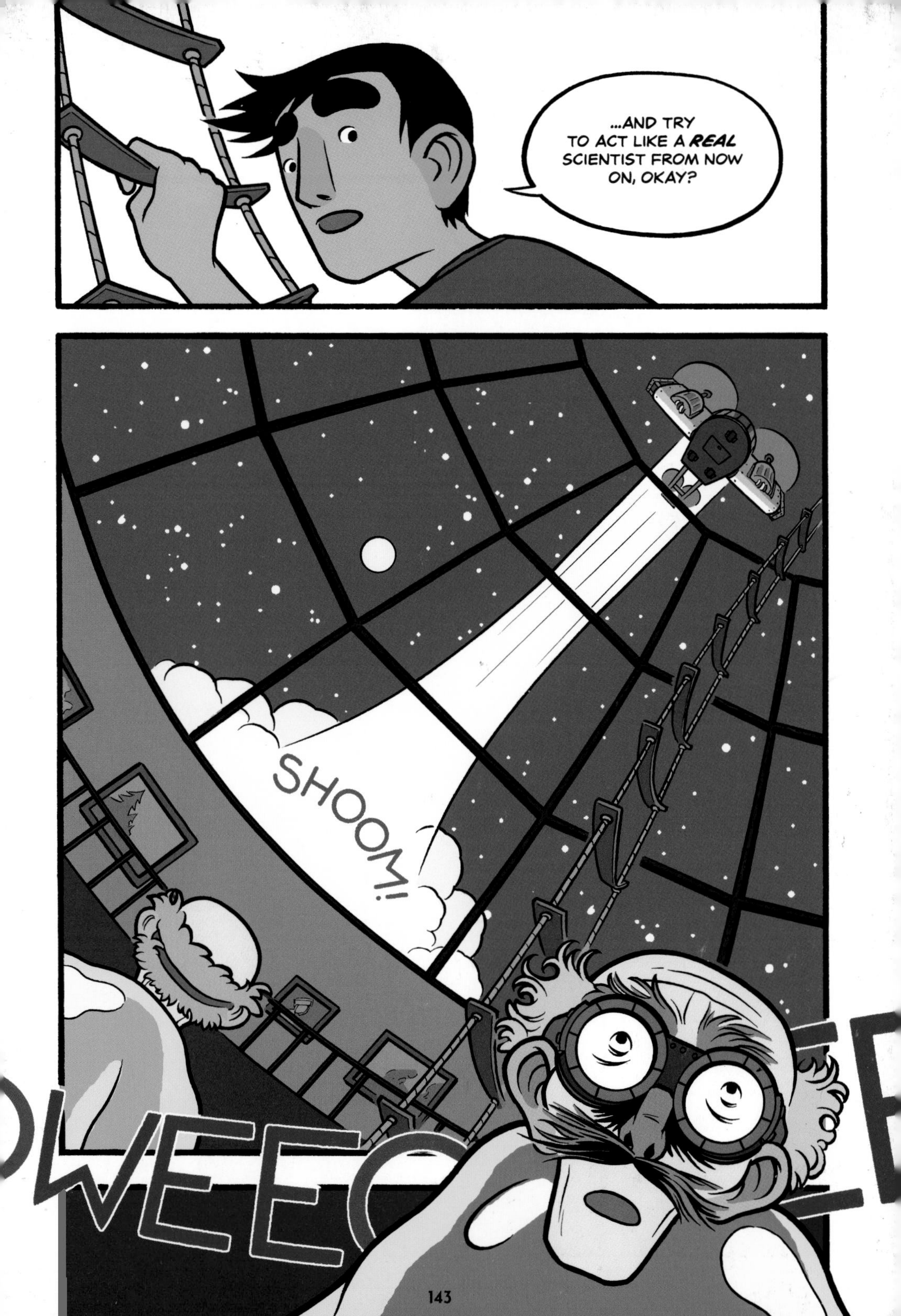
...AND TRY TO ACT LIKE A *REAL* SCIENTIST FROM NOW ON, OKAY?
SHOOM!

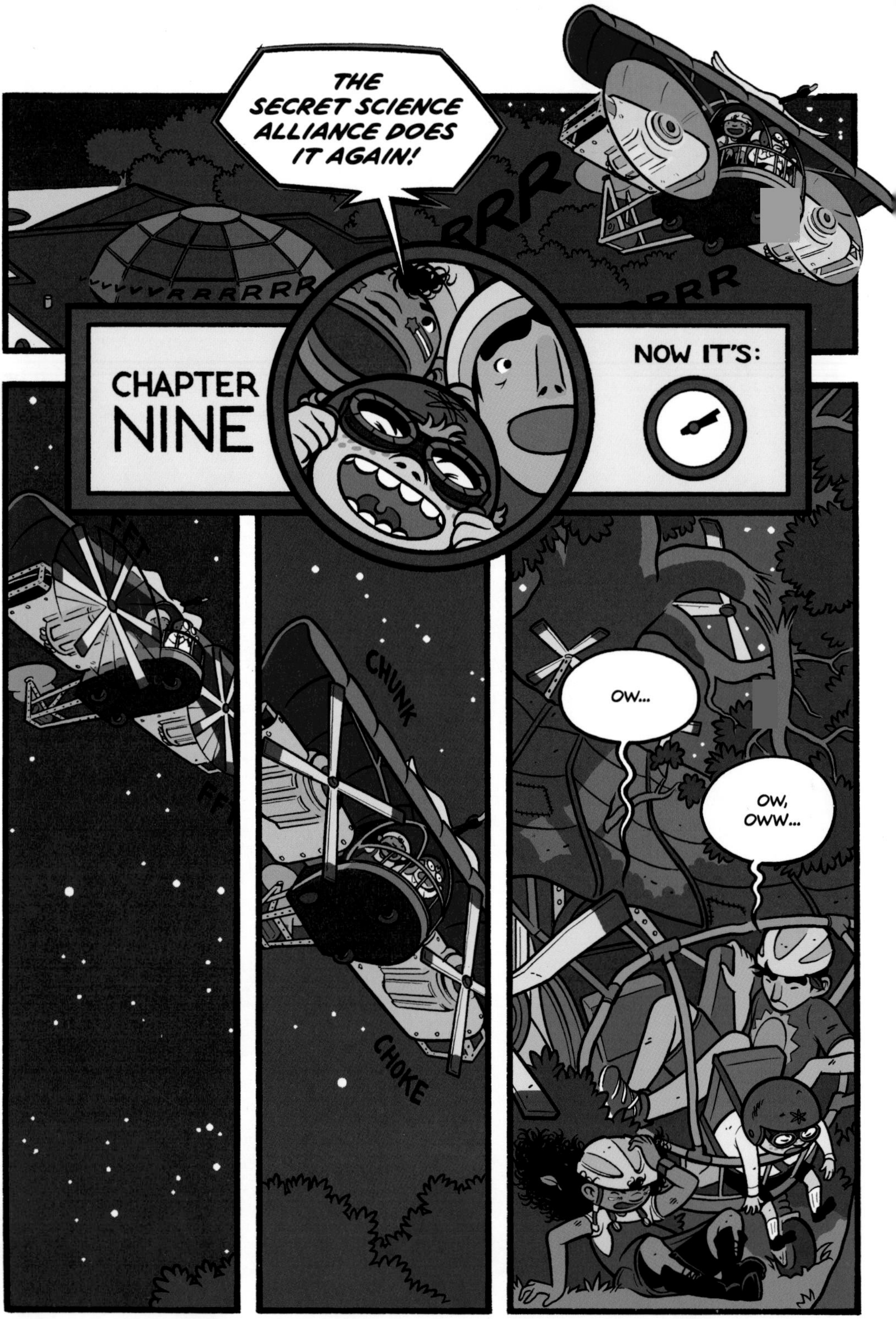
THE SECRET SCIENCE ALLIANCE DOES IT AGAIN!
RRR
RRRRRR
RRRR
CHAPTER NINE
NOW IT'S:
CHUNK
CHOKE
OW...
OW, OWW...

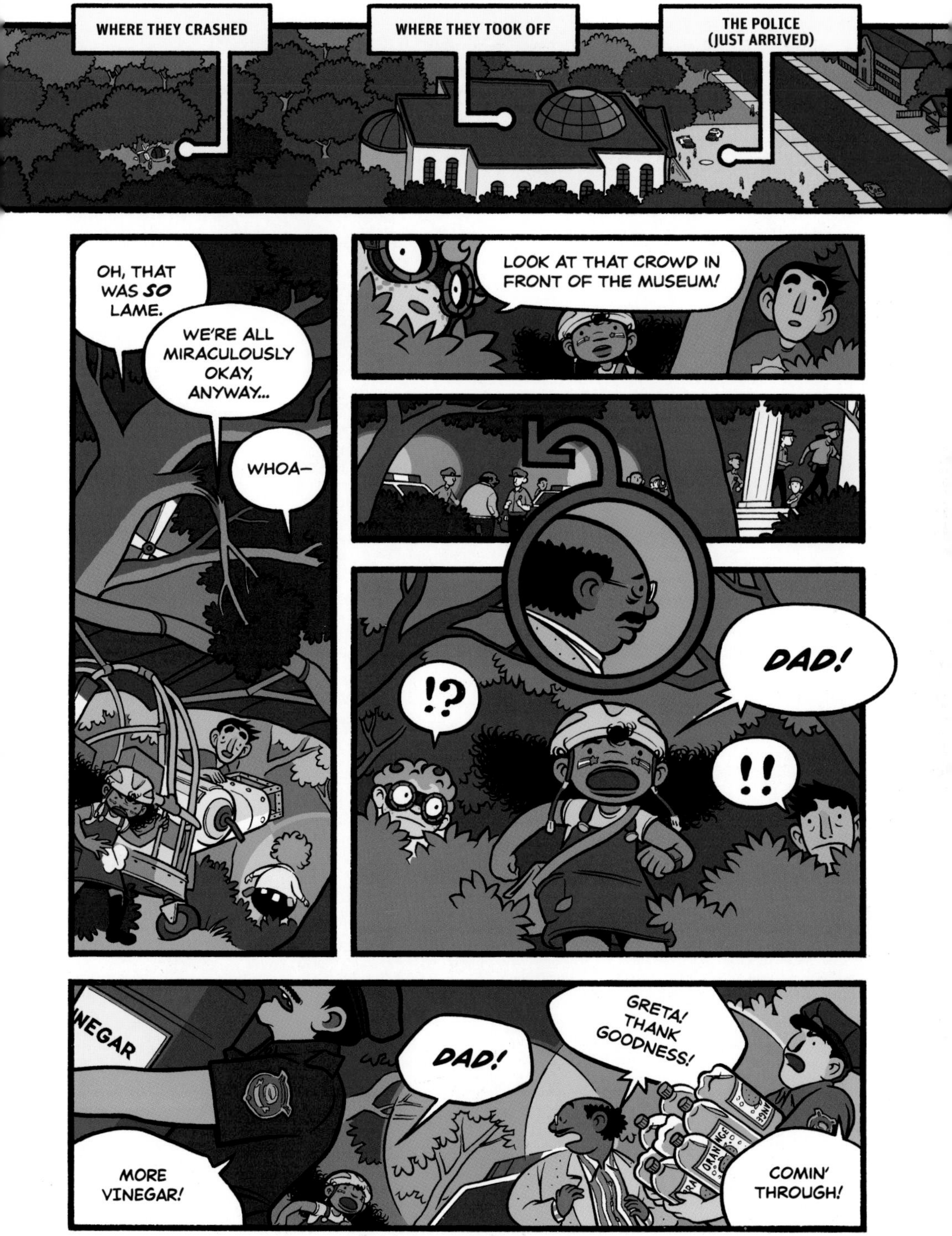

WHERE THEY CRASHED
WHERE THEY TOOK OFF
THE POLICE (JUST ARRIVED)
OH, THAT WAS SO LAME.
WE'RE ALL MIRACULOUSLY OKAY, ANYWAY...
WHOA—
LOOK AT THAT CROWD IN FRONT OF THE MUSEUM!
!?
DAD!
!!
NEGAR
DAD!
GRETA! THANK GOODNESS!
MORE VINEGAR!
COMIN' THROUGH!

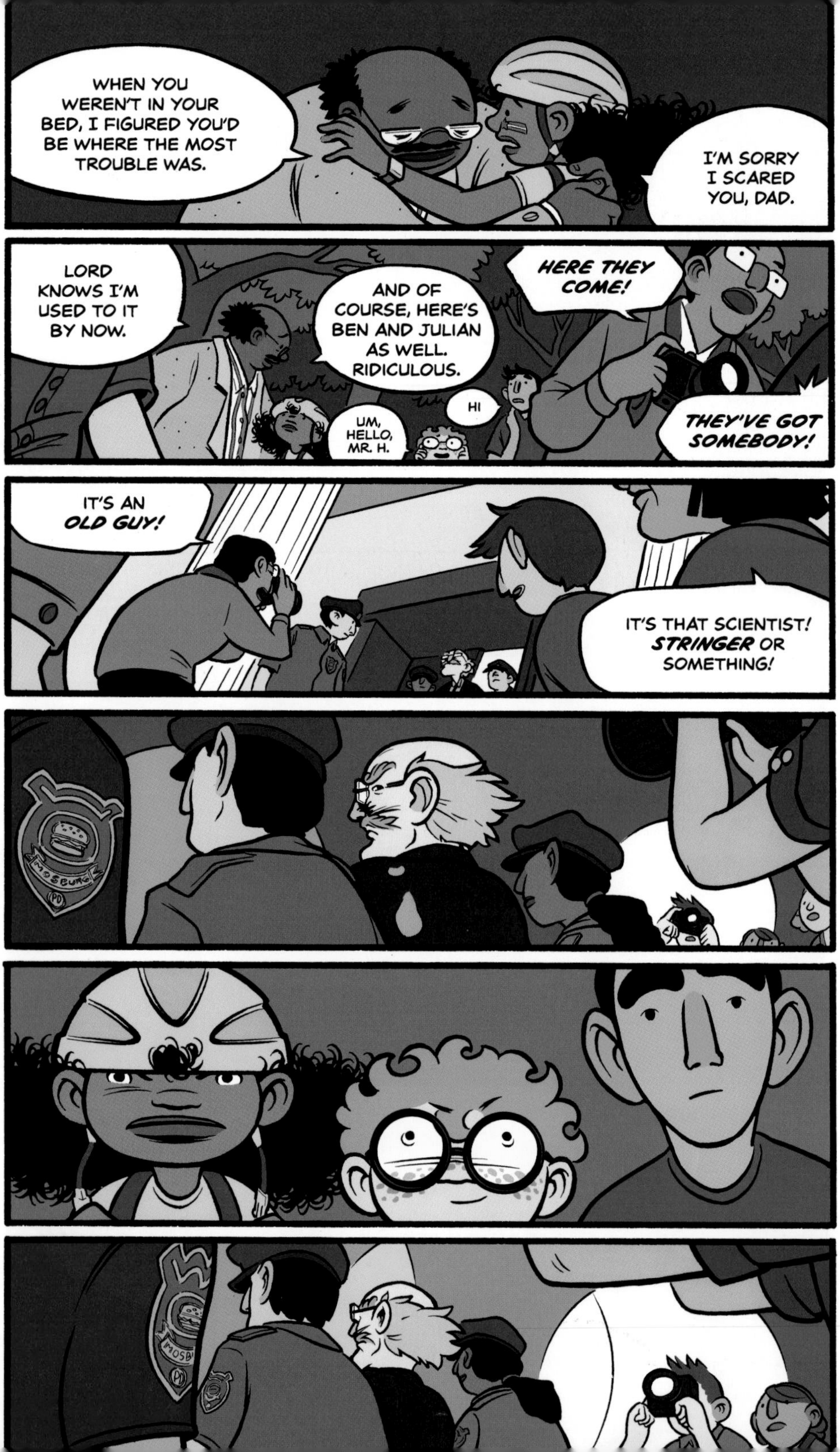
WHEN YOU WEREN'T IN YOUR BED, I FIGURED YOU'D BE WHERE THE MOST TROUBLE WAS.
I'M SORRY I SCARED YOU, DAD.
LORD KNOWS I'M USED TO IT BY NOW.
AND OF COURSE, HERE'S BEN AND JULIAN AS WELL. RIDICULOUS.
UM, HELLO, MR. H.
HI
HERE THEY COME!
THEY'VE GOT SOMEBODY!
IT'S AN OLD GUY!
IT'S THAT SCIENTIST! STRINGER OR SOMETHING!
MOSBURG
PD

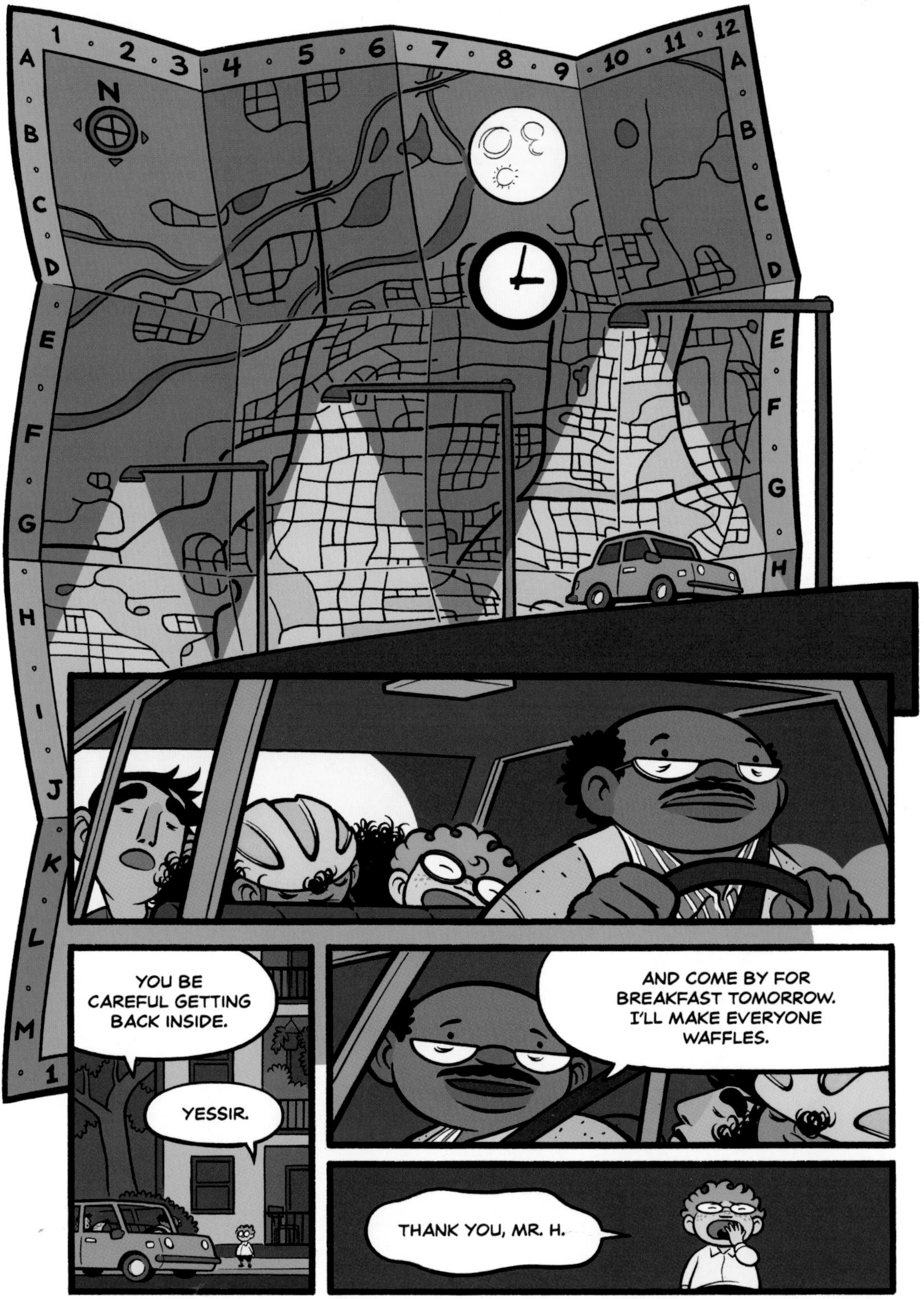

YOU BE CAREFUL GETTING BACK INSIDE.
YESSIR.
AND COME BY FOR BREAKFAST TOMORROW. I'LL MAKE EVERYONE WAFFLES.
THANK YOU, MR. H.

"BREAKFAST."

FINALLY JULY 5

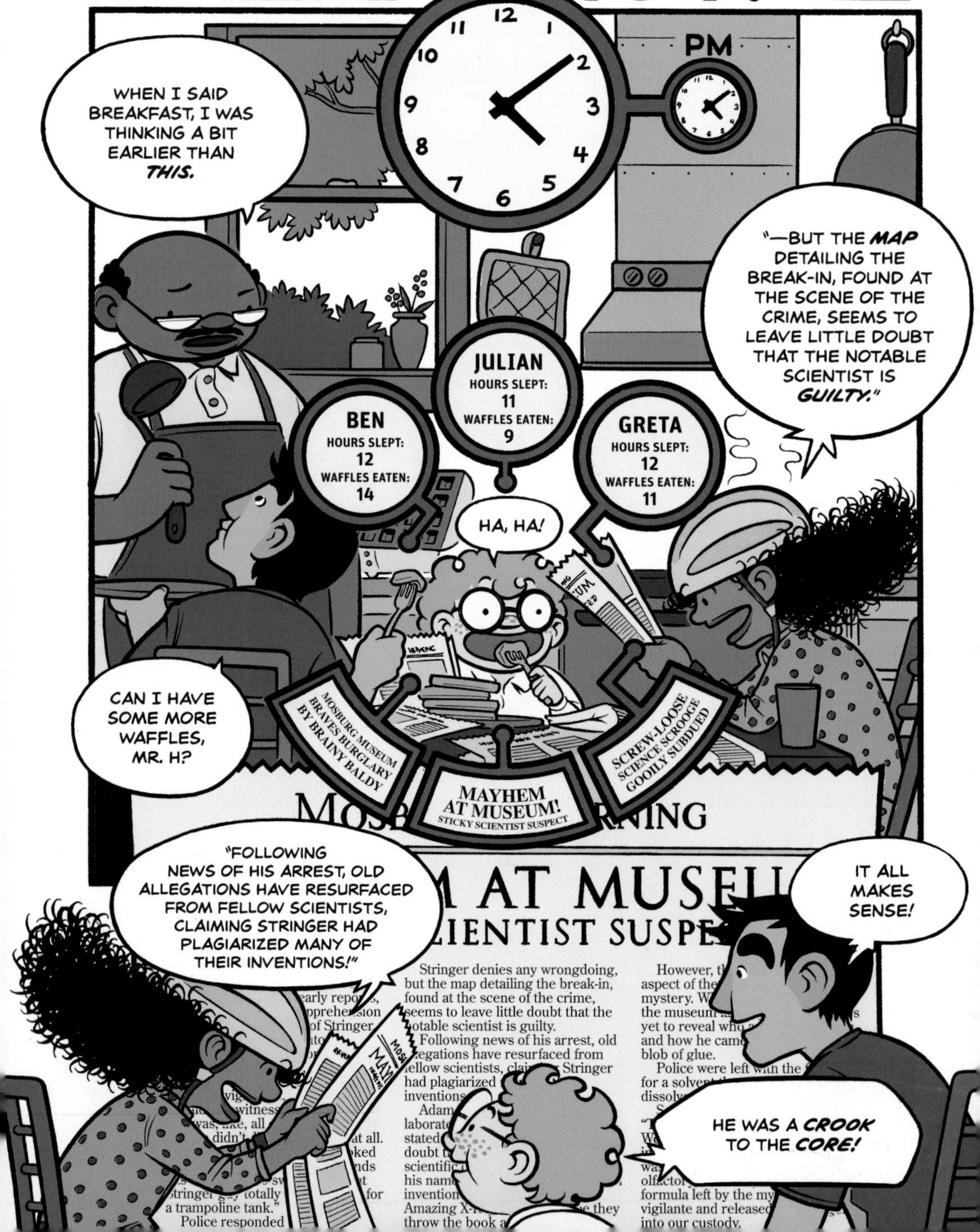
PM
WHEN I SAID BREAKFAST, I WAS THINKING A BIT EARLIER THAN *THIS.*
"—BUT THE *MAP* DETAILING THE BREAK-IN, FOUND AT THE SCENE OF THE CRIME, SEEMS TO LEAVE LITTLE DOUBT THAT THE NOTABLE SCIENTIST IS *GUILTY.*"
JULIAN HOURS SLEPT: 11 WAFFLES EATEN: 9
BEN HOURS SLEPT: 12 WAFFLES EATEN: 14
GRETA HOURS SLEPT: 12 WAFFLES EATEN: 11
HA, HA!
CAN I HAVE SOME MORE WAFFLES, MR. H?
MOSBURG MUSEUM BRAVES BURGLARY BY BRAINY BALDY
MAYHEM AT MUSEUM! STICKY SCIENTIST SUSPECT
SCREW-LOOSE SCIENCE SCROOGE GOOILY SUBDUED
"FOLLOWING NEWS OF HIS ARREST, OLD ALLEGATIONS HAVE RESURFACED FROM FELLOW SCIENTISTS, CLAIMING STRINGER HAD PLAGIARIZED MANY OF THEIR INVENTIONS!"
IT ALL MAKES SENSE!
Stringer denies any wrongdoing, but the map detailing the break-in, found at the scene of the crime, seems to leave little doubt that the notable scientist is guilty.
HE WAS A *CROOK* TO THE *CORE!*

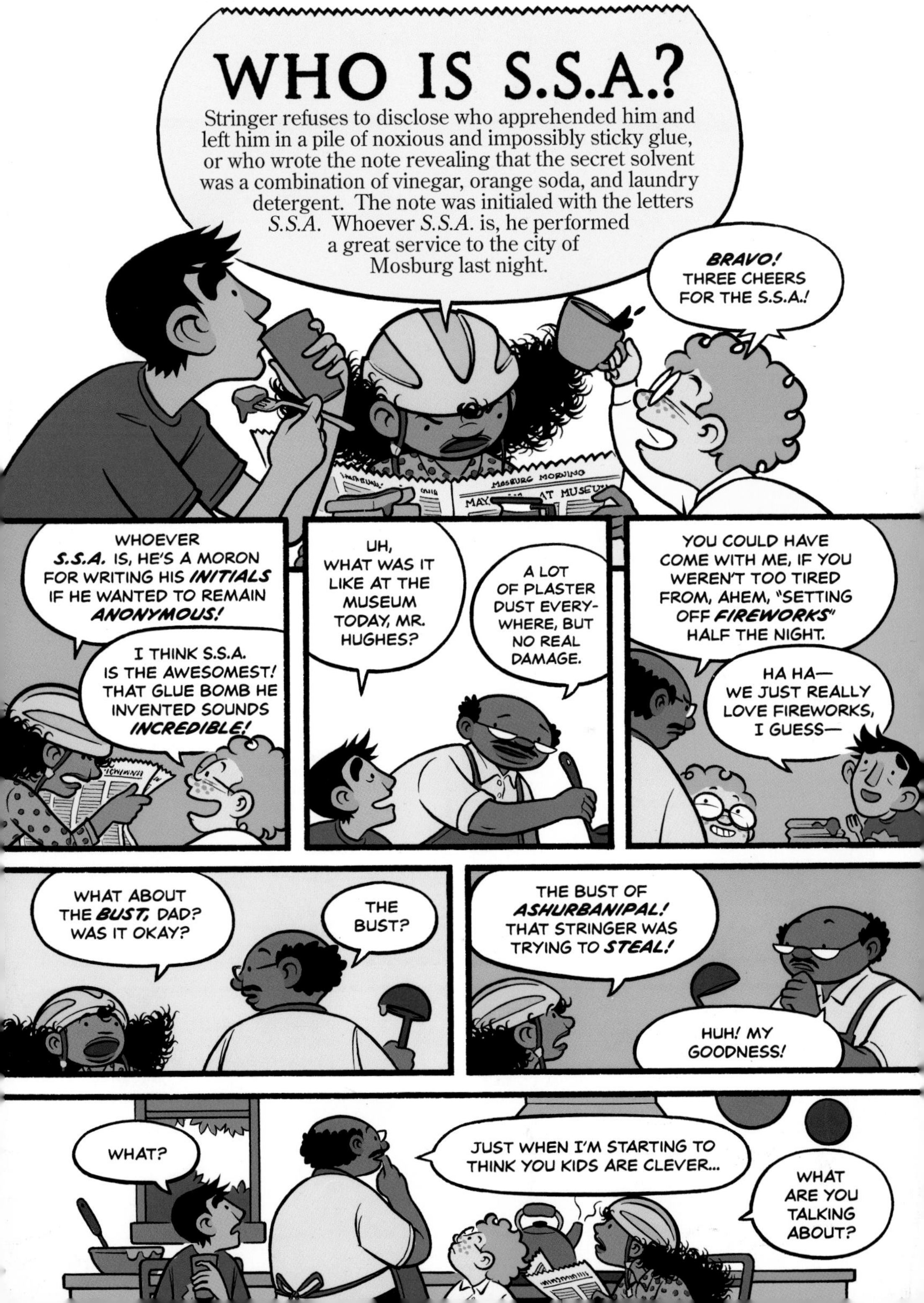

WHO IS S.S.A.?
Stringer refuses to disclose who apprehended him and left him in a pile of noxious and impossibly sticky glue, or who wrote the note revealing that the secret solvent was a combination of vinegar, orange soda, and laundry detergent. The note was initialed with the letters *S.S.A.* Whoever *S.S.A.* is, he performed a great service to the city of Mosburg last night.
BRAVO! THREE CHEERS FOR THE S.S.A.!
MOSBURG MORNING
WHOEVER ***S.S.A.*** IS, HE'S A MORON FOR WRITING HIS ***INITIALS*** IF HE WANTED TO REMAIN ***ANONYMOUS!***
I THINK S.S.A. IS THE AWESOMEST! THAT GLUE BOMB HE INVENTED SOUNDS ***INCREDIBLE!***
UH, WHAT WAS IT LIKE AT THE MUSEUM TODAY, MR. HUGHES?
A LOT OF PLASTER DUST EVERYWHERE, BUT NO REAL DAMAGE.
YOU COULD HAVE COME WITH ME, IF YOU WEREN'T TOO TIRED FROM, AHEM, "SETTING OFF ***FIREWORKS***" HALF THE NIGHT.
HA HA— WE JUST REALLY LOVE FIREWORKS, I GUESS—
WHAT ABOUT THE ***BUST,*** DAD? WAS IT OKAY?
THE BUST?
THE BUST OF ***ASHURBANIPAL!*** THAT STRINGER WAS TRYING TO ***STEAL!***
HUH! MY GOODNESS!
WHAT?
JUST WHEN I'M STARTING TO THINK YOU KIDS ARE CLEVER...
WHAT ARE YOU TALKING ABOUT?

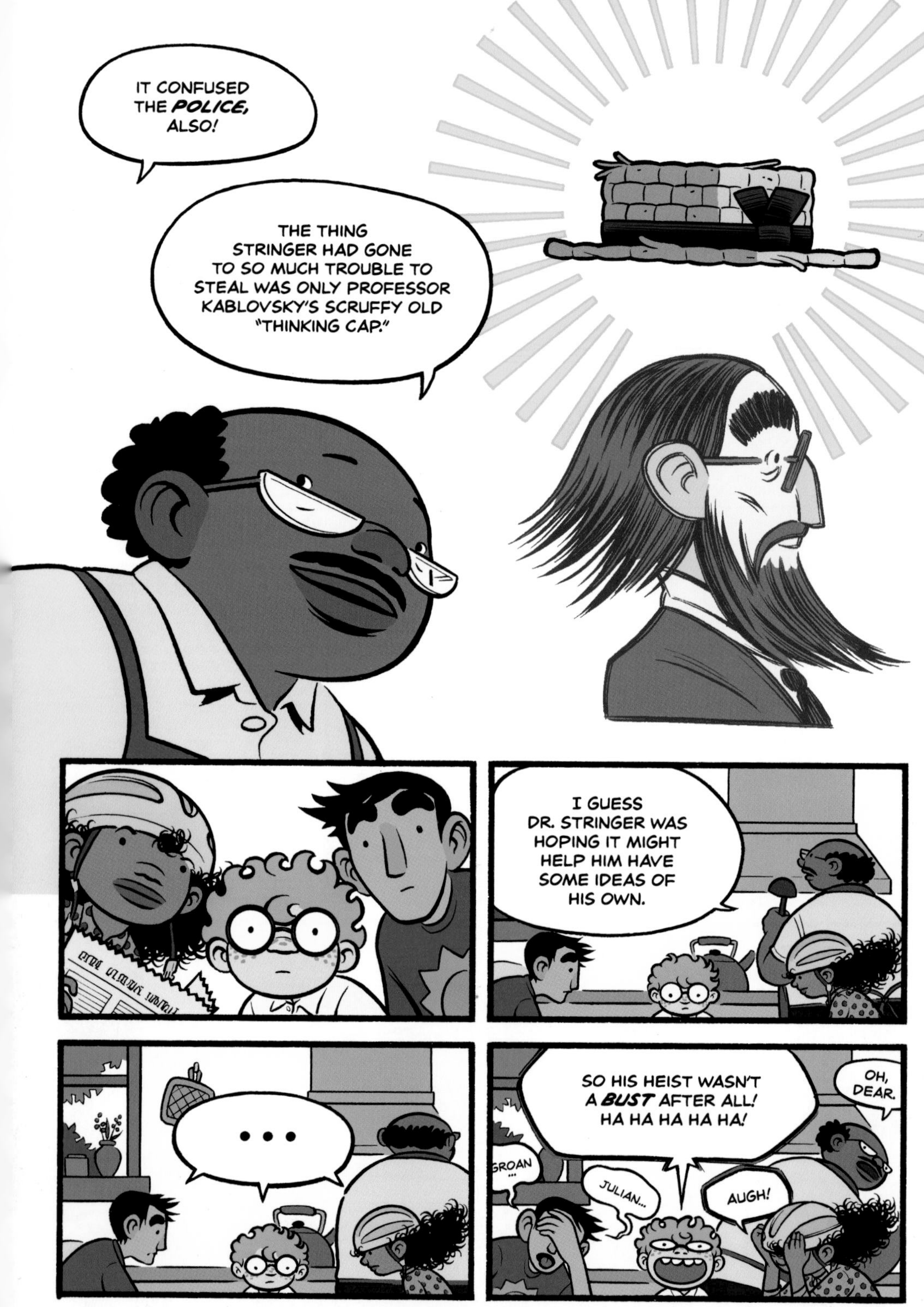
IT CONFUSED THE *POLICE,* ALSO!
THE THING STRINGER HAD GONE TO SO MUCH TROUBLE TO STEAL WAS ONLY PROFESSOR KABLOVSKY'S SCRUFFY OLD "THINKING CAP."
I GUESS DR. STRINGER WAS HOPING IT MIGHT HELP HIM HAVE SOME IDEAS OF HIS OWN.
...
SO HIS HEIST WASN'T A *BUST* AFTER ALL! HA HA HA HA HA!
OH, DEAR.
GROAN ...
JULIAN...
AUGH!

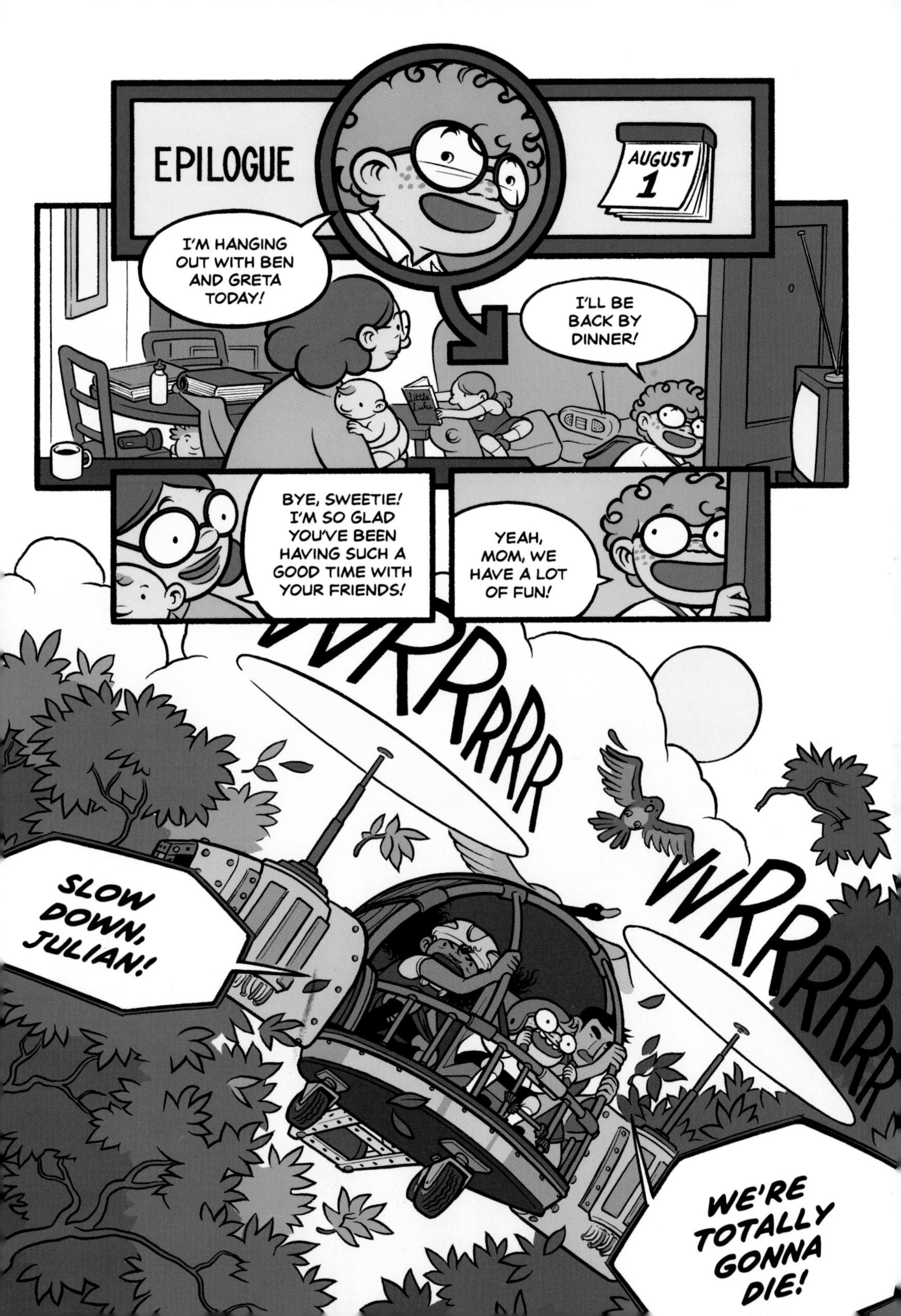
EPILOGUE
AUGUST 1
I'M HANGING OUT WITH BEN AND GRETA TODAY!
I'LL BE BACK BY DINNER!
BYE, SWEETIE! I'M SO GLAD YOU'VE BEEN HAVING SUCH A GOOD TIME WITH YOUR FRIENDS!
YEAH, MOM, WE HAVE A LOT OF FUN!
VVRRRRRR
VVRRRRRRR
SLOW DOWN, JULIAN!
WE'RE TOTALLY GONNA DIE!

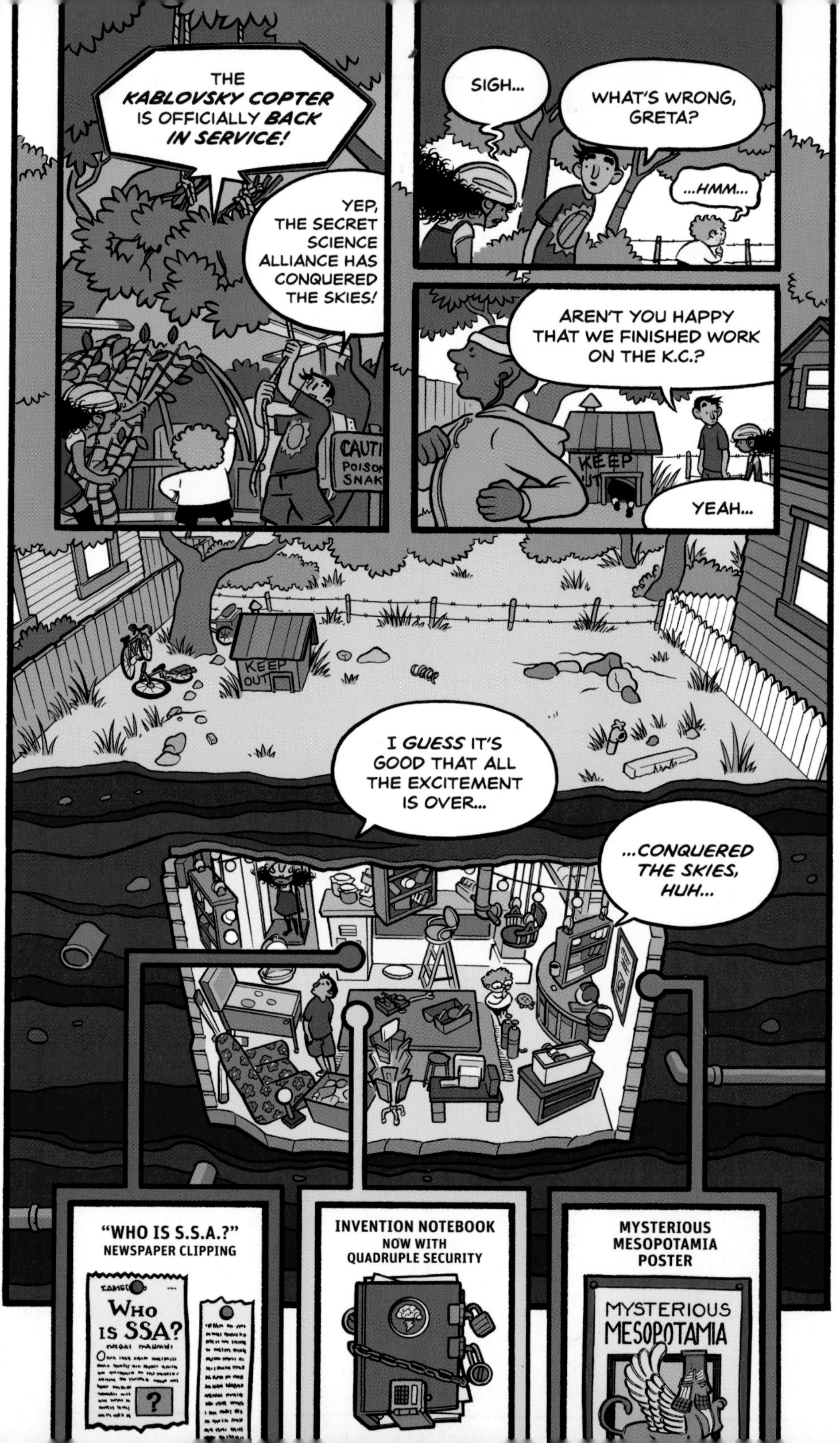
THE KABLOVSKY COPTER IS OFFICIALLY BACK IN SERVICE!
YEP, THE SECRET SCIENCE ALLIANCE HAS CONQUERED THE SKIES!
CAUTI POISON SNAK
SIGH...
WHAT'S WRONG, GRETA?
...HMM...
AREN'T YOU HAPPY THAT WE FINISHED WORK ON THE K.C.?
KEEP OUT
YEAH...
KEEP OUT
I GUESS IT'S GOOD THAT ALL THE EXCITEMENT IS OVER...
...CONQUERED THE SKIES, HUH...
"WHO IS S.S.A.?" NEWSPAPER CLIPPING
WHO IS SSA?
INVENTION NOTEBOOK NOW WITH QUADRUPLE SECURITY
MYSTERIOUS MESOPOTAMIA POSTER
MYSTERIOUS MESOPOTAMIA

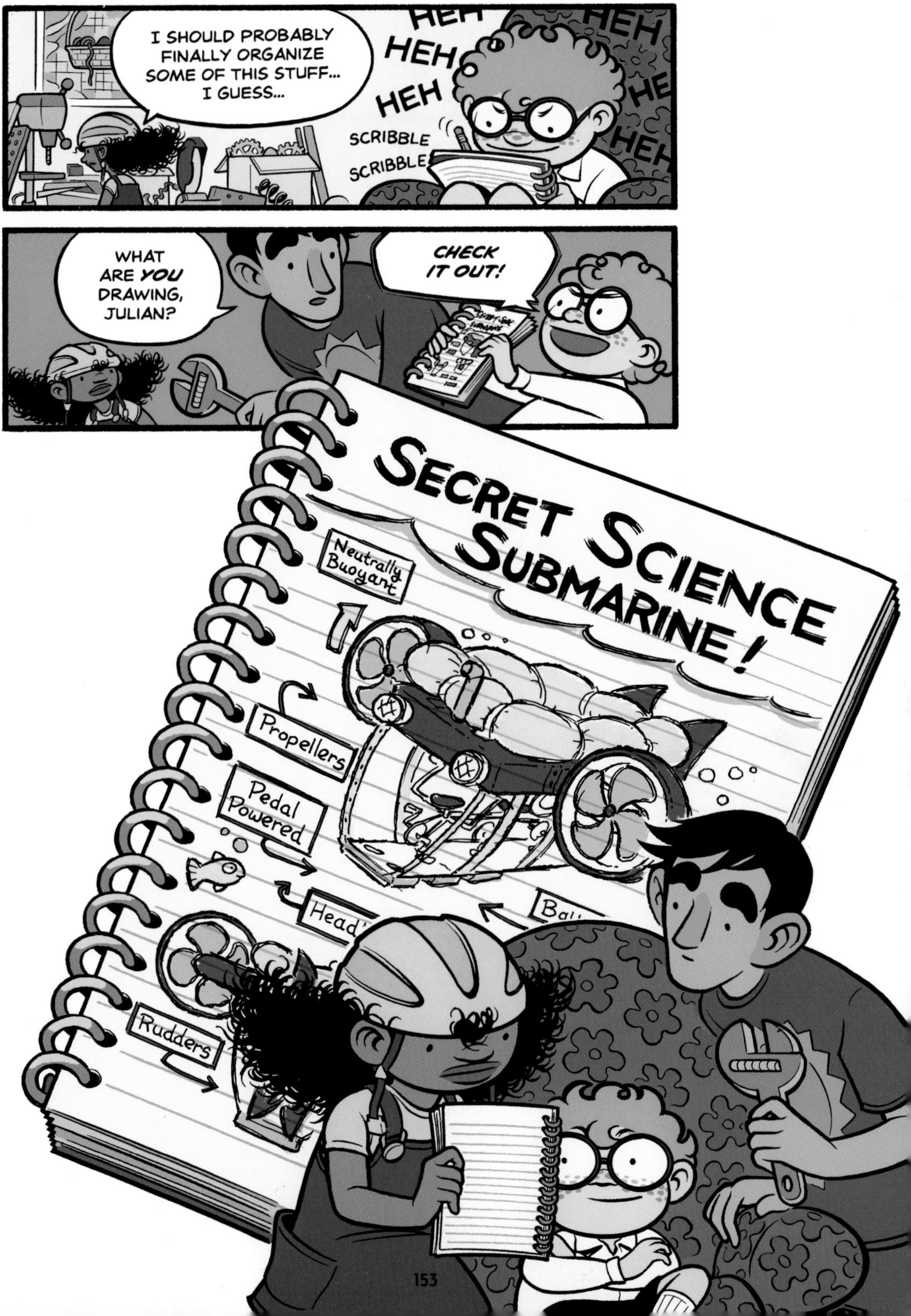

I SHOULD PROBABLY FINALLY ORGANIZE SOME OF THIS STUFF... I GUESS...
HEH
HEH
HEH
HEH
HEH
HEH
SCRIBBLE
SCRIBBLE
WHAT ARE YOU DRAWING, JULIAN?
CHECK IT OUT!
SECRET SCIENCE SUBMARINE!
Neutrally Buoyant
Propellers
Pedal Powered
Rudders

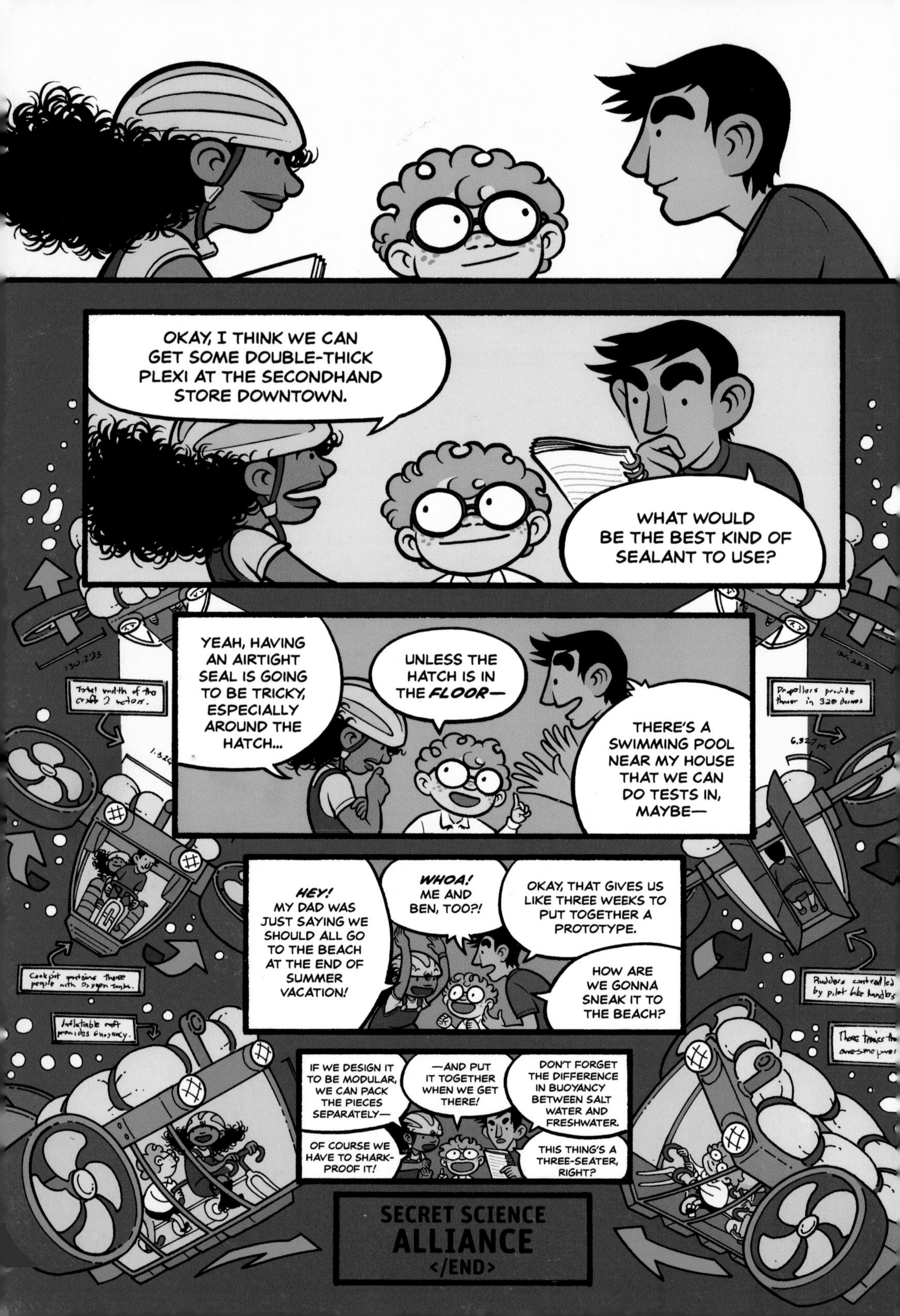

OKAY, I THINK WE CAN GET SOME DOUBLE-THICK PLEXI AT THE SECONDHAND STORE DOWNTOWN.
WHAT WOULD BE THE BEST KIND OF SEALANT TO USE?
YEAH, HAVING AN AIRTIGHT SEAL IS GOING TO BE TRICKY, ESPECIALLY AROUND THE HATCH...
UNLESS THE HATCH IS IN THE *FLOOR*—
THERE'S A SWIMMING POOL NEAR MY HOUSE THAT WE CAN DO TESTS IN, MAYBE—
HEY! MY DAD WAS JUST SAYING WE SHOULD ALL GO TO THE BEACH AT THE END OF SUMMER VACATION!
WHOA! ME AND BEN, TOO?!
OKAY, THAT GIVES US LIKE THREE WEEKS TO PUT TOGETHER A PROTOTYPE.
HOW ARE WE GONNA SNEAK IT TO THE BEACH?
IF WE DESIGN IT TO BE MODULAR, WE CAN PACK THE PIECES SEPARATELY—
—AND PUT IT TOGETHER WHEN WE GET THERE!
DON'T FORGET THE DIFFERENCE IN BUOYANCY BETWEEN SALT WATER AND FRESHWATER.
OF COURSE WE HAVE TO SHARK-PROOF IT!
THIS THING'S A THREE-SEATER, RIGHT?
SECRET SCIENCE ALLIANCE
</END>

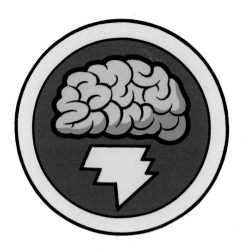

ACKNOWLEDGMENTS

Thank you to the awesome team at Bloomsbury who've worked on SSA (both current and past)—Melanie Cecka, Margaret Miller, Donna Mark, Deb Shapiro, Liz Schonhorst, Julie Romeis, and Victoria Wells Arms, among countless others in production and sales. I'm continually astonished by and thankful for all that you do!

To Joey Weiser, Michele Chidester, Bryant Paul Johnson, John Lind, and Denis Kitchen, profuse thanks and high fives!

Thanks and love to Adam Aylard and my parents, Ann and Ed Davis, for slogging through miles of scrubby thumbnails and giving advice.

For general help, support, love, feedback, blurbs, and a million other things: Françoise Mouly, Tony and Angela DiTerlizzi, Scott McCloud, my grandmother Sue Ellen Groover Davis, my sister Leta Davis, the Davis and McCutcheon families in general, Kate Guillen, Nate Neal, the Savannah crowd of friends and mentors, the Athens crowd ditto, and—nerdily—the LJ comics support team.

And finally, there is no way to adequately thank my husband and partner, Drew Weing. Thank you for getting dragged into being coauthor and coartist of our book. Thank you for tireless months and years of work, and thank you for your inhuman patience. But most of all, thank you for bemusedly loving—and wholeheartedly believing in—Julian, Greta, and Ben.